THE PUPPET PRESIDENT

THE PUPPET PRESIDENT

CLAYTON KEITH

Archway Publishing books may be ordered through booksellers or by contacting:

Archway Publishing
1663 Liberty Drive
Bloomington, IN 47403
www.archwaypublishing.com
844-669-3957

ISBN: 978-1-6657-5502-3 (sc)
ISBN: 978-1-6657-5504-7 (hc)
ISBN: 978-1-6657-5503-0 (e)

Library of Congress Control Number: 2023924721

Print information available on the last page.

Archway Publishing rev. date: 05/20/2024

Special thanks to my wife, son, and daughter for their endless support, love, and insights. May your lives' journeys be full of happiness, joy, health, and making the world a better place. Additional thanks to my parents and siblings for the countless blessings and inspirations that they have given to me. To Jan Vermeer, thanks for being the best political science professor ever, and making election analytics fun! To my friends and co-workers, thanks for including me on the journey. Go Duke and Huskers!

This book is dedicated to my parents. My father was a dedicated public servant for decades who worked across party lines and was always guided by a desire to do what was right for our country, instead of a particular party or person… something severely lacking today. He served on the cabinets of Presidents Reagan and Bush, Sr. and as Chairman of the Republican National Committee. He was renowned as the hardest-working person in government. He was also the smartest and most grounded man I've ever known, and his moral compass was sound. Throughout my dad's tireless government service, my mother was always there supporting him in every way, making all the personal and family sacrifices necessary for him to succeed and our family to thrive in a loving environment. Their marriage was the best I've ever seen, and it seemed to get better with each passing day. The joy they had in seeing each other at the end of every workday and walking their dog nightly before bed continues to make me smile. I will forever miss them. My siblings and I were truly blessed to have them as our parents.

1

OMAHA, NEBRASKA, DECEMBER 2018

"No. No! Stop! I didn't do anything!"

Nick Class sprang forward, nearly tumbling off the couch. Sweat drenched his shirt. He placed two fingers on his carotid as his pulse raced. The mechanical screech of his garage door must've woken him. Nick seldom napped; in fact, he hardly ever slept between his sporadic hospital shifts. And the rare moments he did, it was always *that* dream. *That* recurring nightmare.

That kid, Nick thought, his mind split between the hazy dream and reality. *How do I know him? And what was he running from?*

He leaned over the coffee table, gathering his senses.

No. Not what. ***Who****. Who was he running from...?*

Nick's thoughts trailed off when his wife entered their home.

"Hi honey," Katie Class called from the kitchen, flashing a warm smile as she carried in groceries. "Get a good nap?"

"Guess so," Nick said, wiping the sweat from his brow.

"You needed one. You've been working too hard. And too much."

Nick shrugged. "Maybe. Didn't need that dream, though."

After setting the last of the groceries on the kitchen counter, a wave of worry crossed Katie's face. "Don't tell me. Was it the one with the kid?"

"Yeah. But I'm all right. It's over now."

Nick stood and hugged his wife. Katie's familiar floral perfume made him smile. He always liked her scent, even when they just hung around the house.

"Here, let me help with those," Nick said, proceeding to distribute groceries into their fridge and pantry. "How'd the rest of your errands go?"

"Oh, just fine. The stores were more crowded than I expected. The unusually warm weather definitely brought out the early holiday shoppers." Katie lifted two shopping bags from designer stores. "I'll put these away while you finish the groceries. Then how about I make some fettucine and we watch Tennis Channel the rest of the night?"

"Sounds great! You know how much I love your fettucine."

As Katie hurried off, there was a twinkle in her eyes. "Plus, I may even have a surprise for you!"

Nick couldn't smile any wider. Even after three years of marriage, he still found himself mesmerized by Katie. It was always the little things — the thoughtful texts during long call shifts, flirty banter when he got home, homecooked meals, and adventurous dates in between. Katie's wavy brunette hair, blue eyes, and shapely figure sure made her easy on the eyes, too. But above all, no one loved or understood Nick like Katie did.

Nick sighed and thought, *Life can't get much better than this.*

2

OMAHA, NEBRASKA, DECEMBER 2018

An hour later, the aromas from Katie's signature fettuccine alfredo wafted throughout their house. With it, she prepared a spinach salad with sliced cucumbers, baby tomatoes, chopped carrots, croutons, and craisins. Katie didn't even need to ask before adding Nick's favorite ranch dressing to the side of his salad.

"Everything's almost ready," she called from the kitchen. "How about you get out a bottle of wine?"

"Sure thing," Nick said as he headed toward their basement cellar. "Red or white?"

"Red. Make it a nice one, too."

As Nick retrieved a Napa Valley merlot from the vineyard they visited on their honeymoon, he thought, *Hmm. Fettucine. Nice wine. Plus, a surprise? What's she up to?*

Nick returned with the bottle to find Katie on the couch with two TV trays full of warm food, ready to eat.

"Hope this bottle's a winner," he said as he uncorked the merlot. "Wait. Where's your glass?"

"About that," Katie said, struggling to contain her excitement.

"You would be a terrible poker player. Come on. Spill it."

"Can't you at least *guess* your surprise?"

Nick chuckled. "Guess I need another clue. Come on, Katie. A doctor can't just make a diagnosis without any data."

She rolled her eyes. "Okay. Close your eyes and hold out your hands."

Nick complied. In his open palms, Katie placed two paper strips attached to a plastic device the size of a pencil.

"Okay. You can open your eyes," Katie said.

The second he spotted the familiar test strips, Nick's eyes widened.

"No way!" he cried, nearly dropping the strips.

"So, Doctor Class," Katie said, placing her hand on his shoulder. "What's the diagnosis?"

"I see two lines… one for the control, the other for the beta HCG from your urine. And that can only come from one thing." He looked his wife in the eyes. "You're pregnant!"

She nodded, tears of joy welling in her eyes. "These strips are ninety-nine percent accurate. I tested myself twice just to make sure."

"We're going to have a baby!"

Tears brimmed in his own eyes as Nick embraced his beautiful wife.

I was wrong, he thought. ***Now****, life can't get much better than this.*

3

OMAHA, NEBRASKA, DECEMBER 2018

The sharp buzz of his 5 a.m. alarm heralded the end of another restless night for Nick. It was foolish to think yesterday's excitement and life-changing news meant he'd get a good night of sleep. Besides, Nick knew his subconscious couldn't be trusted. The last thing he wanted was to revisit *that* dream for the umpteenth time.

Instead, he held onto yesterday's high. He forced himself to stay awake by concentrating on abstract rays of moonlight projecting across their ceiling. It was a trick he learned during residency to survive thirty-hour call shifts. As he kept his mind from drifting off, Nick kept his left hand on Katie's stomach — mere inches from their future child.

I'll see you later, little guy, he thought. *Or girl. Whoever you're going to be, I'm excited to meet you…*

Nick gently removed his hand from Katie's belly. He then hopped in the shower and threw on scrubs. Before he left for the hospital, he figured leftover fettucine would make a solid lunch. He reached for the fridge to find a sticky note Katie had written on the sly.

What's up Doc?
Taco Truck for Taco Tuesday?
Text me whenever you get a break.
xoxo
KC

Eight hours later, Nick and Katie met in south Omaha at the aptly named Taco Truck. It wasn't a restaurant per se, but it remained one of their favorite date spots. The mobile truck had the best Mexican food in the city. The menu was diverse, the truck was surprisingly clean, the food was affordable. On top of it all, the Taco Truck was a quick five-minute drive from the hospital where Nick worked. The only downside was that it was a true carryout establishment, but Nick and Katie often made do with the tables at the nearby park.

"Great idea, chica," Nick said when he met Katie outside the Taco Truck.

"Of course," Katie said. "No reason we can't continue yesterday's celebration."

"Buenos días, Miguel," Nick said, waving to the cook inside the truck. "Hoy es un día muy especial para nosotros."

"Ya sabemos," Miguel said with a cheeky grin. "Felicidades, Señora Katie!"

As Katie blushed, Nick raised an eyebrow. "Am I the last person in all of Omaha to know you're pregnant?"

"I only told our family and closest friends," Katie said. "Miguel's known us since our first date. When you were just my *novio.*"

Miguel chuckled. "Que quieren pedir ustedes? La usual comida?"

"Sí," Nick said. "Dos burritos al pastor, un quesadilla barbacoa, y dos Diet Cokes. Por favor."

"Por supuesto, Señor Nick," Miguel said.

Ten minutes later, Nick and Katie grabbed their food, extra salsa packets, and napkins.

"Wow. It's fifty-five out," Nick said as they walked hand-in-hand to their usual park table.

"Not bad for the middle of December," Katie said between sips of her Diet Coke.

"Speaking of December, I meant to ask. How far along are you?"

"I was wondering when you'd ask." Katie grinned. "Six weeks."

"Six weeks..." Nick paused to do some mental math. "That means you'll be due sometime in June or July. Right?"

"Yeah, that's a good ballpark."

"Awesome! A summer baby."

Nick's eyes wandered to the playground and jungle gym at the far end of the park. Several children occupied the area, most only a few years old. Some parents joined them on the slides or swings, others watched their children closely from the nearby picnic table. From their own table, Nick and Katie could hear laughter, cries, and every sound in between. Despite all the babies he helped deliver in medical school, Nick really knew nothing about parenthood. But since discovering his wife was pregnant, he felt eager to learn.

"Just think," Katie said, reaching for Nick's hand. "That'll be us soon."

Nick nodded, gently squeezing his wife's hand. Before he returned to his lunch, Nick spotted three Hispanic men approaching the playground. The trio wore flat bill caps, oversized NBA jerseys, and jeans that sagged well below their waist. Sleeves of tattoos covered their arms. They looked no older than twenty, but they walked with a swagger beyond their years. The shortest of the trio led the pack. He flashed a hand signal to one of the young mothers on the playground; whatever it was, it made her scream, grab her child, and flee the park.

"I don't like the look of this," Nick said to Katie as the trio approached their table.

4

OMAHA, NEBRASKA, DECEMBER 2018

The leader of the trio sat directly across from Nick and Katie. The other two — one very burly, the other lanky — followed suit.

"Why the hurry, *guapa?"* the leader said, his accent as thick as the tattoos on his arms.

"We're just leaving," Katie said, rising from the table with Nick.

"So soon?" The leader turned back to Katie. "That's a lot of queso you're wasting, chica."

He grabbed her Diet Coke, chugged what remained, then tossed it on the grass behind him.

"Come on, guys," Nick said, trying to deescalate the tension. "We don't want any trouble. We're just here for a quick lunch and we're happy to leave now."

Nick rose from the table, but as he tried to take Katie's hand, the heavyset thug stepped in between them.

"Not yet, amigo," said the leader. "You owe us rent."

Nick blinked. "Rent?"

"What, do you own the park?" Katie asked, her brows furrowing.

"Exacto," the leader said. "You use it, you pay rent. Comprende?"

"Even Miguel pays us rent," said the lanky one, pointing to the Taco Truck in the distance.

"And a swallow of Diet Coke es nada. I need something… más."

Nick hesitated before removing his billfold from his scrub pockets. He dropped several fresh bills on the table.

"That's all I got," Nick said. "We're leaving now."

The leader grabbed the cash, counted it, and chuckled. "Just $37? Thought you docs made more," he said, noticing Nick's scrubs.

"Su reloj," the lanky one said, pointing to Nick's Apple watch.

"Yeah. Gimme your watch." The leader glanced at Katie. "Yours too."

Nick and Katie complied, placing their watches on the tabletop. Before they could leave, the leader snatched Katie's left wrist.

"That's a nice rock you got there, chica," he said, admiring her wedding ring.

"Let go of her," Nick growled. Before he could retaliate, the two other thugs grabbed his arms, restraining him.

"Give me the ring," the leader said. He and the others drew switchblades from their pockets. "Unless you want us to cut it off your girl."

"Don't need med school to cut good," the burly one chuckled.

"It's okay, Nick," Katie said, raising her free hand to remove her wedding ring.

The leader swiped her wedding ring, surveying it like a gemologist. His cronies also marveled at it, muttering how much they could get from the pawnshop down the block.

"Just take it," Nick said. "Let us go and you'll never see us again."

The leader reached for Katie's wrist once again. He then examined her head-to-toe with a lusty grin. "I still need más..."

He made a rough grab for Katie's breast, tearing her top.

"No!" Nick shouted, shoving the henchmen.

"NO!" Katie screamed before violently kicking the leader in his groin.

He doubled over briefly from the blow. He laughed before lowering his voice.

"Puta," he muttered before slashing Katie's throat with his switchblade.

Nick's eyes widened. It all happened so fast — Katie collapsing to the ground, blood spewing from her neck like a fire hydrant.

Nick screamed, lunging forward only for the burly and lanky thugs to subdue him once again. As he helplessly watched his wife bleed out, his own blood boiled like never before. He'd never felt an anger this intense, this potent. The paralyzing fear from his recurrent nightmares paled in comparison to the volcano of rage flowing through his veins.

Amidst his panicked thoughts, the frightened kid from his nightmares flashed before Nick's eyes. One second, he'd see his wife's blood-soaked body struggling to survive. The next, the kid from his nightmare, superimposed where Katie's body had been.

The kid, Nick thought, his mind trying to separate his recurring nightmare from this nightmarish reality.

Then the gang leader readied his switchblade, directly above Katie's abdomen as she struggled on the ground to stay alive.

"No. ***Our*** *kid!"*

Suddenly, Nick shut his eyes as if facing a blinding light. His racing, fragmented thoughts evaporated. His neck, arms, and legs went limp. The thugs restraining him nearly dropped him. Windchimes and the sound of rain filled his ears, drowning out the cacophony around him.

"Weather the storm," Nick heard himself chant in a calm, low voice. "*Be* the storm. *Be* a hurricane."

When he reopened his eyes, Nick found his body moving with more agility and efficiency than ever before. His surroundings were in slow motion, failing to keep up with his fluid movements. What followed was nothing short of an out-of-body experience — and a perfect marriage of martial arts and anatomy.

Nick targeted the lanky thug first, driving his elbow upward into the thug's windpipe. He gasped for air, dropping his switchblade in the process. Instead of instinctively lunging for the knife, Nick did just the opposite, waiting for the lanky gangster to reach for the weapon. As the thug bent over to grab the knife from the ground, Nick unleashed a swift, upwards kick with his right leg. The powerful kick connected, crushing the punk's nose with a loud crack and causing the septum wall dividing his nostrils to separate in a bloody mess.

One thug down. Two to go.

Nick turned to the burly gangster. He held up his arms to block an uppercut from the big man and then sidestepped to dodge another punch, making the gangster stumble forward. This bought Nick enough time to kneel to the ground, pick up the knife dropped by the lanky thug, and hurl it in one motion. The knife buried itself in the large man's sternum, killing him before he even had a chance to scream.

Two down. One to go... the leader!

The gang leader stepped away from Katie, his eyes wide as he processed the carnage inflicted by Nick.

"Damn!" he said, turning to face Nick. "Ever heard of 'do no harm,' Doc?"

The macho leader then charged toward Nick, furiously swinging his switchblade that was red with Katie's blood.

A quick side-step enabled Nick to dodge the attack without getting cut by the swiping switchblade. He grabbed the leader's outstretched arm and twisted it, forcing him to drop the blade. Then Nick jammed his elbow into the gangster's forearm until he heard a bone-breaking *CRACK.* The leader cursed loudly, but before he could respond, Nick yanked his fractured forearm outward, dislocating it from the elbow.

The gang leader cried in pain as he fell to the ground. Spotting his dropped switchblade, the thug scrambled to secure it with his unbroken arm. But Nick beat him to it.

"Fuck... you..." the leader said as Nick drove the blade forcefully through his chest and into his heart with a twisting motion. In his last act of bravado, the thug spat blood in Nick's face.

Nick let the leader drop lifelessly to the ground and started to run toward Katie. Before he got there, he heard the first gangster yell something in Spanish. Nick looked at him as he stood wobbly, holding his crushed nose with one hand while brandishing a small handgun.

"You and your family are DEAD!" yelled the thug, raising his gun.

Nick turned sideways to reduce himself as a target. The gunman got off one shot at Nick but missed. He would not get another opportunity. Nick took a quick step to align his throwing motion and slung the knife that he still held. Nick watched the blade that had slit Katie's throat whizz through the air and enter the creep's esophagus, the pointed edge of the blade exiting an inch or two out of the backside of his neck.

"Nick..."

He blinked. His wife's faint voice immediately ripped him from his bizarre trance.

"No!" he said, the panic returning as he rushed to Katie's side. "Katie... Katie!"

She was only a few feet away, lying in a much wider pool of blood than before. Nick shook his head as he held a hand over her carotid, trying in vain to stop the bleed.

"Stay with me, honey," he said. When Katie's pulsed faded, Nick started CPR. Each chest compression felt heavier, more desperate than the last. After many minutes of CPR, Nick's arms twitched with fatigue. Tears ran down his face, landing on Katie's bloody, lifeless body. Wailing in defeat, Nick finally collapsed over his dead wife, losing consciousness.

The storm had passed, but at what cost?

5

BOGOTÁ, COLOMBIA 1999

It was a beautiful, sunny day as the young boy looked out the family room window.

"Mom, I'm going outside to hit some balls," the boy yelled.

"OK," said his mother, "but stay close to the house."

The boy gathered his bucket of whiffle balls and plastic bat, then sprinted to the door. He darted across the street to the vacant lot with an open, grassy patch. He spent most afternoons there, hitting whiffle balls while envisioning his favorite major league stars hitting epic homeruns.

Ken Griffey, Jr. at the plate with the bases loaded and two outs as the Cincinnati Reds are down by three runs in the bottom of the ninth. Here's the payoff pitch, and Griffey rips it. The only question is whether it's fair or foul… and it's GONE! A homerun! Griffey has won the game!

As he retrieved the whiffle balls he hit, the boy noticed a group of four boys approaching. Though they were only a few years older, they all held beer cans they made no attempt to conceal. They were laughing loudly and walking with a tough, cocky swagger.

As they got closer, the leader yelled, "Gringo, queremos jugar contigo."

Although the younger boy didn't understand their language, he could smell trouble. He quickly snatched the plastic bat and whiffle balls before bolting down the street, away from his house. He hoped the gang would just leave him alone, but the young boy could tell from the sounds of their voices that they were chasing him. The boy was athletic and ran as fast as he could. He put some distance between two of his chasers. He made the mistake of looking over his shoulder, where he spotted the other two bullies gaining ground.

The younger boy started to weave, hoping to throw his pursuers off course. He leapt across a small stream; seconds later, splashing and Spanish curse words told him one of his chasers had slipped into the shallow water. The younger boy continued to zig zag as he approached the backyard of the biggest house in the neighborhood. But before he could pivot again, a hard shove to his back sent the boy sprawling. He fell hard, pebbles and gravel tearing up his hands and knees as he skidded across the ground.

Dazed and bleeding, the young boy was soon surrounded by three chasers. They were panting from the chase, and clearly mad that some of their beer had spilled during the pursuit. Their leader soon joined them. He was the maddest of all after his embarrassing spill in the creek. His clothes wet and muddied, he picked up the plastic bat and a ball that the younger boy had dropped.

"You wanna play beisbol?" he said menacingly. "Let's play beisbol!"

The bully took a mighty swing, attempting to hit the ball at the younger boy, but missed so badly he nearly fell himself. Fuming, he tossed his beer can and took a Casey-like swing with the bat.

This time, he connected.

The beer can rocketed into the younger boy's temple, gashing his eyebrow. He fell to the ground, blood and tears seeping from his face.

"Get up crybaby!" the bully yelled. He hoisted him up, gave his face a sharp backhanded slap, then shoved him back on the ground.

"No. No! Stop!" the younger boy cried. "I didn't do anything…!"

6

OMAHA, NEBRASKA, DECEMBER 2018

"No, I didn't do anything!" Nick Class screamed as he woke up in a bed and place he didn't recognize. He was sweating, his pulse was racing, and he was rubbing a scar above his right eye.

"Dr. Class," said a nearby voice, "I am Sergeant August West of the Omaha Police Department. I'm sorry, but I need to ask you some questions."

Nick looked at his surroundings and realized that he was in what appeared to be a sparsely furnished hospital room.

"How did I get here?" he asked the cop. "What day is it?"

"It's Tuesday afternoon," said the cop. "We found you unconscious at the park. You've been out over twenty-four hours."

"My wife… she's gone?" Nick asked, fearing he already knew the answer.

"I'm afraid so," said the cop in a sympathetic voice. "We've spoken with your father. Senator Class was in Europe meeting with some of our NATO allies. When he heard what happened, he immediately canceled the rest of his trip. He should be arriving in Omaha soon."

After a short pause, Sergeant West continued. "I know this is not a great time, but I need to ask you some questions about what happened in the park."

Nick laid his head back and did his best to recount the events at the park. His voice dropped to a mere whisper as he described how quickly things had turned bad, horribly bad, with the three gang members. How Nick lost control of his body. How it was too late to save Katie.

"That's all I can remember," Nick said after describing the senseless slashing of his wife's throat. "To top it off, she was pregnant."

"That is horrible. I'm so sorry," Sergeant West said. "Rest assured, we have forensics and other experts analyzing the crime scene. Right now, you are the only witness of what happened. From what we could piece together, it appears you killed three gang members by yourself. How did you do that?"

"No clue," Nick said. "I got so angry, my mind blanked. Then my body just moved on its own." "I can answer that."

A tall, attractive Black woman stood in the doorway. She looked like she was in her early-to-mid thirties, and very authoritative in her demeanor. She flashed her ID to the cop.

"This is now a federal case," she said. "Thank you, Sergeant West. You are relieved of all duties. I confirmed this with your commanding officer, Sergeant Quinn. Feel free to call him for verification."

The cop blinked, baffled and unsure how to respond.

"This is no longer your case," the woman repeated firmly. "Now if you don't mind, I need to speak with Dr. Class. In private."

Flustered, Sergeant West stood, dialing his supervisor as he exited the hospital room.

"Now I'm totally confused," Nick said. "Who are you?"

7

OMAHA, NEBRASKA, DECEMBER 2018

The woman pressed a hand against the door to Nick's room, ensuring Sergeant West had closed it. Then she pulled a chair up to Nick's bed.

"My name is Samantha Smart," she began, her voice soft yet direct. "I work for your dad. You may not remember me, Nick, but I've known you for almost a decade."

"Yeah. I don't remember you at all," said Nick, rubbing his eyes and straining the recesses of his brain to find any sort of connection to the woman. "So, how do we know each other?"

"Your dad is better equipped to answer that. His flight just landed, so he should be here soon. In the meantime, he asked me to chat with you and assess the situation. You up for that?"

"Sure, I think," Nick hesitated. "Let me guess. You want to know what happened in the park?"

"Yes. What did you do to land yourself in the hospital?"

"Katie and I were having lunch together. We were celebrating. The night before, she told me she… was pregnant." Nick choked back tears and took a deep breath. "Anyway, we picked up some Mexican food and went to a nearby park. Then these thugs approached us, robbed us, and wouldn't let us leave."

“Hold up.” Samantha held up a hand. “That’s why you eliminated them?”

Nick blinked. “What?”

“You eliminated them because they mugged you?”

“It wasn’t just that,” Nick scoffed. “The leader groped my wife and slit her throat.”

“Ah. That was the trigger.” Samantha nodded. “Go on.”

Nick sighed, unsure how much more to share. “After seeing that, something inside of me snapped. The next thing I know, the thugs are dead and I’m doing CPR on my dead wife.”

“Wait. You mentioned something snapped inside of you? What happened between you snapping and their bodies dropping? This is very important. I need to know everything you remember.”

Samantha’s cold and clinical questions shocked him, but Nick still recalled his out-of-body experience from the park. Samantha continued to press him for details on his sudden metamorphosis into a lethal fighter. The more she pressed, the more furrowed her brows became. She was noticeably unsatisfied with Nick’s vague responses. When Samantha asked again for specifics about the battle, Nick finally held up his hand.

“You said you work for my dad?” he said. “You know the placard he keeps on his desk?”

Samantha nodded. “*In anything and everything you do, do it the right way.*”

“Well Samantha, you’re not doing this interrogation right. You keep asking the same questions in different ways. But I clearly don’t have the answers you’re looking for.”

Nick then rolled over in bed, away from Samantha. “I just lost my wife. I’m overwhelmed. I’m tired. And I’m tired of these questions. Please leave.”

8

OMAHA, NEBRASKA, DECEMBER 2018

Samantha Smart stepped outside Nick's hospital room. Thunderous footsteps down the hall made her turn to find Senator Carson Class striding toward her. His suit was wrinkled from many hours on airplanes, but Carson still walked with the energy of a man on a mission. Though bloodshot from jet lag and loss of sleep, his eyes were as alert as his ever-working mind.

"You made it," Sam said, shaking his hand.

"Sam," Carson said. "Thanks for holding down the fort. How's my son?"

Samantha sighed. "I can't sugar coat it. He's sad and confused. Not unexpected after what he went through. But still, I fear he's unstable."

As tears welled in Carson's eyes, a pang of guilt swept through Samantha.

"I'm sure he will be happy to see you," she added. "But first, we need to have a serious conversation about GROSS."

"OK," said Carson. "Shoot."

"Carson, you know I trust you and respect your judgment. I see why you'd consider Nick an asset for GROSS. But let the record show, I think that would be a horrible decision."

Carson paused before calmly asking, "Why do you think so?"

Samantha motioned for Carson to sit at the bench down the hall, well away from Nick's room in case he was eavesdropping.

"Like I said before, he's unstable. And not just emotionally," Samantha said. "Nick may have broken through the Clean Slate Protocol, but his mind remains fragmented. Based on my brief conversation with him, he knows nothing about his past or the extent of his skills. And now that these skills are emerging once again, I fear he won't be able to control them. That makes him a liability, not a partner I can trust."

Carson nodded in understanding. "As always, I appreciate your frankness, Sam. And I appreciate the heads up. But let me speak with Nick first." He stood and walked toward Nick's room. "No decisions for GROSS will be made today. And, my final decision won't be hasty or careless. I don't need to remind you that your new partner has big shoes to fill."

9

OMAHA, NEBRASKA, DECEMBER 2018

Despite his medical background, Nick did not like hospitals, including their unique sanitary smell. Nick couldn't wait for his dad to arrive so he could get out of the hospital quickly.

While waiting for his dad, Nick thought about Katie and how much he wished his mom could have met her. Like Katie, Jeanne Class was a person with a huge, caring heart who was loved by all. Each of them would light up a room with their smiles and easy laughs. Nick would never forget the mutual joy his parents had in their eyes when together, and they had the most loving marriage of any couple that Nick ever knew. However, Nick's mom unexpectedly died of a heart attack in her sleep when Nick was a teenager. No day would pass without Nick thinking of her, smiling at the lasting memories, but saddened by not having her there to share in his life. But now, like his mom, Katie was gone. Pulled from the picture in the blink of an eye.

A soft knock on the door announced that Carson Class had arrived. Carson walked gingerly into Nick's hospital room, not knowing if he was asleep or awake. When he saw Nick move in his bed at the sound of his arrival, Carson picked up the pace and walked briskly to his bedside, reaching over the covers to smother his son with a loving hug that said more than any words could. After the long embrace, Carson pulled out a handkerchief and dabbed his wet eyes before handing it to Nick so he could do the same.

"I'm so sorry, Nick," Carson said and then hugged his son again as another outpouring of tears flooded his eyes. "I know your loss and pain all too well. I promise you, we will get through this together."

Carson pulled up a chair close to Nick. Side-by-side they talked about Katie, life, love, loss, and faith. It was therapeutic for Nick to share emotions with his father, even if it was just a mere band-aid on a gushing wound.

After the tears had stopped, Nick eventually asked, "Dad, something really strange happened in the park. Once the gangsters drew their knives and stabbed Katie, it's like I became a totally different person. Instead of being the one healing wounds, I was suddenly the one who could disable three armed attackers and not get so much as a scratch. Your friend Samantha asked me a ton of questions about the fight, but I didn't have any answers for her. Can you help me understand what happened? I'm very confused."

"That's a long conversation," Carson said. "Let me coordinate with your doctor to get you discharged. Then we'll stay together at the nearby Embassy Suites. We can continue this conversation there. Let me leave you with two thoughts: one, a wise man once said that 'hardships often prepare ordinary people for an extraordinary destiny.' Two, I have a unique proposal for you to consider that may put you on the road to an extraordinary destiny."

10

OMAHA, NEBRASKA, DECEMBER 2018

The layout at the Embassy Suites was perfect for the needs of Carson and Nick Class: two queen size beds, two sinks, and a room located far away from the noise of the elevators. Though both were physically exhausted, more conversations and clarity were needed.

"In the late 1990s, when you were still in middle school," Carson started, "I took a job with the Agency for International Development in Bogotá, Colombia. My job was to help the Colombians develop long-term, sustainable agricultural products other than cocaine, coffee, and marijuana."

"Yeah, I have some vague memories of family activities there and struggling to learn Spanish in the middle of the school year," said Nick shaking his head. "Not much else though."

"This will help," said Carson. "When you were twelve, some local Colombian boys assaulted you. They had been drinking, and things got out of hand. They might have even killed you had one of our neighbors not stepped in. Anyway, after you recovered, we walked over to give a thank-you gift to our neighbor. That's when we found out that our neighbors were Pedro and Paco Salazar, two Colombian brothers that kept a very low profile locally, but had international acclaim as being the best all-around fighters in the world.

"Do you remember Mike 'Steel Fists' Tryson, the self-proclaimed 'baddest man on the planet'? Even though he was a heavyweight boxing champion with one of the most feared knockout punches ever, he admitted that the only men he ever feared were the Salazar brothers. Decades before mixed martial arts ever became popular, the Salazar brothers were recognized internationally as the kings of personal combat. The brothers spent their lives mastering multiple martial arts disciplines. Both brothers beat elite fighters from around the globe to win the 'kumite,' a full-contact freestyle fighting tournament held every five years."

"What does that have to do with me?" asked Nick.

"Well, the Salazar brothers' home was as much a training facility as it was a residence. The Salazar brothers took a liking to you, especially after you showed an interest in learning their craft. Your mom and I also liked the Salazars. After your unfortunate beating, we thought that learning some self-defense skills might be useful.

"So, for the next six years, you trained with the Salazars. The brothers were incredible instructors. I remember them saying that you had the balance of a gymnast, which provided you the foundation for leverage, quickness, defense, and ferocity in your strikes. In a nutshell, the Salazars trained you to be like a hurricane when fighting. Calm and quiet in the center of the storm," Carson said pointing to Nick's heart and head, "but unleashing fury and damage at the extremities.

"Let's fast forward a little bit. It was clear from the start that you had a natural aptitude in multiple branches of martial arts. Unfortunately, you also had this 'bully rage' inside of you that you couldn't control. At your first kumite, you went ballistic when you saw one of the contestants intentionally break the arm of another fighter trained by the Salazars. Things quickly turned ugly, and you had to be restrained before nearly killing him. That was the end of your fighting career. Your mom and I and the Salazars all agreed that your mental health had to be addressed before any further competition would be allowed."

"Wow," exclaimed Nick. "I don't remember any of this… how can that be?"

"I'll get to that. A few years later, our family moved back to the United States when I took a government post in Washington. I used some of my connections to get you a job teaching combat skills to the Navy SEALs and Army Green Berets. Your mom and I thought training our elite fighting units would be a great outlet for you to release your frustrations and control your temper.

"In any event, our plan was working perfectly. While you trained our most advanced soldiers the skills you learned from the Salazars, the branches of the military also let you join in the training of other skill areas. You learned about weapons, marksmanship, demolition, field tactics, and strategy — a perfect blend of tactical training.

"As I said, this was all working perfectly, until it wasn't. One day during a training match at the 'Farm' in Camp Peary, Virginia, you were leading a group of SEAL trainees against another SEAL team. This other SEAL team was led by the Navy's long-time personal combat trainer, Lieutenant Commander Patrick Payne. Unfortunately, Payne didn't like you stepping onto his turf, even though you were just trying to make our soldiers the best they could be. During the team competition, Payne interjected himself into a combat challenge, and broke one of your team-mate's legs. It was a complete bully move, and it triggered you. You went ballistic and beat him up so badly he landed in the ICU."

"Wow! I can't believe I did that," Nick exclaimed.

"That wasn't a wise move on your part, Nick. Payne was a decorated veteran and war hero. I used my influence to keep Payne and the Navy from pressing charges against you, but Payne only agreed to do so if you 'permanently disappeared' from the military."

"What does that mean?"

"The military doesn't like change or loose cannons… and you were both. The military viewed you as a weapon — a weapon to be used, but also a weapon that needed to be controlled. Considering your unique skills, this made you dangerous. Some argued you were a threat to our national security if something triggered you. A friend of mine in the Pentagon alerted me off the record that these perceived threats often 'disappear' or suffer an unfortunate 'accident.'"

"Man, I thought that sort of stuff only happened in Russia!" exclaimed Nick.

"Nick, I had just lost your mother a short time before that. I couldn't handle the thought of losing you, too. Not wanting you to suffer a similar fate, I got the Department of Defense to agree to the 'Clean Slate Protocol.' This is basically an agreement that the government won't interfere in your civilian life if you undergo a procedure developed by the DOD."

"What kind of a procedure was that?"

"It was surgery that effectively wipes the period of your combat training from your memory."

"Wow! The doctor in me really wants to know what they did in this Clean Slate Protocol procedure."

"They assured me the Clean Slate Protocol was safe. It involved a cocktail of midazolam and other drugs in combination with treatments for amnesiacs and those with encephalitis and other cognitive deficits. I was told that this drug cocktail, along with state-of-the-art advancements in cognitive behavioral hypnotherapy, had been scientifically proven to alter destructive patterns, habits, and behavior. As a doctor, you will understand this better than I do, but they did something to the hippocampi in your brain to create an override of the brain's normal memory functions. This override would prevent your short-term memories from the 'fighting' period in your life from being consolidated into permanent, long-term memories. Though I didn't fully trust that any procedure affecting your brain would be completely safe, I acknowledged that it was a better chance for you to lead a full life than meeting an unfortunate 'accident.' In the end, they didn't mislead me. You came out of the surgery fine, with what appears to just be a small wiping of your memory slate clean. Your personality and other loving traits that you possess were left unchanged."

Carson looked at Nick to see his reaction, but found a face full of confusion and pain. Still absorbing, Nick struggled to find the words he wanted to say.

"I know that I just killed three men. I feel… I feel… it's almost inhuman, but I feel… nothing," Nick said, pausing reflectively. "Nothing at all about that. But at the same time, I'm numb from the pain of losing Katie. It's hell… it's pure agony. So, who am I? I don't really have a clue."

Carson responded in a soothing tone, "Trust me, son. I know this is a lot to process, but you are the same sweet, caring person that you were before the Clean Slate Protocol surgery. While there may be a void in some of your memories, look at everything you've done since the surgery. You got into med school. You excelled in that, and in your medicine residency. You became an amazing doctor. Moreover, you married an incredible woman who saw and appreciated all your talents and beauty, both inside and out. You are a complete person, and that should not change after what happened to Katie."

"I don't know, Dad. I'm just really confused right now. Maybe we should just move on to that proposal or opportunity you mentioned at the hospital so I can factor that into everything."

"I have a different suggestion," said Carson. "I think we ought to start fresh tomorrow morning. Mental wounds are as exhausting as physical wounds, so I know that you need sleep. I do as well, so let's try to call it a night. Otherwise, it might keep your mind working in overdrive all night long."

"OK," said Nick. "Thanks for your help. Love you." He turned off the light on his nightstand, and tossed and turned for most of the night as his father snored away in exhaustion.

11

OMAHA, NEBRASKA, DECEMBER 2018

Carson Class, a perpetual early riser, woke up the next morning in their hotel room at six o'clock, and found Nick asleep. Carson went quietly to the living room area and shut the bedroom door, wanting Nick to get as much sleep as his body would allow. Shortly before ten, Carson went down to the breakfast buffet at the hotel and brought two heaping plates of food back to the room just as Nick was waking up.

"This tastes great," said Nick. "So, what's up with this new 'opportunity' you mentioned?"

"In the early 1990s during the George H.W. Plante administration, I was given the opportunity to work as an assistant to President Plante's Chief of Staff, James Bakerton. Though I was very young at the time, Bakerton appreciated my work ethic and policy analysis. He let me be involved in a lot of staff and cabinet meetings. It was in those meetings that President Plante took a liking to me, and a real friendship developed.

"Plante has always had an interest in covert activities. You might remember that Plante was the Director of the Central Intelligence Agency before he became president. Plante also chaired a special task force on international drug smuggling when he was Raygun's vice president. This background convinced Plante of the need to always have adequate checks and duplicative resources to prevent miscommunications and miscalculations.

"After Plante lost his re-election bid to Bill Clanton in 1992, one of his parting acts as a lame duck president was to create with me an off-the-books, covert intelligence entity. We called it GROSS, which stands for 'Government Responsibility, Oversight, and Safety through Surveillance.' The name sounds a little corny, I know. But we formed GROSS without any of the bureaucratic layers that handicap other agencies. GROSS was our way to implement some backup redundancy to the other alphabet agencies if they ever got so confused or competitive that they overlooked something to the detriment of our national security.

"President Plante asked me to serve as the virtual gatekeeper of GROSS. It was intended to be a small, invisible organization, so my role was basically to ensure that GROSS had the right staffing and resources to protect our country. This role did not need to involve me in GROSS's day-to-day activities, so I was allowed to pursue other jobs and interests as long as I could be reached if needed."

"Are you still involved with GROSS even now that you're a senator?" Nick asked.

"Yes, I am."

"So, what does GROSS really do?"

"When it comes to terrorism, technology surveillance is the battlefield of the present and the future. Now, there are more layers to America's current intelligence network than an onion. GROSS's job is to simplify things and be a backstop to the other agencies. I make sure that GROSS has the next generation of technology available."

"Why aren't the CIA, FBI, and the other agencies able to handle things?"

"Let me just say that history has proven how much foresight President Plante had in forming GROSS. America's intelligence community currently consists of seventeen different intelligence agencies. It doesn't take a rocket scientist to know that is a crazy, inefficient structure. Despite using the most sophisticated tools available to analyze, decipher, decode, and filter all this information in the digital universe, there is a lot of critical information that is missed, overlooked, or misinterpreted. The clearest example of this is the September 11 attack on the World Trade

Center in 2001. The failure of the intelligence agencies to identify and prevent the attack, despite multiple warnings, including from us at GROSS, is haunting. It has also been really frustrating to me that all the talk of streamlining the intelligence agencies after 9/11 has turned out to be just that... talk, no action."

"So, are you saying that our intelligence agencies haven't really improved since 9/11?"

"Other than GROSS, not really. Though this was all supposed to change after 9/11, it is clear to me that interagency jealousies and competition still exist. The spy agencies all fight each other for Congressional funding. Especially in times of downsizing and budget cuts, this causes a lot of our clandestine agencies to hoard their own data to try to prove their independent value."

"And that's why GROSS exists?"

"Yes. Unfortunately, today's spy agencies are still more separate than they are coordinated. This confirms the strategic need for GROSS... a small, smart, talented, tightly-knit team that operates out of loyalty and patriotism to protect our country. Our nimble size and anonymity let us operate in ways that the alphabet agencies can't or won't."

"Let's go back to the basics," Nick said. "What role or 'opportunity' do you see for me in GROSS?"

"I have intentionally kept our GROSS team small. The larger a group gets, the greater the risk of infection by a mole, like both Russia and the United States have in the other's intelligence agencies. Here, it's just Samantha, a man we call 'Straw,' and you, if you choose to join the team. You would be replacing a very talented and skilled man, who unfortunately died in the line of duty."

"Oh wow, that's terrible. But do I have the right qualifications for the job?"

"This is a very important job. I would only ask you to join GROSS if I was sure that your skills would help us protect our country."

Nick paused reflectively, so Carson continued. "Look at it this way: you get to join an elite, anti-terrorism agency without having to go through the rigorous application process that the other alphabet agencies would require. No background checks, lie detector tests, or psychological evaluations. This is far removed from the pursuit of a medical career, at least for the time being, and would require a move to D.C. But please consider this opportunity. I can truthfully say that our country could really use you."

"This is all happening so fast. I'll need some time to think. Can you give me a little better idea of what the people at GROSS do daily?"

"Sure. Straw is an analytical genius, and his job is to figure out what terrorist activity is likely to happen. Your and Samantha's main jobs are to prevent it from happening. Hopefully, the CIA, FBI, NSA, Homeland Security, and other agencies also reach the same conclusion as Straw and use their assets to prevent the bad thing from happening as well. But if Straw's conclusion is based on hunches and dot-connecting that only he can do, there may not be enough hard evidence to rise to the level of legal probability. That may prevent the other agencies from acting, leaving just you and Sam to stop whatever it is the bad guys are planning."

"I'm still confused. What happens on a daily basis?"

"Basically, there is a ton of high-level intel that flows into the GROSS office every day. Straw acts as the eyes, ears, and brains of our organization. He is great at deciphering information, but he reads data better than people. Sam's background in psychology has been a huge help to Straw in understanding how a person was thinking. Their joint success in identifying risks to our country has helped prevent numerous incidents, both foreign and domestic, such as stopping the Al-Qaeda plot to bomb New York City subways in 2009. Yet no one knows what they have done for their country, except for me and the president."

"Dad, I've always appreciated your public service work, but I never expected you were involved in anything like this. This is wild! It goes without saying that this is all very intriguing. Can you tell me a little bit more about both Samantha and this guy you call Straw?"

"Sure. Samantha has a very interesting and impressive background, but the bottom line is that in addition to being smart, Samantha is determined, fierce, and unstoppable."

"Yeah, I think I've mainly seen her fierce side. My first impression of her wasn't the greatest."

"I'm confident that will improve over time. You already met Sam, so let me give you the scoop on Straw. He's a very interesting man!

"Straw is a certified genius. He did his undergrad studies at UC Berkeley and his graduate work at MIT. After graduating from MIT, Straw worked for a company where he used algorithms to build a machine to analyze and predict crime patterns. That won him the coveted Squirrel AI prize, which is like the Nobel Prize of artificial intelligence. That caught my attention, and I thought there might be lots of opportunities for Straw to use his skills at GROSS to help predict terrorist strikes. He quickly bought what I was selling, and he's been a dedicated member of the team ever since. Straw is quirky, but when all is said and done, he is an amazing critical thinker under pressure."

Carson paused when his cell phone rang.

"Sorry. I've gotta take this. In the meantime, look at this file. It's something that Straw and Sam are currently reviewing."

Carson went into the bedroom and shut the door to allow them both some privacy for their thoughts.

Nick sat back on the couch and wondered what the heck just happened, and not knowing for the first time in ages where was his life headed.

12

WASHINGTON, D.C., JANUARY 2009

Professor Xavier Moody was enjoying a late afternoon cocktail in his penthouse in the upscale Capitol Hill section of Washington, D.C. The long-time Democrat strategist had been credited by many for the election successes of both Bill Clanton in 1992-2000 and Barrack Olama in 2008. The inauguration of President Olama had just occurred, and Moody was basking in the afterglow of his acknowledged ability to both understand and influence American elections. He was raking in significant money as a member of multiple corporate boards, a visiting professor of political science at Georgetown University, and a valued speaker-for-hire at large corporate events. Life was great. When he got a phone call from his college roommate, Salvador Santos, his life got even better.

"X-man, this is Salvy, though everyone just calls me 'Jefe' these days. How are you doing, my friend?"

"Hey roomie! Doing well, and just enjoying my first drink of the day. It's great to hear your voice! How are you, Verana, and your lovely daughter doing? How old is Abriz now, six or seven?"

"Thanks for asking. Abriz is seven going on seventeen, but the absolute joy of my life. It has been a while since we've seen each other, and there is a lot to celebrate. How would you like to come stay with us this weekend?"

"Your timing is perfect, Salvy… I mean 'Jefe.' My weekend is totally free. When would you like me to come down?"

"I'll have a plane waiting for you at the charter jets section of Dulles on Friday. It will be ready to leave any time between 3-4 p.m. and will get you here in time to have dinner with me and my family."

"That sounds perfect!"

"I look forward to seeing you again, my friend! I also have a business proposal that might be of interest to you."

13

OMAHA, NEBRASKA, DECEMBER 2018

By the time the funeral came, Nick had already cried out all the tears in his body. Nick was very religious, so he clung to God for comfort, but also felt like cursing God in his same breath. Death, more so than life, never seems fair, even if it is a step in the progression to eternal life. Nick almost lost it when he heard his mother-in-law whisper, "You are never supposed to bury your children."

Katie's funeral itself was wonderful as far as funerals go. The emphasis was on an uplifting celebration of the short, but magnificent life of a beautiful and loving person. Nick mentally acknowledged that he was fortunate to have had his wife in his life, but it was impossible not to feel the loss of their bright future together. All feelings were magnified by the sights and sounds of what otherwise would have been a joyous holiday season. Nick was glad that he still felt numb because the pain of his loss would have been too much to bear, and it especially gnawed on him that he had combat skills that could have resulted in a different outcome if he had known or used them earlier.

As he dwelled on this, Nick started to spiral. The façade of the good front Nick thought he was putting on started to fray. As he glanced at the smiling photos of Katie at the reception following the funeral, a flood of memories flashed through his head. To ease his pain, Nick focused on the ornate floral arrangements that surrounded Katie's photos. Nick found strange comfort and parallels from the beautiful flowers: all in the healthy prime of their life, then suddenly cut short with the end to life imminent.

Nick left the reception as early as he could without being disrespectful. "Dad," he said to Carson, who had stayed by his side most of the day, "I need to run by my house and pick up some things. I'll meet you back at the hotel."

Nick departed as stealthily as possible. A chill went through his body when he arrived back at his house for the first time since the disaster in the park.

So much has changed, yet so much in here is the same, thought Nick.

After picking up some clothes to take to the hotel, Nick walked into the kitchen. He threw some rotten bananas into a trash bag and opened the refrigerator to see if the milk had expired. The refrigerator had a rancid smell that Nick couldn't immediately place. He scanned the refrigerator. At the back of the bottom shelf, he found the source: a container of leftover fettuccine. A flood of tears poured out as Nick relived his last meal with Katie in their house.

The tears were therapeutic and eventually stopped. As Nick exited his house, he reached into a pocket to retrieve his keys and lock the door. Along with his keys, he felt a card that had been placed in his pocket. It was a business card with the phone number for Straw at GROSS.

Maybe this is a sign, Nick thought.

14

VERACRUZ, MEXICO, JANUARY 2009

A sparkling new Lear jet was waiting for Professor Xavier Moody when he arrived at Dulles International Airport. He would be the sole passenger on this three-hour flight to Veracruz, Mexico, joined only by the two pilots and a flight attendant.

The Lear jet landed so smoothly at the Aeropuerto Internacional de Veracruz that Moody was barely jostled from his sleep. A shiny black Lincoln Town Car was waiting for him at the end of the stairs as he exited the plane. The driver told him that it would only take fifteen minutes to get to "casa de Jefe."

During the brief trip, the friendly driver gave Professor Moody a proud and short history lesson of the area, indicating that Heroica Veracruz was one of Mexico's oldest and largest ports founded by Spanish settlers in the 16th century. Located on the Gulf of Mexico, Veracruz was just a short helicopter flight to Mexico City and directly across the mainland from Acapulco.

Jefe's house was more in the nature of a large estate, located in a secluded section of Costa de Oro. The road to the house was cut through a swath of trees. As the Town Car got closer, they came upon large wrought iron gates mounted on enormous marble columns on the edge of the road that could only be opened by security personnel on site. Beyond the gates, botanical gardens of flowers came into view in pristinely configured, terraced flower beds. The beautiful landscaping created a "Masters at Augusta" feel to the setting. Two large green marble statues of lions, along with exotic plants and flowers in large stone pots, framed the entryway to Jefe's Spanish-style house that had a red tile roof and Moorish-style windows. The relaxing sound of the gentle ocean surf from the nearby Chachalacas sandbar provided a soothing welcome to all visitors.

Jeez, Professor Moody thought, *Salvy must have a team of gardeners to keep this place lush.*

A glance to the side of the house revealed the edge of a large infinity pool with plenty of comfortable lounge chairs. Further on, there was a pathway to a tennis court, gurgling marble fountains, and a private bungalow. In the distance was a private boat dock for a yacht and three smaller boats.

After parking the Town Car, the driver opened the front door to Jefe's house. He informed Moody that Jefe would meet him soon.

Inside the house were more ornate columns of imported Italian marble. A plush Oriental rug led guests to the Great Room used to entertain visitors. Large windows allowed great views of the exterior and provided natural light to view the many pieces of museum-quality paintings adorning the walls. Eye-catching sculptures were artistically placed where they were visible, but not interrupting the feng shui of the house. An enormous fireplace topped by an extended mantel showcased the view as one entered the Great Room. Through the windows, the grounds in the back of Jefe's hacienda appeared just as immaculate as the front. All the exterior amenities were connected by a flagstone pathway to Jefe's expansive house.

Moody was impressed. While large, Jefe's mansion had an understated elegance. It blended classic Spanish and European architecture to provide both beauty and functionality. Moody thought it was a rare example of a rich person exhibiting good taste, instead of flaunting wealth in excess extravagance.

Before long, Jefe descended the staircase, flanked by his wife Verana and daughter Abriz. As usual, Abriz's energetic personality commanded the stage as she rushed to Moody after reaching the bottom of the stairs, and announced, "Hi, I'm Abriz. Are you really a professor?"

All the adults chuckled, and Professor Moody smiled. "Pleased to meet you, Abriz. Yes, I really am a teacher. But you can just call me Mr. Moody."

"No, I think I like 'Professor' better. That's a lot easier to remember."

"I think that's a great idea," interjected Verana. "I like calling you 'Professor' much better than Xavier. That's always sounded like the name of a mutant in a movie."

"That works for me," said Moody smiling. "'Professor' it is." He reached over to give Verana a hug and said, "Verana! You look fantastic as always. Life with my roommate must be treating you well!"

"It is! I have no complaints, other than Salvador spends too much time thinking about his work."

"Hearing my lovely wife say that is music to my ears," Jefe said as he gave his former roommate a hug. "It's really great to see you again. You haven't changed a bit."

Professor chuckled. "Well, you're nice not to notice my few more pounds and little less hair! It is great to be here. What a fabulous place you have. And, your decorative touch is fantastic, Verana."

"Thank you," said Verana as a maid entered the room carrying a tray of drinks.

"Cheers to good friends," toasted Jefe as the three adults clinked their glasses together. "Tonight is a time for us to enjoy good food, great company, and lots of reminiscing. Tomorrow, we discuss business."

15

OMAHA, NEBRASKA, DECEMBER 2018

Though not a large man, Carson Class was "farm strong." He had broad shoulders and a muscular torso from years of working on the family farm from sunrise to sunset before college. His farming background provided him the work ethic and drive needed to succeed. He excelled during his college and graduate years at the University of Nebraska, finishing top of his class when pursuing both a law degree and a PhD in agricultural economics.

In Washington, Carson was known as one of the smartest and hardest-working people in government. Carson was also well-respected and liked by members of all parties for not having an agenda other than doing what was in the best interest of the country. Carson served in two cabinet posts in the administration of George W. Plante, son of the prior president. When Olama was elected in 2008, Carson returned to Nebraska to serve as managing partner of the state's largest law firm. Two years later, the Nebraska governor appointed him to serve as one of Nebraska's senators in Washington after the prior senator left the post to become a university president. Carson never lost an election since, drawing bipartisan support throughout the state.

Nick loved and respected Carson, both as father and as a public servant. He knew that his dad would always shoot straight with him, and always had his best interests at heart. After the intense emotions of Katie's funeral and the rush of memories at his home, Nick was in a pensive mood when he returned to the Embassy Suites.

Carson greeted Nick with a big hug when he entered the room. "How was everything at your house?"

"Fine," Nick bluffed, flashing back to the fettucine he found in the refrigerator. "Thanks for all your support during the funeral."

"Of course," Carson replied. "I thought it was a very nice service."

"I agree, but it's been quite a day and I'm spent. Before I call it a night, can I ask you a simple question — if you were me, would you take the open position at GROSS?"

Carson paused, carefully wording his response. "Nick, it is ultimately your choice. But here are some more of my thoughts. First, you know that I think you would be a great fit for the position. You, Straw, and Samantha are all different enough in ages and talents to provide unique viewpoints and help us keep up with global events.

"Second, I am a believer that everything happens for a reason. I'm not trying to downplay what happened to Katie. But sometimes, what you think should be the end leads to a new beginning. A great writer once said that 'sometimes we must be hurt in order to grow, fall in order to know, lose in order to gain, and sometimes we have to be broken so we can be whole again.' I think this rings true. You will learn more from pain than pleasure, and failure and adversity will teach you more than success and comfort. GROSS could be a great change of pace for you. When you're trying to solve someone else's problems, you find less time to worry about your own. I don't know if that's good or bad. That's for you to decide."

"Thanks, Dad. It's a lot to think about, but right now all I want to do is try to sleep. Let's pick this up again tomorrow."

"Sure thing. Good night. I love you."

"Love you, too."

16

OMAHA, NEBRASKA, DECEMBER 2018

Nick awoke the next day as tired as he was when he tried to go to sleep the previous night. Inner pain is a stimulus that isn't conducive to good sleep. Nick was a restless wreck the whole night, with frustration growing the more he kept looking at the clock. While he tossed and turned, Nick realized that when he was alone, he quickly felt unraveled and gutted. Nick looked in the mirror and questioned whether this was his new reality, and whether he wanted to live in it.

The sun had not yet risen when Nick went into the living room area of their hotel room, shut the door so his dad could continue sleeping, and splashed water on his face to wake up. Sitting down on the couch to think about the GROSS job offer, he realized it was the opportunity to start a new life... or at least a new chapter in life. While exciting, it was also overwhelming and without any advanced planning — which was very unlike Nick and his orchestrated medical career. On the other hand, Nick wasn't sure he was ready to return to his medical job and other reminders of his old life.

As the debate continued in his mind, there was a soft knock on the door. Carson entered the room and sat next to Nick.

"I thought you might have some trouble sleeping," said Carson while rubbing his eyes. "Want some company?"

"Sure. I'm just trying to figure out the GROSS situation and what to do with my life. Not too long ago, I thought I had everything figured out. I was married to a great woman. I just finished residency. We were going to have a baby. Katie and I had a full life ahead of us. But now, there's this hole in my heart. I feel like I'm back to square one and need to figure out who I really am."

Carson was a skillful listener. He kept his eye contact, but remained silent so Nick would continue to pour out his true feelings.

Nick paused reflectively before continuing. "I've always liked the story about taking the path less traveled. You've given me the option of a path that I never knew existed. For me to start living again, I need to move forward, and that is what I want to do. So, my gut says that joining GROSS is the best next step for me."

"Very well. If you do this, how much will you miss your medical career?" asked Carson.

"That has really torn me up. I don't want to waste all the time and effort that I've put into medicine. But I also need to be realistic. You really need to be sharp in the medical field. I'll admit it… my mind and emotional state are out of whack and may be that way for a long time. So, as you said, when one thing ends, something else begins."

Carson leaned over to give Nick a big hug. "We'll make this work and you'll be a great asset to GROSS. We need all the help we can get to stop terrorists and other threats. But if you ever decide you want to return to medicine, just let me know and we'll make that happen. Just know that whatever you do, I'll always love you and be proud of you."

17

OMAHA, NEBRASKA, DECEMBER 2018

Nick's decision made, Carson went to the bedroom to start coordinating travel arrangements to D.C. Nick stayed in the other room and picked up the file on the Mexican cartel leader that his father had given him.

Reading the dossier was Nick's first exposure to the world of espionage, and it intrigued him immensely. The papers in the file provided a case study that profiled Salvador Santos in great deal. As he read the file, Nick could only imagine what covert resources were used to supply the very specific personal and business information on Santos.

Salvador Santos was simply stated as a person of interest at the top of the "Eyes Only" file. The cover page of the file contained basic biographical information. Santos, a.k.a. Jefe, was listed as 46-years-old, 5'9" tall, and weighing 160 pounds. Born in Mexico City, he has been married for eighteen years to Verana Lopez, age 44, and they have a sixteen-year-old daughter, Abriz. They have resided in Veracruz, Mexico since their marriage. He graduated with high honors from Georgetown University in 1996 with a business finance degree. Santos' occupation was simply listed as "businessman." His net worth was estimated to be in excess of $6 billion, sourced from suspected Los Leones drug cartel operations and significant investments in banks, a trucking company, the major Mexican telephone company, commercial real estate, resort hotels, and a winery. A recent addition to the file indicated that Santos was rumored to be exploring the purchase of a professional fútbol team in the Premier League.

Although the quick-reference cover page of the file was interesting, the real meat of the dossier was contained in the body of the file. Subsections of the dossier provided more detailed analysis of Santos' business holdings and personal life. The file was at least twenty years old. Additions to the file, ranging from newspaper articles about Santos to summaries of intercepted phone conversations, had been made sporadically over time. Nick was surprised that the file was not better organized, and wondered why a paper file even existed.

The most intriguing part of the file to Nick was the information tying Santos to drug cartel activities, first the Los Hermanos cartel, and later as the suspected leader of the Los Leones cartel. Though there was no indication that Santos had ever been indicted, much less convicted of any crimes, the file contained detailed conjecture about his purported involvement. There was an assertion that Santos figured out how to profit from certain actions of the United States military. In 1996, the U.S. military created the Deep Web to provide a system where users could access the internet without divulging their identities, with layers of encryption obscuring the transmitted data. Santos was listed as the first outsider to figure out how to use the Deep Web for the advantage of Los Leones. When Bitcoin later came into play, Santos was able to use the double anonymity created by the Deep Web and Bitcoin to make Los Leones drug money virtually untraceable for decades. After the FBI established the National Domestic Communications Assistance Center to help law enforcement penetrate areas of the internet that were essentially unsearchable, Santos quickly adapted so that the activities of Los Leones continued to remain as hidden and anonymous as in prior years.

Nick looked up from reading the file and noticed that Carson was standing in the room observing him. Carson had a smile on his face and said, "Looks like you are finding some of the info in that file captivating. I think that's a great sign. Happy reading!"

18

VERACRUZ, MEXICO, JANUARY 2009

Jefe was having coffee with his wife the next morning when Professor walked into the kitchen.

"How did you sleep last night, my friend?" Jefe asked.

"Never better. That may be the most comfortable mattress I've ever slept on in my life."

"Glad to hear it. Let's get some coffee. I have pastries and fruit set out by the pool. It's a beautiful morning, so we should discuss business there. Verana, you don't mind if we leave?"

"Of course not, my dear," said Verana with a smile. "Abriz and I will give you some privacy."

Jefe and Professor exited the kitchen and made the short walk to the pool, where a table was set up with a large umbrella and two chairs underneath. An assortment of breakfast rolls and pastries were surrounded by trays of fresh fruits, pitchers of juices, and a pot of coffee. The men each filled up a plate, then sat down to enjoy their beautiful surroundings. The sun provided comfortable warmth, and the soothing sounds of birds chirping and the waves rolling into the nearby gulf created the perfect tranquil atmosphere.

"Jefe, this place is incredible. I obviously was a great influence on you at Georgetown for you to be this successful," Professor joked.

"Thank you, Professor. I have been very fortunate."

"I'd say you've been more than just fortunate," Professor chuckled. "I loved the Newsweek article that nicknamed you the 'Mexican Midas' because everything you touch turned to gold. You became one of the youngest billionaires in the world. It couldn't happen to a better person!"

"Thanks again," said Jefe, as he raised his glass of mango juice in a toast to his friend. "I've also followed your professional successes with a lot of pride and satisfaction. We've both done very well for ourselves. Cheers to us!"

"Agreed. Cheers!"

They clinked glasses, then Professor continued, "Apart from the fantastic influence of your roommate, to what do you attribute your great success, Jefe?"

"Well, you know what they have said about me in various magazines. But there is always a story behind the story, and I want you to know the full facts before I tell you my business proposal."

"Sure. I'm all ears."

Jefe took a deep breath. "As you know from our time at Georgetown, I don't do drugs. Alcohol, on the other hand, is another matter," he laughed, remembering fond times of mutual intoxication with Professor while in college. "However, as you also know, the drug industry has a significant economic influence in both Mexico and the United States. I've never told you this, but the drug industry has played an important part of my life."

Jefe paused to see Professor's reaction. He was pleased when Professor looked more perplexed than judgmental.

"I'm shocked, I'll admit." said Professor. "I remember parties when people would joke that you only got into Georgetown through drug connections. But I always thought you needed scholarship money to attend."

"Yes, my family was very poor. But my parents saw that I was smart, and they knew that an education was the best way for me to escape poverty. Well, high schools in Mexico are big targets for the drug cartels. High schools provide access to new users as well as a pool of cheap labor for the cartels to transport product, collect and move money, and various other tasks."

Jefe paused to take a sip of juice and then continued. "The cartel person in charge of my school wanted me to help with the business-side of marijuana. He introduced me as a young, Einstein-like prodigy to the leader of the entire Los Hermanos cartel at the time, Mario Enrico. Enrico took me under his wing and taught me the inner business of drug trafficking. After I provided some suggestions regarding ways to launder and hide cash, Enrico paid me more money than my parents had earned in their lifetime."

"I've heard of Enrico," Professor said. "Wasn't he known to be a ruthless SOB?"

"Enrico was very nice to me, and he paid his people well. But he also used fear to obtain loyalty. If anyone crossed Enrico, they and their families would suffer grave consequences.

"With respect to me, Enrico supported me going to Georgetown. I always used school breaks to return to Mexico and help the cartel. Even while I was away, Enrico kept elevating my role in the organization. I really appreciated that, and we had a promising career ahead of us.

"However, right before our graduation at Georgetown, there was a massive battle between Los Hermanos and our largest rival. Both Enrico and the head of the other gang were killed. This left both organizations as hugely profitable enterprises without any executive leadership. Both organizations realized that was a horrible structure. So, instead of continuing to shoot each other up, the two gangs called a peace treaty and merged. At that point, I was asked to head the new organization, called Los Leones, going forward."

Professor looked stunned, but not disappointed, so Jefe continued. "I had some reservations, but thankfully both sides supported me. I have tried to lead fairly, develop a positive culture in the organization, and share the immense wealth that we created. For years, Los Leones members have called me 'Jefe.'"

"And that's when you started to become the Mexican Midas?" Professor asked.

"Yes. I used my share of drug profits to make some very good, or lucky, investments. Those investments have grown over the years and now generate more income to me than the money I get from the drug trade done under my watchful eyes."

"Wow!" exclaimed Professor. "That is quite the story. I feel embarrassed that I never expected any connection between you and the drug world. You know how to keep a secret better than anyone I know."

"In this business, that is critical to both success and safety."

19

VERACRUZ, MEXICO, JANUARY 2009

Professor took a deep breath and shook his head in amazement at what he had just heard. He took a long drink of pineapple juice and exclaimed, "I have a million questions, but let's start with just two. First, do Verana and Abriz know any of this? Second, what's this business proposal you mentioned?"

"Verana knows the big picture, but not the details. Abriz is just a happy, innocent girl. I wouldn't have asked Verana to marry me without her knowing the big picture. I have convinced her that I am an executive who is far enough removed from the activities on the ground to be safe… both from legal risks and potential violence. Safety of my loved ones is key. You may not have noticed it, but my house is like a fortress that is protected from attack. All walls are fortified, and all windows are bulletproof. And, though you can't see them, I have a small fleet of well-armed protectors who can react in a moment's notice if needed. I also have protection that discreetly accompanies Verana and Abriz wherever they are, and I've made lots of payments to local police to ensure their support.

"And now to the second question. Why have I asked you to come here? The answer is that I want to use your talents to elect a person loyal to me as President of the United States."

Upon hearing Jefe's bombshell, Professor's face lost a bit of color. He took a moment to compose himself.

"Um, can you give me some more specifics behind this idea of yours?" Professor asked. "Why do you want to control POTUS?"

Jefe took a long sip of his mango juice and looked Professor in the eyes. "Professor, I am really frustrated and disappointed with our elected leaders on both sides of the border, but especially in the United States. It seems to me that Washington has been paralyzed for years by hyper-partisanship that is causing America to be very un-American. Do you agree?"

"I agree," said Professor. "Politicians are intoxicated by power, position, and the glow of the cameras. Political preservation has become more important than running the country, and the fear of alienating any block of voters has neutered Congress. That has led to nothing but short-term thinking, and focusing on the next election or the next poll. That's great for election strategists like me, but what America needs is fewer politicians and more leaders. Fewer policies, more principles."

"Plus, Americans completely underestimate and disrespect Mexico," interjected Jefe, clenching his hands on his pool chair. "They don't see us as a leader of anything or as having the intelligence or resources to be a valued business partner. All Americans see is cheap labor, drug problems, and a disaster at the border. Americans completely dehumanize and undervalue us."

"I agree that our border politics are a disaster," Professor said. "But is your main motivation to increase your drug business in the U.S.?"

"No," Jefe replied. "Most people with money or power are obsessed with getting more. I'm not in that mode. Getting the U.S. presidency is not just a power grab or something that will help my business interests. Those are merely byproduct benefits to having the access and ability to do something worthwhile for the people of my homeland and, secondarily, the people of the United States."

Jefe took another drink of juice before continuing. "Warner Buffett, the 'Oracle of Omaha' and one of the few people with more wealth than me, recently said that 'the disposition of money unmasks humans.' My goal is to follow his guidance. I'm not trying to capture the presidency to increase my assets while leaving only crumbs for others. Ultimately, I want to do what the bottlenecked U.S. government has not been able to do — improve the lives of a great number of people on both sides of the border. If we claim the U.S. presidency, we'll be able to improve relations between both countries and integrate our economies in multiple ways. Growing the economies of both countries will help end the corruption and violence that exists at the border."

Professor nodded his head affirmatively. "Jefe, I am glad that the main goal of your plan is not to just increase your drug profits. If that had been the case, I wouldn't be interested in exploring this any further."

"I would not have expected any other reaction from you, Professor."

"OK. To be absolutely clear, what role would I play in your master plan?"

"I plan to rely on you for the big-picture electoral strategy. You will identify all the steps that need to be taken for us to claim the presidency. In turn, I will supply you all the money and other resources that you need. I already have a ton of loyal connections in America. I don't want to brag, but our distribution network throughout the United States makes us as connected as FedEx or the postal service. Beyond the drug industry, I also have great contacts with banks and hedge funds that have helped my enterprises. These contacts are all at your disposal. Once we are on the inside of the American political structure, then we can start rearranging the power from within."

"Can we rely on the secrecy and loyalty of your contacts?" Professor asked. "In a venture of this sort, we need our assets in America to be as silent and invisible as possible while we amass influence, power, and momentum. Their confidentiality is also needed to keep you and me out of prison!"

"Yes, I assure you that these people are very loyal. There can always be a few fools on the ground level who are short-sighted. However, there will be many layers of protection that will prevent any of their actions from being connected to us."

Jefe took a deep breath. "So, my friend, do you think our goal is attainable?"

"Jefe, anyone who says they can predict political outcomes with certainty is a liar. This is especially true when it comes to electoral politics. What's your expected time frame to capture the presidency?"

"I know that this will take some time, but I would like this to occur no later than the 2024 election in fifteen years," Jefe answered.

"That timing seems reasonable," Professor mused.

"So, Professor, are you willing to provide your talents to help?"

"Well, your timing is great as far as my personal situation. Frankly, I've been pretty bored ever since Olama won a few months ago. And for a political science and election junkie, what could be more exciting than your offer? Like I said, I wouldn't even consider your offer if I thought the goal was just to increase your wealth. But you've convinced me otherwise and that both Mexico and the United States will be better off if we succeed. That will let me work with you and still sleep well at night."

"Professor, you have put a big smile on my face! I appreciate your consideration."

"We'll see if you are smiling as broadly when you see the price tag of our challenge. Running for president takes a lot of money and time. We will need *years* to fully flesh out our strategy. Ideally, we should get more than one candidate from each party in the race in multiple election cycles. Winning a presidential election also involves a lot of luck and just being in the right place at the right time."

"I don't doubt any of that and, in fact, expect it," replied Jefe. "When it comes to money, there are no limits. I want this at all costs, and I trust you as a long-time friend to just spend it wisely. I also know that I really need your planning skills. This will be a massive undertaking, and failing to plan means we are planning to fail."

"Jefe, this is a huge challenge, and I am excited to work with you to meet it head on."

"But do you realistically think we can attain our goal and claim the presidency?"

"With your money and my political brain, I think this is possible. We can look at China for a favorable analogy. For a long time, they have been throwing out money for infrastructure contracts in Africa and the

South Pacific. This expenditure of money has bought them contacts, loyalty, power, and influence in the region ahead of other countries like the United States. We just need to do the same things on a smaller, more targeted scale, to put our people in position to ascend into power."

"Just what I wanted to hear. Oh, by the way, I forgot to mention how much I value your services and dedication. I will pay you $5,000,000 per year, tax-free, into an account in the Caymans in your name, and a bonus of $50 million once our candidate becomes president. A little more than you make as a professor, eh?"

"That is amazingly generous of you, Jefe," said an astounded Professor.

"Here's a toast to our success, and to the day when the president is not known as POTUS, but rather as POTUSOM for those of us who really know the truth... the 'President of the United States of Mexico!'"

20

WASHINGTON, D.C., JANUARY 2019

After Katie's funeral, Nick and his dad spent a couple of days tying up loose ends and getting Nick ready for his move to Washington. GROSS owned a house near the Georgetown campus which was to be used as Nick's residence. However, all old houses sometimes require significant repairs at the worst possible time. This happened shortly before Nick and Carson arrived in Washington, when the HVAC system ceased working and required a complete replacement.

"Nick, I was planning to have you stay with me while your furnace was getting fixed," said Carson. "However, Straw told me that he'd really like to get the chance to know you before you start work together. Is that OK with you?"

"Sure thing."

"OK. We'll go straight to his house from the airport. Straw said you could stay as long as you liked, but your house should be ready for you to settle in this weekend."

"Perfect."

21

WASHINGTON, D.C., JANUARY 2019

Jack "Straw" Berry lived with his wife, Cherise, and 16-year-old daughter, Stella, in a mid-sized, three-bedroom house in a premier Georgetown neighborhood. As Carson walked Nick to the front door, a small black and silver poodle/schnauzer mix greeted them.

"Cassidy, it's OK… they're friends," said the man who opened the door. He appeared to be in his mid-40s, with receding "salt & pepper" hair long enough to be kept in a man-bun. He stood barefoot, wearing loose blue jeans with a psychedelic tie-dyed t-shirt. His glasses gave him a goofy, John Lennon-esque look.

"Nick," Carson said, "this is my colleague, Straw. Straw, please meet my son, Nick. I'd like to stay and see Cherise and Stella, but I've been out of the office and need to catch up on work. So, I'll leave you two to get acquainted."

"Thanks, Carson," said Straw. "Fare thee well now, and let your life proceed by its own design."

"You bet, Straw," said Carson, unfazed. "Let me know if there's anything I can do to help at GROSS."

Nick entered Straw's house, put his luggage on the floor, and shook his hand. "It's a pleasure to meet you. My dad told me lots of great things about you."

"Likewise," said Straw. "Let me show you around the house, but first let's finish the introductions. You met Cassidy, our dog. Let me find my wife."

Cherise Berry entered from the kitchen. She was barefoot like Straw and wore a flattering sun dress. Her face looked younger than Straw, and her bright, easy smile gave off a fun hippie vibe. *Straw married above his level*, thought Nick.

"Nick Class, meet my wife, Cherise. She's my summer love in the spring, fall, and winter, and makes me the happiest man alive."

"It's great to meet anyone related to Carson," said Cherise. "Welcome to Washington. You are always welcome in our house."

"Thanks," Nick said. "I appreciate your hospitality. I'll try not to be in your way too much."

Straw patted him on the back. "Nick, you are a friend, not a stranger. Don't hesitate to reach out your hand if your cup is empty."

Cherise returned to the kitchen and said, "Honey, let me get back to dinner so it'll be ready when Stella gets home from band practice."

Straw led Nick on a quick tour of the house, with Cassidy trotting along at his feet. Music was the clear, common theme of their interior design. Speakers were imbedded in the walls or ceilings of every room.

"Delilah, please play 'Winterland 1972 Box of Rain,'" said Straw, and quickly the house was filled with music from a live concert.

"Wow, that is really cool," exclaimed Nick. "Who's Delilah?"

"She's our version of Siri, but it really goes deeper than that. Delilah is 'fine and fair' in the lyrics of a song we like. In Hebrew, her name is wordplay for 'night.' As the night overcomes the powerful sun, so does Delilah overcome the mighty Samson, who everyone thought was invincible."

As Nick processed the first of possibly many nuggets of hippie wisdom, Straw continued with the tour. Most rooms looked as bizarre as its patriarch. An eclectic combination of Grateful Dead memorabilia, squirrel art, and stuffed toy squirrels were randomly displayed throughout the house, joining the clutter of computer science textbooks, AI magazines, flashing laptops, and a swanky stereo system.

"What are you, a Rocky and Bullwinkle fan?" asked Nick as he picked up one of the larger stuffed toy squirrels. "No, wait. My dad told me you won some elite squirrel award."

"That's right, Nick," Cherise stated as she came in from the kitchen. "Don't let him be all humble with you. Straw's very proud of that award. I've sort of made it our thing by giving fun squirrel artwork or stuffed animals as holiday or birthday gifts."

Straw nudged Nick and whispered, "As you can see, I knew right away that Cherise was not like other girls."

They continued with the tour of the remainder of the house. There were three bedrooms in the two-story structure, but the third bedroom was used as both an office and music studio for Straw.

"This is where you will stay, Nick," Straw said proudly.

The walls in the music studio were filled with posters and pictures of Grateful Dead concerts spanning more than a decade. Centered along the longest wall was a large saltwater fish tank in a custom oak cabinet filled with beautifully colored fish, coral, and crustaceans. The whole room had a light smell of incense. There was no bed, but a large couch sat opposite a glass desk that held three monitors.

"The couch looks a little lumpy, but it's serviceable," Straw said. "Sometimes, I'll just sleep here if I work late. The coolest thing about this room is that it is 100% soundproof. So, as long as you shut the door, you can play music as loud as you want, and nobody will be bothered. Music is like a sunshine daydream… it's inspiration that moves me brightly!"

"Stella's home." Cherise called from the kitchen. "Come and get it."

22

WASHINGTON, D.C., JANUARY 2019

Dinner was an incredible treat to Nick. Cherise had prepared a delicious meal of grilled, wild-caught salmon over balsamic rice, with asparagus and a side salad. Wine flowed plentifully. The satisfaction of the meal was exceeded only by the quality of the company. Stella was a bright-eyed, intelligent teenager who was comfortable among adults. Unlike many of her awkward peers, she wasn't afraid to show how much she loved her parents, giving them both a big hug before they introduced Nick.

During dinner, Nick learned that Stella was sixteen and interested in computer science and American government. She did not yet have a driver's license or boyfriend, although there seemed to be increased interest in both. Stella was named after a Grateful Dead song, which was not surprising since Straw met Cherise at a Grateful Dead concert. Nick also learned that Straw was fluent in Spanish, Russian, and Mandarin. Straw enjoyed the unique way that languages worked, which fit well with the Lego-solving nature of his brain. Learning Japanese was next on his agenda when free time allowed.

As dinner came to an end, Nick snapped his fingers. "Hey, I finally understand your name. You're called 'Straw' because of your last name. 'Straw Berry.'"

Nick's comment brought laughter from the others at the table.

"Nope," said Straw. "It's the other one."

"What? 'Berry Straw?'" asked Nick, confused.

"Nope. 'Jack Straw.' That was my parents' favorite Grateful Dead song. You may know it." Straw cleared his throat. Then, with a far-away look in his eyes, he began to sing. *"We can share what we've got of yours cuz we've done shared all of mine."*

"Sorry, I haven't heard many Grateful Dead songs. My parents were more into classical music, jazz, blues, and classic rock. My favorite music nowadays is EDM."

"Everyone's music preferences are like their heart... each has its seasons, its evenings, and songs of its own," replied Straw, looking like he was going to burst into song again.

"When Dad starts singing, I know it's time for me to leave," laughed Stella. "I've got some homework to do. It was really nice meeting you, Mr. Class."

Stella left as Nick and Straw both helped clear the table. After the dishes were rinsed and put in the dishwasher, Straw grabbed another bottle of wine and said, "Honey, if you don't mind, it's time for Nick and me to listen to some music and get to know each other better."

"Sure thing," Cherise said. "I'll let you know when Stella is about to crash."

23

WASHINGTON, D.C., JANUARY 2019

With a new bottle of cabernet and two glasses in hand, Straw led Nick back to the music studio. Upon entering, Straw said, "Delilah, please play 'Omaha 1978' in honor of our guest."

Once the song started, Straw shut the door and lowered the volume so they could still hear the music, but didn't have to strain to talk. Straw motioned for Nick to sit on the couch for the best view of the fish tank.

"1977 is my favorite year for Grateful Dead concerts," Straw said, "but this Omaha show in '78 had a lot of great moments. It started with a great 10-minute jam of 'Sugaree' to open the first set." As Straw was talking, he opened the top of the fish tank, took some brine shrimp from a small freezer inside the bottom cabinet, and sprinkled the food in the salt water.

Nick was instantly captivated by the beauty and activity level in the tank. The fish and exotic shrimp and crabs hustled to grab bites of the food scattering throughout the tank.

"This is amazing!" Nick exclaimed, watching some of nature's most beautiful creatures.

"It gets even more surreal," Straw said. "If you look closely, you will see that two of my friends haven't eaten since they don't like brine shrimp. One is that beautiful lionfish swimming by the front glass. He knows his dinner is coming soon."

Straw leaned down with a small net and nabbed two small goldfish from a bowl of feeder fish under the cabinet. He dropped the goldfish in the water. The lionfish gracefully tracked each before devouring them within thirty seconds.

"The next feeding is a little more difficult. Do you see that snowflake moray eel sticking its head out under that live rock at the left of the tank? That's 'Jerry.' I've had him over ten years, which is way beyond his life span. However, he can't see very well, so I have to hand-feed him." Straw netted another feeder goldfish, grabbed its tail between his fingers, and slowly lowered the fish until it was inches in front of the eel's face, whereupon the eel lunged slightly forward to capture its prey. "He's crippled but free. He may be blind all the time, but he's learning to see."

"Incredible," said Nick, still transfixed by the beauty and entertainment he had just witnessed.

"There is no ripple in still water," said Straw, sitting down on the couch a few feet from Nick so they could both gaze at the fish tank. "Let's have some wine and talk."

24

WASHINGTON, D.C., JANUARY 2019

Nick started the conversation with Straw. "Before we go into the office tomorrow," he said, "can you tell me more about GROSS and what you do day-to-day?"

"Well," said Straw leaning back into the cushions of the couch, "My job is somewhat like composing music. I find something of interest, and then I look to expand on that theme — note by note, measure by measure — until the entire composition is revealed."

Straw paused to take a sip of wine. "My job is not just to analyze, but to see. National security issues always get the attention of the big agencies — Homeland Security, Department of Defense, NSA, CIA, but most of all, the FBI. However, having all those cooks in the kitchen doesn't mean that all threats are quickly identified and handled. There's always a lot of uncertainty, especially at the start of an investigation. All that I generally know at that point is that we are dealing with a dangerous and unknown foe, and an unknown target.

"Your dad and GROSS give me all the tools I need to dig, and with a very big shovel. I get access to real-time conversations between senior administration officials, military leaders, and heads of intelligence agencies. I basically wade through a tsunami of data every day. Even with all my resources, many leads fizzle out. But I keep digging for information, stress test everything in my mind, and hope that it leads to something important. Basically, it's my job to notice and understand what others can't see. My job is to shed light, not to master. Strategy is my strength, not disaster."

"Well, my dad obviously has a lot of confidence in you," Nick said. "He told me you were a 'certified genius.'"

"Carson called me that? Ha! I'll take that as a compliment. But there's a thin line between genius and crazy. Nick, you had better hope you are not joining a ship of fools at GROSS."

"I don't think that will be an issue," laughed Nick. "However, I am curious about where you get your best intel."

Straw took a deep breath. "In general, the soft underbelly and weakness of all terrorist organizations is communication. They all need to communicate, talk, plan, and organize. We need to capture these communications, identify them for what they are, and then act on a timely basis. Capturing the data is not problematic. Our government has plenty of means of getting data, whether by audio tapes, computer hacks, tips from others, or just basic infiltration of terrorist groups by covert operatives. However, there's also a lot of 'noise' out there that is irrelevant, and it takes time to filter out the 'noise' from the data that is relevant. That's the real challenge, and then being able to act in time. As they say, 'teamwork makes the dream work.' Well, 9/11 is the prime example that we aren't always able to do this."

"Your approach sounds very similar to what I did as a physician," Nick said. "I used to sift through a ton of electronic medical records, and take a thorough patient history to try to diagnose the precise medical conditions. Then, based on all that information, I'd try to develop a plan tailored to cure the problems."

Nick shuddered as his mind flashed back to the Taco Truck melee, when the thug mocked him for breaking the Hippocratic oath shortly before Nick killed him.

"I agree," Straw said. "I think the key difference is that, as a doctor, you actually get to see the patient that you are diagnosing. But me? Sometimes I don't even know the 'patient' that I am supposed to be protecting. While I've got my eyes and ears in the data, my ability to analyze is only as good as the information that is provided to me. More importantly, my 'diagnosis' means nothing if we can't then 'cure' the problem that was identified. That's where Sam and you come in."

"Speaking of Samantha," said Nick. "Can you give me some background on her?"

"Well, Sam is brilliant, loyal, and tough. But if you let her down, she will call you to task. If you lie to her or withhold information, she will make your life miserable. She knows way too well that missteps in our line of work can have disastrous consequences, so trust and reliability are key to Samantha treating you as a full partner. Beyond that, it's obvious that she's very attractive. If good looks were a minute, she would have been an hour."

"OK," said Nick. "Appreciate the tips."

There was a soft knock on the door. Cherise peeked in and told Straw that Stella was ready to sleep.

"I'll be back in a few minutes," Straw said, excusing himself from the room.

Cherise sat at Straw's desk. She chuckled when she noticed the empty bottle of wine. "Having fun getting acquainted?"

"Straw is fantastic," Nick said. "I've only known him a few hours, but I feel we're getting along like old friends."

"I'm glad to hear that. Your father and GROSS mostly know Straw for his brains. His focus sure runs deep when he works. But his love for me and Stella, his family — that's even deeper."

"I've noticed," said Nick. "You have a very tight-knit family."

Cherise grinned. "You know, he spends his days with his eyes glued to a computer, deciphering information on the worst people on Earth. But every night, he comes home happy as ever to see us. He always makes sure to say a prayer with Stella and sing a song before bed."

As Cherise spoke, a duet of Straw and Stella singing 'My Favorite Things' resonated from down the hall.

"Right on cue!" proclaimed Cherise. "I think Straw views these minutes with Stella as his most precious time of the day. How often do you see a 16-year-old and a father do something like that? Straw loves his highly classified job, but that pales in comparison to this."

"That's incredible," said Nick, noticing some tears welling in Cherise's eyes. "Incredible and inspiring."

Moments later, Straw returned, carrying a bottle of bourbon.

"I hope Cherise didn't tell you too many bad stories about me," he joked, giving his wife a hug as she stood up. "Honey, don't wait up for me. Nick and I need to make a dent in this bottle and really get to know each other!"

Cherise rolled her eyes. "I'll leave the Ibuprofen out on the bathroom counter. Have fun, but not too much fun."

25

WASHINGTON, D.C., JANUARY 2019

Straw poured two tall glasses of bourbon over large ice cubes and toasted, "Here's to the start of what I hope will be a great and lasting relationship. We've talked a lot about me, my family, and GROSS, but now let's talk about you. Who is the real Nick Class?"

Nick took a sip of bourbon and leaned back in the couch. "I don't really know how to answer that. As you know, some of my memories were erased to protect me from our own government, the same government that GROSS now wants me to protect. I feel like I have lots of thoughts and history that are tucked away somewhere. How long will they stay in the back shelf of my brain? I don't know."

Straw pondered Nick's conflicted thoughts. "I feel for you. It's like you don't know where you're going, and you don't know where you've been. Some destinations are seen unclearly, and sometimes it's hard to know what to believe in. I can understand why you feel like a stranger, and that things went down that you don't understand, but I think in time you will. One way or another, your darkness has got to give. Maybe you'll find direction, around some corner, where it has been waiting to meet you."

Nick was lost to the vagaries of Straw's response. He took a long sip of bourbon while gazing at the fish tank. The combination of the exotic fish, wine, and bourbon was mesmerizing, but Nick was still in need of answers.

"Straw, sometimes it's like you're speaking in a foreign language. It's like I'm a first-year med student again. Listening, but struggling to understand. Can you just speak in plain English?"

Straw grinned. "Right now, I think you just need to keep on keeping on. You need to be all the things you are able to be."

Nick still looked dazed and confused, so Straw continued. "Do you remember the first song Delilah played when you came into our house?"

"Not really. I was more focused on meeting you and your family."

"That's totally understandable, but I played that song for a couple of reasons. The song is 'Box of Rain.' One of the reasons I play it is because it is very mellow arrangement, much different than the acid-based rock that many people improperly associate with the Grateful Dead. But the main reason I played it is for its message. Let's listen to it again. Delilah, play 'Box of Rain' from the album."

Nick sat back on the couch as the song filled the studio. Listening to the music while watching the fish tank was sublime. Nick could feel his entire body and mind begin to relax for the first time in a long time.

"The Grateful Dead usually play their best music live in concert," Straw said. "The studio recording of this song is the exception. But that's not as important as the message of the song. 'Box of Rain' is about an appreciation for life, its beauty, and the journey where everyone is simply trying to find their own way. Another message is to take life's challenges as they come and, if you do so, you just might find yourself in a place you least expect. As the band said in a later song, 'once in a while you get shown the light in the strangest of places if you look at it right.'"

"Thanks Straw. That's really beautiful... and poignant." Nick chuckled. "'Poignant' is a word I don't know if I've ever used in my life, much less after drinking."

Straw laughed as well as they toasted their glasses once again.

26

VERACRUZ, MEXICO, JULY 3, 2009

Six months after their initial meeting, Jefe flew Professor down to Veracruz once more, ostensibly so the former college roommates could enjoy a long holiday weekend together. Though Professor had been provided burner phones, Jefe preferred to take no chances. He wanted a meeting in person to discuss Professor's progress.

After greeting Verana and Abriz, Professor followed Jefe to their favorite meeting place, an isolated table by Jefe's swimming pool. Jefe had instructed his staff not to work in the area or intrude on their discussion.

"So, my friend," Jefe started. "Tell me what you have to report."

"As you know, we need to play the long game," Professor said. "Running for president takes a lot of planning and organization. Since we last spoke, I've been laying the grassroots foundation for that organizational backbone. With both your contacts in the U.S. and mine from the Clanton and Olama campaigns, I think we are off to a good start. But realistically, our goal is still to win the 2024 election."

"Any chance of accomplishing our goal before then?"

"I doubt it. I expect Olama to be a two-term president. He's got enough momentum and support from a diverse set of voters to get re-elected in 2012. There's a chance our first viable option arises in the 2016 election, though it's too early for solid predictions. I think our best shot in 2016 is to try to get our candidate as the vice president on either party's ticket. Getting a VP slot then would position that candidate well for a successful run at the presidency later."

Jefe nodded in understanding. "Who are the likely frontrunners in 2016?"

"Great question. Among the Democrats, I see either current VP Burden or Hillary Clanton. On the Republican side, I frankly have no clue. The party is in an identity crisis now, so it's hard to predict."

"Ah, I see. Perhaps we study the political climate through 2016. See how the parties unfold — or implode — before diving into those murky waters."

"My thoughts exactly. This is where patience comes in. Realistically, unless the economy is in the tank right before the 2016 election, I would suspect that Democrats will win again in 2016 and hold the presidency for the next eight years. That pushes us to the 2024 election. By that time, the Republicans will have had enough time to address the weaknesses in their voting base and diversify their support. That's why I project 2024 is our ideal — and perhaps only — shot at securing a potential presidential candidate."

"Noted, Professor. But it's only 2009. A lot could change between now and 2024." Jefe stood and began to methodically pace in front of their lawn chairs. "You said that you expect Olama to serve two terms, no?"

"Correct. Pending any health issues or other unforeseen circumstances."

"Hmm. Yes. 'Unforeseen circumstances.' You know, racism remains one of America's many vices. As our first Black president, I would not be surprised if some white supremacist didn't try to assassinate Olama."

Professor spat out his cocktail. After a brief coughing spell, he said, "Jefe! You don't suggest an assassination attempt to secure a ticket."

"No, no. That would not be my plan A." Jefe handed Professor a napkin before switching gears. "So, what's the key to attracting the Hispanic vote in the U.S.?"

"Interesting question. Hispanic voters are now the nation's fastest-growing demographic group. Second only to the African American vote, it was record turnout among Hispanic voters that helped push Olama over the top. I think Latinos will surge for any candidate who protects their interest, particularly if that candidate is Latino or speaks Spanish."

Jefe grinned. "Like President Plante Jr. At times, he spoke Spanish better than English."

"Indeed!" Professor chuckled. "If we energize the Latino vote, they will show up to the polls. Among their other efforts, the Olama campaign spent over $20 million to court Latino voters. As a result, about one in five new voters were Hispanic. We need to implement similar proven tactics as we prepare for our future candidate's race. The clout of Hispanic voters is only going to grow in future elections."

"This is all very interesting and seems to open up some nice possibilities for us," Jefe said. "Any more keen insights at this time?"

Professor nodded. "I have a couple more tricks up my sleeve. First, it's worth noting that the number of females who won elective seats nationwide skyrocketed in recent elections. Now, with the 'Me Too' movement, female candidates — especially female minority candidates — are very relevant.

"Second, governors are the only people in politics getting things done. The political bottleneck in Washington has almost forced them to be active and successfully govern at the state and local levels. That's why I think the next 'new' presidential candidate will likely come from the ranks of the governors, not someone already inside the Washington establishment. There's a lot of precedent for this, with Carter, Clanton, and Raygun being the most recent. And, for what it's worth, sitting governors with successful track records are much better fundraisers than other politicians."

"Hmm," Jefe said. "So based on all this, our 2024 candidate should be a female Latina governor?"

Professor snapped his fingers. "Bingo."

Jefe sighed. The pieces were slowly but surely falling into place.

27

WASHINGTON, D.C., JANUARY 2019

Five hours after crashing in Straw's studio, Nick awoke to his blaring phone alarm. His head still buzzing from the bourbon, a hot shower helped sharpen his senses and keep his hangover at bay.

After showering, Nick put on dress khaki pants, a blue and black patterned sport coat, and a button-up shirt for his first day at the office. Straw wore blue jeans, Converse, and one of his many tie-dyed t-shirts.

"Way to stick to the dress code," he chuckled as Nick entered the kitchen.

"Is this business casual to you?" Nick asked, taking in Straw's hippie apparel.

"Unlike field agents, I don't need to look good in public." Straw held up to-go cups and a brown bag. "I already got us coffee and bagels. Let's hit the road."

"Sounds good." Nick nodded to Cherise, who sat across the counter near her husband. "Thanks for all your hospitality, Cherise."

"Of course," she said, smiling back. "Glad you survived your first night drinking with my husband!"

"Ha. Barely."

"Come on, Nick," Straw said. "Don't wanna be late for your first day at the office. I'll drive since you look like you could be going down the road feelin' bad and lost and lacking in some direction."

"That's probably a good idea."

"And here's your first surprise of the day." Straw opened the door to his garage. "Let me introduce you to your company car."

In front of Nick stood a large metallic black Mercedes Benz SUV. "GROSS provides you some special wheels as part of the job," said Straw. "We call her 'Sadie' and she has some very special features. Her super turbo charged engine can exceed 200 mph. She's fortified with a bullet-proof exterior. Her weaponry includes the ability to shoot fifty-caliber rounds out of an adjustable front grill gun port. Your dad choose Mercedes because most people wouldn't think that an American intelligence agency would ever use a foreign-built car."

Straw paused to catch his breath. "Sadie is also equipped with high explosive armor-piercing ordnance that can penetrate tank armor and concrete walls. Her moon roof can be elevated into a rotating and tiltable surface with three mounted and modified Heckler & Koch MP5 .40 caliber submachine guns. She also has a launcher that can be used for grenades or tear gas or smoke cover. I can control all of Sadie's weaponry wirelessly through my laptop."

"Wow. Sadie's got more gadgets than James Bond's ride!"

"We haven't even got to my favorite part of the car. Sadie has a juiced-up, military-grade drone with lots of features, like heat sensors, wall-piercing listening capability, top-end cameras, and the ability to fire two mini, but very powerful, rockets. I play with that drone a lot, after taking off the rockets of course, mainly because it's fun but also so I can master its flight capabilities."

"Man, that's impressive," exclaimed Nick. "Is there anything else?"

"Yes, I haven't even gotten to the rear of Sadie. In her hatch area there are a trove of weapons available for you and Samantha. This includes two fully automatic Colt M-16 5.56mm assault rifles with high-capacity drum magazines and four .40 caliber UMPs. As you probably already know, these are universal machine pistols... the specialized weapons used by SWAT squads that have thirty-round magazines. Considering your sniper training, GROSS added a Remington 700 .308 caliber sniper rifle. But the coolest thing in the back is an adjustable-aiming pod that can fire two turbo-boosted, heat-seeking, state-of-the-art SAMs… surface to air missiles that can take out any helicopter or plane that is giving us trouble. The bottom line is that we never want the bad guys to have better firepower than the good guys."

Nick pointed to Sadie's license plate which read WALSTIB. "What does that stand for?"

Straw could do nothing but smile, smile, smile as he said, "What A Long Strange Trip It's Been!"

Nick chuckled. "I get that reference!"

"You're learning, Young Grasshopper. Hop in. It's a pretty short drive to GROSS."

28

WASHINGTON, D.C., JANUARY 2019

The GROSS office was in an unassuming commercial building in a nondescript strip mall in Alexandria, Virginia. As Sadie entered the mall's parking lot, Nick noticed a small sign on the entrance door reading "Real Estate Consultants, Inc."

Straw parked Sadie close to the entrance and led the way into the building. Consistent with the dingy exterior of the building, the interior décor of the building was an obvious afterthought. The main hallway wreaked of stale cigarettes. The entry door to the GROSS space begged for some WD-40 when Straw opened it. Upon entering the office, Nick's eyes went first to the dented metal file cabinets lining the back wall. For a second, he thought they contained files of legitimate commercial real estate listings.

Samantha's desk sat closest to the door, letting her serve as both real estate consultant and receptionist to anyone who might stray into the office. Samantha's desk had a large red octagon stop sign, but instead of the letters "STOP" there was the word "FRAGRANCE" with a line drawn through it. Nick surmised that Samantha suffered from fragrance allergies and made a mental note not to wear fragrant deodorant to work. An empty wooden desk was placed to Sam's left. Beyond that was Straw's desk, unsurprisingly decked out with Grateful Dead posters and other paraphernalia. Each of the three desks had two chairs in front of them to allow for face-to-face conversations.

Straw's "desk" was different than the others. It was more of a long table with five large, interconnected monitors, each with pictures of exotic foreign real estate taped on the outside to give the appearance of a commercial realty focus. Straw had a phone at each end of the impressive display of monitors. The monitors and keypad consumed most of the space on Straw's table, with just enough room for pictures of Cherise, Stella, and Cassidy to frame the ends of his desk along with a Terrapin Station coffee mug on the side. Behind Straw's chair was a sign that read, "So I give you my eyes and all of their lies, please help me to learn as well as to see."

Nick looked over the entire office. It was very pedestrian for a commercial real estate company, even a fake one. Each desk, table, and drawer had only standard office supplies. The office artwork consisted of cheap prints in inexpensive frames. The only plants in the office were fake. Real estate pamphlets were strewn around the office in case they had an unintended walk-in from the mall. The office had a welcome bowl of candies and mints on the window ledge near the entry door that were probably hard as rocks for never being replaced. The most expensive items in the office were the computers and the high-tech adjustable chairs that made make work comfortable for the three GROSS employees.

Straw dropped the bag of bagels and on Samantha's desk. "Morning, Sam. Here's breakfast to celebrate Nick's first day."

"Same to you, Straw," she said. She gave Nick a curt nod. "Welcome. Glad to have you on board." She then returned to the paperwork she was idly sorting.

"Thanks," Nick said. "Look forward to working with you both."

"But first, we must eat," Straw said, distributing paper plates and placing a plastic knife in the container of cream cheese. "So, Nick, what do you think of the office?"

Nick shrugged. "It's certainly spartan. Kind of underwhelming. Maybe that's intentional?"

"Indeed! Everything about the location of our office was carefully selected by Carson," Straw explained. "The goal is for GROSS to be overlooked. Unlike real businesses, we don't want to attract any attention or customers. Every now and then, we get some nosey walk-ins. But Sam's a pro at shooing them away."

"All in a day's work," Sam said.

"Our appliances are communal," Straw said between bites of bagel. "We got a microwave, fridge, coffee maker, and toaster in the breakroom back there." He nudged Nick in the shoulder. "You're always welcome to the energy drinks I stock in the fridge. After a few hours crunching data, I need a little jolt."

"No wonder you've had tremors lately," Sam said, letting a brief smirk cross her face.

Straw chuckled. "Guilty as charged."

"Let me get this straight," Nick said. "GROSS stays invisible by hiding in plain sight?"

"Exactly. What you call 'spartan,' I call invisibly high-tech. All our comms, shared networks, NSA feeds, and other data have been deeply firewalled and encrypted. Just like Sadie, all our windows are bullet-proof, and all walls have been fortified to withstand any vehicular attack."

Nick's eyes widened. "Has that ever happened?"

"Not yet."

"But it never hurts to have security," Sam said. "If anyone on the outside learned about our operations, the consequences could endanger the entire country."

"As you know," Straw said, "we have access to a treasure-trove of information here. After the 9/11 terrorist attacks, the key tech companies agreed to an open-surveillance system that provides the U.S. government and GROSS any critical audio, video, or other intelligence data needed to thwart further terrorist attacks." Straw beamed, enjoying every morsel of this topic. "There are as many cameras as there are snowflakes in a Buffalo winter. With our access to all the government feeds, plus my state-of-the-art facial recognition technology — we can usually find anyone on the planet, at almost any time."

"Wow," Nick said. "Sounds like a real challenge to hide nowadays."

"Especially when *we* are the hunters," Sam said emphatically.

"Anyway, I could talk about surveillance all day," Straw said. "But it's time to get to work. Sam, will you help Nick settle in? He'll need to be onboarded, too."

"Will do." She opened one of the back cabinets and retrieved a laptop, monitor, keyboard, and mousepad. She handed Nick the monitor while she connected the other hardware.

"So," Nick said, "do you prefer Samantha or Sam?"

"Either is fine."

"Gotcha. Where are you from?"

"All over." Sam tapped the newly assembled computer. "Turn on the laptop and create a password. Minimum of twelve characters, including uppercase, special characters, etcetera. Once you log in, please read the List."

"Okay. What kind of list?"

"Not just any list. *The* List. It contains all potential domestic threats the alphabet agencies are looking into." She handed him a flash drive smaller than her finger. "This will bring you up to speed. Then, Straw and I can include you in future discussions."

"Understood. So, how do we handle the List?"

Sam looked Nick straight in the eye. "Look. I know we're a team now. But your only job is to follow the orders that Straw or I give you. If we assign you someone on the List, that name is your sole focus. Depending on how things develop, we may ask you to 'engage' with that name."

"What does that mean?"

"It could be anything from locating, detaining, fighting or destroying the name if we say it's necessary to protect our country."

Taken aback, Nick studied the flash drive closely.

"So, I'm just a glorified lap dog?" he said.

"You broke the Clean Slate Protocol. You're a highly trained lap dog." Sam pointed to the far window, where Sadie was parked outside. "Straw probably showed you Sadie's weapons. You'll also find some firearms in your desk."

Nick opened the top desk drawer to find the normal panoply of office supplies. In the lower right drawer, he found the weapons Sam had mentioned: two Glock .45s and ample magazines.

"Let me know if you have any questions," Sam said, returning to her computer screen.

29

WASHINGTON, D.C., JANUARY 2019

Nick spent the remainder of the morning reading the List. He was shocked to see the variety of potential terroristic threats, and how many more came from domestic groups instead of foreign sources.

At the top of the List were radical Islamist extremists, followed by various white supremacist and far-right extremist groups. The List also indicated that Straw was closely tracking a number of U.S. citizens who he believed were being recruited and radicalized by Islamic or other terrorist groups.

As Nick dug deeper into the List, it became clear that Straw had also analyzed a lot of the activities and communications of many foreign groups. Separate files were kept for Al-Qaeda, ISIS, and other militant Islamic-affiliated spin off groups such as Hamas, Hezbollah, and al-Shabaab. The List also contained a memo Sam wrote describing how GROSS had identified an opportunity for the U.S. to kill a senior ISIS leader in an April 2018 strike in Syria.

While reading through the expansive List, at times Nick asked Sam about the status of the threats they tracked. She seldom answered in sentences exceeding one or two words. She was certainly concise, but Nick wondered if there was more behind Sam's curtness. Unlike the start of his relationship with Straw, Nick found no easy flow to his conversations with Samantha.

After a few hours of work, Straw stood from his chair to stretch. “I took the liberty of ordering a pizza. It should be delivered soon. I’m going to the restroom now, but if it comes while I’m gone will you put it on our GROSS credit card and give a good tip, Sam?”

“Sure thing. I’m getting hungry too.”

“I think I’ll let you show me where the restroom is,” Nick stated while rising from his chair. “I was starting to wonder if you two ever ate lunch!”

Nick followed Straw into the main corridor of the mall and found that the public restroom was just a short walk away, surprisingly clean, and well-maintained. Straw went into a stall and closed the door, so Nick waited for him outside after urinating and washing his hands.

Straw came out of the restroom a few minutes later. “That sure felt good! Lots of room for pizza now!”

“Hey, Straw. Is it just me, or does Sam always act this cold?”

Straw smiled. “I get it. Her focus is intense when we work. She does tend to shut out a lot of things, just like me and my headphones.” Straw snapped his fingers. “How about I try to break the ice during lunch.”

“Thanks. That would be much appreciated.”

30

WASHINGTON, D.C., JANUARY 2019

Straw and Nick re-entered the GROSS office and Nick could tell by the lack of aroma that the pizza had not yet arrived.

"Straw, before the pizza comes, can I ask you some questions about the List?"

"Sure thing. Ask away."

"How do you prioritize your targets? For instance, the far-right extremist groups in the U.S. don't seem to be getting as much attention as other threats."

"With any threat, I generally focus on three factors: imminence, severity, and intended target," said Straw.

"Ah. I understand the 'imminence' and 'severity' factors. But what do you mean by the 'target' of the threat?"

"My biggest concern at GROSS is threats against the U.S. government or its elected officials. That's why I don't spend a ton of time looking at our domestic extremist groups. Most of their targets are hate-based and either racial or religious in nature. While that stuff is horrible, it generally doesn't threaten our government or its leaders. My attention to some of the white supremacist groups has increased since the 'Unite the Right' rallies in Charlotte a few years ago, but I generally leave potential hate crimes for other intelligence agencies unless I see some direct national security implication."

A knock on the door meant the pizza had arrived. Sam paid the delivery man while Straw took the two boxes of pizza and spread them out on Sam's desk. Straw filled up a paper plate with food and then sat in one of the visitor chairs opposite Sam's desk.

"So, Sam," Straw began, "Nick learned a lot about me when he stayed at our house last night. Why don't you give him some of your background?"

Sam shot him a slight glare before a reluctant sigh.

"Well, my father was in the military," she said. "We traveled all over the world. It was a great experience and I learned multiple languages along the way, but it's hard to make friends when you move every couple of years. We never had much money, but I never felt that we were poor or missing out.

"I later went to Stanford for college. That's where I really noticed for the first time all the material things that I didn't have growing up, but that didn't bother me. While I like having the nice things that this job allows me to afford, that's not what it's all about. I try to keep perspective about what's important in life, and that's relationships with family and others. Do you agree, Straw?"

Straw grinned. "For a long time, my family didn't have a need for possessions beyond a good stereo, a car to get to the next Grateful Dead show, and enough money to clothe, shelter, and feed us… and we were happy as clams the entire time! It's always better to focus on what you have instead of what you don't have. Everything you gather is just more that you can lose."

"So, what did you do after college Sam?" Nick asked.

"Sort of the opposite of what we just talked about… I chased the almighty dollar in New York City. I worked eighteen-hour days and became the youngest Managing Director of Global Finance at Goldman Saks. However, after three years there, the money wasn't worth the burnout. So, I floated my resumé on Capitol Hill to try the public sector and actually do something to benefit our country. Your dad heard about me from some Senate Finance Committee staffers who had my resumé. Carson interviewed me off-the-record about a unique opportunity to help the country at GROSS. The rest, as they say, is history."

"Thanks for sharing, Sam," said Straw. "The pizza was great, but I need to get back to my screens. After work, how about we try that new ice cream store nearby?"

"Sounds like a great way to celebrate my first day on the job. My treat," Nick said.

"Count me in," Sam said, quickly turning to her monitors.

31

WASHINGTON, D.C., JANUARY 2019

"You survived your first day at GROSS," Straw said, tossing Nick the keys to Sadie. "Time for your inaugural drive."

Nick gulped. He'd never driven a car this nice — or high-tech — in his life. Straw hopped in the passenger seat so he could interface his laptop with Sadie's core processor. Sam made herself comfortable in the back seat.

Straw handed Nick a credit card. "Also, your inaugural GROSS credit card! Well, it really says 'Real Estate Consultants, Inc.' But you get the picture."

Nick started the car and Sadie's engine immediately purred. Nick adjusted his mirrors and then looked at Sadie's dash.

"Hey, Straw. It looks like we're almost out of gas."

"Good catch, Nick. I haven't put any gas in the car for a long time. There aren't many places to get gas on the parkway, so let's fill up at a station in a couple of blocks. Just turn right at the exit."

Nick put Sadie into drive and slowly crossed the mall's parking lot. He approached the exit, signaled right, and waited for the traffic to clear. The oncoming car failed to signal before abruptly turning onto the mall access road. Nick slammed his hand on Sadie's horn.

Straw and Sam said nothing as Nick eventually pulled onto the road and followed Straw's directions.

"The gas station will be on the right side of the street in two blocks," Straw stated.

Nick turned into the gas station and parked Sadie along a row of gas pumps. Nick grabbed the credit card, stepped out, and started pumping gas. Though Sadie's engine was off, her battery provided enough power for Straw to play more Grateful Dead tunes.

"These speakers are next level!" Straw hollered, twisting the volume knob.

While Straw grooved to the music, Sam peered out the window.

"Straw," she said, motioning to the vehicle in front of them.

Straw turned down the music and looked where Sam was pointing. Parked ahead of Sadie was a black semi-truck with an enormous grill in front and custom-painted flames on the sides. Near the monstrous vehicle was its equally intimidating driver, a six-five bearded man missing his front teeth like a hockey player. For some reason, Nick stood toe-to-toe with the behemoth, their voices loud, their faces red with stress.

"I live here now," Nick yelled, pointing to a smoldering cigarette butt on the ground. "My city is not your ash tray! Pick it up and put it in the trash where it belongs."

"Make me, asshole!" the large man growled.

Before the situation could escalate further, Sam stepped out of Sadie. She forced herself between the two angry men.

"Shut up, both of you!" she ordered. "Stop fighting like children. Just get your gas and go."

As the two hot-headed men separated, Sam reached down, picked up the cigarette butt, and threw it in the adjacent trash bin.

"There you go, Nick," she said. "Problem solved."

A man at the far pump clapped his hands and yelled, "You show them, girl!"

Sam chuckled and gave a brief wave to her admirer. She then pushed Nick back to Sadie.

"Get in," she demanded. "I'll finish with the gas."

Nick rolled his eyes. Samantha shot him a razor-sharp glare before turning to the gas pump. Nick turned to Straw, whose eyes were wide.

"You're toast, man," he said. He turned off the music, also fearing Sam's wrath.

"Let's go," Sam said, returning to the back seat once Sadie was gassed. Nick sat in the driver's seat but didn't start the car, waiting for his reprimand. Silence filled the car until Sam slapped Nick on the arm.

"Nick! What the hell was that?"

"Sorry," Nick said with a sigh. "Not sure what came over me. Things just got out of hand."

"*Out of hand?* You were about to fight that mountain man. And over what? *Littering?* Are you crazy? I felt like I was putting a 2-year-old in a timeout!"

Nick nodded as the gravity of his outburst — and Sam's reprimand — sunk in.

"Sam's right," Straw said, but in a gentler tone. "In our business, we can't let things get out of hand. We need to stay invisible. Not only to our enemies, but also to any of the locals."

"Staying invisible also applies to driving," Sam said. "Earlier, you consistently drove ten over the speed limit. Unless we are in an emergency, follow the rules of the road. Don't draw any attention from police or other locals. I mean, just think how they'd react if they pulled us over and found all the weapons in Sadie? The best questions are ones that are never asked of us."

"Bottom line, we don't need the heat coming round," Straw said. "They'd bust us for smilin' on a cloudy day."

"Sorry, guys," Nick said. "I've always hated bullies, littering, and bad drivers. Guess I saw two of the three in the last five minutes. But that's no excuse. I shouldn't have let it get to me."

"On that, we agree," Sam said.

"Still, how come I just *lost it* with that guy?"

Seeing the guilt wash over Nick, Straw held out his hand.

"How about I drive home?" he said.

Nick nodded, handed him the keys to Sadie, and stepped out of the SUV. After he closed his door, Sam said something to Straw. Sadie's reinforced windows blurred most of the words. Moments passed and Straw remained inside, talking with Sam, clearly about Nick. He stepped close enough to hear Sam saying, "He's unstable! He's a liability to both you and me…"

Nick took a deep breath. Sam was not wrong, and deep down he knew it. But he needed to hear her say it.

Some team we are, he thought. *Day one, and they're already cutting me out.*

Straw finally stepped out of the vehicle, an unsettled look on his face. As he took the driver's seat, Nick walked around Sadie to the passenger's side. As he reached for the door, Sam suddenly stepped out and looked him straight in the eye.

"Nick," she said, her voice firm. "Pull it together. I get that you've been through a lot of shit recently. But that doesn't give you an excuse to be reckless. Your pain can't compromise the mission."

Nick slowly nodded. "I get it."

"I'm not sure you do." Sam placed her index finger on his chest. "*You* shouldn't be here. *You* should not be in GROSS. But thanks to nepotism and your reawakening, *you* are supposed to be my partner now."

Jeez, tell me how you really feel, Nick thought, taken aback by Sam's blunt remarks.

"As partners, I need to be able to trust you," Sam continued. "But your fuse is too short. I can't trust what I can't control. So, either get your shit together, or get out."

"Fine," Nick said. "Call me a short fuse. Call me a shoo-in because of my dad. But have you considered maybe I'm all those things *because* of all my recent shit? You couldn't even imagine what it's like to watch your partner die in front of you."

Sam turned her head. Nick took a deep breath, hoping he got his point across.

"Believe it or not, I can," she said. Before Nick could react or further question her, she turned back to him. "Look, Straw and I need the man who broke the Clean Slate Protocol. But we don't need a time bomb. Got it?"

Nick nodded. "Got it."

Following Sam's lead, Nick got in Sadie so Straw could drive them back to GROSS. Ice cream would wait for another day.

32

WASHINGTON, D.C., JANUARY 2019

After dropping Sam off at her car in the GROSS parking lot, Straw turned to Nick.

"Day one, man," Straw said. "Day one, and you already set off Sam."

"I'm off to a great start," Nick said, still shell-shocked from earlier.

"Look, I know you're still grieving and figuring out your life. But Sam's not wrong. Better change your act. I'm living proof that you can be a little crazy and still succeed at GROSS. But, you can't act insane."

Nick nodded. "Fair enough."

"Just keep your temper under control. 'Cause I'd like to keep you around GROSS."

"Thanks. Glad to know at least one of my partners likes me."

Straw chuckled. "Take it from personal experience: Sam's a slow burn when it comes to connections. She's been through a lot herself, so she's got a lot of walls up. Just lay low, give it time, prove that you're — what'd she call you, a lapdog? If you do that, she'll be your fiercest, most loyal friend."

"Hope so."

Straw clapped his hands to change the subject. "So, Stella and Cherise are out with their friends. How about we make it a guys' night? We could grab a bite at my favorite Chinese restaurant."

"I'm game."

"Then after, maybe we catch the new Mission Impossible movie at the old theater next door."

"Count me in."

"Plus, you know the good thing about theaters?"

"What?"

"They're so dark, you can't see anyone littering!"

Nick gently punched Straw in the shoulder, a small smile returning to his face.

33

OCTOBER 5, 2009

Jefe and Professor had established a routine for a standing call to be held at noon on the first Monday of every month. More frequent contact was allowed if urgent, but Jefe did not want to raise any eyebrows of a Mexican or American intelligence agency.

Professor used one of his many burner phones to call Jefe promptly at noon. It took only one ring for Jefe to answer on his own burner phone.

"Good afternoon, Jefe," Professor started, hearing the sounds of seagulls and waves in the background. "Sounds like another beautiful day in Veracruz. Which boat did you take today?"

"Hello, my friend," Jefe said. "Indeed, another day in paradise. I took Verana, the yacht named after mi amor. I brought the real Verana too, along with Abriz, for lunch on the water."

"That's great. Sorry, I don't want to interrupt your family time."

"Esta bien. Go on."

"Well, I have some exciting news. After studying your plethora of associates stateside, I think I found a great potential candidate."

"This *is* exciting news! Who did you have in mind?"

"Silvia Luisa Anna Maria Rodriguez."

"Ah, yes. Silvia."

"Have you met her?"

"Yes. I have point people at every major university, just like I was at Georgetown. For years, Silvia was my point person at Arizona State."

"Oh, I see. Well, her background is very impressive. Graduated summa cum laude from ASU. Joint degrees in political science and business finance — music to my ears! After graduation, she got a job with the Arizona Department of Commerce, all while doing law school at ASU. She graduated near the top of her law school class and landed a job at a prominent law firm. On track to make partner next year. That is, if she doesn't run for local office."

"That's right. She led ASU's Young Republicans for years."

"Exactly. Her rising status in the party is very promising," Professor proclaimed.

"Silvia was always so busy, so accomplished, so high functioning. But I'm grateful she always made time for our organization. She has been indispensable to the expansion of our Arizona branch."

"Just like I hope she will be indispensable for our plan."

"So, what do you propose we do with Silvia?"

"Our candidate needs to first gain traction at the gubernatorial level. Through my connections, I can get her a senior position on the current governor's staff, if she is interested."

Jefe paused to process the news. "She's strong, you know. She knows what she wants. Professor, you think you can sway her to join our team?"

"Only with your permission, Jefe. But she already seems very loyal to you. I'm confident she'll get on board with our plan."

"Yes. Please tell her I fully support her career change." Jefe's daughter Abriz tugged at his shirt and handed him a snorkel. "Professor, I need to go. Time for a family swim."

"Sounds good. Enjoy! I'll update you next week after I meet with Silvia."

"Excellente." Jefe tossed his burner phone overboard before rejoining his family.

34

WASHINGTON, D.C., JANUARY 2019

Straw's favorite Chinese restaurant did not disappoint.

After parking Sadie in a residential area, Nick and Straw scaled a long flight of stairs to reach the dining area. Entering the restaurant felt like time-traveling back to 19th century southern China. Ornate pagoda chandeliers hung above lavish teakwood tables inlaid with mother-of-pearl. Handcrafted golden camphor carvings decorated the trim of private booths and tearooms. Silk embroideries adorned walls. The original furnishings appeared accurate for the era, and there was no attempt to incorporate a trendy motif. Neon signs and TVs were nowhere in sight, not even in the bar area. The hostess and waitresses all wore silk yellow and red dresses with intricate patterns of Chinese dragons flowing through the material.

Nick had never experienced an atmosphere like this in his life, and it set the tone for the magnificent meal that followed.

The King Fong cuisine was another time-warp experience. The food was distinctively Cantonese. The chow mein and egg foo young were exquisite.

As they were enjoying their meal, Straw turned the conversation back to the incident at the gas station. "Nick, I'd like to get some closure regarding what happened earlier today. At one point, after all your rage had subsided, you asked why you 'lost it' like you did. I'm not a psych major, but I'd guess that it all goes back to Katie's death. That's one topic that we've never discussed, but doing so might help both you and our team."

Nick's eyes immediately welled up. He had a lot of thoughts and feelings that had been festering, but he never felt comfortable discussing, even with his father. But now, though he just met Straw the day before, Nick felt ready to spill his heart.

"Katie and I had an unfinished life together. I'm still in shock about what happened at the park. In a matter of seconds, the love of my life was taken from me forever. When I'm alone with my thoughts, I hurt in places I didn't even know I could."

"That's a good thing," Straw said. "If you felt nothing, you wouldn't be human. Don't let the day come when you can't feel at all."

Nick nodded pensively. "I know that I shouldn't let that thug kill both Katie and me with one swipe of his knife. But it sure feels like a big part of me stopped living the day Katie died, even though life all around me continued like nothing ever happened."

Straw absorbed the pain behind Nick's words. "Nick, there are things you can replace and others you cannot. Love is an amazing force, and I can tell you've already cried enough tears to flood a big river. Death has no mercy in this land, and there's nothing worse than this pain in your heart that you continue to carry wherever you go."

Straw paused to finish his drink. "Your landscape seems empty 'cause Katie is gone and I know you'd trade all your tomorrows for a single yesterday. But don't let all you got to live for be what you left behind. You may feel lost and lacking in some direction, but I'm confident that you will eventually find love again… maybe not the same love you have for Katie, but love, nonetheless. You have time to make it on the dreams you still believe. Just don't give up. You've got an empty cup that only love can fill."

As Nick reflected over his advice, Straw added, "Remember 'Box of Rain?' It was the final song that the Dead played in their last concert. The last words sung by my favorite band were 'such a long, long time to be gone and such a short time to be there.' I think their message is to not waste our fleeting time on this earth. This world is not our own. We are just passing through."

"Thanks, Straw. I appreciate the lyrical wisdom and caring."

Straw patted Nick on the back. "I get your pain. Just don't carry the world upon your shoulders and you will get by, you will survive. Pretend you are strong in the hopes that you can be. And do not be afraid to lean on Sam or me, because he who loves loneliness loves it alone."

At that point, both Straw and Nick had finished all the food on their plates. The enormous portions disproved the urban legend that everyone got hungry an hour after eating Chinese food.

"Straw, I can't eat another bite," Nick said as he broke his fortune cookie in half. "But I don't want to leave this great restaurant without reading my fortune."

"*Forget about the past, leave your worries behind,*" he read aloud. "A bit on the nose, don't you think?"

"I've got you beat," Straw said. *"Sometimes the wisest man is deemed insane."*

On their way out, Straw grabbed a handful of mints, saying under his breath, "You can never have too much free stuff. One man gathers what another man spills."

Nick laughed. "Well, that hit the spot, Straw. Thanks. I needed that."

"Happy to help. Just know, Nick, there are times when I can help you out, and times you must fall. There are times that you must live doubt, and I can't help at all."

Nick raised an eyebrow. "When you don't work, do you write fortunes for fortune cookies?"

"Destiny is the true author; I am but a scribe."

"So true," replied Nick. "I'm really starting to come down from all the excitement of the day. Raincheck on the movie?"

"Sure thing. Sometimes, it's best to be thankful for living and just go home."

35

SCOTTSDALE, ARIZONA, OCTOBER 9, 2009

Not long after speaking with Jefe, Professor contacted Silvia Rodriguez to arrange a meeting. Her hesitation of talking with a stranger quickly ended when Professor indicated that they shared a mutual friend in Salvador Santos.

Professor landed in Phoenix the following afternoon. This gave him plenty of time to check into the Biltmore Hotel and freshen up for dinner. He then taxied to Francine's, the Mediterranean restaurant near Old Town Scottsdale that Silvia recommended. Professor arrived a half hour before the 7 p.m. reservation and was seated by the maître d' at an inside booth that offered little visibility to the other restaurant patrons.

Professor had not even touched his martini when Silvia Rodriguez arrived promptly at seven, carrying a bag from Nieman Marcus.

"Mr. Moody! I'm Silvia. It's a pleasure to meet you." She flashed Professor a big smile and gave him a firm handshake. Then she placed her purse and shopping bag on the booth before sitting opposite of Professor. "Sorry, there was a Nieman Marcus next door. Hard for me to resist a little shopping!"

As anticipated, Professor found Silvia immediately likeable, both in her looks and in her engaging, unpretentious personality. She had a Roman nose, perfect skin tone, shiny deep brown eyes, and high cheekbones. She wore a blue gabardine skirt with a white silk blouse. Professor thought to himself that she had the face and smile of a woman who never took a bad picture.

"Can I first say, Mr. Moody, I owe you an apology," she said.

"For what?" Professor asked.

"For not immediately recognizing your name when you called me Monday. I was a political science major in college, and I didn't connect the dots. Maybe it's because I'm a Republican and I didn't expect a call from a renowned Democrat election guru."

"Thank you for the complement. But I'm part-time now, so not much of a 'guru' anymore."

"Still, your reputation precedes you. Also, are you a seafood fan?"

"I love seafood."

"Great! I don't want to be brash, but please let me order our entire meal. Trust me, it won't disappoint."

Oh, I don't think you could disappoint, Professor thought when they raised their glasses in a toast.

Over the next hour, the two drank a bottle of Merlot while enjoying a phenomenal octopus appetizer and an even better Branzino fish for two prepared tableside Sicilian-style. The food was exquisite, but their conversation was even more stimulating. Professor certainly had the advantage, having diligently studied Silvia's background. But hearing her story firsthand — the daughter of impoverished Mexican immigrants — was inspiring.

"I'm curious," Professor said after Silvia had told her life story. "With everything you did in college, why did you agree to associate with Los Leones?"

Silvia pursed her lips, hesitant to discuss that part of her life, especially to a relative stranger. Sensing her unease, Professor leaned forward and lowered his voice.

"It's okay. Jefe's my friend. We were college roommates and now are business partners."

Silvia exhaled and smiled. That was all the reassurance she needed.

"Los Leones liked that I was very active at ASU," she said. "I was a cheerleader, I was President of Young Republicans, and I was involved in a lot of political science and business clubs. That's why they recruited me. I had tons of connections on campus.

"I initially turned down their offer because I wanted to study abroad in Rome. That's when my dad was diagnosed with a 'double hit' lymphoma."

"I'm sorry. I've never heard of that."

"It's an incredibly rare and aggressive cancer. Chemo couldn't touch it. He needed a stem cell transplant, but that would require several trips to the Mayo Clinic and NIH for treatment and monitoring. Well beyond what my family could afford." Silvia took a sip of wine. "So, I did what any daughter would do. I canceled my semester abroad and took the offer to work for Los Leones. They were nice enough to fund my father's treatment."

"Incredible," Professor said. "Jefe is a lifesaver."

Silvia nodded. "I never told my parents where I got the money. That's the only lie I've ever told. But that lie saved my dad. He's still alive, and now happily retired in Mexico City. In addition to financial support, Los Leones have always looked after me."

"Of course. You spearheaded their expansion into Phoenix."

"Yes. ASU is a notorious party school, so it didn't take much to strum up new business. But that was years ago. I'll admit, I haven't kept in much contact with Los Leones since law school. And now, I'm being considered for partner at the law firm."

"That's amazing. Congratulations!"

"Thank you. It's overwhelming, for sure. Tax law is not glamorous, so I doubt Jefe would have any interest in my associates at the firm."

"No. But not to worry, Silvia. Your connections are not what interests us." Professor folded his hands. "We are more interested in your political aspirations. Jefe and I are discreetly arranging some important political positions. We think you would fare very well in the political arena. Assuming, of course, you'd be willing to put your law practice on hold."

"Hmm," Silvia said, refilling her glass of wine. "I'm intrigued. The law firm pays well, but the grind of the practice is not something that I could see doing long-term. What kind of political position did you have in mind?"

"At first, state government. You know Arizona. It would play to your strengths." Professor grinned. "But for you, Silvia, I see no ceiling on how far you can go in politics."

"I'm flattered. Just to be clear: when you say 'no ceiling,' what is your ultimate goal?"

"The President of the United States of America."

Professor waited for Silvia's bewildered expression to subside. "That's obviously long-term, and several election cycles from now. You'll have quite the ladder to climb. But Jefe and I can offer you the first rung: assistant on the staff of the Arizona governor. Just say the word, and it's yours."

Silvia stared at her wine glass for several seconds, which felt like eons to Professor.

"I'll give my two-week's notice tomorrow," Silvia said. "Let me know when I start and what I can do to help."

Professor raised his glass once again and echoed Jefe. "Excellente."

36

VERACRUZ, MEXICO, JANUARY 2010

"Happy New Year, Professor!" Jefe greeted his guest upon his arrival at Jefe's home.

"Happy first anniversary of your 'plan,'" responded Professor. "It's always good to see you, especially at these marvelous accommodations."

As in their past meetings, Jefe had their poolside "office" fully stocked with appetizers and beverages.

"Help yourself, Professor, but don't eat too much. Verana is preparing an authentic Mexican dinner. My mouth is already watering!"

"Thanks for the advance notice, Jefe," Professor said as he helped himself to a small plate of platanos, fresh pineapple, and mango. "Traveling does make me hungry."

After adding beverages to the equation, Jefe and Professor sat down to discuss business.

"Jefe," Professor started. "We are off to a good start after one year of operations. This was really a year to build our foundation. We made a lot of grass roots connections that we will expand over the course of our plan when it's most advantageous to do so. I will note that the common denominator in all my meetings was the universal respect and gratitude your team members have for you, Jefe. Even if they have never met you. That's a great testimonial, and perhaps uncommon in your line of business."

"Gracias," Jefe said humbly. "I'm grateful you had successful dealings with my associates. Tell me, Professor. Has your assessment of the political climate and the timing of our plans changed at all?"

"Not really. We are still at the first part of our marathon. 2024 is still likely the first election cycle in which we have a viable chance of winning the presidency. Patience will be required, but 2024 will come sooner than you'd ever think. Look how fast Abriz has grown up!"

Jefe smiled. "Yes. It seems like it has just been a blink of an eye since she was born."

"Blink twice and 2024 will be here." Professor raised his glass to toast Jefe. "Of course, if opportunities arise before then, we will take advantage of them."

"Como no. By the way, how have things gone with our mutual friend, Silvia Rodriguez?"

"She is off to a fantastic start," proclaimed Professor. "By all reports, she has quickly become very useful to the governor's team, and she is elevating her profile and reputation throughout Arizona. She also seems to be working well with both Republicans and Democrats. The media loves her and frequently asks her to provide insights on current issues. This is all awesome, especially since the governor has declared that he won't run for re-election in 2012."

"That's great news. It looks like Silvia has a good chance to be the next governor of Arizona!"

Professor grinned. "Bingo."

37

VERACRUZ, MEXICO, JANUARY 2010

After a night of delicious Mexican cuisine and plentiful fine wine, Professor awoke from an excellent night of sleep. He opened the blinds to his guest room to check the weather. He spotted Jefe already lounging by the pool.

It looks like it will be business for breakfast, Professor thought.

Professor strolled down to the pool and his prediction proved to be correct. Jefe greeted him with coffee, juices, and breakfast pastries.

"Once you get set," Jefe said, "I'd like to get your thoughts on the electoral strategies we need to use to win the presidency."

"OK," Professor said between bites. "Let me start with some general observations and then get into specifics. Let me warn you. It's currently too soon to identify our approach on specific issues until we figure out the pulse of the voters heading into the actual election."

Professor took a sip of juice and continued. "For Republicans, electability requires that we have a center-right candidate as our nominee. This has almost always been the case since the days of Garry Boldwater in the 1960's. The traditional election playbook is for a candidate to run to the left of Democrats and to the right of Republicans in the primaries and, after prevailing there, come back to the center in the general election. We probably should not stray too far from that general philosophy, all while trying to diversify the Republican voting base.

"My next general observation is to quote long-time former Speaker of the House, Trip O'Neill. He famously said 'all politics is local.' I agree that it's hugely important to generate grassroots support and enthusiasm for our candidates. A star candidate without solid ground support will not get elected. Star quarterback Tom Brady could not win a Super Bowl if he wasn't surrounded with a great offensive line."

Jefe interposed, "Thanks. I understand the analogy, but I'm still more of a fútbol fan than a football fan!"

"Sorry, Jefe. I'll try to remember that! My real intent was to emphasize that campaigns are long, ugly, and expensive grinds. The main calculus for many presidential candidates is whether they can raise enough money to enter and stay in the race. It can cost hundreds of millions of dollars. The Golden Rule rules, but not like in the past. Now it's 'he who has the gold makes the rules.'"

"Thankfully, we are the ones with gold!" Jefe said with a big smile.

"The final general rule for today is something we can't control, but still need to consider. This rule is that the most important issue for voters in elections is always the wallet. If a person has plenty of money in his or her pocketbook, the incumbent always looks appealing. However, if the economy is bad and inflation is high, people will feel the pain and hold the person at top accountable. Even if it is not his fault, a bad economy translates to bad approval ratings and it's hard for a sitting president to get reelected."

"This is all interesting, but very basic," Jefe said. "Anything specific you'd like to add, Professor?"

"As I said before, it's way too early to develop specific issue positions for our candidates. Right now, I'm more concerned about ensuring our candidates can easily pass any background check. History shows there are lots of things that can derail any election strategy, usually in the last month of the campaign. It could be releases of damaging emails by Wiki Leaks. It could be dirt on the candidate that is dug up by the RNC or DNC's team of character assassination investigators. Or, it just could be stupid candidate behavior, like engaging in monkey business during the campaign. In today's era of social media visibility, everyone is looking for any skeletons in a candidate's closet. Jefe, I will do background checks on my end, but I would ask that you also do it for any candidate we start to push forward, starting with Silvia."

Jefe nodded. "Happy to assist. Any other thoughts you'd like to share?"

"I'll just throw out one more. From day one and every day going forward, our candidates should always support the police, support the military, and thank each of those members for their service and patriotism."

"I agree. Just curious, but what position should our candidates take on drugs?" asked Jefe.

"Unless something changes, I think our candidates need to take a hard stance against drugs and the legalization of marijuana. This will be most convincing if our candidate can say that he or she has seen firsthand the devastation that drugs can cause to families and communities. Is that acceptable, Jefe?"

"Yes, if it will help us claim the White House. Part of my real goal, of course, is to stop the states from legalizing pot and creating an accepted, regulated product. I don't like the competition! The U.S. will always have an insatiable demand for drugs. However, we profit most when the drugs are illegal, and we are the main supplier. It's simple economics."

"Understood," said Professor, his stomach starting to tighten.

38

VERACRUZ, MEXICO, JANUARY 2010

Two days later, Jefe was driving Professor to the Aueropuerto Internacional de Veracruz when Professor decided the time was right to open conversation on a difficult subject.

"Jefe, this has been wonderful. As always, you, Verana, and Abriz treat me like family. However, before I head home, there is one topic that I would like to discuss because I need to know my guardrails."

"You have my total attention," Jefe said. "What is it my friend?"

"Winning an election is not the only way to become president of the United States. When we initially discussed your objective, you told me to do 'all things necessary' to get one of your people to be POTUS, regardless of cost, party affiliation or viewpoints." Professor gulped. "What exactly did you mean by 'all things necessary?'"

Jefe blinked. "I truly meant all things necessary. As long as nothing is traced back to me, of course."

"To be clear then," said Professor, "a sitting president can be replaced in a number of circumstances. He can be removed from office for cause, like Richard Dixon before he resigned due to Watergate. There are also various succession policies in the event POTUS is incapacitated or dies. If our candidate is not elected president, am I to use succession strategies to obtain our objective?"

"Let's not discuss this in vague generalities. What are you asking?"

Professor hesitated. "If our candidate is not elected, do you want me to pursue killing the president as a fallback strategy?"

"I strongly prefer that our plan be executed without bloodshed. But I am not unfamiliar with the need to use violence to accomplish one's goals. So, as I said before, the answer is 'yes' as long as it's not traceable back to me. However, I do want to know the details of any plans to replace the president."

"Thank you for clarifying. It is good to know the boundaries of my authority, because I can foresee a possible situation where we have a candidate who becomes the vice president. If our person stays in the background supporting the president, an opportunity could arise later to become the successor in office."

Jefe grinned. "That would be fine with me."

Professor sighed. "Let's hope we don't have to employ such tactics. But I assure you that I will look at all possible options to attain the presidency for you, Jefe."

39

PHOENIX, ARIZONA, NOVEMBER 6, 2012

It was a hard-fought and closely contested race for the 2012 Arizona governorship. At the election watch party of Silvia Luisa Anna Marie Rodriguez and her team of supporters in the Arizona Biltmore Hotel main ballroom, the mood was upbeat and hopeful. It was almost 11 p.m. when a national news network came on the TV screens throughout the ballroom and indicated it was ready to call the race. The room quickly fell silent before the election anchor spoke.

"With 98% of the votes counted, Republican newcomer Silvia Rodriguez is the governor-elect of the State of Arizona, gathering slightly over 50% of the total vote."

The ballroom erupted in applause and the victory celebration started in earnest.

Moments later, Silvia left her hotel room after receiving the traditional concessionary phone call from her opponent. She left with her inner circle of advisors to go to the ballroom to make her acceptance speech. Backstage, Professor approached her before she took the stage. He handed the new governor-elect a glass of champagne.

"I am very proud of you, and Jefe will be very pleased," Professor whispered to Silvia as he gave her a hug. "I am going to call him immediately and share the good news."

Silvia thanked him before taking the stage. After waiting for the clapping and celebratory yelling to subside, Silvia thanked all her campaign supporters for their help.

She then said, "My parents always taught me to dream big, work hard, and stay humble. This was not just a saying to them; it was a way of life. Success was something to be earned. It was not something that was guaranteed or entitled. I hope that I have lived my life in a way that makes my parents proud, and I hope to govern Arizona in a way that makes all of you proud."

Professor smiled, basking in their first of hopefully many election victories. After listening to the rest of Silvia's heartfelt acceptance speech, Professor left the celebration and returned to his hotel room. He pulled a burner phone out of his suitcase and called Jefe.

"Sorry to call so late, Jefe, but Silvia just won the Arizona governor's race. I am very happy and proud."

"That is great news," Jefe said. "I hope this is the first of many steps in her political career."

"I think you can count on it!" promised Professor.

40

WASHINGTON, D.C., JANUARY 2019

Washington had always been a beautiful, welcoming city, and a wonderful place to live, especially for people with money, power, or fame. Home to multiple colleges and universities, Washington was also full of young people looking to climb the ladder of success. The magnetic draw of politics and power provided a unique and spellbinding energy to the city. It was easy to feel like you were living in the most important city in the world, and the surroundings made every day feel like you were living an American history textbook.

After leaving Straw and his family, Nick drove Sadie to his new home. It was a brownstone row house in the East Village of Georgetown, not far from Straw's home. The residential portion of Georgetown was renowned for federalist architecture, historic brick and frame row houses, cobblestone streets, and grand estates dating back to the 18th century. Straw's house fit in perfectly.

As Nick approached his house, he enjoyed driving on the narrow residential street, shaded from the sun by a canopy of branches from century-old trees. As he pulled into the driveway, Nick's first impression was that the house appeared inconspicuous, yet had distinct charm unlike many other suburban homes. Dormer windows beneath the roof line gave the impression the house had more living space than it did.

A large bay window to the left of the front door added to the unique aesthetics of the house.

Upon entering the front door, Nick's eyes were drawn to the parquet wood flooring that extended throughout the ground level. Asian rugs adorned the floor. A large, elegantly carved wooden crucifix was displayed over the entry door in the interior, helping illustrate the grand ceilings in the house.

The home was tastefully decorated like it was straight out of an episode of HGTV. There was a clear emphasis on having an open floor plan and spacious kitchen. All furnishings looked new and expensive and provided a sense of freshness to the historic home.

The kitchen had state-of-the-art appliances, a double sink, granite countertops, a rectangular island large enough for four bar stools, and a spacious pantry. Next to the kitchen was a dining nook with built-in banquette seating and bar space that flowed into a comfortable Great Room with a vaulted barrel ceiling. The interior was decorated with tasteful oil paintings, modern light fixtures, and large windows providing lots of natural light. The Great Room was furnished with comfortable chairs and throw pillows on a large sofa. The backyard was small, with fencing and perimeter trees that provided both privacy and security.

Nick received a pleasant surprise when he did the walk-through of his house. Nick's dad had arranged for his bedroom walls to be painted green, Nick's favorite color since early childhood. A photo of Nick and Katie was placed on his nightstand. In addition, Carson left a care package in the kitchen: a large platter of fresh fruit and a refrigerator full of milk, vegetables, and Guinness beer. The freezer was full of frozen Valentino's pizza and ice cream.

Nick smiled and felt a little bit at home knowing that his dad had carefully stocked the kitchen with his favorite foods.

41

WASHINGTON, D.C., JANUARY 2019

After returning home from an uneventful second day of work, Nick heard a knock on his front door. He opened the door to find a pregnant African American woman and her two children.

"Hi, I'm Miriam Hawkins and these are my children, Alana and Grant. We are your neighbors just down the street," she said, pointing to a house on a corner lot. "We wanted to welcome you to the neighborhood."

Alana, a nine- or ten-year-old with pigtails and a big smile on her face, handed Nick a plate of fresh-baked cookies. "We saw you jogging yesterday, and you run really fast!"

Nick laughed. "Thank you! I'd like to run even faster, someday. My name is Nick."

"My mom always gives cookies to new neighbors," said Grant, an energetic boy wearing a jersey with the number 33 on it.

"Well, I appreciate the gift. You are the first people I've met in the neighborhood. I hope I can rely on you for great tips on fun places to go in the area."

"You can count on us," said Alana. "We've been here my entire life!"

"Those talks will have to wait for another time though," said Miriam. "We have to leave now for Grant's basketball game."

"That's very exciting," said Nick. "Play well and have lots of fun. Thanks again for the cookies."

42

WASHINGTON, D.C., JANUARY 2019

It was near the end of Nick's second full week of work at GROSS. He noticed that several mornings, Straw would arrive at the crack of dawn, eager to receive clues and information from places in different time zones. One of those mornings, Nick decided to come into the office earlier than usual so he could watch Straw work.

Nick knew that Straw was already at work when sounds of the Grateful Dead reverberated as he opened the door. Straw's best work was always done listening to music. Whenever Straw tapped his foot and had a far-away look in his eyes, it was because a Dead jam session had opened a transcendent new universe of analyzing the data in front of him.

Nick entered the office to find Straw, looking like his normal fashion victim, in the zone. His eyes were glued to his desktop monitors while his fingers drummed to the music. Straw jumped when he noticed Nick take a seat at his desk and he turned down the volume of his music.

"Sorry, Straw," Nick said. "I didn't mean to surprise you. Is this a good time to talk?"

"The time is good," Straw said. "I am tracking some interesting stuff, but none of it is time-sensitive right now."

"Gotcha. What are you looking at?" inquired Nick.

"One of my strategies is to follow the money, because that often takes me where I need to go. Right now, I'm seeing hundreds of payments just under $10,000 going from Banco Internacional de Mexico to individuals and pass-through businesses across our country. And that's in just the past couple of weeks."

"But why so many payments less than $10K?"

"It's the amount that triggers banks to report it when received as deposits. This bank is owned by Mexican businessman Salvador Santos. Whoever he's paying, he's trying hard to stay under the radar."

Straw took a chug from his glass of tap water… he was too environmentally conscious to drink from plastic bottles. "My gut tells me something is happening. But I have no hard clues, no defined suspects, and no clear motive. I'm stuck in quicksand and can't see much difference between the dark and the light. But what would you like to talk about?"

"Straw, I've been here almost two weeks now. I know that I didn't get off to a great start with Samantha, but I was hoping that I'd see at least a little thaw in our relationship by now. Any suggestions?"

Straw sat back in his chair. "Let me think about that a little more. You made Sam throw you out in the cold rain and snow on your first day, so I think you've got to have more patience. Just keep on keeping on. Do what you are asked, and I think things will get better over time. I'll let you know if I come up with any better ideas."

43

CHASE FIELD, ARIZONA DIAMONDBACKS STADIUM, AUGUST 2016

Four years after being elected the youngest governor in Arizona, Silvia Rodriguez continued to grow her reputation as an up-and-coming Republican at an extraordinarily fast pace. Under her leadership, taxes in Arizona were reduced, the state attained record low levels of unemployment, and a budget surplus was generated. She also worked with the Arizona legislature to provide enough state and local incentives to entice Amazron, Goggle and SuperSolar, the largest U.S. manufacturer of solar panels, to locate significant new facilities in the state. The Arizona Republic, the state's newspaper with the largest circulation, called these accomplishments the "governmental grand slam."

Her achievements as the chief executive in Arizona not only provided the state with a strong base for future economic growth, but they also sent the approval ratings of Governor Rodriguez through the roof. Her success was so undisputed across party lines that Silvia essentially ran unopposed in her bid for reelection.

With no real challenger against her in the upcoming election, Silvia spent her free time helping other Republican candidates throughout the country in their election bids for state or federal offices. Silvia was quickly developing a reputation as a "secret weapon" to Republican candidates, her endorsement carrying significant weight beyond the borders of Arizona. More importantly, she was a fundraiser with no equal. At fundraising events for Congress or Senate positions, Silvia produced donations from supporters in amounts rarely seen in prior campaigns. Of course, Professor was behind the curtain of these efforts, using Jefe's contacts and bank account to donate funds whenever Silvia requested.

One day, Silvia accepted an invitation from the mayor of Phoenix and the owner of the Arizona Diamondbacks to watch an inter-divisional baseball game against the New York Yankees. Silvia was an avid sports fan, and the lure of watching the Yankees was exciting to her, especially since it would be the last time that Yankee superstar, Andres Rodriguez, would play at Chase Field. The handsome slugger, known as A-Rod, had previously announced he was going to retire at the end of the year.

Unlike many politicians who only make cameo appearances at sporting events for publicity, Silvia stayed the entire game. She was rewarded as the game between the Diamondbacks and Yankees was a nailbiter. Despite A-Rod hitting a homerun, the Diamondbacks won 6-5.

Seeing that Silvia had cheered when A-Rod connected on his homer, the owner of the Diamondbacks asked if she'd like to meet A-Rod after the game.

"Of course!" Silvia said. "Even though he plays for the wrong team, I've always been a big fan."

After the game, the owner walked Silvia to the outside of the Yankees locker room, where he introduced her to his counterpart with the Yankees. A message was relayed to A-Rod about the request from the Arizona governor to meet. He showed up shortly after his shower, his hair still wet.

"Andres," said the Yankee owner, "please meet Arizona governor Silvia Rodriguez. Governor, please meet Andres Rodriguez."

"The pleasure is all mine," Silvia gushed, not trying to hide her fangirl excitement. "I've been a fan of yours for a long time."

"I'm also a big fan of yours," Andres said, "and that was before I even knew you were a baseball fan! And, I'm not just saying that because we share the same last name, although I think that's very cool."

"That is a neat coincidence. By the way, impressive homer today. Hope you get to 700 by the end of the year."

"Thanks," A-Rod said. "I'm also impressed with what you've been able to accomplish as governor. I read in the paper today that you've hit the 'governmental grand slam.' Congratulations! I also know that your full name is Silvia Luisa Anna Marie Rodriguez. So, my question for you is, why aren't we calling you 'SlamRod?'"

To A-Rod's surprise, Silvia smiled. "I would be honored to have that nickname!"

Local TV crews captured the exchange between Silvia and A-Rod. The video clip soon went viral nationwide. The nickname stuck and thereafter, Silvia was often referred to as "Governor SlamRod."

44

VERACRUZ, MEXICO, JANUARY 2017

Jefe summoned Professor to Veracruz to discuss Donald Triumph's surprising 2016 presidential election victory. Instead of being met at the Veracruz airport by a limo driver, Jefe himself was there to greet Professor as he exited the Lear jet.

The greeting was in pure style. Jefe did not often make flashy shows of his wealth, but one of his indulgences was his love of elite sports cars. Jefe's favorite was his metallic blue Bugatti Chiron, a toy for billionaires with a base price of $2.4 million euros. The Bugatti purred and seemed to float on air as Jefe enjoyed the drive to his estate.

"Professor, how were you able to predict Triumph's victory?" asked Jefe when they were out by his poolside office. "It seemed like all of the pollsters and other experts were shocked by the outcome."

"Well," Professor said, "I think my distance from the campaign let me view the election more objectively than other prognosticators. This let me identify the frustration felt by much of the electorate. I understood the fallibility of polls in an election where voting was an emotionally charged choice, and public support of Triumph in polls may have been unpopular."

"So, how did Triumph win the presidency?"

"In my view, Triumph brilliantly took advantage of American frustration with government. He used his TV personality, business profile, and extremist reputation to garner all the far-right voters. These are people who embrace Triumph's brashness, bigotry, and divisiveness. On the flip side, Triumph's opponents dislike him mainly based on his character. Alarms go off every time he tweets or speaks off-script. He's a liar and a bully who disrespects people and lacks morals.

"For years, experts thought that winning elections came down to character and trust. Neither Triumph nor Hillary Clanton had those in the last election. Just think what either party could have done with a candidate that possessed even one of those traits! Triumph had a 60% disapproval rating and still won the election. That's incredible! He also became the first-ever president with no military or political experience. Although many voters did not think he was qualified to be president, most of them ended up voting for Triumph. A huge factor in the outcome was the number of independent voters who went with Triumph, contrary to Hillary's expectations. Ultimately, Triumph got 100% of the U.S. presidency in 2016 even though he got less than 50% of the popular vote."

Jefe nodded. "Let's focus on what this means for us. What are the key lessons for us to learn and act upon from this election?"

"Triumph's victory was very unconventional," Professor replied, "but I don't want to overreact and think we need to throw away the traditional playbook on winning the White House. The Democrats are going to be very determined to create gridlock and make Triumph fail, so I don't anticipate the Triumph administration will get many legislative successes in the coming years. This makes it very important for competing candidates in upcoming elections to have a successful track record."

"Won't that be good for us based on Silvia's successes as governor?" Jefe asked.

"Absolutely," Professor said. "What we need to do is stay on course with Silvia and continue to increase her recognition. I've already started to put plans in place to increase Silvia's profile by arranging for her to become the chairperson of the Republican Governors Association. This will allow her to hone her party-building chops while broadening her network beyond Arizona."

"Fantastic. Silvia seems by far like our front-running horse in this race, isn't she?"

"Without a doubt, and my appreciation of her talents and potential grows every day."

45

VERACRUZ, MEXICO, JUNE 2018

Jefe's burner phone rang at an unplanned time. He knew that it was not good news by Professor's lack of small talk.

"There are always potholes in every president's road to the White House," Professor started. "We have hit two setbacks recently."

"Please, go on," Jefe said.

"First, as you know, I've always wanted a multi-pronged strategy heading into the presidential election cycle. Realistically, I'm still looking at 2024 as the election in which we are most likely to be positioned for success, but I've been working hard to see if there are chances for us in the upcoming 2020 election. This strategy would optimally have us with competitive candidates loyal to us on both the Democrat and Republican sides of the ticket. Unfortunately, I have not been able to cultivate any Democrat candidate as capable as Silvia is on the Republican side.

"Camila Flores, our first term Congresswoman out of California, is our best Democrat option. While the Democrat nominee has not yet been determined, the clear frontrunner is Joe Burden. He has the name recognition and visibility from being Olama's VP for eight years. I really don't see him having any serious contenders. Bernie Sanderson is even older than Burden, and America will never elect a socialist. Elizabeth Warrent may enter the race, but she's too far to the left of Burden. If Hillary could not win last election, then Warrent really has no chance."

"So, is there any role for Camila?" Jefe asked.

"Not in the near term. I talked to my contacts in the Burden organization to see if he would be open to Camila as a potential VP. While it was too early to commit, the honest answer was that she didn't have enough of a political resume or name recognition to add value to the Burden team. I hate to say it, but I agree with them. Hopefully, we will be able to increase her profile looking ahead to 2024."

"OK, I understand," Jefe said. "Please continue to cultivate growth there. What is the other setback?"

"Well, it may be both a setback and an opportunity. As you know, I couldn't be more pleased with the trajectory of Governor Rodriguez. In 2020, there's no doubt that Triumph will be the Republican candidate, and he'll have a lot of advantages as the incumbent. I've noticed some friction beneath the surface between Triumph and his vice president, so I made some subtle inquiries whether Triumph would be open to replacing Spence on the ticket with Silvia. Triumph's team said he really likes Silvia, but unless something happened to Spence, Triumph would not break up his winning team."

"So, where does that leave us?"

"I thought about the response from the Triumph team and wanted to clarify something with you." Professor hesitated. "Do you want to see if we could make something 'happen to Spence?'"

"What are you thinking?"

"There are two things that could cause Spence to be replaced. The first is if he were implicated in a scandal. The problem here is that Spence doesn't really have any vices or skeletons in the closet. While it's always possible to get an innocent man accused of scandalous activity, considering Triumph's background, it would be quite a stretch for Triumph to disassociate with Spence merely because he was the subject of some unfounded accusations."

"What is the other option?"

"A health issue that makes him incapable of serving."

"But, isn't he in great health? He looks very fit."

"Yes, he is."

Jefe thought it over. "Well, we may just have to change that. I think we need to talk in person."

46

VERACRUZ, MEXICO, JUNE 2018

The next day, Professor arrived in Veracruz on one of Jefe's planes. Soon they were back at Jefe's poolside "office" so they could discuss the topic alluded to in their last conversation: the assassination of Vice President Spence.

"If we hope to attain the presidency in 2020," Professor said, "it will require the termination of Spence as VP. But it does no good to terminate Spence unless he will be replaced with our candidate, Silvia. Based on my initial inquiries, I think this is likely the case."

"Let me ask a few questions," Jefe started. "First, do you have a plan to assassinate Spence? Second, to even think about doing that, I would need a *much* stronger assurance that Silvia would replace Spence as VP. Have you had any direct conversation with Triumph himself?"

"On the first question, yes, I do have the broad outline of a plan, but I obviously won't go any further without your involvement and approval."

"What about my other question. Has Triumph been contacted about Silvia being his VP if the opportunity arose?"

Professor chuckled as he opened a laptop. "I anticipated your need for proof that Silvia is on Triumph's VP short list if Spence were out of the picture. I arranged for Silvia to have a Zoom call with Triumph yesterday. Here's a recording of the call."

Professor hit a few keys and a video appeared on his screen. Jefe watched closely as Silvia described her desire to assist Triumph at the national level. After Triumph agreed that Silvia would be a welcome addition to his campaign, Silvia interjected, "To be clear, I don't just want to work on your campaign for reelection. I want to be your running mate. While I have a lot of respect for Vice President Spence, there is noticeable friction between the two of you. If voters see that as well, it will cost you votes."

The video showed Triumph as he responded, "Right now, Spence is my VP, but you never say never in this business."

Professor stopped the recording.

"Here's the key part of the conversation, Jefe," Professor said while pushing the "play" button.

The video continued, showing Triumph say, "Silvia, you've given me lots to think about. If for any reason the vice president and I split as teammates, you will be the first to know."

"Amazing," Jefe proclaimed as Professor turned off the video. "But how do we know Triumph's not lying, or just thinking with his penis instead of his brain?"

"We'll never know if we can fully trust Triumph. But apart from Silvia's physical attractiveness, the beauty of our plan is that Silvia really is the best fit for the VP slot if anything takes Spence out of that role."

47

VERACRUZ, MEXICO, JUNE 2018

"Silvia won't land on Triumph's ticket as long as Spence lives," Jefe said. "So, what can we do about the VP?"

Professor hesitated. "Jefe, I am not an expert on the logistics of assassinations. I will leave that planning to your connections in the U.S. who have done that before. But, unless your planning experts say otherwise, I think a great opportunity to take out Spence will occur December first. That's when Spence will be the keynote speaker at a fundraiser in Scottsdale that will be attended by none other than our own Governor Rodriguez. It seems like a perfect opportunity for our paths to cross."

"Professor, it seems to me that it would be very difficult to assassinate one of America's leaders. You seem to think otherwise. Why?"

"History proves that it's not hard to kill an American president. Look at what John Hincklebee did to President Raygun in 1981. Hincklebee was just a teenager with mental health issues who thought he could impress actress Jodie Fostner by killing the president, and he almost did it! His plan was simple… be on the street outside of the Hilton Hotel in Washington where Raygun was giving a speech. As Raygun was walking to his limo after the speech, Hincklebee opened up with a handgun, shooting Raygun and three others. Raygun survived, but just barely."

"Wow," exclaimed Jefe. "I remember that."

"If Hincklebee could penetrate presidential security by the most basic of maneuvers, just think what can be done with a sophisticated, well-financed, and conceived plan."

"I'm counting on that," Jefe said. "I'm curious. Has a VP ever been assassinated?"

"No. We will be making history."

"Cheers to that!" Jefe said. "But let me summarize. Our goal is to open up the VP slot and have Triumph fill it with Silvia. Then together, they win the 2020 election. Sometime thereafter, Triumph will be assassinated so Silvia becomes president by succession."

"Exactly. I never said this was going to be easy."

"Just remember. This must not be traceable back to me. Beyond that, you have my blessing to do whatever is necessary. No matter what the cost. No matter the casualties."

48

WASHINGTON, D.C., JANUARY 2019

It was a Sunday morning, so Nick slept in before going on his daily run through the neighborhood. Upon arriving back home, Nick noticed the entire Hawkins family shooting baskets on a hoop in their driveway. Though in need of a shower, Nick thought it was the perfect time to repay the neighbors for their hospitality. He grabbed a bottle of red wine from his house and walked to the Hawkins' house.

"Sorry to interrupt your game of H-O-R-S-E, but I wanted to thank you for the delicious cookies," said Nick, handing the bottle of wine to Miriam. "This probably isn't the best gift, but hopefully you can enjoy it after you have your baby."

"Thanks, Nick," Miriam said. "Let me introduce you to my husband, Blair."

Miriam's husband, a slightly built African American man with glasses, extended his hand to Nick and said, "Pleased to meet you. Welcome to the neighborhood!"

"Thanks. You've got a great family. What kind of work do you do?"

"I'm a pulmonologist at Georgetown University Hospital. Miriam is a corporate finance partner at the Logan Hovells law firm. Between those jobs and our kids, we stay pretty busy!"

"I can imagine."

"Hey kids," Miriam said, "your dad and I concede in H-O-R-S-E. Continue without us so we can get to know Mr. Class a little better." Turning to Nick and noting his jogging clothes, Miriam said with a smile, "It's getting hot out here, so let's go inside and chat. I've already got a pitcher of lemonade prepared. You look like you could use a drink!"

Despite the upper-class salaries of both parents, having young kids and a dog meant that the main floor of the Hawkins house was decorated like it was from a Pottery Barn or Crate & Barrel catalogue. The modern sectional couch, floor rug, coffee table, and chairs all looked comfortable, but also not expensive enough to worry if damaged by the playful activities of children or a pet.

For the next half hour, Nick had a great talk with the parents while Alana and Grant shot baskets. Nick gave a Reader's Digest version of his story, indicating that he moved here to work for a small real estate consulting company. In return, he learned lots about the Hawkins family, including that Miriam and Blair met while they were in grad school at Duke University, and they were avid Duke basketball supporters.

"That's why our son is named Grant Hill Hawkins and why we choose Alana as the name for our daughter," explained Merriam.

"Have you picked out the name for your next child?" asked Nick.

"Children," Merriam clarified. "We're going to have twin boys! Greyson and Allen are expected to arrive next month."

"Congratulations. You are really going to have your hands full!"

A short time later, Nick excused himself so he could go home and shower. As he walked home, Nick reflected on his time with the close-knit Hawkins family. His mind was soon flooded with thoughts of what could have been... a joyous family that he and Katie were so close to starting. Nick entered his house and broke down in a waterfall of tears.

49

VERACRUZ, MEXICO, NOVEMBER 30, 2018

"Happy Black Friday, Professor!" Jefe greeted Professor when he arrived at his estate.

"Thank you for inviting me," Professor said. "Hope you and your family had a nice Thanksgiving together."

The two men soon found themselves alone by Jefe's magnificent pool, with the rhythmic sound of the nearby surf providing a relaxing backdrop.

"Tomorrow's the big day. Is everything set?" Jefe asked.

"Yes, everything is in order. We hired an ex-Army sniper specialist who needs the money. He's our trigger man. All payment is in untraceable cash, fifty percent up front and a final payment a week after a successful event." Professor hesitated. "I feel bad, though. Spence seems like a stand-up guy."

"That may be. But sometimes, sacrifices must be made for the greater good. Collateral damage cannot be avoided. I'm glad the hard work and planning have all been done. Now we can just relax and wait."

"Sure thing," said Professor, his hand shaking as he raised his glass to toast with Jefe.

50

WASHINGTON, D.C., JANUARY 2019

Straw went to the office earlier than usual. He arranged three of his monitors to show different time-synched angles of a Republican party fundraiser in Scottsdale, Arizona. The event was held on the golf course of a resort hotel. A makeshift stage for the VIPs was placed on the 18th green, allowing plentiful room for deep-pocket donors to mingle between the clubhouse and the green.

Straw looked closely at the background for any anything unusual or unexpected, no matter how minor.

The fundraiser was well-attended and the stage at the event was filled with Arizona Republican royalty: both U.S. senators, the senior member of Congress, the governor, and the mayor of Phoenix were seated in a semi-circle of chairs on the stage. The chair for the featured speaker, Vice President Mike Spence, was in the middle of the stage. Straw easily identified Secret Service and FBI agents dressed in black as they tried to blend in with the event patrons.

Straw watched carefully, but saw nothing of interest during the speeches of the initial speakers. Governor Rodriguez then gave a rousing speech that energized the crowd. She then introduced Vice President Spence, who gave her a quick hug when he approached the podium. With Spence's right hand holding Rodriguez's left hand, they extended their arms to the sky as the crowd stood to give them a deafening ovation.

Straw was so focused on his screens that he paid no attention when Nick and Sam entered the office. They ventured over to Straw's desk to see what he was watching. It was then that chaos erupted on his screens.

Multiple gunshots went off. One bullet hit the stage, barely missing the vice president. As Secret Service agents quickly covered Spence, another bullet hit one of the agents in the neck. He writhed in agony, blood spewing from his neck. Then Governor Rodriguez leapt over him, shielding him from any further shots. She pressed her hand on the agent's wound, trying to stop the bleeding. In a matter of seconds, other agents rushed the stage and grabbed the governor to escort her out of the danger zone.

"Straw," Sam said. Her voice trembled, but her hands rolled into fists. "Why are you watching this..."

Before Straw could remove his headphones to answer, Sam buried her face in her hands and screamed. She grabbed her coat and kicked her chair so hard it flipped twice before landing upside-down. Then she bolted through the door.

Nick stood in stunned silence. "Yikes. What was that about?"

Straw sighed. "I can't really say."

51

WASHINGTON, D.C., JANUARY 2019

Nick bundled up before exiting the GROSS office. It didn't take him long to find Sam pacing along the sidewalk bordering the strip mall. In the short time they had worked together, Sam always appeared in control. She almost never lost her cool, except when Nick did on his first day of work. But for her to break down out of the blue, Nick knew something was off.

Was it something to do with that video? he thought as he followed Sam. *That looked like the VP assassination attempt from last year. It sure looked gruesome. But what's it got to do with Sam?*

As Nick approached her, Sam slowed her pace.

"What do you want?" she asked, turning away to hide her tears.

"Just checking on my partner," Nick said.

Sam chuckled and shook her head. "Go ahead. Say it. Pot calling the kettle black? How can she tell me to keep my cool when she just lost it?"

Nick held up his hands. "Not my intention. Kinda caught me off guard, though. Do you want to talk about it?"

"Not. At. All." Sam wiped her tears with her coat sleeve before sitting down on the edge of the sidewalk.

"That's all right." Nick joined her on the pavement. "You don't have to talk about the video. But something on it is hurting you. You once told me you needed to know *everything* about your partner. Their ticks, their triggers." He shrugged. "I'm just trying to help, Sam."

She pursed her lips and thought it over.

"Ticks and triggers are important," she eventually said. "How about we focus on triggers?"

"I'm all ears."

"Actually…" Sam stood and brushed the snow off her coat. "Before we talk about triggers, I say we *pull* some triggers."

Nick raised an eyebrow.

"You got the keys to Sadie?" she asked.

Nick nodded, pulling them from his pocket.

"Good," she said. "Take a left and head north. Stop when you reach the Marksman."

52

WASHINGTON, D.C., JANUARY 2019

The Marksman was a massive warehouse and the largest indoor shooting range outside D.C. proper. Over the years, the old military training grounds urbanized. One of the owners opened a pub on the second level, welcoming the locals to eat and drink. As long as they did so *after* exercising their Second Amendment rights, of course.

"Here we are," Sam said, breaking the awkward silence that had filled their half-hour drive.

Nick parked and locked Sadie before following Sam inside the warehouse. Neon lights and military banners hung over the lobby and check-in. A large oak double staircase separated the bar and grill upstairs from the shooting range on the lower levels.

"Sam!" said the mustachioed man behind the front desk. "You're here early."

"Hey Rich," she said. "Sorry for not calling in advance. Just got an early morning trigger finger."

"Understood. All lanes are open. You can grab brunch upstairs after."

Rich pulled out two over-ear headphones and a metal briefcase. He opened the latter to reveal two .40 caliber Universal Machine Pistols with ample magazines. Nick's eyes widened at the heavy yet compact artillery.

"The usual?" Rich asked as he displayed the supplies.

"Please," Sam said. "Mind if I show my colleague around first?"

"Not at all." Rich closed the briefcase and waved a hand for them to proceed downstairs.

Sam took the gear and led Nick to the shooting range. SWAT team, police academy, and other training fliers adorned the walls as they descended to a long hallway. This connected each of the twelve lanes with various targets and obstacles.

"Lanes one through three are beginner courses," Sam said, explaining each lane they walked past. "Four through six emphasize distance. Ideal for snipers. Otherwise, lanes seven on up are military-grade courses. They're the most advanced and customizable. The targets differ every week."

"Gotcha," Nick said.

They eventually stopped at lane eight. Nick's hands were already clammy, and he hesitated to reach for the door when Sam held it open for him.

"What is it?" she asked.

"Sorry," Nick said. "I've just... never held a gun before."

"Actually, you have. Before the Clean Slate Protocol, you trained with Navy SEALs." Sam ushered him inside. "Come on, Nick. Shooting will come back to you. Just like riding a bike."

Nick scoffed as he stepped inside the lane. His efforts to help Sam were beginning to backfire. Something about the video clearly traumatized her. But, Nick would have *never* broached the subject with Sam if it meant reliving some of his own repressed trauma. Besides, what if holding a gun made Nick spiral into the same "hurricane rage" that killed the thugs who killed Katie?

"I'll go first," Sam said, setting the briefcase on the tabletop near the door. She put on her protective headphones, grabbed a UMP, and loaded a magazine. "FYI, these are the same pistols we carry in Sadie."

Nick nodded, donning his own headphones as Sam approached a black line. Several human-shaped targets stood at the opposite end of the lane. Their torsos were labeled with circles of varying sizes. Some targets were even animatronic, moving in fixed patterns above or lateral to fake boulders and other terrain.

Sam rotated her shoulders and took a deep breath. When a *BUZZ* erupted from the lane's overhead speakers, she sprang into action.

She planted her legs firmly behind the black line and extended her gun arm, steadying it with her non-dominant hand. She unclicked the safety on the UMP and fired ten shots in rhythmic succession. Her shots pierced the target twenty yards away, dealing fatal blows to the head and heart.

Holy cow, Nick thought. *Sam has stellar aim!*

She took another deep breath, side-stepped, and reloaded. Her gaze shifted to the next target thirty yards away. Half her shots connected with the torso, but she missed more of the headshots. After finishing her second magazine, Sam shook her head.

"Come on, Sam," she said as she reloaded again. "Get your head in the game."

Her last target stood at least fifty yards away. This one was a moving target, rotating in a circle above and to the side of a rusted sedan littered with bullet holes. Sam straightened her postured, relaxed her shoulders, and took another deep breath. Then, she planted her feet and thrust her arms forward.

Before the moving target could take cover behind the sedan, Sam fired ten clean shots straight through its head. The last few shots dented the target's metal support rod, halting its cyclic motion. She removed the empty magazine, placed her gun on the shelf, and removed her headphones.

His eyes wide with admiration, Nick applauded her.

"That was sick," he said.

"Thank you," she said. "After this morning, I needed that."

"Do you always come here to blow off steam?"

"Yeah. The Marksman has been my safe haven for the past few months." Sam handed him a UMP and a few magazines. "Your turn."

Nick gulped. "You sure?"

"Yes."

"But what if I black out? I don't want to lose myself to the 'hurricane' like I did at the park."

Sam looked him straight in the eye. "Focus your feelings, Nick. Zero in on each target in front of you. Channel everything you got into each bullseye. Even if you feel the hurricane, don't give into it. Focus your feelings."

Nick nodded, donned his headphones, and took the pistol and ammo. When he arrived at the black line, he tried to relax his body like Sam did before she shot. Untensing his back, shrugging his shoulders, and steadying his breathing still didn't seem enough to calm his nerves. Nick grew even more concerned when the sounds of wind and rain cut through his protective headphones.

No, no, no… he thought as he recalled hearing those sounds before his "hurricane" blackout at the park.

He was tempted to quit, but then he felt the pistol in his hand. The black handle fit snugly in his palm. The trigger and safety required but the smallest, subtlest movements of his index finger and thumb, respectively. There was an odd, almost comforting familiarity to the weapon. It felt like a natural extension of Nick's body, a limb long neglected but now reawakened.

Focus your feelings, he thought, echoing Sam's words. *Just because you hear the hurricane, doesn't mean you have to give in to it.*

He then loaded the gun, cocked it, and unloaded the entire magazine. He fired the consecutive shots even faster than Sam. Though his first few shots sprayed, Nick made quick adjustments to connect with the closest target. Seconds later, he reloaded and shot the further targets with ease and efficiency. Since Sam already took out one of the moving targets, Nick zeroed in on the other target jetting side-to-side over a hill seventy yards away. He only had two shots left in his magazine. Unfazed by the sounds of the torrential storm raging inside his head, Nick steadied his arms and unloaded.

The first shot ricocheted, but the second connected. Clean headshot.

This time, Sam applauded him.

"Impressive," she said when he returned the weapons and empty magazines.

"Thanks," Nick said. "And thanks for the advice."

"That's what partners are for." A slight smile crossed Sam's face. "Okay. Round two. Count the number of headshots you hit. The loser has to buy brunch. Deal?"

Nick nodded. "Deal."

53

WASHINGTON, D.C., JANUARY 2019

Though Nick managed to hit the furthest targets, Sam was the more consistent shooter. She tallied over thirty headshots to Nick's seventeen. After they returned their weapons and other gear, Nick and Sam grabbed a booth and ordered brunch.

"So," Nick said once they were settled in. "Now that you pulled some triggers, how do you feel?"

"Better. Not 100% by any means. But better." Sam sighed, looking down at the menu as she searched for the right words. "Nick, you remember when I told you I knew how it felt to watch a partner die in front of me?"

Nick nodded. "Both Straw and my dad mentioned GROSS lost a valuable member recently. They said I had big shoes to fill."

"Yeah. His name was Derrick. He was a great man. An even better partner. And not just at GROSS." Sam pulled out her cellphone and handed it to Nick. He examined a photo of a younger Sam holding hands with a clean-cut man with kind eyes. "He was my fiancé."

Nick blinked. "Wow. Sam, I had no idea."

"I asked Straw and your dad to keep it that way. I knew whoever would replace Derrick would come around to asking about him. I asked for their discretion so I could heal on my own terms. Tell my new teammate when the time was right."

"I see." Nick paused as his mind put the pieces together. "So that video Straw was analyzing earlier, the assassination attempt against Mike Spence…"

Sam nodded somberly. "Derrick was the agent who took a bullet for the vice president."

Nick's eyes widened. Everything he knew about Sam — her strictly business demeanor, her reservations about him joining GROSS, and her ferocity behind a gun — suddenly made a lot more sense. He knew she had a chip on her shoulder, but never knew why.

"Sam," he said. "I… I don't even know what to say. I'm so sorry."

"I appreciate it, Nick. But you know better than anyone that apologies can't bring back our partners." Sam's gaze drifted to the bulletin board behind the bar. "You know, Derrick took me here on our first date. We sat in this very booth."

"Oh wow. Well, the Marksman is pretty cool. It's a great safe haven, like you said earlier."

"Yep. It was years ago, but seems just like yesterday." She pointed to the top of the bulletin board. Derrick's name was listed atop one of the Marksman's sharp-shooting contests. "Derrick was a regular here. I've come back every week since he died. Sometimes multiple times a week."

"That's really special, Sam. Derrick sounds like a great guy."

"He was. He truly was." She blinked back some tears and cleared her throat. "At first, I started coming back here because I missed him too much. I'd sit in this booth for hours on end, mentally replaying some of our happiest memories. But some days, that made the pain even worse."

Nick sighed. "I can relate. After Katie died, I tried to avoid going back home. But one day before I left Omaha, I came home and found leftover fettucine in the fridge. Katie made that the night she told me she was pregnant. When I found those leftovers — the last thing she ever made — I just lost it."

Sam nodded in understanding. "Jeez. Sounds like we're partners in both GROSS and grief."

Nick half-chuckled, half-choked back a sob. "Dang. Grief's a bitch, isn't it?"

"Couldn't have said it better myself."

"I appreciate you sharing this, Sam. Since you've dealt with this longer than me, I have to ask. Does grief ever get easier? Will there ever come a day when we won't be triggered by anything that sounds, smells, or remotely reminds us of our loved ones?"

Sam idly ran her hand over her empty ring finger. "That's a great question. Sadly, I'm not sure these feelings will ever go away completely. They're a part of us, just like Derrick was a part of me. Just like Katie was a part of you. Grief can be potent, but it doesn't have to be a weakness. I'm trying to make my grief my number one weapon."

"What do you mean?"

"Think back to the shooting range. When you focused your feelings, your aim improved. Right?"

"Right. I felt the hurricane, but didn't give in. I focused all my energy on the targets."

"Exactly. In my limited experience with grief, I've slowly gotten better by owning it, rather than letting it own me. But I needed some way to channel my grief into something productive. So, one day I came here and went straight to the shooting range. Sure beats sulking in a booth all day."

"Good point. If we can't escape grief, might as well weaponize it."

Sam nodded. "Look, Nick. We're both far from healed. I thought keeping Derrick and his death from you would make it easier to heal, and easier to compartmentalize at work. But maybe we can be more open about our grief journeys. Maybe we can learn from each other."

"Hey, I get why you kept this from me. We didn't exactly have the best first impression."

Sam chuckled and shook her head.

"But I agree," Nick continued. "We can both learn to make the most of this new world without our loved ones. I mean, that's all we really can do, right?"

"Right." She held out her hand for a fist-bump. "Sounds like a plan, partner."

Nick obliged, fist-bumping his partner in GROSS and grief.

54

VERACRUZ, MEXICO, DECEMBER 1, 2018

Professor had arranged for a live broadcast of the Scottsdale Republican fundraiser to be aired on the local news station, which Jefe could access at his estate. The upbeat mood at Jefe's household was soon shattered as the sobering scenes of the failed assassination attempt played out on live TV.

"Thank goodness the vice president wasn't killed!" exclaimed Verana as she watched on the couch next to Jefe, unaware of his plan to the contrary.

"Indeed," Jefe said, feigning a somber expression. Jefe shook his head and locked eyes with Professor, who sat at the opposite couch.

Professor could tell from Jefe's body language that he was infuriated by the botched assassination attempt. Later, when they were alone, Professor broke the ice.

"This was clearly disappointing, Jefe, and I will find out what went wrong in the coming days," Professor said. "But all is not lost. Those images of Silvia jumping to cover the wounded security agent and standing up with her white clothes covered in blood are priceless. If people didn't know Silvia before today, they surely do now. We couldn't buy better advertising to increase her national profile and voter recognition."

"But will that recognition help her become VP?" asked Jefe curtly.

"Not in this election cycle. The benefits probably won't be seen until 2024. That is the downside. After this attempt, the security detail for all candidates will increase exponentially, so our window of opportunity to replace Spence has probably closed."

"At least Silvia didn't get hit by a stray bullet," Jefe sighed. "Please give me your update when you learn what happened. And most importantly, make sure none of this can be traced back to us."

55

WASHINGTON, D.C., JANUARY 2019

Nick had only been home a short time after his outing with Sam when his phone rang.

"Nick, this is Straw. I saw that you and Sam left together after the drama in the office. Is everything OK?"

"Better than OK," Nick said. "We went to 'The Marksman' and shot away a lot of stress. But most of all, we had some excellent conversations."

"Glad to hear it. Whatever you wish to keep, you have to grab it fast. It will be good to have less stress at the office."

"Hey, Straw. One of the things we talked about was that I'm filling the slot of Sam's fiancé."

"Phew," Straw said with a sigh of relief. "I'm glad that finally came up. That was really hard for me not to tell you about Derrick, but I made a promise to Sam. Sounds like you covered a lot of ground in your time together."

"We definitely did. I do have a request… can you show me the video of how Derrick was killed? I'm not trying to be morbid, but since it was in the line of work, I want to see if there's anything I can learn from it."

"Sure thing. Let's do it early tomorrow morning before Sam arrives. As we just learned, it's still something that can set off a lot of emotions."

56

WASHINGTON, D.C., JANUARY 2019

Nick arrived at GROSS early the next day as he and Straw had discussed.

Straw's largest monitor showed a video file that was date-stamped December 1, 2018. Nick watched as the Republican fundraiser in Arizona go from traditional political speeches to utter chaos after Vice President Spence took the stage. Nick also remembered how much this video triggered Samantha.

"Spence was lucky to get out alive," Nick said. "And I remember that some photographer won a prize for his photo of Governor Rodriguez standing up after the shooting, with blood all over her face and white blouse with the dead agent... Derrick... at her feet."

"That is all true, and so sad," Straw said. "But, now let's watch it again with different camera angles. I'll fill you in on some details that aren't readily apparent to the naked eye."

As the video of the attempted assassination played again, Straw supplied key background information.

"GROSS had received some patchy data that I thought indicated an attack was possible. I just wasn't sure about the target. Sometimes false alarm is the only game in town, and other times the obvious is hidden. Nothing was adding up for me. I still don't know who wins if Spence is killed, or even the motive to kill him. Nevertheless, my radar was up, so out of an abundance of caution I talked to Carson. He used his connections to get Derrick and Sam added to the security detail.

"Turns out we needed a lot more. The sniper was atop a nearby hotel roof that was otherwise vacant. A GROSS helicopter spotted the sniper. I immediately notified the Secret Service but, unfortunately, I couldn't notify Derrick in time." Straw sighed. "You know, there are always unknowns in my business. I'm constantly in search for the rest of the story. Unfortunately, I didn't find it fast enough here, and there's a very thin line between success and disaster.

"In any event, the Secret Service got my notification and took some long-distance shots at the sniper. That made him miss Spence. That's why you heard a lot more shots being fired than the number of bullets hitting the stage area. The sniper was killed a short time later by agents as he tried to exit the building. He was ex-Army. Fell on some tough times and became a gun for hire. We don't know who hired him to kill Spence, but we're still digging. The press is painting him as a lone wolf, acting alone."

"But you don't buy it?" Nick asked.

Straw shook his head. "Now, we know what happened on the stage, but look what happened just off the stage. Whenever there's gunfire, people usually panic, flee, or take cover. Two people don't. One is Sam, standing to the left. The other is this tall blonde. I call her 'Blondie.' Like Sam, she's looking where the shots were fired."

Straw zoomed in close on the mysterious blonde and his description did not do her justice. She was tall and slender, with an athletic frame and curves she tastefully did not flaunt. Her long blonde hair flowed naturally past her shoulders. She was dressed simply but stylishly. Her makeup was light, just enough to compliment her natural beauty in an almost unnoticeable way. She had an understated elegance in all aspects of her appearance. She looked like a healthier and prettier version of a fashion magazine cover model.

When Nick finally pulled his eyes away, he asked, "Straw, do you know who she is?"

"I've got my suspicions, but I don't yet know for sure. I tried the biometric facial recognition software the FBI uses at airports and customs checkpoints, but I couldn't ID her. I almost admire how successful Blondie's been in keeping herself anonymous."

"What do you think that means?" Nick asked. "Does she work for the bad guys? Or, does she work for one of our intelligence agencies?"

"I don't know," Straw said, "but I'll keep looking."

57

PHOENIX, ARIZONA, FEBRUARY 2019

Ever since he was on stage with Vice President Spence when the errant assassination attempt occurred, the senior congressman from Arizona had been suffering from panic attacks, nightmares, and other signs of post-traumatic stress disorder. Despite being reelected for his sixth consecutive term a few months earlier with a wide margin of victory, he was feeling older than his sixty years of age. He was already having second thoughts about how long he wanted to remain in politics when he received a call from Xavier Moody, the renowned Democrat election strategist.

"Mr. Moody," started the congressman. "You have really piqued my curiosity. What interest does a well-known Democrat strategist have in a senior Republican congressman?"

"Thank you talking with me, Mr. Congressman. While we historically represent different sides of the aisle, my call to you today has nothing to do with politics," lied Professor. "Instead, I come to you as an intermediary for an anonymous party who admires you and your service greatly. My associate appreciates your tenure in office, but is concerned that the trauma of the Spence assassination attempt has impaired your health. This seems to be proven by the results from your recent visits with your physician."

"How did you get those reports? The relationship I have with my physician is supposed to be totally confidential."

"That is not important," Professor said firmly, not wanting to lose control of the discussion. "What is important is that my source is a great supporter of you and wants me to extend an offer to you. This offer will preserve and memorialize your selfless contributions to Arizona and the country forever, while also providing you a nice retirement in economic comfort, free from the stress of Washington."

"Oh. That is not where I thought this conversation was going," replied the congressman. "Please continue."

"Here's the proposal: due to unforeseen health reasons that will prevent you from adequately representing Arizona, you will retire from congress next week. In exchange, and in honor of your notable history of service, a $5 million grant will be made in your name to your alma mater, the University of Arizona. The donation will re-brand the political science department and place your name on the building."

"That's a very nice honor, but it doesn't help me pay the bills."

"There's more. You will also serve as a professor emeritus, working how little or much as you desire in the realm of academia. For your services, you will be paid $250,000 per year for the remainder of your life. This basically immortalizes your name and legacy, and provides you a comfortable life style and retirement."

"That is both enticing and generous. But while I know you, Mr. Moody, I do not know your associate. How do I know the funding you promise will actually be there?"

"I have an escrow account already funded with $10 million. You can access it now to make the $5 million donation, then withdraw $250,000 annually thereafter. However, this offer requires satisfaction of two conditions: one, that you retire your congressional seat within seven days. And two, the escrow account agreement will have nondisclosure language indicating that we can terminate the agreement, remove your name from the political science building, and claw back any monies if you ever disclose that the proceeds for this opportunity arose from meeting me or because of my anonymous benefactor."

"I will need to discuss this with my wife, Mr. Moody. I will also read the escrow contract. But, I can say with almost one hundred percent assurance that you have a deal."

58

WASHINGTON, D.C., FEBRUARY 2019

Straw was doing his daily data dive when he saw a notification that Arizona governor Silvia Rodriguez had scheduled an impromptu press conference to make "an important announcement."

I wonder what that's about, Straw mused. *Maybe I'll watch… she's been on my radar ever since that photo of her at the Spence melee went viral.*

Straw watched later that day when Governor Silvia Rodriguez arrived for her press conference. Her attire was immaculate, yet understated, as she approached the microphone at the podium of the press room of the governor's mansion.

With bright lights and a multitude of cameras everywhere, Silvia began, "Ladies and gentlemen and all Arizonans, thank you for joining me today. As you know, a week ago our senior congressman announced his surprise retirement from the U.S. House of Representatives due to health concerns. I would first like to thank the congressman for his lengthy and invaluable service to Arizona and the country, and to wish him a fast and full recovery. His shocking announcement creates a big void that needs to be filled. I am here today, in my role as governor and using the authority granted to me under the Arizona constitution, to announce that I am appointing myself as the interim congressperson for the remainder of his term."

Silvia's announcement piqued Straw's interest. Silvia continued, "I know this is a shock to many, if not all, of you. But it all makes perfect sense to me. Many of my advisors have told me that being governor of this state is a much more important and prestigious position than being just one of four hundred thirty-five members of the House of Representatives. But, under the circumstances, I think it is just the opposite.

"I have had the distinct pleasure of serving as governor to the great citizens of Arizona since 2012. We have accomplished many great things together. Today, I feel that Arizona is the most economically stable, secure, and prosperous state in America. Unfortunately, I feel just the opposite about Washington, D.C. The political bottleneck that prevents progress for our great country is both concerning and appalling. Someone needs to step forward and break the stagnation that permeates our Capitol. I would like to take the track record of success that we have in Arizona and move it to Washington. I want to be a change agent for the good of our country. And now, I strive to make that happen as part of the U.S. Congress. I will always be loyal to Arizona, but I now feel that it is time to give my heart and soul to the entire United States. Please wish me well in my efforts. Thank you."

Very interesting, thought Straw. He closed his eyes and tried to connect possibilities, no matter how remote or unlikely. *Hmm. Silvia... Salvador. Are you connected?*

59

WASHINGTON, D.C., MARCH 2019

Nick liked jogging in the early morning when the cool air would cleanse both his lungs and his brain. It gave him a sense of calm comfort to run alone through the neighborhood before the sounds of the city would drown out the silence.

It was still dark when Nick started his run. Upon passing the Hawkins' house, Nick spotted the burning orange end of a cigarette being smoked by a man in a parked car across the street. The car was running but had no lights on. Nick's suspicion was aroused, so he decided to circle around the block to take a closer look. At the end of his loop, Nick noticed a side window in the Hawkins' house was broken.

Nick peered through the window to find Blair Hawkins lying motionless on the floor in his blue scrubs, a trickle of blood coming from his head. Two teenage-looking boys wearing black hoodies and brandishing street guns were taping the mouths, hands, and feet of Miriam, Alana, and Grant. They were all attired in Duke basketball pajamas and looking very scared.

Nick felt his pulse speed up and his fingers subconsciously clench and unclench. Acting fast, Nick left the window and approached the parked car from behind. He opened the front door to surprise the driver, knocking him unconscious with two fast punches to the head. Nick frisked the driver and took his only weapon, a small .38 pistol. Nick then turned the car off, took the keys out of the ignition, and ran back to the Hawkins house. He entered quietly through the broken window and stepped into the doorway to intentionally alert the two thieves of his presence.

"Everyone stay calm!" he said. "I'm not a cop and I haven't called 911. But I knocked out your driver and have his gun. We need to think through your next move so no one else gets hurt."

Both youngsters aimed their guns at Nick, but neither pulled a trigger. Nick hugged the side of the doorway to give them as little of a target as possible in the event they changed their minds. Nick was surprised at how young the boys were. The oldest looked old enough to have facial hair, but young enough to still enjoy shaving it.

Nick continued to assess the situation. Nick could easily kill both boys with clean shots to the head or heart, but this risked one of the boys getting off a stray shot that might hit one of the Hawkins' family. Instead, Nick looked directly at the oldest teenager and calmly asked, "Do you want to know how to get out of this situation without going to prison or a grave?" Nick wanted the boy to think instead of just act. Triggers are not often pulled by thinking people.

"Here's what is going to happen," Nick said authoritatively. "You two are going to walk out of this house, shut the door, and not look back. I'm going to give you thirty seconds before I call an ambulance. This plan lets you get out of here alive and without going to prison. You'd better take it."

"What if we don't want to leave without some loot?" asked the oldest hood, raising his gun slightly.

"That would not be smart. I can put a bullet between both of your eyes anytime I want," Nick said convincingly. "Time's running. You've got ten seconds to get out of here. GO!"

Both boys looked at each other and made a dash out the door. Nick locked the door after them, quickly assessed Blair's condition, and called 911. Though unconscious, Blair had a pulse and was breathing.

The rest of the Hawkins family was hugging each other in a circle around their fallen father when Alana spoke up, "Those guys are going to get away!"

"They won't get far," said Nick, holding up the car keys he had taken from the driver he knocked out. However, Nick's plan backfired when the two boys realized they didn't have any wheels to make a getaway. Instead of running away as Nick expected, they turned and headed back to the Hawkins' house.

"Get on the floor," Nick ordered as he ran to the front door. He turned off all the inside lights before stepping outside.

"Don't come any closer," Nick yelled at the two boys. They both shot at Nick, but the bullets ricocheted off the house brick. Crouching, Nick aimed at their knees and pulled off two clean shots. Both boys crumbled to the ground, shrieking in pain.

The sounds of sirens approaching in the distance gave Nick the chance to check on the two boys and pick up their dropped weapons. One of his bullets had severed an artery, so Nick took the belt off the boy and made a tourniquet to contain the bleeding until the ambulance arrived.

Nick returned to the Hawkins' house, where everyone was still laying on the floor.

"You can get up now. Everything is okay," Nick said. "An ambulance and the police will be here soon."

Nick then excused himself, stepped outside, and made a call.

"Dad! Sorry to call you so early in the morning, but I'm in the middle of a situation and need your help."

"What can I do to help?" asked Carson Class.

Nick described what had happened and asked his dad to use his connections to intervene with the police to minimize attention and preserve Nick's anonymity.

"I understand," said Carson. "I'll have the Chief of Police come personally to your location. He'll make sure the officers on the scene stand down with respect to your role in what happened, including in the official report that is filed. I'll tell them we can't afford to have your identity compromised for reasons that can't be disclosed."

"Thanks, Dad. Always appreciate your help."

Nick returned to the room as an ambulance and police car arrived outside the house, lights flashing. Blair Hawkins was sitting up, groggy but conscious. Miriam saw Nick and immediately wrapped him in a tight hug.

"Thank you so much for helping us. I don't even want to think of what might have happened if you didn't show up."

"I'm just glad I was jogging past your house when they broke in," Nick said.

Miriam returned to her husband and children. Nick stood, alone with his thoughts. Feelings of relief and pride swept through his mind. He had both applied and controlled the hurricane forces within him.

60

VERACRUZ, MEXICO, SEPTEMBER 2020

Jefe welcomed Professor once again to their poolside office. When drinks were in hand, Jefe sat back in his lounge chair.

"Professor, even though we don't have a horse in this race, I'm very interested in your thoughts about the upcoming presidential election. You predicted Triumph's surprise win four years ago. I'd like your insights on this one."

"Jefe, you know I never mind giving predictions on election outcomes!" Professor took a drink of his piña colada and continued. "I'll start with my conclusion: based on the latest polls, Burden will be the next POTUS."

"But how can you trust polls? Most polls predicted that Hilary Clanton would beat Triumph in the last election."

"I've analyzed the 2016 polling data closely and have concluded that it wasn't that far off. Heading into the election, Clanton had 3.2% polling advantage, and she ended up winning the popular vote by 2.1%. So, the polls were pretty accurate. We just ended up having one of those rare, inverted elections where a candidate like Clanton wins the popular vote but loses the election based on the electoral college."

"I forgot about that," said Jefe. "How rare is that?"

"Pretty rare. Before Triumph's win, there had only been three prior inverted elections. Two of those were in the 1800's and the other was when Plante, Jr. beat 'Environmental' Al Glore in 2000."

"So, what do you see from the polls now?"

"Taking a lesson from 2016, Burden needs to win the popular vote by 3-4% to make sure Triumph can't repeat what he did in the last election. Right now, Triumph is behind 8% in the polls. He's also behind in key battleground states. Michigan, Pennsylvania, and Wisconsin are all states that Triumph won in 2016, but look strong for Burden. Burden also looks safe in all the states that Clanton won. Triumph is also spending a lot of money and time just to hang onto traditional Republican stronghold states like Texas, Ohio, and Georgia. Based on all of that, I don't think Triumph can win this election."

"What happened to all the advantages incumbents have in elections? Shouldn't that help Triumph?"

"Sure. But again, everything about Triumph is unique and adds an element of unpredictability to elections. Historically, in an incumbent presidential election, the incumbent will win if he has an approval rating of at least 48%. Well, Triumph is a 'love or loathe' president to an unprecedented degree. His approval range is only 35-45%. These ratings don't improve much for Triumph even when things are going great with economy and unemployment. Conversely, when a scandal occurs, those ratings don't really drop much either."

"So, where does that leave Triumph?"

"Things could always change. In the last election, a lot of voters made up their minds the day or two before voting, and the overwhelming majority went to Triumph. However, I'm skeptical that will happen here. People generally view Triumph's strength as being his management of the economy. But right now, the economy is soft and COVID is the biggest issue in most peoples' minds. Triumph's approval rating on COVID is not good. My prediction is that, in two months, Burden will win modestly, and possibly win big."

"We shall soon see," said Jefe. "I look forward to seeing how accurate your predictions are. Then, we can fine-tune our plan to get a candidate in play for 2024."

61

VERACRUZ, MEXICO, THANKSGIVING 2020

"Professor," Jefe began at their Thanksgiving celebration. "You have once again proven your crystal ball is very clear. It is very impressive how accurate you were in predicting Burden's victory over Triumph. Congratulations!"

"Thank you, Jefe. But even a broken clock is correct twice a day."

"It's not bragging if it's true," Jefe replied. "But predicting the last election isn't our goal. Our victory only occurs when we have one of our candidates seated in the Oval Office. Let's talk about what it will take to make that happen in the '24 election."

"OK. Republicans have lost three of the last four presidential elections. But they have never done a thorough autopsy of why, what went wrong, and how they need to change to be a more inclusive and attractive party. Their only win in this period was Triumph in 2016, and he promptly lost to Burden a few weeks ago. Whether Republicans can repair their divisive and fractured cliques within the party remains to be seen. In my mind, the best way to get back on track is to unify behind a candidate who is nothing like Triumph."

"Very interesting," mused Jefe. "Please continue."

"At a very basic level, the trouble with American politics is the polarity. Republicans campaign on being anti-Democrat, and the Democrats run on being anti-GOP. I sense the public is fed up with this negativity.

Voters want plain-talking, budget-hawking candidates who will run a positive campaign.

"History has shown that, except for Triumph in 2016, the Republican party is most successful when it supports a viable center-right candidate. Raygun, in particular, knew how to win and how to govern by appealing not just to narrow sectors within his party, but to the nation as a whole.

"However, right now, the Republican party is clearly at a crossroads. Triumph, Tea Party activists, and the far right have only led to the elevation of extreme candidates and positions that have damaged the party's brand nationwide. The Republican party can either continue to splinter into its various factions and die. Or, it can unify behind an attractive candidate and present an alternative to the economic malaise often caused by the spend-easy Democrats."

"Sounds to me like the Republican party is in big trouble!" exclaimed Jefe.

"That's not wrong, but I also wouldn't say that a stake has been driven through the heart of the Republican party just yet. Republicans can't win unless they secure most of the white vote, a significant chunk of the Hispanic vote, and prevail in most of the battleground states."

"Professor, that sounds like a pretty high hurdle. Is it likely to occur, and where does Silvia fit into the equation?"

"I think it's possible, but Republicans will really have to work hard. Republicans will need a strong, inclusive president and vice president team that can gather the majority of the white vote by promoting fiscally conservative positions on the economy. To garner a big chunk of the ethnic vote, that team will need to show enlightened, sympathetic positions on topics such as immigration policy. With respect to Hispanic voters in particular, Republicans under President Triumph literally drove this fastest-growing group of new voters into the arms of the Democrats. Republicans will need to change this."

"How would they do that?"

"Having Silvia on the ticket would be a great start. Spending lots of money on Spanish-language television and radio will also help court Latino voters."

"So, what is your strategy, Professor?"

"We continue to do everything possible to elevate Silvia's profile and visibility. The best way to do this if for her to announce her bid to be president. This gives us two opportunities. One, even if she doesn't win, a positive performance will enhance her status as a potential VP candidate to Triumph or anyone who gets the Republican nomination. Second, she might actually win the nomination and have a good shot at being the first woman president of the U.S.!"

"And the first Latina in the White House!" said Jefe.

"Stranger things have happened."

"But do you really think that's possible?" asked Jefe.

"While it's a long shot, you never say never in electoral politics, especially when the election is four years away. I also don't want to underestimate Silvia. In her last gubernatorial election, not only did she sew up an unheard-of sixty percent of the vote, but she also scored decisive victories among the demographics we are keenest to claim, namely Hispanics, women, and independents. She has great skill at converting voters otherwise hostile to the Republican party."

"I'll drink to that!" Jefe said. "You've given me a lot to digest. Let's head inside for some air conditioning and to refresh our drinks. We can continue this discussion after dinner."

62

WASHINGTON, D.C., JULY 2020

Nick entered the GROSS office and could immediately sense that something was happening.

Straw was sitting upright in his chair, his eyes glued to the screens in front of him.

"The Department of Homeland Security is about to issue a 'heightened threat' of domestic terrorism warning to the public," said Straw as Nick sat down at his desk.

"What does that mean?" asked Nick.

"As you know, they and the DOD have teams of analysts to survey the threat landscape. Lately, there's been an increase in chatter by domestic extremist groups. Mainly white supremacists. Targets have generally been churches, malls, or electric substations."

"Are we going to get involved?"

"Probably not if it's one of those targets I just mentioned. Most of those threats are from lone offenders or small groups. Considering our small size here at GROSS, I tend to focus on mass-casualty events or threats to our democracy. That's what I'm trying to determine now."

From his desk, Nick marveled at how Straw worked. Even with the benefit of his preliminary information filters, he still sifted through enormous columns of data. Straw was always obsessing in his search for a missed clue, a pattern, or an anomaly that would put into focus the myriad of facts at his disposal. He had to determine if his bits of evidence amounted to a legitimate threat.

For the next ninety minutes, Straw focused intently on his screens. Sam did the same, only interrupting Straw a few times to show him some information she thought might be relevant. Finally, Straw stopped clicking the keys of his keyboard and sat back in his chair with a satisfied grunt.

"I think I've got it." Straw pulled out a burner phone and dialed a number. "Jason, this is Dark Star. I think I know DHS's heightened threat. You need to get to Knoxville, Tennessee. I think a spin-off faction of the white supremacist Proud Patriots gang is expanding into anti-Semitism. And, I think they are planning an attack in the next few days on the Heska Amuna synagogue."

The person on the other end of the line made some comments that Nick couldn't decipher.

Straw then said, "I'll send you my supporting data. Let me know if there's anything else I can do to help."

Straw hung up and turned to Nick and Sam, who sat in the chairs opposite of Straw's desk.

"There's a lot I want to unpack here," said Nick, "but let's start with who you just called. And, who is Dark Star?"

"This threat involves domestic security and intelligence," Straw said. "So, I called up a contact at the FBI. I've selected a few officers that I trust inside our alphabet agencies. Sometimes, I share with them my analyses on an anonymous basis. Jason, in particular, is a really good intelligence officer at the FBI, even though I've never met him in person. Over the years I've given him tips like today. It's made him look like a rising star at the FBI when his intelligence stops terrorist plans before they happen."

"OK," said Nick. "This sounds like the type of coordination that would make my dad happy. It's exactly why he and President Plante formed GROSS in the first place."

Nick continued, "So... Dark Star? Let me guess... a Grateful Dead song?"

Straw grinned. "I was going to go with 'Deepest Throat' in homage to the Watergate informant. But Dark Star is one of my favorite cosmic

Grateful Dead songs, so I thought that was more in tune with my personality."

"Makes sense," said Sam. "Now, can you explain why you think the Proud Patriots are going to attack a synagogue?"

"Analyzing hate groups is hard for me, since my soul and mind always look to find love and light in the darkness. Hate groups are full of cloudy dreams unreal and lights no eye can see. In fact, the darkness never seems to go from a hateful person's eyes. That's why they are so challenging for me to figure out and make sure their deals don't go down."

"So, Straw, what clued you in on the synagogue attack in Knoxville?" Sam asked again.

"Secrets make the best stories and that's why they are so hard to keep. Hate groups are no different than anyone in this regard... they have secrets they struggle to keep. That's what led me to the Proud Patriots' plan today."

"Can you give us any details?" asked Nick.

"Everything is made of patterns," Straw began. "I analyzed the frequency of Proud Patriot communications over the past weeks. Compared to other known domestic terrorist organizations, there were enough coincidences involving Proud Patriot members to not be a coincidence."

Straw reflected for a moment, then continued. "Emails, texts, and cell phone calls always leave behind a trail of digital breadcrumbs. Even cell phones that are wiped clean can still reveal plenty of information if you know how to look for it. If someone uses a burner phone or tries to use encrypted messages, the cell phone will always ping the closest cell tower. If you map the phone's pings, then you can readily determine where the phone has been or where it is heading.

"Based on cell phone data alone, it was clear that the Proud Patriots spent a lot of time last month near Knoxville's Heska Amuna synagogue. The recurring cell pings of white supremacists in the vicinity of the synagogue created the theory that something was going to happen there. But, I needed more information to elevate my theory into something more reliable. Here's where I got lucky. One of the Proud Patriots casing the synagogue was recently arrested for destruction of property of a prominent Jewish store owner who worshiped at the synagogue. He sent a text, which we intercepted, to one of the other Proud Patriots saying that he will get his retribution against the Jewish store owner 'in his holiest of houses' this week."

Sam clapped. "Strong work, Straw."

Straw's cell phone buzzed and he answered it. He listened intently to the person on the other end of the line for about thirty seconds. He then said, "Yes, Jason. We will be there."

Straw patted Nick and Sam on the back. "Go pack your bags. We're leaving for Knoxville ASAP."

63

KNOXVILLE, TENNESSEE, JULY 2020

The GROSS team boarded a private jet early that afternoon to Knoxville. During the flight, Straw gave his team the update about their mission.

"In its infinite wisdom," Straw began, "the FBI and its internal counsel determined that the evidence supporting my theory about the attack may have been derived from an illegal wiretap. Accordingly, the FBI won't preemptively arrest any Proud Patriots because the FBI doesn't think it has enough admissible evidence to get criminal convictions. Instead, the FBI and local police will have to wait and try to capture the culprits 'in the act.'"

"What does that mean?" asked Nick.

"Basically, law enforcement is staying on the sideline until *after* the Proud Patriots have put their plan in motion but *before* any killings occur."

"That's the dumbest threading of a legal needle I've ever heard," said Sam.

"I agree," said Straw. "And it really pisses me off. They are putting people in danger because of a legal technicality."

"So, what do we do?" asked Nick.

"Like usual, we're here in a very unofficial capacity. Jason, my contact at the FBI, wants me to keep digging. If I can find some additional evidence about the plot, he might be able to convince the FBI and law enforcement to intervene before things get nasty. He also wants me to actively monitor events near the synagogue. The quicker I can provide intelligence updates, the faster the security response will be. Minutes, if not seconds, can make a difference between a mass shooting and a foiled act of terrorism."

"How can Sam and I help?"

"Law enforcement has been notified that undercover agents will be on site. That's where you two come in. Most likely any attack will occur during a worship service to maximize fatalities and shock value. There is Shabbat evening service tonight, so I think that is when the Proud Patriots will attack. We'll land in plenty of time for you to case the perimeter and interior of the synagogue before the service starts. Pick your positions inside the sanctuary as strategically as possible once people start arriving. Hopefully, agents outside the synagogue will stop any threats before they get into the building. If not, you will be part of the protection inside."

64

KNOXVILLE, TENNESSEE, JULY 2020

The GROSS team landed at Knoxville Downtown Island Airport about two hours before the Shabbat service was to start. Upon exiting the plane, they were greeted by a fit and muscled man with a military-style crew cut wearing khakis and a button-up shirt.

"I am Sergeant Ray Vaughan of the Knoxville police department. Confirming that you are Nick, Samantha, and Straw?" he asked reading the names from a piece of paper in his hand.

"Yes, we are," said Sam.

"Welcome to Knoxville. At the request of Senator Class, the Knoxville PD has asked me to drive you in an unmarked police car to the Heska Amuna synagogue." He pointed to a black Cadillac parked nearby. "Let's go. Time is of the essence."

After a short fifteen-minute drive, Sergeant Vaughan parked the car on the outskirts of the synagogue parking lot.

"Before anyone exits the car," he said, "make sure you are all wearing protective gear."

"Yes," replied Sam. "We all put on Kevlar vests during the flight."

"Good. I only have two other orders. First, I am to stay in this car with the person named Straw and provide him anything he needs."

"That's me," said Straw, who had almost finished setting up his laptop and other electronic devices in the backseat of the car.

"Second, I am to give this to Nick. That must be you." The Sergeant handed a Kippah brimless cap to Nick. "This will help you blend in with the other worshipers."

"Thanks," said Nick as he and Sam exited the car. "Good luck, Straw. Keep us updated."

"Will do. Stay safe."

Sam and Nick did a quick walk around the synagogue and the block on which it was located. Each had holstered two Glock pistols under the light jackets they wore over their Kevlar vests. Since cell phones were not allowed to be used in the synagogue, Straw had given them state-of-the-art mini earpieces that served to both transmit and receive conversations among the GROSS trio.

Nick put on the Kippah as they surveilled the site. The synagogue itself was an old, quad-shaped building of terracotta orange brick. The whole facility appeared drab. Its only architectural distinction was five white columns of stained glass that wrapped the front corner of the building in the shape of a semi-circle and extended ten feet above the roofline. The main sanctuary was parallel to the street, with the rest of the quad being used for offices, a library, and meeting rooms.

"Straw," Sam said, "can you confirm the people trimming trees at the rear of the parking lot, the guys in the cable TV van across the street, and the two young couples that keep walking on the sidewalk are all law enforcement in disguise?"

"Sergeant Vaughan and I believe so," Straw said through their earpieces.

"I can't believe anyone would pick this site for an attack," said Sam. "The synagogue is right off Kingston Pike, a two-way street that runs in front of the building. The only way in and out of the synagogue are the two small entry drives that circle around to the parking in the back. Although the neighboring residential area has lots of trees, the landscaping around the synagogue is very sparse, giving no opportunity to hide. Directly across the street is a large residential house with a steel fence extending the full length of the large lot. No opportunities there either."

"I agree," said Straw. "This is very perplexing. But you guys better go inside and check it out. Some people have already arrived."

65

KNOXVILLE, TENNESSEE, JULY 2020

Sam and Nick entered Heska Amuna trying their best to look like they belonged. Before entering the main worship area, they walked through other portions of the facility. At first glance, nothing appeared out of the ordinary. Sam was grateful to see another person of color reading in the internal courtyard area.

"I didn't expect to see that," whispered Samantha. "You can pull it off with your Kippah, but I didn't think there was any chance I could blend into the surroundings here."

Entering the main sanctuary, Sam and Nick split off and went to different ends of the worship area. The sanctuary had two long columns of pews separated by an aisle. Sam sat in the back pew on the left and Nick sat in the back pew on the right, giving each optimal vision into the place of worship. Rays of late afternoon sunlight shined through the stained glass into a quarter of the sanctuary, adding to the holiness of the space.

Several people were already seated in pews throughout the room when Nick and Sam arrived.

I wonder how many of these people are cops instead of worshipers, thought Nick.

People started to file in rapidly as the scheduled worship time approached. Young adults, frail elderly, and parents with children all sat in pews throughout the synagogue. Nick profiled the people as they arrived, but he thought the only ones who stood out were likely with law enforcement.

"Look for someone seated on the outside of the pew," Samantha said quietly. "That gives them the best exit opportunity."

Sunset arrived and the service began. Nick looked over at Sam. They shared a smile, watching each other try to fake knowing the communal prayers the worshippers recited.

Everything about the worship service seemed ordinary until a loud explosion shook the building. Seconds later, another explosion resonated from the back of the synagogue.

"What's happening, Straw?" Sam yelled over the anxious crowd.

"It looks like car bombs exploded about two blocks from each side of the synagogue," Straw said excitedly.

The car bombs effectively shut down Kingston Pike, preventing access to the synagogue from the main thoroughfare. Just then, a van screeched up to the front of Heska Amuna from the residential street perpendicular to Kingston Pike. Five hooded men jumped out of the van, each brandishing an assault rifle. They started running to the front of the synagogue when gunfire came at them from multiple angles.

A man and woman walking on the sidewalk had pulled handguns and were shooting rapidly, dropping one of the gunmen to the ground. Machine gun fire from a cable TV truck dropped two more before they could reach the door. The remaining gunmen returned fire, shattering windows on the TV truck and hitting the man on the sidewalk in the shoulder. Before the gunmen could fire any more, they were shot dead, one by an agent posing as a greeter at the front door of the synagogue and the other by Sergeant Ray Vaughan as he stood by the side of a black Cadillac on the entry drive to the synagogue.

Seeing what happened, the driver of the van screeched his tires in an attempt to escape. Before the van moved far, the woman agent on the sidewalk shot out its windshield and both passenger tires. Seeing that escape was futile, the driver slammed on the brakes. He jumped out of the van and laid prone on the street, surrendering.

66

KNOXVILLE, TENNESSEE, JULY 2020

Inside the synagogue, everything had stopped when the blasts from the car bombs shook the building. The relief that people initially felt when seeing no structural damage to the synagogue was quickly replaced by chaos once the sound of gunshots erupted.

"What's going on Straw?" yelled Nick.

"They are trying to get into the front entry," Straw said. "Lots of gunfire."

Nick and Sam were both standing, watching the chaos unfold. Some people were lying under the pews for shelter while others rushed to the back or front of the synagogue in search of a safe exit. The continuing sound of gunfire from outside the building further terrified the crowd.

Chaos all around him, Nick noticed a young man at the end of one of the front pews stand up and reach inside his light outer jacket. He pulled out a handgun and aimed at a young mother as she was leading her two children out of a pew. Before he could get off a shot, Nick pulled his own gun and shot him between the eyes.

His gun still drawn, Nick approached the young family to make sure they were unharmed.

"No!" Sam screamed loudly as Nick walked toward the family. He turned to look at Sam, just in time to see her shoot at a target behind Nick. Turning totally around, Nick saw Sam's shot knock the gun out of the hand of a man who was seconds away from shooting Nick point blank.

"Drop your gun and raise your arms, Nick," commanded Sam. "They think you're a terrorist."

Nick did as he was told. Sam ran toward him, yelling, "He's an undercover cop. He's an undercover cop."

67

KNOXVILLE, TENNESSEE, JULY 2020

Straw, Sam, and Nick were ready to be taken by Sergeant Vaughan to the Knoxville airport after getting clearance to leave the crime scene. As they were about to step into the Cadillac, the officer who had almost killed Nick by mistake approached the car.

"Hey man, I'm about to head to the hospital to get this treated," he said, holding up his bandaged hand that had been wounded by Sam's shot. "But first, I wanted to apologize for my mistake. I was screened from seeing who you shot, and it looked to me like you were just shooting into a family. But I know better than to jump to conclusions, especially when I knew other undercover cops were on site. My bad."

"Thanks, but I know how easy it is to make mistakes when everything around you is going crazy. We're good," said Nick, giving him a left-handed fist bump.

"That was nice," said Sam once they were in the car.

"What's even nicer was the shot you made to knock the gun out of his hand. Thanks!"

"I guess our time at the Marksman paid off," Sam laughed.

Just then, a breaking news story flashed on Straw's laptop. The GROSS trio watched as the network showed video of the FBI arresting numerous Proud Patriots in Knoxville, Tennessee after a thwarted attack on a Jewish synagogue. While watching the broadcast, Straw's phone buzzed as he received a text that simply said, "Thanks… again! Jason."

"Thanks everyone," Straw said. "Congrats on a day of success and working together. May we have many more to come."

68

VERACRUZ, MEXICO, JANUARY 7, 2021

"So much for the United States' famed peaceful transition of power!" exclaimed Jefe to start his unplanned call to Professor. "What happened at the Capitol yesterday, and how does it affect our plans?"

"Yesterday was a very sad day," Professor said, "and I think history will show it is one of the worst days ever in our country. Let's be honest. Yesterday was nothing less than a Triumph-instigated insurrection against the Capitol to overturn Burden winning the election. Triumph's actions, and especially his inactions, were pathetic, if not criminal. This is something you might expect to see in a third world country, but not the United States of America! Yesterday truly sickened me."

"I don't disagree," said Jefe. "But what do you think this means to us? Oftentimes, there is opportunity in times of chaos."

"Yes, we should look for those opportunities, but right now it's too early to gauge the fallout of yesterday's events. I would be shocked if there isn't a Congressional investigation into everything that happened. Not to mention lawsuits by the victims."

"So, any changes to our plans going forward?"

"Not at this moment, but we will clearly adapt as things play out. We're still four years away from the next presidential election. Yesterday's events, as monumental as they were, will quite possibly be nothing more than a distant memory to voters when they enter the voting booths. We'll see how yesterday's events affect the midterm elections in a couple of years. We can then react and change our campaign strategies as needed."

"Hold on!" Jefe exclaimed. "Do you think Triumph is still a viable candidate? How can that be after what happened yesterday?"

"As crazy as it sounds, I think there's still a very good chance that Triumph will be the Republican frontrunner. Remember, he's often called 'Teflon Triumph' because none of his crazy actions, legal problems, or tweets stick to him. He also has a very large base of loyal supporters who will never leave him."

"Does yesterday have any direct effect on Silvia?"

"Yes, I think the events will work to Silvia's advantage. We just need to play our cards right. The VP position on the Republican side is wide open now. Triumph almost got Spence killed yesterday, so you can rest assured that Spence will never team up with Triumph again."

"Does this make Burden the prohibitive favorite to get re-elected 2024 as the incumbent?" Jefe asked.

"Too early to tell, but yesterday sure doesn't hurt Burden's chances."

"Professor, I do not dislike President Burden. However, I also don't think he should be a candidate in 2024. Serving as a president in his 80's is not right, and he is already frail in both mind and body. There's a good reason for mandatory retirement age policies. That's why there are virtually no CEOs of major companies in their 80's."

"You make very valid points, Jefe. I'm sure age will be an important factor in the next race. But we should not underestimate Burden. He's a winner. Lots of people viewed him as a lightweight in the Senate, but he got the party nomination in 2020 and won. While there will be lots of concerns about his age, the fact is that he was old when he just beat Triumph and was elected. He's not yesterday's news. The other key fact is that if Triumph got elected, he'd be the second oldest president in office ever."

"I hadn't realized on that," Jefe admitted.

"You know, it's unfortunate for the country, but candidate quality issues abound for both parties at all levels. The new administration hasn't yet taken over, but I think it's clear that it will have an uphill battle in the coming years. With Democrats controlling the White House and Senate in 2020, it's going to be virtually impossible for House Republicans to get any of their legislative initiatives enacted. Therefore, the main goals of House Republicans will be to stall Democrat proposals and try to make Burden a one-term president."

"When it comes to politics, I think I am happy that I live in Mexico." Jefe sighed. "Let's talk again soon my friend. Adios."

69

MARCH 1, 2022

Professor answered his burner phone on the first ring, having expected a call from Jefe for the past week.

"Professor," began Jefe without any introductory small talk. "It's been a week since Russia invaded Ukraine. What impact does this have on our plans?"

"Good morning, Jefe. I have been expecting a call from you! Yes, we are watching history unfold before our eyes. I think Putrid is surprised the invasion hasn't already been successful. It's clear that he totally miscalculated the fervor and preparedness of the Ukrainians. Unless this war ends much sooner than I anticipate, how the U.S. supports Ukraine will be at the top of foreign affairs issues in the '24 election."

"Do you think the Ukrainian battle will be done by the election?" asked Jefe.

"I'm a political strategist, not a war expert, my friend. It would be malpractice to offer anything but an uninformed opinion on that question. However, I am willing to offer my thoughts on the political implications of Putrid's invasion."

"Please, let me hear them."

"First, I was shocked and appalled that in a recent interview, Triumph called Putrid's invasion 'brilliant.' Let me rephrase. I am no longer shocked by anything Triumph does anymore, but I do find his comment appalling. How can the former leader of the free world compliment Putrid for an unprovoked incursion into a sovereign foreign country?

His comments dangerously undermine U.S. foreign policy. This is even more incredible than when Triumph praised neo-Nazi demonstrators in Charlottesville in 2017."

"I don't disagree with your outrage, Professor. But what does it mean for our current plan?"

"Foreign policy will clearly be one of Triumph's weak spots in the next election. Silvia needs to capitalize on this weakness by showing she is strong on supporting our military, our national defense, and our NATO allies throughout the world. If I were a Democrat or even a Republican candidate in '24, I would run TV ads showing both the 'Putrid's invasion is brilliant' and the Charlottesville comments of Triumph to remind voters of his behavior that is unimaginable for a national leader. Add on his actions during the January 6 insurrection, and you have a trifecta of proof that Triumph is not qualified to be president of his local homeowner's association, much less president of the United States of America."

"Thanks," said Jefe. "Glad to hear that you are all over the electoral implications of the Ukraine war."

70

NOVEMBER 9, 2022

Jefe called Professor on burner phones to get his reactions to the midterm elections the previous day.

"Hola, Professor! How are you doing?"

"Well, I'm a bit tired," Professor admitted. "A lot of midterm results are still not known, and keeping tabs on tons of races is frankly exhausting."

"Would it be better to wait until a later day to talk?"

"No. I'm ready to chat."

"Great, let me hear your thoughts."

"Let me start by giving some historical perspective: past elections show that it is almost a foregone conclusion that at the half-way mark between presidential elections, voters routinely give the incumbent party a beating. Accordingly, it was highly expected that the Democrats would get thrashed in these midterms and that they might end up without control of either the House or Senate. As it turns out, the Democrats will retain control of the Senate by a slim margin. And, on the House side, it looks like the Republicans will get control, but not by the landslide margin that many expected."

"So, what does this mean to us?"

"On the Republican side, they took back a majority of the House mainly because of their successful gerrymandering of election districts. I don't view any Republican midterm wins as a testament to the health of the party or the strength of former President Triumph. This may create some opportunities for Silvia who, as you know, won in a landslide vote to continue as an Arizona congresswoman. She also provided a lot of your financial support to Republican candidates who won in tight races. The donations that Silvia raised for them may have been the difference between winning and losing. That should bring Silvia a lot of loyalty in the future if she ever needs to call in a chip."

"So, where does this lead us?"

"It's still too early to tell, but some important voter tendency insights can be gleaned from the exit polls. These polls clearly show the importance of having a candidate who is not too extreme. Some experts say this is evidence of 'Triumph fatigue' and that Triumph's presence as a divisive candidate may be the Democrat's best weapon to stay in power. I think it's fair to question whether Triumph will have a positive influence on his party, or whether he will be a drag on the ticket. Look, the facts are that while Triumph was on the ballot or in office, the Republicans lost the House, Senate, and White House. Under normal circumstances, those underwhelming results and his other divisive qualities would make him the past of the Republican party.

"However, let me say that I disagree with that analysis. First, with Triumph or his supporters, there is nothing 'normal.' Second, it's only 2022 and any Triumph hangover in the aftermath of the dismal midterms may long be forgotten when the race heats up for the White House in 2024."

"Those are good insights, Professor. But I'm getting a little lost in the weeds here. What is your ultimate takeaway from the midterms?" asked Jefe, sounding a bit exasperated.

"I think my takeaway is don't read too much into the midterm results. I don't think they foreshadow the death knell to Triumph or that Burden is on the right track."

"So, do the midterms affect our strategy?" Jefe asked.

"I still think our best strategy is for Silvia to announce her candidacy for the presidency in early January. If I'm wrong, and Triumph really is the past of the Republican party, then Silvia could be viewed as the future of the party. As Olama and Bill Clanton showed, sometimes a new and refreshing face and approach is just what voters want. Silvia also seems very electable in a race against Burden. On the flip side, if Triumph retains his powerful base of support, Silvia seems well-positioned to be selected as his running mate."

"What's our next step?"

"As a newcomer to the national stage, and as a woman, Silvia needs to be more prepared and professional than the other candidates to win votes. Jefe, it's time for us both to engage in some intense training with Silvia. I know she was planning on going to Mexico City to see her parents over Thanksgiving. I think we need to sneak her to Veracruz for at least two days of hard-core training at your house. Can you do this and keep your involvement invisible?"

"If you think it is critical, I will make it happen," Jefe said.

71

VERACRUZ, MEXICO, THANKSGIVING 2022

It was great that Silvia Rodriguez, a rising star in the Republican party, was so likeable and recognizable. Voter recognition and acceptance was always important in the world of electoral politics. However, being a public figure also came at the expense of personal privacy, and the hotter the star became the less privacy was available. Jefe knew very well that ushering the famous Silvia Rodriguez away in the middle of her Thanksgiving vacation would be a challenge. As expected, there was a constant media and paparazzi presence surrounding Silvia from the time she landed in Mexico City and continuing at her parents' house.

Often the best plans are the simplest plans. After spending Thanksgiving Day with her parents, Silvia was to escape to Jefe's residence the following morning. She would spend the rest of the four-day weekend there in intensive training and strategy discussions for the election that would occur in less than two years.

Jefe's escape plan for Silvia was brilliant in its simplicity. At approximately 10 a.m. on Friday morning Julia Jimenez, a trusted female member of Los Leones, arrived at Silvia's parents' house in a Town Car from a local car service. Jimenez was selected for her role because she was close to the same height and weight of Silvia. Wearing sunglasses and a business-oriented pant suit with fat pads from her butt up to her shoulders that put on an extra twenty or thirty pounds, she exited the Town Car carrying a briefcase with her long, red hair flowing as she approached the front door and rang the bell. The media and paparazzi that were present witnessed Silvia open the door and welcome the visitor inside while waiving to the press and making the quick comment that "work never ends!"

Once inside, Julia quickly stripped out of her clothes and wig and Silvia donned them. With the fat pads imbedded in the clothes, the carefully placed wig, and the sunglasses, Silvia's disguise was complete. Silvia waited approximately fifteen minutes and then exited the house through the front door, carrying the briefcase and a to-go cup of coffee. The disguise worked, and Silvia entered the Town Car without being recognized by the media outside the house. With Jimenez staying behind at Silvia's parents' house to spend the next three days getting paid to read books inside the house away from windows, the Town Car drove to the airport where a helicopter flew Silvia, still in disguise, to Jefe's house two hundred forty-five miles away in Veracruz.

72

VERACRUZ, MEXICO, BLACK FRIDAY 2022

"Welcome, Silvia. Happy Black Friday. Thank you for interrupting your family vacation to meet with Professor and me," greeted Jefe as Silvia entered his house.

"Happy to do it, Jefe. But I'm surprised you could even recognize me in this outfit! Do you have a place where I can change clothes?"

"Yes, of course. I've arranged for comfortable clothes in your size to be put in your guest bedroom. Let's get you changed out of your disguise and then we can start our work."

Silvia returned about a half-hour later dressed in casual beach attire. Jefe and Professor guided her to their office by the pool. After getting iced teas and pre-lunch appetizers, the trio got down to business.

"Thank you for coming, Silvia," Professor started. "Let me begin by saying how impressed and proud I am of your accomplishments to date. Your trajectory as a rising star in American politics has been nothing short of incredible. So, thank you for all your great work and efforts to date. I foresee a great future for you!"

"Thank you, Professor. I couldn't do anything without the support of you and Jefe, so you clearly share in all my success. It has truly been a team effort."

“Indeed,” piped in Jefe. “Now, with the grand prize in reach, we want to make sure we are all in synch. Professor, will you please outline your thoughts about the next two years?”

“Of course,” Professor said. “Jefe and I think the best approach is to keep as many options open as possible during the election journey. We’ll start by announcing in early January that you want to be the Republican nominee for president in 2024. I anticipate that you will be joined in this race by Triumph and a number of other Republican hopefuls. If there’s a path for you to win the nomination and then the general election, we’ll take it. I never want to put a ceiling on what you can accomplish, Silvia.”

“Thanks Professor. That is very exciting!” Silvia proclaimed.

“However, if Triumph stays as the favorite to win the nomination, then we need to make sure your campaign has made you an enticing VP candidate to join the Triumph ticket. This will force us to thread the needle with our campaign positions. Finally, if Burden or some other Democrat is likely to win the general election, then I have a fallback plan where we will get you reinstated as one of Arizona’s members in the House. At that point, we will make an all-out push to get you elected as Speaker of the House.”

“Any questions?” asked Jefe.

“Just a million of them,” replied Silvia with a laugh. “Let’s start with me in the race to win the presidency. Do you really think I have a chance?”

“Stranger things have happened. You poll well across many different demographics. The Republicans had disappointing results in the mid-term elections. This creates an opening for you as a new, more positive, and attractive candidate. However, you don’t possess the name recognition or other advantages that both Burden and Triumph have as people who have been POTUS. So, if I had to handicap your chances now, they would be in the ten to fifteen percent range. I think the more realistic opportunity is to get aligned with Triumph and be his VP. That’s going to take some fancy footwork on your part, but that’s part of our discussions this weekend.”

“I’m ready to get started if you are,” said Silvia enthusiastically.

73

VERACRUZ, MEXICO, BLACK FRIDAY 2022

"OK, let's jump into the key issues that you will confront as a national candidate. You've had to address some of these during your roles as governor and a member of the House, but now we need to focus on positions that we think will put us in the best place for success. Before we go any further, Silvia, I want you to be very honest with us and tell us whether you are uncomfortable with any of the positions we promote. This is critical. American voters generally have a good bullshit detector, with Triumph being their one blind spot.

"Let me be very direct," Professor continued. "To win the White House, you will need to broaden your appeal nationwide. You must be someone who combines passion for the country with brains, blunt talk, and charisma. You must be someone who will willingly campaign in Black and minority precincts because it's the right thing to do, not just because those votes are needed to win. If voters think you are thoughtful about an issue, then the voter can still disagree with you but be willing to cast a vote for you. Authenticity attracts voters, and that's why we need you to tell us if you strongly disagree with any of the stances that we propose."

"Don't worry," chimed in Silvia. "I will let you know. I agree that I need to be believable to be respected and accepted. I remember how my stomach felt like it was tied into knots when I had to do that suck-up Zoom call with Triumph!"

"Fantastic. Let's get started. You just mentioned your stomach being tied into knots. Well, I think that there will be two leading issues in this election. The first is the abortion issue, which twists Republicans into knots, and the second is the gun and crime issue, which twists the Democrats into knots. Which of those issues would you like to discuss first?"

"Let's tackle the abortion issue first," replied Silvia quickly. "I don't know if you saw this, but while I was in the Phoenix airport a few days ago, a local TV reporter cornered me and turned the situation into a mini press conference about my views on abortion. Want to watch it and critique how I handled the question when it was sprung on me?"

"That would be great," said Professor. He and Jefe huddled around Silvia to watch the video on her cell phone. The news segment commenced with the reporter catching Silvia as she walked through the TSA pre-check line with other passengers. It was clearly an unplanned interview in which Silvia had to respond spontaneously. Silvia handled the interruption with ease and grace, without even the smallest hint she was annoyed by the reporter's intrusion into her private space. The entire time Silvia walked slowly toward the TSA checkpoint, never giving the appearance that she was a prima donna who would delay other passengers in line just because a camera and microphone were shoved in her face.

Silvia was also impressive with her response. "I grew up in a Catholic family and feel strongly about the right to life. However, I also grew up in a family where my mom, who I am about to visit for Thanksgiving, was a very strong person. She made sure that I, as a woman, felt empowered and capable of making big decisions. I learned not to take a back seat to anyone simply because of my gender."

Silvia continued after a short pause. "Based on my background, I can't envision a situation where I wouldn't carry a pregnancy to term. I think a lot of women feel this way. If they had insufficient means or other reasons why they couldn't raise the child, they would put the baby up for adoption. The bottom line is this: women are smart and fully capable of making decisions about critical issues. Clearly in cases of rape, incest, or where the health of the mother is at risk, it should be the woman who makes the ultimate decision, and it is *not* the job of the federal or state government to dictate the outcome. Despite my Catholic background, I also don't support the attempts by many states to limit access to contraception. Finally, here's an important point to me: as much as I appreciate a woman's right to make decisions about her body, I don't think women have the unfettered right to use abortion as a delayed form of birth control. Though it was overruled by the Dobbs case, I think Roe v. Wade was smart when the court recognized that, at some point of viability, the fetus becomes a 'person' and has rights that deserve protection. It is at this point when the issue no longer becomes just a woman's personal decision."

At that point Silvia was near the front of the TSA line and ended the interview with a quick, "Thank you for talking with me and I wish all of you a happy Thanksgiving holiday." A number of bystanders who witnessed the interview, clapped their approval of Silvia's handling of the situation.

"So, what do you think?" asked Silvia as she turned off her cell phone.

"I think you did a great job!" Jefe exclaimed. "You were much more composed with that asshole of a reporter than I would have been! I really liked your approach, but I'm not the expert here. Professor, what did you think?"

"I'd give you a grade of 'A' on this issue," Professor said. "As you know, there is a big division over 'pro-life, anti-abortion rights' as Republicans like to call them, or 'pro-choice reproductive rights' as Democrats like to call them. This is such a divisive and emotional issue that if you take a strong side, you will automatically lose voters on the other side. So, the goal is to walk the tightrope and try to be responsive, thoughtful, and caring, while at the same time not alienating either side. I thought you did a great job in this regard. Your stance was not as far right as many conservative Republican voters, but it was also not as far left as many liberal Democrat voters either. I think that means you successfully positioned yourself as a thoughtful moderate on the issue. I also really liked the personal touch you gave about your mom, and how your upbringing has affected your views."

"Thank you both. I have really given this issue a lot of thought."

"That's great. As we discussed, it's important for you to be thoughtful and authentic, and you did that on your response. Too many candidates are scripted and can only give a '10-second sound bite' response to questions."

"Any suggestions on the best way to respond to the question of when abortion is absolutely not allowed?" asked Silvia.

"I think some thoughtful waffling on this issue is best. I know that some Republican-dominated states want to impose a ban on abortions after six weeks. That seems a little extreme. Something in the twelve-to-fifteen-week range seems to be a better balancing of a woman's need to digest all the factors and options involved in this critical decision with the rights of the unborn child once it is viable. I would want the medical experts to weigh in on this issue instead of suggesting an arbitrary line."

"Got it," Silvia nodded affirmatively. "How about we go to gun rights issues, because I'm very curious about your thoughts on how to best approach that topic, Professor!"

"OK," started Professor. "Like I said, I think the second most divisive issue in the next election will be gun rights, especially if a mass shooting has occurred recently. I think it is important for you to take a firm stance on this issue to show that you are fed up with gun violence and want to be proactive in developing solutions."

"Hold on, Professor!" interjected Jefe with a note of shock in his voice. "Won't taking such a view automatically cause us to lose lots of votes?"

"Maybe. Those on the far right of the Republican party may drop Silvia or any other candidate taking this stance immediately. However, they always say that there's 20% of the people that you'll never be able to convince or change so you might as well just concern yourself with the other 80%. I think that's what we need to do here. I think Silvia can distinguish herself among Republican candidates by having 'Responsible Gun Safety' as a major plank of her platform. This position makes her look like a thoughtful moderate, which is where we want to be."

"Won't we get blasted by the NRA?" Jefe asked.

"Yes," Professor said. "But, unlike other Republicans, we don't need the NRA's campaign donations. This lets us take a stance on guns that will separate us from the pack."

"Can you give me specific suggestions about my gun safety platform?" Silvia asked.

"I would say something like this," Professor started. "The crime rate throughout the country is scary and must come down. I will never take away the Constitutional right of people to protect themselves and their families. However, preventable gun violence is way too prevalent, and Congress has not taken any significant action to stop it. Gun violence is now the leading cause of death among children, and it has been this way for years for Black children. I want to be proactive in helping develop solutions that increase our peace and safety while not preventing gun ownership by responsible citizens. Now, use of the term 'solutions' is too optimistic, since we'll never be able to totally end gun violence. But if we enact progressive, multi-faceted policies we should be able to make a dent and save lots of innocent lives.

"Here is where I think we just need to be reasonable as a nation, including in how we interpret the rights to gun ownership afforded by the second Amendment to the Constitution. Let's start with something we should all be able to agree on: that the second Amendment to the Constitution does *not* mean that citizens are allowed to own tanks or nuclear bombs. There are limits on the rights that people have to own weapons and it's now time to set forth in reasonable terms what those limits should be. Let's start with assault weapons...we should ban those nationwide. These weapons are never used for hunting and civilians don't need the capacity to make multiple kills. Likewise, civilians should not be able to get high-capacity magazines and those should be banned nationwide. The size, caliber, speed, and destructiveness of bullets available to citizens should not exceed that of the weapons used by our military and police. Look, the weapon used in the 2022 Highland, Illinois mass shooting was a Smith & Wesson M&P 15… that 'M&P' stands for military and police. Should a disturbed teenager be able to buy a gun intended for use by our military and police? I don't think so. But, in addition to banning assault weapons and large capacity magazines, what can we do? Let's start with the basics. Let's toughen the red flag laws and restrict gun purchases by known criminals and other dangerous people. Let's require gun permits and training before a gun purchase is allowed. We won't let anyone drive a car without passing a driver's test and showing a basic comprehension of the rules of the road. I don't think it's asking too much to have similar rules apply to the purchase of firearms. Then let's also enact programs to reduce some of the underlying causes that lead to gun violence… everything from mental health programs to poverty. All of this should help parents not have to worry when they drop off their children in school. With these suggestions, we won't be able to stop all gun violence, but hopefully we can reduce it considerably."

Jefe reflected for a moment before commenting. "Professor, I am still concerned that we are a lone wolf on this issue and will lose many votes."

"I don't disagree that there is risk here, Jefe. I'm sure that there are some 'single issue voters' who will automatically vote against Silvia for our positions on gun control and abortion. But I think it is worth taking the risk. Hopefully, the rest of the voters will appreciate Silvia taking stands that represent reasonable approaches to tough issues."

"Silvia, what do you think?" Professor asked.

"Personally, I support breaking the Republican mold on guns. You may not know this, but I know a thing or two about guns. I've gone hunting with my father ever since I was a young girl and I've been a registered gun owner all my adult life."

"Silvia, you never cease to amaze me!" exclaimed Professor. "I think that is an important fact you should make known when discussing your views on gun rights. I would wager that there aren't many women who have extensive experience in using and owning guns. This really adds to your authenticity on the issue."

"That also gives me comfort," added Jefe. "Now, let's head to the house for a cocktail. We can continue the discussion tomorrow, but right now all this talk about issues is making my head hurt!"

74

WASHINGTON, D.C., AUGUST 24, 2020

"Hi Dad!" greeted Nick as he opened the door to give his father a hug. "I made it easy on you this year."

"You sure did," replied Carson Class, carrying two large Manny & Olga's pizza boxes as he entered Nick's house in Georgetown. "I like not having to travel far to see you."

It was an annual tradition in the Class family. On the anniversary of the passing of Jeanne Class, Carson Class would visit Nick and the two would share a meal of pizza and ice cream to reminisce and celebrate their blessings of having her as an angel in their lives.

"I've got two different kinds of ice cream waiting for us if we have the willpower not to get too stuffed eating pizza," Nick said.

Nick cleared space on his couch and adjoining table for Carson's arrival with the pizza. Carson sat on the couch opposite Nick, and they feasted on the pizza while exchanging heartwarming memories of Nick's mom.

Nick was feeling warm inside from the pizza and the bonding with his father when Carson asked, "So, how are you liking things at work? Are you happy at GROSS?"

"Well, I'm learning every day. The attacks we helped prevent in Knoxville really showed me how important GROSS is. A lot of people are alive in Knoxville because of us. That really makes me feel good."

"That's great!" Carson said. "However, I'd much rather you be bored instead of busy!"

"I also like that Straw and Sam have been trying to get me more involved, sort of like an intern to investigate things they think might be of interest. I'm nowhere close to where they are as far as their analytical skills, but I'm enjoying it."

"How are you and Sam getting along?"

"Things have really improved since our rough start. Heck, she saved my life in Knoxville! However, a part of me still doesn't know whether I'll ever meet her expectations. She wants somebody who is *totally* dependable. I don't know if she thinks I'll ever be that person. Strangely, I think it helps that Sam and I share the same emotional wounds."

"Nick, successful comebacks happen all the time. Look at all the movie sequels, reunited rock bands, and elected politicians who previously lost races. Son, I have no doubt you can come back too."

"But it's hard to come back when you don't know where you've been. Dad, I want you to know that I still struggle with my lost memories… and how you let that happen."

Carson didn't know how to respond to the comment, so he shifted the narrative. "Nick, trust me. You don't need to shed your skin like a snake and be reborn. You are great just the way you are."

Nick sat quietly for a second, soaking in his father's words. Carson took advantage of the break in the conversation to add one more thought.

"Nick, it's also very natural for you to continue to mourn Katie. Don't treat that as something that makes you weak or unreliable. The worst thing you can do is to incarcerate yourself in an emotional prison over Katie. Don't hesitate to reach out to me, or a pastor, or a shrink, or a friend if you ever just need to talk. I also think you are right. There is a unique bond that you and Sam share because of the similarities in your situations. I think Sam appreciates and supports you more than you will ever know."

Nick let Carson's words sink in and felt a sense of comfort and relief.

"Let's have some ice cream," said Nick. "I'll go fill up some bowls."

"I'll join you," Carson said, picking up both of their wine glasses to take to the kitchen. "Make my bowl a big one."

"Ha!" Nick said. "Ice cream has always been your Achilles heel!"

"I don't dispute that at all," Carson replied with a laugh as he watched Nick scoop out two types of ice cream into large bowls.

After finishing dessert, Carson stood up to leave.

"I probably don't say it enough, Nick, but I appreciate everything about you. Your mom would also be very proud of you. But now, I think it's time for me to leave. I love you, and may the sun never set on your dreams."

Shortly after Carson left, Nick crawled into bed. He looked at a picture of Katie on the nightstand and found himself smiling instead of regressing.

No one lives forever, and I have been so blessed to have both my mom and Katie in my life. They both loved life to its fullest each day, thought Nick. *It's about time for me to realize that being alive and living are two different things. I need to focus only on the latter.*

75

VERACRUZ, MEXICO, SUNDAY AFTER THANKSGIVING 2022

Jefe, Professor, and Silvia were gathered by Jefe's pool after an active and productive Thanksgiving weekend.

"Silvia, it has been a pleasure having you here for the last couple of days and getting to know you better. I only wish we would have had more free time for relaxation instead of training," Jefe said.

"The pleasure has been all mine, Jefe," Silvia replied with a smile. "It was great meeting your wife and daughter. Of course, it's always educational and entertaining when Professor is around!"

"Before you put your disguise back on and return to your parents' house, Professor and I thought we would put you through one final training exam… something called a 'Lightning Round.' It's where I ask you about a topic and you give us your response. It will be a great way for us to judge how much more preparation we need to do once your campaign for president starts for real in January."

"I'm game! Let's start!" Silvia said, positioning herself on her chair as if she were on a hot seat.

"OK, first question, Congresswoman Rodriguez, is what would you do to improve immigration policy and the situation at the border with Mexico?" asked Jefe.

Silvia jumped right in with her response to Jefe's question. "The United States and Mexico share a border more than 1,900 miles long. Yet

U.S. politicians have historically done nothing but play political football with border issues, and some candidates from our party have painted migrants as human rats that bring nothing but disease and crime across the border. The fact of the matter is that there is a lot of suffering at the border, and most of it is felt by people who are hardworking, proud, kind, and family oriented. This is a human rights disaster. The vast majority of immigrants are not dangerous. They are just poor people who are desperate to get away from drug cartels, human traffickers, and horrible living conditions in Central America and Mexico. What we need is a thoughtful, humane, and secure immigration policy, and this should be a win-win for both the United States and Mexico."

Silvia paused for a second and then continued. "Americans should not be anti-immigration. All Americans are immigrants. I think Republicans have forgotten the wisdom of Ronald Raygun. While recognizing that steps must be in place to ensure border security, in President Raygun's last formal statement at the White House in 1989, he said: 'We lead the world because, unique among nations, we draw our people...our strength...from every country and every corner of the world. And by doing so we continuously renew and enrich our nation. Thanks to each wave of new arrivals to this land of opportunity, we're a nation forever young, forever bursting with energy and new ideas, and always on the cutting edge, always leading the world to the next frontier. This quality is vital to our future as a nation. If we ever closed the door to new Americans, our leadership in the world would soon be lost.'

"Like President Raygun, I think immigrants should be valued, not belittled. So, what's the big problem? I think the answer is simple; the concern is lawlessness and our collective security. We *cannot* let people into our country who are terrorists, such as the people who carried out the attacks on 9/11. So, while compassion at the border is important, the first prong of my immigration policy is ensuring the safety and security of the border. We need to fund additional ICE and border patrol agents. Let's use more technology. Laser beams can now extend over four miles in length. Let's use lasers, sensors, drones, and AI to create a 'virtual border fence' that lets us quickly detect intrusions and rapidly respond to them. This will be a much better approach than trying to put the Wall of China on the border of Mexico. This wall will never be built, much less paid for by Mexico. We can combine this technology with the arsenal of surveillance tools already used by border agents, including airplanes, helicopters, satellites, and other ground-based sensors, to make the border safe. The bottom line is, we need to take strong actions to solidify our Mexican border and preserve our national security as the first and foremost element of a new and comprehensive effort to address immigration. After that, we can address the many other social problems at the border."

"Wow," replied Jefe. "That was quite a good response. It was just a lot longer than what I expected in something I called the 'Lightning Round'!"

"I agree with Jefe," added Professor. "Overall, a great answer, but way too long. I thought it was great that you came off with an approach to immigration that seems tough, but fair, as well as fiscally conservative. However, I think you can condense a lot of your conclusion to something as simple and memorable as 'We do NOT need to put the Wall of China on the border of Mexico. We just need to use our technology with lasers, drones, AI, and satellites to determine breaches of the border. Securing our border has to be our top priority, but then we must follow that with a humane approach to the immigrants involved.'"

"Great. I'll try to be more concise with my future responses. I just get a little compassionate about immigration issues in light of my background."

"And, that's great," Jefe said. "Don't be afraid to mention that."

"So, what's the next question, Jefe?"

"How about this: All the candidates for president seem to be wealthy or privileged, including you. How can you and the other candidates connect and truly represent low and middle-class voters under these circumstances?"

Silvia replied without hesitation, "I am a blessed and fortunate person. In a country of 'haves' and 'have nots' I am definitely a 'have.' Even though my family did not have much money when I was growing up, I have benefitted from the advantage of having loving parents who provided me great educational and work opportunities. While I worked hard to get where I currently stand, I also acknowledge that most of you in the country didn't enjoy the advantages that I had. It would be wrong of me not to acknowledge that our country needs to be the country of opportunities that are as open and equal to all as possible, and that's not happening very much these days. Now, don't misunderstand me... I am not in favor of giving the less fortunate an automatic handout. But I promise you here and now, I will give you the opportunities and resources that you need to succeed. That means more training, more healthcare, and more educational programs... and I sure don't expect you to pay taxes at the same rate as someone like me! In this regard, I'm a clear supporter of the Buffett Rule, named after Omaha billionaire Warner 'the Oracle' Buffett, that would require those making more than $1 million to pay at least 30% of their adjusted income in taxes."

Silvia paused briefly and then continued. "Here's an example of one of the places where I think former President Triumph is disconnected from mainstream America. Mr. Triumph has made frequent comments that his best barometer of how the economy is working is how well the stock market is performing. While stock market performance is important to some Americans who have 401K investments, there are lots of middle and low-income people who are being hurt and squeezed by existing policies even if the stock market is making Mr. Triumph happy. And President Burden is the worst offender of all. He doesn't seem to understand the pain and difficulties caused by the double whammy of his inflationary policies and the fact that wages for most working people have stagnated and not kept pace with the increased cost of living. There are way too many people in America who have jobs, but who are having a difficult time paying rent, buying groceries, or clothing their children. This trend needs to be reversed!"

"What do you think, Professor?" Jefe asked. "How did Silvia do on that question?"

"Excellent! I like how you brought your background into play as affecting your values and approach to the common man. It really showed

empathy. I also liked your criticism of both Triumph and Burden on this point. Neither will like it, mainly because it rings true. It should also be another point that proves to Triumph how valuable of a counterbalance you could be to his campaign if he needs to select a VP."

"Great!" Silvia said. "Any more questions, Jefe?"

"Always, but I don't want you to miss your flight back to the States. Here's the final topic for today: Please give us your thoughts on the Ukraine conflict."

"With respect to Ukraine," Silvia started, "it is critical that the United States and our allies continue to supply needed weaponry and technology support to the brave Ukrainians. The outcome of this conflict has consequences for the democratic world that extend way beyond the borders of Ukraine. We need to continue to condemn Putrid's actions in the strongest ways possible. Russia's unprovoked invasion of Ukraine violated every rule of acceptable international conduct and it is clear that Putrid did it to see how the United States would react. History shows that Russia's actions are not surprising. When Russia took the Georgian provinces in 2008 and Crimea in 2014, it is now clear that those were mere appetizers to Putrid, and Ukraine was always the main course he wanted to consume. If he is not stopped in Ukraine, that might also not be his last meal. That's why it is so important that he fail in Ukraine and, thankfully, he totally miscalculated the pride-filled ferocity of the Ukrainian response. We need to do everything possible apart from putting U.S. boots on the ground to ensure that no part of Russia's actions can be viewed as a triumph instead of a tragedy. My only real complaint with the U.S. support to date is that it has been too slow."

"I think that's a great response, Silvia," Professor said. "But Jefe is right. You need to get back to Phoenix. Safe travels and I'll be in touch soon!"

76

VERACRUZ, MEXICO, SUNDAY AFTER THANKSGIVING 2022

"Professor, I think that was a very productive weekend with Silvia. But before you return tomorrow, I have another very important topic to discuss with you."

"Of course, Jefe. What is on your mind?"

"While Silvia presents us some great opportunities, I think that we need to discuss in greater detail our contingency plans in the event Silvia does not win the election."

"We've already discussed having Silvia be Triumph's VP, if that is necessary. And, if that strategy doesn't work because the Democrats win the election, then another fallback is to get Silvia in place as Speaker of the House."

"I'm curious. Have these rules been used before?" Jefe asked.

"Yes! Nine vice-presidents have become president under these rules upon the death or resignation of a president, and two VPs have temporarily served as acting president. However, no other officer has ever been called upon to act as president. Our contingency plan could possibly change that."

"All of our contingency plans still require assassination, correct?"

"Correct."

Jefe took a moment to collect his thoughts. "After our failed assassination of Spence, this plan needs to be big and bulletproof. Professor,

in my line of work, I have learned that violence can be an effective tool. History has shown that killing innocent people may be acceptable if it is ultimately for the 'greater good.' Take the Nagasaki and Hiroshima bombings in World War II. Sure, there was an enormous death toll. But the violence ended the war and prevented further bloodshed. While my violence, should we need it, will not be military in nature, the ultimate goal is not dissimilar."

Jefe continued, his voice rising with passion. "I really want to emphasize one thing. I am *not* a terrorist! Terrorists only try to destroy things by creating terror and fear. My goal is to build things and better things, not destroy things. I want to use our power to help, especially at the border. While I expect our drug profits to skyrocket, I don't force the weak Americans to buy them. After the election, I plan to increase the manufacturing and distribution of Narcan, so fewer people will die of drug overdoses. A win-win situation for us!"

"Jefe, I would not have accepted your job offer to get you a puppet president if I thought you were only motivated by profits," Professor said. "But, let me ask you one thing. When you said we need to go 'big' in your contingent plan, what did you have in mind?"

"My contingency plan involves the use of a small nuclear weapon, the goal of which is not to cause massive casualties but just to ensure that it accomplishes our strategic objectives."

Professor shuddered and his eyes widened. Before he could compose himself, Jefe continued.

"I promise to cause no more death than is necessary. If we need to use this fallback plan, then I will view it as another example of killing for the greater good and I will have no remorse."

"Jefe, you have clearly done a lot of thinking about this backup plan. I'd like to hear the details."

"Let's go outside and have a drink."

77

VERACRUZ, MEXICO, SUNDAY AFTER THANKSGIVING 2022

A gentle ocean breeze along with a picturesque sunset made a perfect setting for Jefe and Professor to continue their discussions as they headed poolside. Verana and Abriz were just finishing a swim as Jefe and Professor approached the pool. Abriz gave Professor a goodbye hug before heading back to the house.

"Professor, Verana and Abriz both adore you. Which brings up an important question. Why haven't you been able to find a beautiful American woman who adores you as much as they do?"

"I wish I had the answer to that," replied Professor with a chuckle. "But we don't have enough time to discuss my romantic failures."

"Well, maybe after we get Silvia to the White House, we can see if the two of you can become the next power couple in Washington!"

"Ha! I could be so lucky, but I also make it my practice not to mix business and pleasure."

"Like I said, let's get her in the White House, and then your business with me is over and you can pursue the relationship with no regrets. You've always liked women who are super intelligent, and she clearly passes that test, plus she's gorgeous!"

"I won't argue with you on either of those points, but let's get back to business before those thoughts distract me too much!"

"I agree," Jefe said. "Let me summarize where I think we are. If Silvia is not elected president, she may still ascend to that position if she is either the vice president or Speaker of the House. But, both of those latter options require the assassination of the president, and possibly also the VP. Our experience with Spence shows that is a tricky thing to do. The degree of difficulty will, I assume, increase considerably if we must take out both the president and the VP, and this has never been done before. However," Jefe said with a smile, "I've been thinking of a plan that will increase our odds of success under all circumstances."

"I want to hear about your plan," Professor said, "but let me remind you that presidential security details are dense and multi-faceted. With all those layers of protections, I don't see how it will be possible to make any attack on the White House. The White House has fortified underground bunkers that can withstand even a nuclear attack. I also think it would be hard to make sure that both the president and VP are taken out, especially with limited civilian casualties like you said was mandatory."

"That's part of the beauty of my contingency plan, Professor, because I won't attack the White House or any part of Washington. Your concerns are all correct… there is too much security, too many civilian casualties, and too many variables we can't control."

"So, where would your attack occur?"

"Camp David. I researched an informal tradition after each presidential election. The first weekend in February, the president, vice president, and the president's entire cabinet traditionally take a weekend retreat at Camp David to discuss their business initiatives for the coming year. Both Triumph and Burden followed this tradition. If Silvia is not elected president, I think this presents a perfect opportunity for us."

"You know, Jefe," Professor said, his brain racing. "That retreat would be a great opportunity, if we need it. But still, how would you carry out a nuclear strike?"

Jefe grinned. "The beauty of the plan starts with Camp David. Unlike the congestion of a city, Camp David is located at the top of a mountain range, which is a good security move that ensures that no one can look into the camp from a higher elevation. The mountaintop location and the heavily forested topography essentially makes Camp David very isolated, even though the nearest town is only a few miles away."

"I don't get it. How does the isolated location of Camp David help us?"

"This is all very favorable to my goal! My plan is to build a fake business not too far away that can serve as a launching ground for our attack. And even though Camp David has a lot of security, it is not as fortified as the White House. Basically, no matter what precautions are taken by the White House secret service to ensure the president's safe arrival at Camp David, once he arrives, he is a sitting duck. There is not much that can be done to protect him if a nuclear weapon is dropped on his head with little to no advance warning."

"Your contingency plan does have potential," Professor mused.

"And I think there is some big icing on the cake that you may not have even considered."

"What would that be?" asked Professor.

"If my plan is needed and works, it will wipe out the president's entire cabinet. So, not only will Silvia be appointed as the successor president, but she will also be able to select a new cabinet that is loyal to me. I can effectively take over the entire executive branch of government in one fell swoop under this contingency plan!"

"I had not thought about that," Professor exclaimed. "I feel like the student has just taught the Professor a lesson! However, you've glossed over one small detail… tell me your plan to get a nuclear weapon, since those things aren't exactly available on the open market."

78

VERACRUZ, MEXICO, SUNDAY AFTER THANKSGIVING 2022

"In chaos there is often opportunity, Professor. Putrid's invasion of Ukraine is the chaos that will supply us the opportunity to get possession of a nuke. A lot of the details will need to be worked out, but here's a rough outline of my thoughts.

"For years, the Russians have asked for me to partner with them. They want to use my drug pipelines and resources to move Russian drugs into the U.S. market. I have always refused because I did not trust them. However, Putrid desperately needs access to new capital to continue to fund his war. His oil revenues are declining because of the embargo and there is global pressure on countries not to purchase Russian commodities. This gives me a chance to partner with Russia in a way that provides us a critical piece of our puzzle with limited risk exposure."

"What are you thinking?" Professor asked.

"Well, I want us to get one of Russia's small nuclear weapons. We don't need one of their nukes that is attached to a huge intercontinental missile. Putrid also won't do anything that directly ties him to putting one of his nukes on the market. However, one of his contacts in the shadowy part of his military could help us accomplish this goal."

"I'm intrigued," Professor said. "Tell me more."

"Aleksandr Rublev Medvedev, a man famous for his huge biceps and tattoos, is the commander of a large faction of mercenaries that comprise the Vagner Group, Putrid's private army. They have surreptitiously tried to help Putrid accomplish his geopolitical goals throughout Eastern Europe and the world at large. By necessity, Putrid has required Medvedev and the mercenaries to become increasingly active in the Ukraine war. Medvedev is known to be money hungry. He is willing to use his position and influence if the payoff is large enough, especially if Putrid is also on board. If things fall into place under my plan, we will get a 'baby nuke' in exchange for some upfront cash payments to Medvedev and Putrid, plus promises of future Russian access into the U.S. drug markets."

"I'm still unclear how you end up with the nuke in your hands," Professor said.

"Here's a rough outline of the plan. Putrid has talked for months about the possible need to use nuclear weapons in the Ukraine conflict. Accordingly, it wouldn't be viewed by the world as unusual if Putrid moved some of his mobile nuclear weapons closer to the border with Ukraine. My sources in Russia have informed me that Medvedev has some unexploded long-range ordnance that Ukraine used to bomb a Russia-based resupply station a few weeks ago. My plan is that Medvedev and his team will go to the new location of two of Russia's baby nukes. They will gain access via written orders signed by Putrid, but, as a precaution, Medvedev and his team will kill all the Russians charged with guarding the site. Medvedev will place the Ukrainian ordnance at the site and remove one of the two nukes. They will then use timed explosives to ignite the site after Medvedev and his team are a safe distance away.

"The huge explosion will be blamed on a Ukrainian missile hitting the Russian site, and Putrid will confirm that two weapons in its nuclear arsenal were destroyed. Putrid will require review of the site by nuclear professionals to ensure that any nuclear fallout will not endanger Russian citizens. Putrid will declare that heads will roll for those responsible for exposing Russian's most valued weapons, and he will chastise and condemn Ukraine for its unprovoked and dangerous escalation of the war. The second nuke that no one thinks exists anymore will then be transported to a ship bound for Mexico, where we will obtain possession."

Jefe paused to let his plan sink in and then asked, "So, what do you think of my plan?"

"Jefe, my expertise is in electoral politics, not foreign or military affairs. However, everything you've laid out seems plausible. I think the international community will accept Putrid's explanation for having two of his nukes destroyed in the conflict. Other than North Korea, Russia is acknowledged to be the nation with the least amount of control and security over the nuclear weapons in its arsenal. So, as crazy as it sounds, I find no holes in your plan to get a nuclear bomb. But what do we do after getting the baby nuke in Mexico?"

"Here's what I propose. While waiting to get our nuke, I will start to build a facility a few miles away from Camp David to purportedly provide underprivileged children the opportunity to enjoy camping and other outdoor activities in the mountains. I will do this through a foundation that I control, but it will be impossible to trace back to me due to the many layers of the corporate onion structure that need to be peeled away. This facility will serve as the launching ground for our baby nuke once we have transported it there. I have already acquired a modified, large drone that can fly just above the level of the forest trees and carry the baby nuke to be dropped on Camp David when the time is right. In an homage to the biblical story, I thought we name this facility of ours 'Goliath.' However, unlike in the Bible, this time Goliath will prevail in victory over David."

"I like the outline of your plan, including the 'Goliath' name," Professor said.

"Clearly, a lot of details remain outstanding. But my contacts inside Russia have already started to work on the plan. I would halt everything immediately if you did not support it, Professor. But I am glad that you are on board."

"Hopefully, we will never have to use this weapon," Professor said. "But I have always instructed you about the uncertainty of presidential elections and the need to have backup plans. Looks like you have done exactly that."

79

WASHINGTON, D.C., DECEMBER 23, 2022

Nick arrived at the GROSS office to see Sam and Straw huddled around one of Straw's monitors, gazing intently at a CNN breaking news update.

"What's happening?" Nick asked as he hurried to join them.

"CNN is reporting a missile strike into a Russian munitions depot about fifteen miles inside of Russia from the Ukraine border," Sam said. "They have satellite footage showing quite an explosion in the area last night."

"Good for Ukraine!" exclaimed Nick. He turned to Straw, who had a very quizzical look on his face. "Straw, you look puzzled. What's up?"

Straw had a far-off, glazed look in his eyes as he studied the feeds of military intelligence that were flowing into the alphabet agencies about the missile strike.

"I don't know yet, Nick," Straw said while maintaining his focus on the screens. He continued to mutter to no one in particular, "Everybody wants something they might not get and the whole world is full of petty wars, saying I got mine, and you get yours. It's nothing but glorified insanity."

Nick met Sam's gaze, who gestured to leave Straw alone. They moved over to Sam's desk where she streamed other broadcasts for any different information.

"This doesn't seem that unusual to me," Sam said, lowering her voice to not interrupt Straw. "In the last month, there has been a significant increase in the number of cross-border strikes into Russia."

"I thought Ukraine has denied responsibility for the strikes," Nick said. "Isn't it possible that the strikes are from anti-Putrid Russians?"

"Either way, the strikes are capturing the attention of Putrid. However, the only thing unusual about this strike is the enormous size of the fireball from the munitions site... it was huge!"

Sam and Nick continued to monitor the various news transmissions of the missile strike when, after about thirty minutes, a live feed started from Moscow. Putrid, dressed in his typical expensive, dark blue pin-striped suit, stood at a microphone, surrounded by Russian generals and other leaders. Putrid's presentation was short and succinct. Through an interpreter, Putrid indicated that an attack by Ukraine had hit a Russian munitions storage facility and destroyed, among other weapons of conventional warfare, two mobile, mini-nuclear bombs that Russia had deployed closer to the border. As news footage showed fragments of exploded Ukraine ordnance at the gruesome site, Putrid publicly condemned Ukraine for the attack on Russian soil and the risks of escalation of the war. He noted that no detonation of the nuclear weapons occurred, nor was there any significant leakage of radioactive material. He assured his comrades there was no risk to the health of Russian citizens in nearby cities and villages. Russian nuclear scientists had made this conclusion, but Putrid was going to invite an international inspection team to the site soon to confirm no spreading of nuclear contamination. Putrid promised to prove to the world that he and Russia were conscientious guardians of these powerful weapons and were good caretakers of global safety.

"What do you make of Putrid's broadcast, Straw?" Nick asked.

"It's a crock of crap," Straw responded. "Just another politician throwing stones and talking a lot about less and less!"

"Anything bother you about the bombing?" Nick asked.

Straw stretched his back. "It's still too early, and it's bending my mind trying to figure out what to find. I try to see what's goin' down and read between the lines. But when governments are involved, the needle's eye is thin since the ships of state sail on a mirage, making things fuzzy and so obscure."

"Anything you can tell us?" prompted Sam. "Preferably in plain English, not Grateful Dead lyrics."

"Sorry, sometimes lyrics flowing through my brain also come out of my mouth," Straw grinned. "Here is what I have been able to piece together from the intelligence blasts I've received. The Russian military leader closest to the bomb site, and who has been providing reports of the event to Putrid, is Aleksandr Medvedev. This is interesting, because our intelligence had him located with a Vagner team under his command deeper into Ukraine just a few days ago. It's also interesting because, in addition to his role as a key Vagner commander, Medvedev was previously influential in the grupperovka, the Russian mafia. Lots of our analysts think he's also likely an officer of the SVR, the Russian foreign intelligence counterpart to the CIA. This all may just be coincidence, but my radar is up. I've always felt that it's been easy to go rogue in Russia, especially in the military, because of lax security, including on oversight of their nuclear arsenal."

Straw paused as a CNN broadcast showed Ukraine military officials neither confirming nor denying involvement in the strike.

"The other thing that really strikes me as odd is how rapidly Putrid went public about the event. The normal Russian playbook is to delay, deny, and deceive. But here, Putrid was immediately out in front with a public condemnation of the event. This is a very unusual reversal of roles."

"What do you mean, Straw?" Nick asked.

"Prompt responses never come out of Moscow for normal news events that may make Russia look bad. It's unheard of that Putrid himself would quickly address a successful attack on Russian soil that takes out two of their nukes."

"Could that be because anything involving nukes scares everyone?" Sam asked.

"I don't buy Putrid's public health concern about the spread of radioactive residue as a believable reason for his quick actions. I'm sure there is a lot more information to come in, so I'll keep you updated."

"Could it be that Putrid wants to get in front of the issue in the hope that it will die down quickly?" Nick asked. "I could see them wanting to do that if the attack on the munitions site came from disgruntled Russians instead of Ukraine."

"I guess that could be possible, Nick. Glad to see you thinking like an analyst!"

80

VERACRUZ, MEXICO, JANUARY 1, 2023

"Happy New Year!" Professor greeted Jefe over their burner phones.

"And to you as well, Professor. Did you bring in the new year with the wildness of a lion or the tameness of a lamb?"

"It was more 'lameness' for me. I saw the ball drop in NYC on TV at my home, but was fast asleep shortly thereafter."

"What else have you been up to?"

"I've spent a lot of time getting Silvia ready for her announcement that she will be a candidate for president. I've also been making sure that we will quickly have a visible presence on the ground in key states across the country. It's been exhausting, but we are in a good position to start gathering momentum once Silvia makes her announcement. What about you, Jefe? Did you have a big celebration?"

"No, Verana and I just watched the new year arrive in the cozy comfort of our home. My father always said that New Year's Eve was for amateurs, so it was wisest to stay home and be safe."

"Fantastic! You know, Jefe, that's truly inspirational. You have the means to easily travel to Paris or some other exotic destination for a romantic celebration, but you are grounded in your priorities and can enjoy the simple pleasures of life. Very commendable, my friend!"

"Thank you. I give all the credit to Verana. She cares very little about material things. Faith, family, and helping others are her only real priorities in life."

"She is definitely a keeper. Maybe one day I will be fortunate to have a wife like her."

"In time, my friend. Probably when you least expect it. Anyway, before you give me your progress report, let me give you a quick update on our little venture with the Russians. Our 'baby nuke' should arrive in the next four or five weeks on a cargo ship bound for Matamoros, our Mexico border town just across from Brownsville, Texas."

"What happens then?" Professor asked.

"When it gets to Matamoros, our people will take control of the nuke. They will wait for my instructions on when to use our system of tunnels to get it across the border. It will then be put on a truck to our Goliath campus near Camp David."

"Do your people know that they will be handling a baby nuke when they take it off the ship?" asked Professor.

"No, absolutely not. That type of news would portend to undesirable gossip, among other complications. All they know is that a crated item of great value to me is being delivered, and to treat it with the utmost care and caution."

"Sounds like you have everything under control, as expected. Sometime I would like you to educate me about the tunnels and transportation devices that you use to move your products so flawlessly to and throughout the United States. You have clearly mastered the mechanics of black-market commerce."

"Yes. Another time, old friend. For now, please give me your annual update. Are we where you expected to be fourteen years into our project?"

"Yes and no. In the ever-changing arena of politics and elections, that is probably not surprising. The biggest downside is we were not able to cultivate any top-level Democrat candidate. However, that would have been more important if Burden had not beaten Triumph in 2020. If Triumph had won in 2020, then his two-terms would have ended and the 2024 race would be between hungry Democrats and Republicans, with neither party having an incumbency advantage. With Burden winning in 2020, he will almost surely be the Democrat nominee in 2024 despite concerns over his age."

"Sounds like not having a talented candidate within the Democrat party is meaningless to us?"

"Correct. The downside is that all our eggs are in one basket, so to speak. Silvia is our best and only hope to ascend to the presidency. But I am more optimistic and hopeful than ever with Silvia. She is exactly what the voters in the U.S. should be looking for. Our wildcard on the Republican side is, of course, Triumph. But if Silvia can't win the election outright, then I'm confident that our fallback plans to have her become Triumph's VP or the Speaker of the House give us a great opportunity to put her in the Oval Office."

"Can you give me the odds that this will happen?"

"If I were a betting man, I would say that we have about a two-thirds chance that Silvia will be POTUS before the end of the first quarter of 2025."

"That is the most optimistic I've ever heard you sound."

"That is all due to how impressive I think Silvia is and your contingency plan. She's a winner, and the type of person that people just gravitate towards. That magnetism is not something that is taught. It's just who she is."

"What's next in the short-term?"

"As we've discussed, Silvia will make her formal announcement that she's a candidate for the Republican nomination in Des Moines, Iowa in a few days, on January 6. That is the two-year anniversary of the attack on the Capitol by Triumph's supporters. We want the symbolism of that date to help Republicans realize that, in 2024, they are not just choosing a candidate to represent the party in the general election, but they are selecting the future direction of the party."

Jefe interrupted, "Professor, you have more confidence than I do that Republican voters will select intelligently as long as Triumph is around."

"You may be right, and we will have to deal with matters as they evolve."

"What's next on Silvia's agenda?"

"She will spend the rest of the week campaigning throughout Iowa. That will let her connect with voters across the state. As you know, we had Silvia spend New Year's Eve campaigning in New Hampshire. We've lined up media coverage for all her travels, so she will be the first candidate that people see as a viable alternative to both Triumph and Burden."

"Why so much focus on those two states?" Jefe asked.

"Our goal is to generate momentum. Iowa and New Hampshire are the first two states to hold primaries in 2024. Then we will try to grow the momentum through Super Tuesday."

"What is Super Tuesday again?"

"It's about a month after the New Hampshire primary, and it's when fifteen states hold primaries. About one-third of all delegates to the nominating convention are chosen that day. Once the dust settles after Super Tuesday, we'll have a much clearer picture of which direction the election is heading."

"So, all those primaries occur early in 2024. After Silvia announces her candidacy, what does the rest of 2023 look like?"

"Making strategic campaign appearances, increasing her visibility and name recognition, and positioning herself to shine in debates. We need to be organized and show that we are serious about winning the election. Getting volunteers and grass roots support is hugely important. We'll also do lots of fund-raising, since we don't want her main source of financing to be traced back to you. When the time is right, we'll also do advertising and phone-calling blitzes, while hopefully lining up endorsements ahead of time from people of influence."

"Don't you think it will be hard to get endorsements while Triumph leads in the polls?"

"I agree, Jefe. That will be a challenge. But I hope we can count on celebrities like A-Rod to help with campaign ads and promotional appearances. I'm afraid that if candidates fear criticizing Triumph, he will continue to dominate the conservative media and the Republican party. To be a viable challenger, Silvia must address this uphill battle straight-on. She will need to challenge Triumph's policies and behavior, but do so while offering reasonable, alternative plans for the future. Otherwise, if you tip-toe around Triumph, he will steamroll you."

81

DES MOINES, IOWA, JANUARY 6, 2023

The press conference was to be held in Des Moines at the entrance of the Iowa State Capitol, a majestic building with 23-karat gold leaf covering its picturesque main dome.

Promptly at 12:59 p.m., Silvia Luisa Anna Maria Rodriguez walked confidently to a microphone surrounded by large banners of a photo of her and the words "MA PA 2024." She wore a professional-looking blue pant suit with red accents from her scarf, flag pin, and shoes. A crowd estimated at three hundred people surrounded the platform and cheered every step that Silvia took. Both local and national media had camera crews that captured every moment.

Silvia smiled and waved to the crowd.

"Thanks for showing up on this cool, crisp January day in beautiful Des Moines, Iowa," Silvia started, with the cold 18-degree Iowa air showing with every word she spoke. "I thought it would be very important for me to make this historic announcement at the site of a Capitol building. I'm doing this at exactly the time when, two years ago, the Police Chief at the U.S. Capitol in Washington received the first reports that rioters were trying to break into the Capitol. Like in Washington, D.C., the Capitol building behind me houses the legislative bodies of this proud state of Iowa. The timing of my announcement is symbolically important because I want America to never forget the travesty to our democracy that almost occurred that day. January 6, 2021 is a day that we should think carefully about when we elect the next wave of leaders for our country. January 6 has inspired me to make sure that nothing like that ever happens again. We can do better to make America proud. Accordingly, for that and my pledge to Make America Proud Again, I am hereby announcing my candidacy to be the next president of the United States."

The crowd erupted in applause at Silvia's announcement, with many of them raising placards with the slogan "SlamRod 2024! Make America Proud Again" or simply "MA PA".

Sylvia continued with a passionate presentation about her background and her dreams for America. She deftly touched on a few key issues for the country. She ended her speech by saying that she had selected the slogan "MA PA" because it held for her the dual significance of her Mama and Papa in her life, as well as the need to Make America Proud Again. Silvia noted that we didn't need MAGA, since we were always the greatest country in the world, but we just needed to bring back pride in our country and the people who are its leaders. She ended with a pledge to work tirelessly to accomplish these goals, and to make both America and her parents proud.

82

WASHINGTON, D.C., JANUARY 15, 2023

The winter wind was biting, and a bitter gust hit Nick flush in his face as he exited Sadie. He walked quickly to the GROSS office entry, regretting that he didn't dress more appropriately for the frigid weather. Before entering, Nick saw Samantha get out of her car. Unlike Nick, she had dressed for the winter weather. She wore an insulated ski coat, gloves, a stylish hat, and earmuffs. Nick waited to hold the door for Sam, and then followed her into the office.

"Thanks for the coffee, Straw," said Sam upon seeing a cup of steaming hot coffee sitting on her desk.

"Ditto," said Nick.

"I've got some more intel on that Ukraine strike that eliminated two nukes from Russia's arsenal," said Straw as soon as Nick and Sam had settled into their chairs. "But something isn't sitting very well with me."

Nick and Sam grabbed their coffees and walked over to Straw's platform of monitors. Straw's screens displayed various satellite pictures of the Russian weapons compound. Straw studied them closely, zooming in and out, focusing on specific frames to isolate items of interest while muttering to himself, *"Darkness always hides the light. This looks like a song of Gomorrah... blew the city off the map, left nothing there but fire."*

Nick looked at the photos, but only saw the devastating debris of a munitions armory that had been bombed, igniting the weapons on the ground like firecrackers. The explosions had scattered remnants of the structure that had housed the weapons, and the unfortunate soldiers who had been nearby, over a charred area about the length of a football field.

"So, what are these pictures telling you, Straw?" asked Sam.

Straw emerged from his zone of Zen-like focus and looked up at Nick and Sam.

"Well," Straw began, "it's a combination of things that are driving me insane. First, even though the nukes on site did not detonate because of the strike, a damaged nuclear device will always have some amount of radioactive discharge. Based on my intel, the radioactivity level coming from the bomb site, strangely enough, only represents the expected fall-out from one such weapon, not two. The second troubling thing is that the corpses of at least three of the Russian guards had what appear to be critical bullet wounds. Of course, the Russians quickly wiped the site clean, so this can never be verified. But I suspect some of those soldiers did not die from the blast at the site. In my attempt to read the signs and connect the lines, I've also investigated the real-time radar data for the region at the time of the explosion."

"What does that show?" asked Nick, intrigued as he tried to follow Straw's thought process.

"It shows nothing, which I find to be hugely significant. There is no sign of any long-range Ukrainian weapon being fired or in flight in that area at the time."

"So, what does that mean?" Sam asked.

"I don't know for sure. But I suspect Ukraine never touched the Russian armory. Something — or someone — else must have destroyed it."

"But didn't the U.S. intelligence community confirm that remnants of a Ukraine missile were found on the armory bomb site?"

"Yes, they did, and I could see the remnants on some of the satellite photos. But how could the Ukraine missile trigger the explosion if there is no radar record of any such flight path over the region at the time? That is something our military technology tracks very closely."

"So, what are you saying?" Nick asked.

"I have a hunch that the Ukrainian missile was just unexploded ordnance that the Russians had on-site along with their own weapons. I don't know the reason for this, but it could be to pin the cause of the blast on the Ukrainians instead of others."

"Who else would be interested in blowing up the armory? The Russians themselves?" Sam asked.

"That's my suspicion."

"But why would they do that?" Sam asked. "There's a lot of friction internally in the Russian military, but how does an explosion at the weapons site help any Russian faction when it comes to the war with Ukraine?"

Straw shrugged. "Heaven help the fool, but my guess is that it relates exclusively to the nuclear weapons at the site and has nothing to do with the war in Ukraine."

Straw let his revelation sink in, then continued, "This is just a theory, but it's the only thing that makes sense to me. Why else would some of the guards have bullet wounds? Why else would there be no radar evidence of incoming Ukraine missiles? Why else would the radioactive discharge be less than expected for two nukes that were supposedly destroyed at the site? And why was Putrid so quick to publicly acknowledge and condemn the attack? My fear is that someone inside of Russia, possibly with Putrid's knowledge, now has possession of a baby nuke that the rest of the world community does not think exists. One man gathers what another man spills."

The gravity of Straw's theory that a rogue nuclear weapon was in the hands of unknown people, who had the skills and resources to perpetrate the camouflaged bombing of the Russian armory, hit everyone at GROSS like a Bud Crawford uppercut.

Nick's eyes were bulging and his heart racing. "Straw, does anyone else in the intelligence community think this?"

"Not that I know."

The GROSS office became as quiet and somber as the Dean Smith Center after losing to Duke in basketball. After a few seconds, Straw got a faraway look in his eyes and reverted to reciting Grateful Dead lyrics.

"Some folks trust in reason, others trust in might. When life looks like it's on easy street, there is danger at your door. Trouble ahead, trouble behind."

Before he could get too isolated with his own thoughts, Sam broke in. "Straw, what can we do to help?"

"First, let's hope I'm wrong. Second, let's continue to stay vigilant and try to figure out what is really happening. Third, pray!"

Nick put his hand on Straw's shoulder.

"Straw, you once told me your job was to shed light, and that strategy was your strength, not disaster. I don't fully know what all that means, but I've got one hundred percent confidence that you will figure this all out."

"Thanks for the vote of confidence."

"You got this, Straw," Sam added. "But never forget, we're here for you."

83

MATAMOROS, MEXICO, FEBRUARY 10, 2023

Delayed a few days by inclement weather, the ship containing cargo that was highly valued by wealthy businessman and drug overlord Salvador Santos arrived in Matamoros, Mexico. Hefty advance payments to port officials provided assurance that the valued cargo would be transferred to the possession of business associates of Santos, the 'Mexican Midas', without incident or inspection.

Everything with respect to the transport and transfer of the precious container went perfectly according to plan until possession was handed over to Jefe's trusted first assistant, Miguel Ramirez. Assisting with the physical transfer of the crate was an intimidating, muscular man from the cargo ship that everyone thought was just an employee of the shipping line. He had short brown hair, broad shoulders, a chiseled face with protruding cheekbones, and a two-inch scar on the side of his left eye. At the point of transfer, the man spoke up.

"I have an urgent message for your boss, Salvador Santos."

The mention of Jefe's real name shocked Miguel Ramirez. Jefe had made it emphatically clear that all actions with respect to the cargo were to be totally confidential.

"I don't know who or what you are talking about," started Ramirez, "but I can assure you that any attempt to change our plans will meet with your immediate death. I have snipers in strategic positions throughout these docks."

"Cut the bullshit," said the man in a Russian accent.

The man held out his hand to show a device the size of a small cell phone, with a blinking red light on the front.

"I have this message," he said holding a sealed envelope in his left hand, "from Russian President Putrid. I am to deliver it personally to your boss, along with this cargo. If I am prevented from doing this, my instructions are to push a button on this device. This will explode your cargo and kill us all."

"What do you want?" Ramirez asked.

"We either go to your boss's house in Veracruz or you can ask Mr. Santos to meet us here in Matamoros. In all events, I am never to leave this crate. Just so you know, if this device drops from my hand without a code being entered in five seconds, the detonation will occur. Do not even think about killing me before I've met your boss."

Ramirez's face went white, but quickly responded, "I have to make a phone call." He walked beyond earshot of the Russian and pulled out a burner phone.

Ramirez was shaking slightly when he hung up the phone and turned to speak to the Russian. "My boss is not happy about this surprise."

"Happy or not, he has no choice," replied the Russian matter-of-factly.

"He has agreed to meet, but it's too risky for us to drive the twelve hours to Veracruz. Based on what just happened, he's not comfortable meeting here at the docks in Matamoros. He has agreed to meet at one of our safe warehouses in Reynosa, which is just about an hour drive from here. He will go by helicopter and meet us there."

"That is acceptable," said the Russian.

84

REYNOSA, MEXICO, FEBRUARY 10, 2023

A truck used to transport avocados was loaded with an added cargo, the crate containing the baby nuke, along with Ramirez and the Russian in the back of the vehicle. It began its unplanned journey to Reynosa as Jefe boarded his helicopter with the same destination. During the flight, Jefe ordered extra guards to provide security at the Reynosa warehouse.

Jefe's helicopter arrived first at the warehouse. He exited the chopper and entered his secure warehouse, which had been used for years as a center for drug distribution into the United States. He confirmed the location of the added security men at the facility, then stood in the middle of the entry road. His wait was not long as he received a text from Ramirez that the truck was just a minute away. Jefe gave Ramirez the 'go ahead' to continue and enter the warehouse.

The doors of the warehouse opened for the avocado truck, then closed quickly after the vehicle had entered. Jefe motioned the driver to continue to where he was standing. The driver obeyed, stopping a few feet from Jefe before turning off the engine. The rear of the truck opened, and Ramirez and the Russian stepped out.

"I never deal with someone whose name I don't know," said Jefe to the Russian. "Tell me who you are."

"Dmitri Federov, at your service," said the Russian, extending his hand to Jefe.

"I need to know more before I will shake your hand," replied Jefe sternly. "I do not like surprises."

Federov extended an envelope to Jefe, who opened its contents and began reading:

> *Sr. Santos,*
>
> *I look forward to a long and prosperous partnership. As part of this partnership, I require that my associate, Dmitri Federov, accompany the cargo wherever it goes and assist you in all your efforts.*
>
> *Vladimir Putrid*

Jefe paused, and then extended a hand to Federov.

"Welcome, Mr. Federov. I guess we are partners. But if you ever cross me or my men, you're dead."

Jefe walked back to the helicopter. He entered it while muttering, "I hate doing business with freakin' corrupt Russians."

85

VERACRUZ, MEXICO, FEBRUARY 14, 2023

Jefe and Professor had just finished an election status update call on burner phones when Jefe said, "Professor, I know you are curious, so here's the update on our special cargo from Russia. Tomorrow is moving day into the U.S."

"Do you mind me asking how you plan to get it across the border, and then to Goliath?"

"I'm glad you asked that. Let me answer by giving you some background regarding our product distribution network. A significant portion of our business in the U.S. is very similar to that of American farmers. Our marijuana harvest happens primarily in the fall, and we need to quickly get our inventory to the U.S. However, the U.S. has increasingly fortified the border since the Triumph administration, and it's harder than ever to transport our drugs 'over' the border without being detected. Accordingly, we've adjusted and built large tunnels to transport our drugs 'under' the border. Unfortunately, the Drug Enforcement Agency isn't that far behind us, and is using ground penetrating radar and seismic technology to find our tunnels. We used to have four tunnels to move our product into the U.S., but border agents have found two of them. Thankfully, they have not located our two most sophisticated tunnels, one that crosses over into Nogales, Arizona and the other that goes under the Tijuana airport runways into San

Diego. I've coordinated with my allies on both sides of the border, and tomorrow night looks like the best time to move our valued product with the least risk of any detection during its journey. We will use the tunnel that goes into Nogales. Once we get the baby nuke to the U.S. side, it will be picked up by you and our Russian 'friend', Dmitri, in a U-Haul truck, along with miscellaneous items of furniture that will be used at Goliath."

"What?" asked Professor with shock in his voice. "You want me to drive the nuke from Arizona to Goliath?"

"Yes," replied Jefe. "This is the most valuable cargo that we have ever transported, and you are the person I trust most. Let's be honest. If you were pulled over by police, you are the person in my employ who is least likely to be suspected of moving illegal items across the country. I don't think you even have a parking ticket on your record."

"How do I explain about Dmitri if we are stopped?" Professor asked uncomfortably.

"That is easy," replied Jefe. "As you know, he has been instructed by those in Russia to accompany the 'asset' wherever it goes, and I've reluctantly agreed. However, sometimes the Russians are more thoughtful than I usually give them credit for. Dmitri has a visa permitting him to reside in the U.S. Your story, if you're ever asked, is that he is a friend of one of your politician friends in Washington, and you are helping him move to the area."

"How did he ever get that visa?" ask Professor.

"He's had if for a while under America's EB-5 program."

"What's that?"

"It's a program whereby foreign immigrants can get accelerated visas for permanent residency if they are willing to pay the price and meet a background check. This is basically a way for rich foreigners to buy their way into the U.S."

"Unbelievable!" exclaimed Professor.

"I thank you for assisting me in transporting this valuable cargo, Professor. My plane will pick you up tomorrow afternoon at 5 p.m. at the normal location. Sorry if this forces you to juggle some appointments."

"I understand and will be at your service, Jefe," Professor said, trying to hide the anxiety he was feeling.

"Great. Once you get to Nogales, my people will give you the details of when and where the U-Haul will be ready for you to begin your trip. Drive safely my friend, and enjoy your time with Dmitri," Jefe said with a laugh.

86

GROSS OFFICE, FEBRUARY 15, 2023

It had been a full month since Straw first postulated that a nuclear bomb may have been stolen as part of the attack on the Russian munitions armory. Intelligence work took patience. Straw could only work as fast as the other U.S. intelligence agencies gathered useful information. But Straw's patience was noticeably waning. He sensed he was alone in his theory of the stolen nuke, and he detected no urgency or interest in the intelligence community regarding the event. It seemed, in their view, that it was just another event in the course of a war, and even the destruction of nuclear weapons did not merit more focus.

Whenever Straw was annoyed with the progress of his intelligence analytics, he would ask Nick and Sam to sit with him. They would serve as a sounding board for Straw to discuss the case and his theories. That day was one of those times, and Straw asked both to gather around his desk while they all ate Taco Bell.

"Thanks for letting me bounce stuff off you guys," said Straw as he took a bite of a bean burrito. "I'm sure you've sensed my frustration that I haven't been able to prove a rogue nuke is out there that nobody thinks is missing. Unfortunately, this is still just a theory. My gut tells me that something big is happening, but I'm not getting any helpful data from the intelligence services. I feel like I'm not just looking for the needle in the haystack, but I'm looking for the unique pebble of sand on a resort-sized beach. I've bent my ear to hear and closed my eyes to see, but everything is still fuzzy and so obscure."

"Is there anything we can do to help bring clarity?" Sam asked.

"Just being my backboard helps."

"We're happy to help," Nick said. "Where can we start?"

"When I'm stuck in a funk, I usually go back to the basics. Why do terrorists get caught?"

"Greed?" suggested Nick.

"No. The biggest reason terrorists are caught is they make a mistake. Most of the mistakes involve an unintended conversation. This can be from email, because even with encryption safeguards and sophisticated operating systems, nothing is totally secure. But, most often, the mistake is just human-oriented. People are imperfect. No matter how tightly contained an organization thinks it is, one slip of the tongue to a spouse or a friend, or due to alcohol or drugs, can create an opening for the good guys to stop the bad guys."

Straw paused, reflecting on his words, and then continued. "We must also always consider that power and money are great corruptors, and, in my mind, the Russian sky stinks with greed. It is very unusual that people seeking power or riches can ignore their temptations, and ultimately a weak link will show itself. When this happens, we must not miss the opportunity to learn, capitalize, and react. As the saying goes, 'loose lips sink ships' and that's very true. It's often the lazy or lax communications that upend even the best laid plan."

"So, have you seen any suspicious conversation that might support your theory?" asked Nick.

"Not really, at least nothing that I've been able to connect yet. It's the trouble with me… I've got two good eyes but I still don't see."

Samantha interjected, "That might be because our Flame malware has not yet been implanted very extensively in Russia."

"What's Flame again?" asked Nick.

"Flame is a government-developed spyware computer program that allows us to see and hear all communications on another person's computer or cell phone," Sam said. "So, if we are looking for an errant conversation that identifies a big mistake, that's often when our Flame malware can be most helpful."

As Sam and Nick were talking, something caused Straw to sit up straight in his chair.

"You know, maybe there has been some recent chatter that is interesting… or at least strange. Sometimes the obvious is hidden."

Straw started typing furiously on his keyboard. After a short time, he motioned for Nick and Sam to look at his screens.

"I recently received information from STRATCOM and its headquarters in your home city of Omaha, Nick. STRATCOM does lots of things, including coverage of weapons of mass destruction and cyber and information warfare. Until talking with you, I think I was blind all the time I was learning to see. There's nothing definite here, but this transmission from STRATCOM is interesting and merits more of our attention."

"I can't read it very well from here. What does the STRATCOM transmission say?" Nick asked.

"Nothing that is directly helpful, but it confirms that Medvedev was the primary person in contact on multiple occasions with Putrid about the explosion at the armory and the loss of the two nuclear weapons. It also tracks known conversations that Medvedev and, to a lesser extent, Putrid had in the months before and after the explosion. Some of the communications of Medvedev that were intercepted by STRATCOM were with a party in an undetermined place in Mexico. That would make for some strange bedfellows, since there isn't a whole lot of commerce that gets done between those two. Hmmm, I wonder if the missing nuke is now in Mexico?"

Straw paused, and then concluded the lunch by saying, "Thanks, guys. You've helped me focus. This may not be a smoking gun, but it's at least something for me to look at more closely, which may connect with something else. I might as well try. Once in a while you get shown the light, in the strangest of places, if you look at it right."

"You're welcome, we think," said Sam, exchanging a confused expression with Nick as Straw dove back into his data.

87

TUCSON, ARIZONA, FEBRUARY 15, 2023

Professor arrived at Tucson International Airport in Jefe's plane, where he was greeted by a man who simply introduced himself as Roberto. Roberto led him to an unwashed 2017 Honda CRV parked nearby.

After they got in the car, Roberto spoke. "Mr. Professor, Jefe sends his apologies that you will be traveling in neither class nor comfort on this trip. But he reminds you that it is for the best. Nobody will pay any attention to this car."

"Of course, Roberto. No apology necessary. I once owned a Honda CRV and was very fond of it."

"Feel free to relax. I have water available for our drive, which should take us about an hour to get to Nogales. When we get there, we are to park at the Mariposa Hotel and have dinner in the Latin Steakhouse inside the hotel. It is actually a very good restaurant. After dinner, a U-Haul will come to the hotel parking lot where you will exchange places with the driver. I'll be sure to pay the dinner bill."

88

NOGALES, ARIZONA, FEBRUARY 15, 2023

Professor was just finishing his meal when Roberto received a text.

"Our friends are five minutes away," informed Roberto, as he motioned to the waitress to bring the check.

Roberto paid for their dinner in cash, then walked with Professor to the hotel parking lot. A twenty-foot U-Haul truck entered the lot and stopped next to the Honda CRV. The driver of the U-Haul exited the big truck, got a nod from Roberto, and handed the keys to Professor without saying a word. He and Roberto then got into the Honda CRV and drove away.

Professor climbed into the U-Haul and saw, for the first time, Dmitri Medvedev sitting in the passenger seat. Dmitri extended a hand and introduced himself with a smile, "Professor, I'm Dimitri. It is nice to meet you. I have heard many good things about you."

Professor shook Dmitri's hand and said, "Nice to meet you as well."

Before Professor could say anything more, Dmitri said, "Let's get going. I have all the directions for our trip. We have 2,300 miles to cover before we arrive at Goliath. We are never to exceed the speed limit and we are to stop for gas any time our fuel gauge reaches one-quarter of a tank. Every time we refuel, we are to switch drivers so that our driver is fresh and never drowsy. We will drive a little more than half of our journey now, until we stop to spend tomorrow night at a Holiday Inn in

Little Rock. Jefe has arranged for some of his people to watch over our truck while we sleep to make sure that it is not subject to any random break-in or theft attempt."

Dmitri then started typing on his laptop. Professor drove in silence for much of the next three hours, other than getting an occasional instruction from Dmitri regarding directions or upcoming construction work on the interstate.

Professor glanced at the truck's fuel gauge.

"Dmitri, we'll be at a quarter of a tank of gas soon. I'll stop at the next gas station at an interstate exit. Let me ask you two questions. First, and I'm embarrassed that I don't know the answer to this, but do you drive in the right or left lane in Russia? And second, do you need a license to drive in America, just in case we are ever stopped?"

Dmitri looked up from his laptop.

"Professor, we drive on the same side of the road in Russia as you do here. You do not need to worry about me having any head-on collision. On the second question, I am allowed to drive in the U.S. with a valid foreign driver's license, which I have. I also carry an International Driving Permit along with my foreign license because some states require that."

89

FEBRUARY 15, 2023

After they had filled the tank and switched drivers, Professor thought it was the right opportunity to get to know Dmitri better.

"So, Dmitri, I think you know a lot more about me than I do about you. Please tell me about yourself."

Expecting a short and curt answer, Professor was surprised with how open Dmitri was with his response.

"I was born and have lived all of my life in Moscow," started Dmitri, speaking with just a slight Russian accent. "I am the son of civil servants, and my father is one of the 450 elected members of the Duma. That is Russia's Parliament, although you know the real power all lies with President Putrid. Because of the position of my father in the Duma, I was able to avoid conscription into the Russian military and I studied at Russia's best university, Lomonosov Moscow State University, specifically its Institute of Physics & Technology. I graduated with dual degrees in computer science and physics."

"Did you enjoy your studies, and is the Russian education system good?" Professor asked.

"I did. And, the Russian education is not just good, it's great. Most people don't appreciate this, but Russia has a long-standing tradition of high-quality education for all citizens. Russia's education system produces a ninety-eight percent literacy rate, one of the highest in the world."

"I did not know that. What did you do after graduation?"

"The first thing I did was get married to Svetlana, my best friend from university. She and I now have two beautiful children, a boy aged nine and a girl aged seven. After university, my father 'blat'... oh, how do you say in English? My father used his connections and pulled strings to get me a job with the Ministry of Foreign Affairs. That is the main government institution charged with leading the foreign policy and foreign relations of Russia. As you can see, I really have not put my university degrees to very good use!" Dmitri said with a real laugh and smile.

"And you have worked there ever since?"

"Da. Since the Ukraine invasion started, I have served as an intermediary between those in Putrid's inner circle and the leaders of the Vagner Group. That is where I met Colonel Medvedev."

"So, if you don't mind me asking, what do you think of the war with Ukraine?" asked Professor tentatively.

"War of any nature is horrible, and this war did not need to happen. Putrid is, at his core, a power monger... a small man with a Napoleon complex."

Dmitri's frankness caused Professor to laugh. "Wow! I did not expect that response!"

"But it is true. The Russian people hate this war and the unnecessary killing, on both sides. But nobody can stand up to Putrid and call him out for his outlandish actions. It seems to be the same in the U.S. and the crazy behavior that your Triumph gets away with."

"You know, Dmitri, you are not the person I envisioned you to be. I saw a Russian with a scar on his face and I immediately thought you would just be a robotic, stone-cold killer like in the movies. Instead, you are an educated, multi-faceted family man with views on foreign events that I never expected. By the way, how did you get the scar on your face?"

"It was not a knife fight with the Russian mafia, if that is what you were thinking. I was cut by the blade of a hockey skate when I fell while playing youth hockey. I never was very good in that sport."

"Dmitri, I really like you. I think we are very similar even though we are from very different parts of the world."

"Da, we are good guys who just happen to work for ruthless bosses."

The comment caught Professor by surprise. While he hadn't viewed Jefe as a ruthless person, he could see how Dmitri would think along those lines. Likewise, he truly sympathized for the uncomfortable position in which Dmitri was operating, serving both Putrid and Medvedev, who truly were monsters in human skins. Dmitri's comment made Professor continue to think as the U-Haul drove down the interstate. *Here I am transporting a nuclear bomb across the country to help Jefe take over control of the entire executive branch of our government. Maybe Jefe is more ruthless and selfish than I thought,* mused Professor to himself.

90

GOLIATH FACILITY WOODSBORO, MARYLAND, FEBRUARY 17, 2023

The Goliath facility, located approximately twelve miles from Camp David, was still in the process of construction when Professor and Dmitri drove in with their U-Haul as sundown neared. Though the final campus was far from complete, the contractor had done expedited work to finish a large, secure underground storage room for the valuable cargo that had just arrived. With the assistance of the well-paid and loyal construction team, Professor and Dmitri helped unload the crate and carefully placed it in the storage room.

After the crate and the storage room were secure, Professor placed a call to Jefe.

"Jefe, we have arrived at our destination. Our cargo has been unloaded and is secure."

"That is great news, Professor. Thank you for your services. How was the trip with Dmitri?"

"Actually, it was very enjoyable. He has a fascinating background and is someone I now consider a friend. Like you, he is a highly educated family man, and nothing is more important to him than his wife and children. He even taught me some Russian during our trip."

"Excellent, though your impression of him is vastly different than my first reaction. All for the better, I suppose. Now, go get some sleep because tomorrow I would like to get your update on Silvia's race for the presidency."

"That sounds great. Thank you, Jefe."

Professor and Dmitri then got in the U-Haul for their last trip together. Professor dropped Dmitri off at a nearby Hampton Inn, where Dmitri would stay while he oversaw the construction of Goliath.

"Spasiba," said Professor to Dmitri as he exited the U-Haul.

"Your Russian is excellent, Professor. Thank you as well. I'm sure our paths will cross again."

"I hope so. Best wishes my friend," Professor said as he shook Dmitri's hand. Professor then drove off in the U-Haul to his house in Washington where his own bed would welcome his tired body.

91

FEBRUARY 17, 2023

"Hello, Professor," said Jefe as he answered his burner phone. "I trust you got a good night of sleep after your exhausting drive across the country. I can't imagine those U-Haul trucks are very comfortable."

"I admit that I've traveled in more comfortable vehicles, but I was happy to trade that for a safe and uneventful trip."

"I agree!" exclaimed Jefe. "I'm very thankful that our valuable cargo has been delivered to Goliath. But now let's discuss what we need to do so we don't have to use that fallback plan. Please give me your assessment of Silvia's challengers for the Republican nomination."

"Happy to do so. While more people are likely to enter the race, the frontrunner is obviously Donald Triumph. Ever since he formally announced his campaign in 2023, Triumph has been working hard to reassemble the voting coalition that supported him in 2016."

"Is he succeeding in that effort?" asked Jefe.

"I don't think so... at least not yet. Triumph is very polarizing and people either hate him or love him. Today there are about thirty percent of Republican voters who are "Always Triumphers". These voters are like lemmings and are willing to follow him over a cliff without any hesitation or second thoughts. The rest of the voters are probably split, with about thirty percent of people being in the "Never Triumpher" class and forty percent being in the "Maybe Triumpher" category."

"I'm still shocked he's a viable candidate after his actions inciting the attack on the Capitol on January 6," Jefe said.

"I agree. That would normally make lots of voters see him as a dangerous, self-centered candidate. However, he has a unique ability to weather storms that others do not possess. Triumph has proven that we should never underestimate the power of money, celebrity, and fame in American politics. It worked in the past for Raygun, Schwarzenhamer, and Triumph himself in 2016. Even when things go bad for Triumph, he will be able to use his money, notoriety, and core supporters to stay in the race. In fact, he plays the witch-hunt victim better than anyone. He always gets a big boost in fundraising every time he is subpoenaed or indicted. It's really incredible and shows the measure of his hold on the Republican party!"

Jefe spoke up. "It sounds to me like we need to focus our efforts on getting the thirty percent Never Triumphers and the forty percent Maybe Triumpher voters to favor Silvia. What do we need to do that?"

"As we strategize for the upcoming election, we must focus on many things, but one of the most important is what I like to call the 'Diploma Divide'. The 'Diploma Divide' is the education factor that is reshaping national elections and the statistics are staggering. White voters who do not have college degrees have turned into the backbone of the Republican party. In both 2016 and 2020, Triumph had more than a 35-point advantage over both Hillary and Burden in getting non-college white voters. The reverse is true on the flip side of the coin... Democrats now routinely win by significant margins the votes of white people with college degrees. As a challenger to Triumph, we need to have distinctive marketing plans based on whether the target of the pitch is college educated or not. I will strategize with Silvia to tailor her campaign pitches accordingly."

Jefe nodded in agreement before saying, "Let's do a deeper dive on campaign issues and strategy later. Let's just focus now on the candidates. But before doing that, here's a question I've had for a long time about America's two-party system. Do you think there is any chance that an independent or third-party candidate could ever prevail?"

Professor replied, "That is a very interesting question. The short answer for the 2024 election is 'no', but beyond that there may be possibilities. The United States is amazing in that almost half of adults identify as independent instead of being loyal to either the Republican or Democrat parties. I think this shows great frustration with the two-party system, the bottleneck that has occurred in Washington, and the plain fact that the parties have not nominated quality candidates for the highest office in the world in the last couple of elections. How crazy is it that voters will likely be given the option of selecting between Triumph and Burden? Is that really the best we can do? Choose between Triumph, a man facing numerous lawsuits and likely criminal indictments, or Burden, whose academic credentials include being near the bottom of his law school class and who would be the oldest elected president ever? It's crazy!

"Sorry," Professor said. "I got a little emotional and carried away there! Let me get back to your question. While America may really need a third-party alternative, currently nobody speaks for or represents people who identify as independents. There has never really been a serious third-party candidate in the past. All prior third-party candidates, like Ralph Nadero, were really just 'protest' candidates who didn't have a real chance of winning. With the amount of public discontent with Washington right now, there may be a new lane for an independent or no-label third party. However, until a third party gets its organization and political machinery in place across the country and offers a desirable candidate, it won't be a viable challenger. For our purposes, that's not really the key analysis. Even though a third-party candidate can't win in 2024, the votes that a third-party candidate gets would most likely otherwise go to Burden. This could have an impact on the final outcome of a close race."

"OK, let's discuss some of the other candidates and their chances of winning."

"Excellent. Let's start with Florida Governor Ron DeRantis. Somewhat like Silvia, he is another governor who is trying to use his success in governing at the state level to propel him to the presidency. I look at DeRantis like he is a mini version of Triumph, but without all the baggage. He is going to bring the conservative, 'anti-woke' crusade policies he championed in Florida to the national stage. However, DeRantis has a lot of hurdles to overcome. First, he does not relate well to people, and he's not nearly as likeable as his wife. Second, even before DeRantis formally entered the election, Triumph came out with attack ads that effectively painted DeRantis as a person who is unprepared for the presidency. Third, DeRantis is positioning himself as super conservative and on the far right of the party. But this is where the loyal 'Always Triumpher' voters live, not the more moderate voters who are more likely to leave Triumph. No challenger can beat Triumph by trying to be more conservative than Triumph."

Professor let his analysis sink in and then concluded, "So, my ultimate prediction about DeRantis is that voters won't find him ready for prime time. He is starting in second place, and I think he's destined to go no higher. His most critical role may be to use his money and large campaign organization to compete effectively in the early Iowa and New Hampshire primaries. If he doesn't do that, the main concern I have is that Triumph could win the early primaries by a large margin and then steamroll through the entire remaining slate of primaries, which would be bad for Silvia. So, in a strange way, it may be best for us in the long run if DeRantis gains some traction and makes the early primaries competitive."

"Thanks for that insightful analysis, Professor. What about some of the other candidates?"

"Sure. Let's discuss Nikki Hayley. Like Silvia and DeRantis, Hayley is a governor with an impressive resume. She was governor of South Carolina before serving as United Nations ambassador under Triumph. I expect that this past relationship with Triumph may result in some unique dynamics and fireworks between her and Triumph on the campaign trail. Triumph usually implodes when challenged by a strong woman. Hayley is also a woman of color as the daughter of immigrants from India, and she's the only female candidate in the race other than Silvia. She's a very effective speaker and does great face-to-face with voters."

Professor paused for a second and then continued. "All of those factors lead me to believe that Hayley may really surprise and do well in Iowa and other early primaries. Polls don't show her connecting with voters enough yet to be a real challenger. But, at a minimum, Hayley will shift the debate and allow people to consider whether the next generation of Republican candidates is ready to step in. Silvia does this as well. I think that Hayley, DeRantis, and Silvia are all hoping they can convince voters that Republicans need a generational change, a nod to both Triumph's age and his temperament. Ultimately, however, I don't envision Hayley making a strong challenge. Silvia's involvement in the race hurts Hayley since Silvia is more enticing in many respects. Silvia has the same or better credentials as a successful governor. Silvia will get more of the important Hispanic vote. Silvia has better notoriety and recognition from the press that she received during the failed Spence assassination and her SlamRod nickname from A-Rod. And, pardon my sexism, Silvia is simply better looking than Hayley. Overall, it would be to our benefit if Hayley were to drop out of the race quickly since I don't want Hayley to take any support of women voters away from us."

"Speaking of Spence, what do you think of his chances in the race?" Jefe asked.

"Unfortunately, I don't think he has much of a chance. I say 'unfortunately' because I respect Spence for having the courage to resist Triumph's attempt to use Spence to overturn the results of the 2020 election. However, ever since then, Spence has been reluctant to criticize Triumph for his January 6 actions even though they put Spence in fear of his life. That is a huge strategic error by Spence and makes him look like he lacks spine. As they say, 'nice guys finish last.' However, with his credentials in office, Spence may be someone that Silvia should consider as her VP if she wins the Republican nomination."

"What about any other candidates?"

"I think only two of them really merit any attention right now, Chris Christee and Trim Scott. I will say that I'm a bit surprised that New Hampshire Governor Sununu didn't join the race. He's also part of the next generation of Republicans and he has a great record of getting things done in New Hampshire, an important early primary state that could have given him a big boost. However, he chose not to run so his role will be limited to being a potential VP candidate.

"With that said, let me start with Chris Christee, the rotund former governor of New Jersey. I initially thought he joined the race just to derail Triumph. But now, I don't think his mission is purely Kamikaze-like. I could see a narrow path of success for Christee. He's a great debater who is not afraid to go on the attack on the debate stage. In the last debate he effectively gutted candidate Marco Rubioh and ended his presidential aspirations. This alone may make Triumph not participate in any debates under the guise that he's far enough ahead that he doesn't have to get on the stage. If they both end up on the debate stage, watch out for the fireworks because I think Christee will treat it like the start of World War III."

Professor continued, "With that said, the fact remains that Christee has been out of office and out of the spotlight for the last five years. I think the New Hampshire primary will be critical for Christee if he is to have any chance of being a long-term factor in the race. I think people will like the fact that he's very direct, but he treads a fine line between being direct and being too confrontational. Time will tell."

"OK, let's conclude this session with my analysis of Trim Scott. Basically, he's a great story… a nice guy with a good tone and the only Black Republican in the Senate. This could make him an excellent VP for whatever candidate wins the Republican nomination, except for Silvia."

"Why do you say that?" interjected Jefe.

"Because if Silvia is the Republican nominee, I don't think America is ready to elect a ticket that is comprised of a Hispanic woman and a Black man."

"OK, that makes sense. Please continue about Scott."

"Scott is from South Carolina like Hayley, and he offers a completely different tone than Triumph and an alternative to DeRantis. He has a respected and fresh conservative perspective. His positive demeanor and approach will resonate with voters, but I think he's going to have a hard time standing out from Triumph's shadow. It's hard to stand up to Triumph when Scott's record in Congress shows that he voted ninety-seven percent along with the Triumph line."

"Thank you, Professor. Where do you think this leaves us at the current time? Does Silvia have a chance of winning? And, is America ready for a president who is a female?"

"I think when the dust settles, the race will be between Silvia and Triumph to win the Republican nomination. In the end, I think Silvia is the only real candidate who is moderate enough to win against Burden in the general election due to her ability to attract minority and independent voters. We need to impress upon Republican voters the importance of her electability in contrast to Triumph, who is a magnet for drama and distraction. Let's hope Chris Christee asks Republican voters how they could ever elect Triumph to the most powerful position in the world when he could be facing prison time once pending legal trials get concluded. And, yes, I think America is ready for a female president if it is the right woman. Hilary almost got elected and she had a lot of negatives that Silvia doesn't have. Silvia will be an inviting alternative to the other candidates on the slate."

"I'm happy to hear your optimism, Professor," Jefe said. "But I've learned that there are a lot of moving parts in electoral politics, so I'm glad we have some fallback plans if needed. Now, assuming we can get Silvia on the Republican ticket, either as the presidential candidate or as a VP on the Triumph ticket, what do you think our chances are of beating the Democrat candidate, who I assume will be Burden, in the general election?"

"Here is where I think the power of Silvia's ability to attract moderates and voters of color will really make a difference. If she competes directly against Burden for the presidency, then I think she will get a groundswell of support for what she represents, much like the support Olama received when he ran for president. On the other hand, if it's Triumph against Burden, then I think that race is too close to call right now. Triumph has baggage that will follow him through the entire campaign. Burden is aging fast, but has already beaten Triumph once before.

If Silvia is Triumph's running mate, she may be able to pull in enough votes to swing things in Triumph's favor. If Triumph picks a different running mate, it will be a tight race, but I don't see how he beats Burden. Since this is not a business in which outcomes can be predicted with precision, I am also glad that we have our fallback plans."

92

MINNEAPOLIS, MINNESOTA, JUNETEENTH 2023

Silvia Rodriguez arrived at the Minneapolis-Saint Paul International Airport after flying coach from Phoenix on the morning of June 19. She got into a cab at the airport and asked the driver to take her to the location where George Floyd had been painfully murdered. Silvia thought back to the horrifying images of a white policeman who played judge, jury, and executioner. A white policeman who slowly strangled to death a Black man, suspected of using a forged twenty-dollar bill, in front of a crowd of bystanders, other cops, and countless cameras.

Silvia noticed that the cab driver kept doing double-takes of her in his rearview mirror. After exiting the airport grounds, the cab driver finally got the nerve to speak up.

"Pardon me, ma'am, but aren't you SlamRod?"

"Yes, I am," she said with a genuine smile. "And you can call me either Silvia or SlamRod, whichever you prefer."

For the duration of the cab ride, Silvia put her cell phone away and engaged in pleasant conversation with the driver, an African American man in his mid-30's named Tyus Tatum. Tatum told Silvia that he had been laid off from his corporate job during Covid and was now working multiple jobs to keep his wife and two children afloat. When they arrived at their destination, Silvia gave him her autograph at his request and added a nice, personal message to it. She shook his hand from the back seat, wished him well, and then exited the cab.

Waiting for Silvia was a camera crew that Professor had lined up to do a publicity shoot in which Silvia would honor the nation's Juneteenth celebration. Professor told her the segment would be distributed to key TV and broadcast stations across the country in a 'media blast' that would continue to elevate her profile and recognition to voters. Silvia remembered Professor telling her that "we need to emphasize our color and embrace and highlight diversity as positive points in our favor."

When the video team was happy with the lighting, sound, and location of Silvia, a local news station reporter selected by Professor began the interview.

"Governor and Congresswoman and presidential candidate Silvia Rodriguez, thank you for coming to Minneapolis to talk with us. What are your thoughts on this national holiday, Juneteenth?"

"Thank you for welcoming me to Minnesota. It is a pleasure to be here," started Silvia. "This is a very historic day, and we are in a very historic location that I really wanted to see and feel for myself... the place where George Floyd was killed about three years ago. There are lots of lessons to be learned from the murder of George Floyd and the history of racism in our country. That is especially true today as we reflect on and celebrate Juneteenth, the day the end of slavery was finally communicated to slaves in Texas in 1865. We all need to open our eyes, minds, and hearts, and take transformative action to eliminate inequality and racism. This is not a topic to be avoided, but one that should be discussed openly and often, not only in this upcoming election, but in everyday life. We need to call on employers, businesses, and schools to take steps to diversify in hiring and to address pay inequalities. Only by discussing the topic in a mature and responsible way can the system and narrative be changed."

The staged interview continued a few minutes longer and Professor quickly had adequate material that could be edited for news 'bites' of varying durations. Members of Professor's election team made the edits and circulated the material to numerous broadcast and social media outlets. When Professor watched clips of Silvia later that day, he was pleased with the outcome, and happy that Silvia's natural beauty and engaging nature made her instantly likeable to a broad swath of viewers. Professor was just about to call it a night when he saw an unplanned piece of publicity about Silvia courtesy of WCCO-TV, Minneapolis' largest TV station. Somehow, they had located Tyus Tatum, the cab driver who took Silvia to the George Floyd location.

"She is the nicest and most caring person I've ever met," raved Tyus. "She didn't act like a 'big shot' at all and paid total attention to me our whole trip, where most of my other passengers just stare at their smart phones. She'll get my vote for sure. I hope she's our next president."

Wow! thought Professor to himself. *With all the work we did today to get Silvia on multiple broadcasts, that unplanned bit from a Black cab driver is the absolute BEST publicity we could ever get.*

93

GROSS OFFICE, JUNE 30, 2023

Nick entered the GROSS office and sat at his desk. Before engaging in any friendly chit-chat, Straw went straight to business with an energized but serious look on his face.

"Remember the calls that STRATCOM intercepted a while ago regarding the two nukes that were supposedly destroyed by a Ukraine missile?" Straw asked. "STRATCOM indicated there were calls before and after the event between Medvedev and someone in Mexico. Even though the calls were always on a burner phone in Mexico, I've finally been able to triangulate the rough location of the calls in Mexico. They all went through a cell tower in Veracruz, Mexico."

"There are a lot of people who live in Veracruz. How does that help us?" Nick asked.

"Sometimes it's like a game of connecting dots," Straw replied. "It seems like every day in the past couple of months, new information would arise that alters my theory of the missing nuke in vital ways. It's like working on a puzzle or piece of art that changes its appearance when you look at it from a different angle."

Straw looked at Nick to confirm that he was still following him and then continued. "The source of information often colors how I analyze it. For instance, military intelligence is usually pretty straight forward since you generally know who your adversary is. That may have thrown me off a little here, considering the connection of Medvedev with the Vagner Group and the Russian military. In contrast, the world of finding and fighting terrorism is often quite different… the bad guys can come from outside or within and their gameplans have no limits. It makes me feel like I'm playing a high-stakes game of chess at times.

"In any event, I spent a lot of time looking for a military connection between Russia and Mexico with respect to the nuke that I thought was missing. I haven't come up with any military connection that makes sense. Russia has plenty of nukes in its intercontinental ballistic missiles that can easily reach the United States, and no one in North America would let Mexico become a nuclear power. It would be like the Bay of Pigs all over again. So, looking for a military connection really sent me down an unproductive rabbit hole. However, when I found that the calls from Medvedev went to Veracruz instead of Mexico City, where the Mexican government is located, this led me to start thinking about a non-military connection to the nuke."

"So, what are you thinking? Some sort of terrorism sourced in Veracruz that is directed at the U.S.?"

"I honestly don't know… yet. The truth is that all the communiques to and from Veracruz are still a mystery to me. No plan or motive is clear… yet. What I do know is that the calls all go to a cell tower in Veracruz that is close to the residence of Salvador Santos. Whenever things go on in Mexico, I've always had him on my list as a person of 'High Interest.'"

"Why?" Nick asked. "I know he's one of the richest people on the planet, but I read in a dossier my dad gave me that he also used lots of his wealth to do good things for others."

"Exactly right! He's a little too 'do gooder' for me," responded Straw, scratching his head. "I'm pretty sure that a lot of his wealth comes from drug trafficking. I've always thought the most dangerous enemy was one who could hide in plain sight… someone who everyone respected and nobody feared. He falls into that category for me. I hope I'm wrong, because if he's as dangerous as I fear, I dread what he might be able to accomplish with his wealth. Sometimes it's hard to tell the flowers from the weeds."

"But why would he ever need a nuke? And why would he do business with a guy like Medvedev?"

"I don't know… yet. But Medvedev's reputation for corruption is exceeded only by his reputation for deadliness. Connect that with a Mexican who has unfathomable wealth and drug interests, throw a nuclear device into mix, and you end up with a very scary combination."

94

MILWAUKEE, WISCONSIN, AUGUST 23, 2023

Professor's burner phone rang, and he quickly answered it.

"Good afternoon, Jefe. How are you?"

"Fine, fine," Jefe said. "More importantly, how is Silvia? Is SlamRod ready to hit a homerun in the debate tonight?"

"I think so, and we shall soon see. As you know, we've had her working with the best debate professionals in the country the last couple of weeks on her presentation style and strategy. In the last few days, Silvia and I have spent a lot of time on the issues and points to hammer home. She is a very quick study and I really think she will do well."

"Do you expect any big surprises in tonight's debate?"

"Obviously, the big news is that Triumph has decided not to participate in the first debate. He says this is because people already know him and he has a big enough lead in the polls that he doesn't feel challenged for the nomination. However, there's more to it than just that. With all the indictments and over ninety criminal charges pending against him, Triumph knows that he would be a massive target for criticism and concern."

"Even without Triumph, it looks like this could be a very interesting debate," Jefe said.

"Absolutely! The entire 2024 election looks like it will be one that captivates voters. This will increase the importance of televised debates, like the one tonight. It would surely smash previous viewership records if Triumph participated. But, even in his absence, I expect lots of people to watch just to see which candidates are willing to stand up to Triumph, and which ones want to cower in his shadow in the hope of being a potential VP selection. It's kind of a tricky line to walk, since the debate stage can provide the largest audience yet for many presidential hopefuls, but it also can trip up candidates."

"So, what will Silvia's approach be tonight?"

"Well, we know that Triumph has followed his history of going low during the campaign, adopting a scorched earth policy for everyone who confronts him. Even though he won't be there in person tonight, he will be a centerpiece of discussion. We need Silvia to take the high road of positivity where possible, but not be afraid to lock horns with Triumph when the opportunity arises. When it comes to divisive issues that don't pertain to Triumph, like reproductive rights and gun rights, I expect Silvia to be responsive, thoughtful, and caring without alienating any side if possible. I'm confident she'll do a great job."

"We'll soon see," said Jefe. "I'll talk with you after the debate is over."

95

MILWAUKEE, WISCONSIN, AUGUST 23, 2023

Seven candidates other than absentee-Triumph met the RNC's qualifications to participate in the first Republican debate. Silvia was located second from the far end of the stage, as the RNC positioned the candidates with the highest polling numbers in the center of the stage. Though not optimal, it did allow her to make a great first impression to viewers as she was the second candidate to walk on stage before the nationwide TV audience. Walking on the stage behind the rotund Chris Christee, Silvia presented quite an aesthetic contrast. She was impeccably dressed in a designer red Burberry-patterned knee-length skirt with a coordinated scoop neck three-quarter sleeve Marni blouse. Red patented leather pumps from Louboutin with the famed red lacquered soles put the finishing touches on her outfit.

Silvia was captivating, looking elegant but not presumptuous. She looked like she belonged on the stage, yet still made the other woman, Nikki Hayley, look frumpy. In comparison, all the male candidates looked stiff in their stale dark suits, light shirts, red ties, and American flag pins attached over their hearts.

Score the first point for Silvia, thought Professor as he watched the entrance of the candidates on his TV. *The camera seems to love her… beauty combined with class. She could have been a model on the runway, yet she did not look overstated, in part due to her understated makeup and jewelry. Beauty can be a powerful and attracting force, but it can also be a double-edged sword. We don't want to over-focus on Silvia's beauty and distract from her intelligence and record. And we definitely don't want to risk alienating the stay-at-home working mothers or other women voters watching the debate. I think we threaded the needle just right with respect to her appearance. Let's just hope she performs well in the debate,* mused Professor as he focused intently on his TV screen.

The moderator from Fox News started the debate with a discussion about foreign policy. Initial questions were addressed to frontrunner DeRantis and former VP Spence. Trim Scott then offered some additional thoughts, but the responses from all the candidates were very vanilla. When Scott had finished talking, Silvia saw an opening and injected herself into the conversation.

"I appreciate the views expressed by the other candidates so far," Silvia started diplomatically. "But, I think that many viewers tonight are looking to see how those of us on this stage distinguish ourselves from each other… and from Mr. Triumph."

She looked four inches above the Fox News camera with the red light on it as instructed by Professor and continued. "Foreign policy is a very important area. There is a huge difference in my approach to foreign policy and the approach of others on this stage. Unlike Mr. Triumph and Mr. DeRantis, I think we need an active and engaged America in global affairs. Foreign policy should not be a partisan issue, but many candidates are making it one. America is the leader of the free world. We cannot just put our heads in the sand and deny what is happening around us. The world is at a critical juncture today. Autocratic countries like China, Russia, North Korea, and Iran are all making strategic moves to increase their influence and power. It's not an understatement to say that the future of the world will be determined based on how we and our democratic allies respond to these challenges. And let me make it clear. I will NEVER abandon our friends in Ukraine. The stakes in Ukraine and around the world are extremely high. We need to establish international order in a manner that maintains world security and our leadership."

Polite, but not emphatic, applause came from the crowd when Silvia finished her statement. *A good start,* thought Professor. *Now she needs to keep gaining momentum.*

The debate continued. Silvia stood patiently and respectfully as the other candidates finished giving their views on foreign policy issues. The moderator then shifted the debate to domestic economic issues. Trim Scott was given the first question and DeRantis interrupted him toward the end of his response. Chris Christee, who had been very controlled so far, interrupted DeRantis with some biting comments on how he did not wish the entire country to follow what DeRantis had done in Florida. However, without Triumph in attendance, Christee seemed deflated and disinterested, despite his reputation as a master debater.

When Christee finished his comments, Silvia jumped at the opportunity to inject herself into the discussion.

"I think it's time that we address the elephant in the room tonight," Silvia said. "The absence of Donald Triumph from this debate stage."

A hush of excitement seemed to come over the audience as Silvia continued.

"There are just two reasons why Mr. Triumph is not here tonight. The first is that he thinks his lead in the polls is insurmountable and he will automatically be the nominee. The second is that he's embarrassed about his indictments and legal entanglements. Voters will ultimately decide whether Mr. Triumph is right on the first point.

"On the second point, I'm unlike a lot of the candidates on this stage who want to avoid talking about Triumph's indictments under the guise that we just need to look forward. I disagree. Like foreign policy, this is another example of where a presidential candidate cannot just stick his head in the sand and avoid the topic. Where there's smoke, there's fire. Mr. Triumph's legal problems are generating more smoke than the Canadian wildfires. Triumph's actions on January 6 were, at best deplorable, and at worst, criminal for trying to overthrow our democracy. Nobody, not even a former president, is above the law."

A combination of applause and boos greeted Silvia for her statement. She paused for a second as the hypocrisy of her "overthrow democracy" statement almost made her laugh. She quickly composed herself and continued.

"Voters across America should not just summarily dismiss a charge that one of our presidential candidates tried to overthrow the federal government by not abiding by the will of the voters. If he truly tried to sabotage democracy for his personal fame and promotion, then he should be held accountable. This is an extremely serious charge. If he were to be convicted, I would think that it would automatically disqualify him in the minds of voters from being someone they would want as the next president. But that is only if he is convicted, and Mr. Triumph is entitled to his day in court."

A mixed reaction of applause and a smattering of boos again emanated from the audience.

Those 'Always Triumphers' are a tough and loyal crowd, thought Professor as Silvia continued to control the dialogue in the debate.

Silvia continued, "That's my view of how we should approach the past actions and legal problems of Mr. Triumph. I really wish Mr. Triumph was here tonight to participate in these debates. America is at its best when people are informed about issues, and can debate them. We may never find two candidates, and possibly not two people in the entire country, who agree on everything. However, it is now more important than ever that people be able to respectfully disagree for our common good. I also agree that our party and America need to focus on the future. In this regard, I note that I am the only candidate who has released a detailed plan to move America forward, with specific proposals on the economy, immigration reform, guns, taxes, and foreign affairs."

At this point the debate moderator from Fox interrupted Silvia and asked, "Ms. Rodriguez, you are one of the few candidates to support a tax increase. How do you justify your position?"

"My proposed tax increase is fair because it will only affect the wealthiest. Under my tax proposals, I would increase the tax rate on corporations, I would decrease the tax rate on individuals earning less than $100,000, and I would increase the rate on individuals earning more than $1 million, with big increases to those earning more than

$10 million. Look, our country has for years been spending a lot more money than it is taking in. We need wealthy corporations and wealthy individuals to start paying their fair share of taxes. Along with my economic growth package, this approach should let us reverse the huge budget deficit over a reasonable period of time."

Modest applause followed.

While the applause was far from thunderous, thought Professor, *I'm surprised anyone applauded at all when the topic was tax increases. Silvia is showing she is a candidate to be reckoned with.*

The debate continued, but there were few fireworks or memorable moments in the absence of Triumph. At the end of the debate, each candidate was given time to provide final comments. When her turn came, Silvia gave a warm smile to the crowd and thanked them all for coming and participating in the 'important event'. She concluded her remarks by saying, "In the upcoming election, I think the people of the U.S. are looking to find a party and a president who will put the country ahead of themselves. We need a president who respects our country, who reveres our country, who protects our democracy, and who appreciates the power we give to voters in our electoral system. It seems like *five-ever* since we've had a president like that, who above all will love and protect America more than he loves and protects his own interests. The United States is the greatest country in the world, and it needs and deserves a president whose only focus is to preserve, protect, and expand its greatness. I hope you will consider me to be that person."

The reaction from the audience was heart-warming to Silvia. While she still received a few boos from the 'Always Triumphers,' the genuine applause she received was more than received by any other candidate. She even got a standing ovation from some in attendance, which no other candidate received.

As Sylvia stepped down from the stage at the end of the debate, a reporter from NBC approached her for an interview.

"Congresswoman Rodriguez, you seemed to generate as much interest and applause as any candidate on stage tonight. Are you surprised by that and happy with your performance?"

Silvia grinned. "I'm happy to have the opportunity to participate in an event that lets the voters get to know the candidates better. With respect to how I performed, that's for the voters to decide. All I try to do is speak truthfully about my desires for this country."

"Well, I think they really liked you," said the reporter. "And I really liked your 'five-ever' statement. I hadn't heard that before!"

"Yes," Silvia chuckled. "It seems like a lot longer than 'forever' that we've had a president who focuses only on what is best for our country. I hope to change that!"

96

AUGUST 24, 2023

"Well, Jefe, how do you think Silvia performed in the debate last night?" asked Professor over the phone.

"I thought she did fantastic. She made me proud... just the right balance of promoting her views on matters of policy and the backbone to stand up against some of her arrogant opponents, including Triumph. What did you think?"

"I was also very happy, and I told her as much after she returned to the hotel after the debate. The best news seems to be in the 'rapid polls' conducted immediately after the debate. Silvia universally received the biggest boost among all candidates on stage. While I would like to have seen Triumph's approval rating drop more than it did, he did lose a few points of support. He's still the heavyweight favorite, and DeRantis is still in second place, but Silvia has moved past Trim Scott into third place. Unfortunately for Nikki Hayley, she appears to be the big loser after Silvia's performance last night. She just doesn't outshine Silvia in any area, and I don't expect her to stay in the race very long. Bottom line, this is a great start for Silvia. I think voters are now starting to see that she is a bona fide candidate who merits their attention and respect. She is no longer just the pretty governor who has A-Rod as a fan and who was on stage when Spence survived the assassination attempt."

"So, what's next?" Jefe asked.

"We need to continue the momentum and the connection that voters have to her. The Iowa caucus is earlier than usual, January 15, 2024, so this gives us less than five months to attract voters and make inroads into Triumph's lead. One strategy would be to get the endorsement of popular Iowa Governor Kim Reynoldswrap, but it appears that she won't back any candidate now because she is fearful of getting on Triumph's bad side. Iowa can be important, as shown by the big boost that candidate Olama received from the state. So, now is the time to ramp up our media campaign and grass roots efforts. We will be heading to the Iowa State Fair soon, and Silvia is lined up to do a CNN interview with Kate Boldowin tomorrow. We're also already putting together a video montage of her debate highlights, coupled with the A-Rod and Spence moments to flood social media tomorrow, including nontraditional sources like Tik Tok and Instagram."

"Sounds like a lot of that is directed at young voters. Will they be important in the upcoming election?" Jefe asked.

"In what looks to be a tight race, every vote is important. When it comes to the young, Gen Z vote, they are looking for their voice and a candidate to support. Based on the stage last night, Silvia is clearly the most attractive alternative to young voters, who are almost evenly split between Republicans, Democrats, and independents. These young voters get their political information from social media, so it's important to connect with them quickly to take advantage of the great things Silvia did last night. I'm trying to arrange for Silvia to make some guest appearances on social media with prominent 'influencers.' I've also inquired about appearances on Saturday Night Live and The View... anything we can do to increase her visibility and connection with voters!"

"Sounds good," said Jefe. "Buena suerte and keep me informed."

97

GROSS OFFICE, SEPTEMBER 15, 2023

Nick walked into the GROSS office and was glad to see Straw had a smile on his face. Though Straw put on a good show of being chill and laid-back, Nick could tell Straw was bothered by the fact his desired trail of clues to support his stolen nuke theory had gone completely cold. Yesterday, as Nick left the office, he heard Straw mutter, "Sometimes the dark star crashes and there are times we all must fall. There are times I must live doubt and I can't help at all. I'm the boy without all the clues and I feel like I need a miracle every day. My trail of clues has gone so cold I could die of freezing in the heat of the sun."

Straw's previous gloom had taken an abrupt turn. Nick soon learned the reason.

"Nick, I'm sure you remember Blondie," Straw said. "The only person in the crowd during the Spence assassination attempt who reacted similar to Sam?"

"How could I forget her?" Nick exclaimed. "Have you been able to identify her?"

"No. Darkness still hides the day, and it seems like she has stolen her face right off her head. But, while I still don't know who she is, I have found her again. Come take a look."

Nick walked behind Straw to look at his largest monitor and Sam followed. Straw had isolated various shots of the crowd at Triumph's rally on January 6 and the subsequent attack on the Capitol. He showed Nick and Sam the clips and zoomed in on a tall, attractive woman.

"Her hair was brown instead of blonde," Straw said, "but my facial recognition software confirmed a ninety-nine percent match. That brunette is the same person as Blondie."

In light of the jam-packed crowd at the event, it was difficult to get a clear view of the woman, but Nick knew immediately it was Blondie.

"Would you please show me those video clips again?" Nick asked.

Nick watched intently and then asked, "Straw, what do you think she's doing there? Is she there protecting Triumph? Is she a supporter of his? Or, do you think she might have been part of a plot to take him out?"

"Slow down, cowboy," Straw said with a chuckle. "I don't know what she was doing there. I think she may have been just an observer, either on her own volition or for whomever she represents. I don't think she's a Triumph supporter because you never see her clap during his rally speech, and she never came close to entering the Capitol. There are a couple of times when she seems to be talking, presumably on a microphone to one of her partners. But with all the other noise in that large crowd, it's impossible to isolate her conversation. I also don't have any reason to believe that she, or anyone else there, was part of a plot to take out Triumph. If she was there for a business reason, I'd wager she was part of a secret protective force in the crowd, making sure things didn't reverse course."

"Were you able to track where she went after things got crazy?"

"Alas, I couldn't. She's pretty stealthy and escaped all of the video surveillance after things got hot at the Capitol."

"Well, with that riled up crowd, she could not have done anything to stop the attack on the Capitol. We've now seen her twice at significant political events. I hope she's one of the good guys instead of on the other side."

"I'm going to reserve my judgment until more facts are known," said Straw. "But I thought you would be interested in my find of the ever elusive and mysterious Blondie."

"I am! Thanks Straw."

Sam piped in as she returned to her desk. "I think I'll let you guys be alone. This is turning into too much of a boy's locker room talk for my taste."

Nick looked at Straw for confirmation that Sam was just kidding.

"Don't worry," said Straw when he saw that Nick needed some reassuring that he hadn't re-entered Sam's doghouse. "She just thinks that we've been playing the cool fools."

"Good. I don't want anything to make my relationship with Sam take a step backwards. We're really getting along well right now."

98

VERACRUZ, MEXICO, THANKSGIVING 2023

It was a beautiful day in Veracruz when Professor arrived at Jefe's estate to spend the Thanksgiving holiday. After the usual greetings with Verana and Abriz, Professor and Jefe went to their poolside "office" as was their custom.

Professor grabbed a tall glass of iced tea and a variety of tapas appetizers before sitting down in a comfortable chair by the pool. Jefe did the same, and the two friends sat in silence for a moment, enjoying the beautiful and tranquil surroundings.

"You have a little slice of heaven here, Jefe… a beautiful family and a home in paradise. It's too bad we must discuss business here!"

"Thank you, Professor. I count my blessings every day. Let's get an update on our business developments so we can then just enjoy the rest of the holiday."

"Of course, Jefe. Let's discuss the current status of electoral politics. On the Democrat side, it's clear that Burden will be the nominee in 2024 unless his health fails. He's the horse the Democrats are going to ride, and the Democrats won't put him out to pasture just because he's run a few races. However, there are some warning signs for Burden, even though he is the incumbent. His approval rating is below 45%, 75% of voters feel the economy is in fair or poor shape, and 60% do not want him to run again. These challenges will continue to affect Burden during the campaign. However, the lesson from the 2022 midterms is that an unprecedented number of voters will vote for Democrats even though they may be disappointed with the economy or Burden's performance if the Republican alternative is too extreme. In 2024, this extremism exists automatically if Triumph is the Republican nominee, and also exists for most other Republican challengers as a result of their stance on abortion. Thus, there are a lot of reasons for Democrats to feel optimistic about winning the presidency in 2024 even if there is pessimism about the economy."

"OK. How are things progressing with Silvia?"

"On the Republican side, during the debate and afterwards, Silvia and Chris Christee have painted Triumph as someone who has bullied his way out of accountability and who is a plague on the party and our democracy. Christee has done this with a sledgehammer, while Silvia has been more subtle in her criticism to preserve a potential VP role. It seems very logical that Republicans need to come up with a non-toxic leader who can unite the nation. However, logic doesn't always apply when it comes to politics, especially when Triumph is involved. He is uncanny in his ability to turn lemons into lemonade."

"Forgive me, Professor, but I'm struggling to understand what Americans see in Triumph. From my vantage point in Mexico, all I've seen is that when he was president, he alienated, without apology or remorse, women, Hispanics, African Americans, and most of America's traditional allies abroad. So, why do so many still like him?"

Professor paused and then replied. "Some of Triumph's issues are not totally unexpected. When Triumph won in 2016, he did so as the candidate with the highest negative ratings of any candidate in history. That distinction would have gone to Hillary if the Republicans had nominated anyone other than Triumph."

"That may help explain his troubles in office, but it doesn't answer why he still has such support. It seems like it should be just the opposite."

"When Triumph won in 2016, it was in part because he was a businessman and not a politician. He gave voters hope for an aspirational path toward prosperity for the country. His 'Make America Great Again' slogan was Raygun-esque and hopeful. I think a lot of people still see that, or at least hope for that, and their hope blinds their view of reality. But two impeachments, four indictments, and ninety-one felony charges all show the intoxicating corruption of power, and how much Triumph desires to cling to it at all costs. Eventually, I think lots of those Americans will wake up and say 'Emperor Triumph is wearing no clothes.' But I haven't seen that happen yet."

Jefe shook his head. "America really is loco! Let's get back to the real topic. Where does Silvia really fit in? Can she beat Triumph and then Burden?"

"Silvia continues to exceed my expectations, and she has a message that will continue to resonate with voters. She is now consistently in the top two or three in polls, even though she has been less in the public eye than other candidates. Voters like that she is a straight-shooter. On the political spectrum, she's more moderate than most candidates, yet she is a foreign policy hardliner. She also has an impressive track record, with her 'Governor's Grand Slam' in Arizona. Not many candidates can tout such a record!"

"But is that enough for her to win?"

"There's a saying in politics that if you are always coming in second, then you are never coming in first. Elections are winner-take-all contests. So, despite how well Silvia has done, right now she hasn't turned enough of Triumph's base away from him for her to win. There is still a lot of time left and things can change quickly, especially considering Triumph's legal troubles. But it's good for us to have our contingency plans."

"OK, it sounds like we really need to look at our fallback plans. If Silvia is not the Republican nominee, our first fallback plan is for her to be VP. How likely is that?"

"As VP, she would be the proverbial 'heartbeat away from the presidency,' and we would take advantage of that. Of course, getting Silvia as Triumph's running mate only works if he beats Burden. That is far from assured, and Burden has already beaten Triumph once. If Silvia is on the ticket, she'll bring a lot of Hispanic and other votes that Triumph would not normally receive. That's why I think she would be a strong selection for the position. Even with her impact, I don't think it lets Triumph unseat Burden, though the election would be very close."

"If that happens, then we are left with trying to get Silvia in as Speaker of the House and using the succession rules of the Constitution to put her in the presidency, correct?"

"Yes."

"What are the chances of Silvia becoming Speaker?"

"Well, first we would have to get her back in the House. She would then have to be elected Speaker by the members in the House. We've laid a great foundation for that to happen, but a lot of the dominos still must fall in place."

"What if they don't?"

"Then we probably have to wait another election cycle and try to get Silvia elected president in 2028."

"Aaargh, I don't want to wait that long," Jefe groaned.

"I'm going to do my best to make sure you don't, but there are no sure things in electoral politics."

"I understand," Jefe said softly. "One final question on this topic. How would things change if Burden wasn't the Democrat candidate?"

"The only way I see that happening is if Burden had to drop out due to health reasons or a scandal with his son. That would likely leave his VP, Camelot Harris, as the Democrat nominee. That would be quite a change, because Harris has been invisible as Burden's VP. She was supposed to be the point person to solve the issues at the border, but it was quickly apparent that she wasn't ready for that huge task. It's interesting, and this is very unusual for a VP, but Harris is currently polling below Burden. That means she is probably a slight drag on Burden's chance to be reelected. Burden is very loyal, so I don't think he'd ever replace her on the ticket. If Harris somehow became the Democrat nominee, I don't think she would have a snowball's chance in hell to beat any Republican for the presidency."

"Thanks, Professor. You've answered all my questions. Let me say it again. I really appreciate all your efforts to attain our goals."

"Likewise, Jefe. Before we celebrate the holiday, I must ask. How is Goliath? And, how is my friend Dmitri doing?"

"Dmitri is doing an excellent job overseeing construction of Goliath. It's a big facility, so we have about a 2-year construction schedule. We're about a year into this and slightly ahead of schedule. Enough segments have been completed to allow Dmitri to move in and live there, along with some of my friends from the Los Leones gang who are helping with construction and providing security. It is actually looking like a beautiful facility for children. As you will remember from when you and Dmitri delivered our important 'package' there, its location is perfect… far enough away from Camp David that our construction doesn't generate much scrutiny, yet close enough to Camp David to let a drone carry the baby nuke without detection before it's too late to stop it."

"And far enough away to not be affected by nuclear fallout," Professor added.

"Indeed," Jefe agreed. "I still hope that we never have to use the Goliath strategy. As I've told you before, I want Americans to thrive and have plenty of disposable income to buy our products! I don't want my legacy to be the person who used a nuke on American soil to attain his goals. But all great goals require sacrifices."

"I have also been pondering the morality behind our Goliath plan," said Professor. "Here's an interesting line of thinking that should give us some comfort. Triumph tried some novel ways on January 6 to overturn and steal the 2020 election. Goliath represents a plan to accomplish the same objective of overturning 2024 election results and putting an unelected person in the presidency."

"I like the way you rationalize things, Professor! Let's have another drink!"

99

VERACRUZ, MEXICO, DAY AFTER THANKSGIVING 2023

After eating a delicious brunch with Jefe and his family, Professor was getting ready to go to the airport where one of Jefe's private jets would fly him home. Before departing, Professor pulled Jefe aside.

"Jefe, as always, the hospitality of you and your family has been top-notch. I want to give you a small token of my appreciation before I leave." Professor pulled out a gift bag with crumpled, colorful tissue paper covering the top of the bag so the contents inside could not be seen.

Jefe reached into the bag and pulled out three t-shirts of different colors and sizes. The front of the shirts had printed in bold letters:

The back of the shirts read:

"As you might remember, Jefe, Silvia's original campaign slogan was MA PA… Make America Proud Again. But Silvia's comment in the debate that it's been 'five-ever' since we had a president who cared more about our country than himself, went viral after the debate. We worked quickly to capitalize on the attention and offered these t-shirts for sale on Silvia's campaign website for a donation of $20. These shirts sold like hotcakes and raised almost a million dollars in the first two weeks. People love it when Silvia hands out the t-shirts while campaigning. It's really been a great, inexpensive device for her to connect with crowds. We also thought you might appreciate not having to finance the entire campaign yourself!"

"Thank you," said Jefe. "We'll wear these with pride."

"Well, I was hesitant to give them to you since we don't want to publicize your interest in the election. It's probably best to just frame them or put them in storage until the election is over."

100

DES MOINES, IOWA, JANUARY 15, 2024

For the night of the Iowa caucus, Professor and Silvia stayed at their campaign headquarters, the Hilton Des Moines Downtown Hotel. This 330-room hotel is the only hotel in downtown Des Moines that is directly connected to the Iowa Events Center, a world-class convention center, and the Wells Fargo arena. Professor admitted that four years in advance, he reserved the hotel's 10,000 square-foot ballroom for the evening mainly because he knew that this was the hotel that Triumph would have preferred as his Iowa-based campaign headquarters.

Professor and Silvia had adjoining rooms. This let them stay in constant communication as results from the 1,700 Iowa caucus locations were tallied, while keeping Professor's involvement invisible to the outside world.

Unlike the primaries in other states where people go to polls and cast ballots, Iowans gather at a set location in each of Iowa's precincts. Typically, these meetings occur in schools, churches, public libraries, or even individuals' houses.

"I usually don't like this antiquated caucus Iowa uses," Professor said to Silvia, "but in our case, it just might work to our advantage. I think we are very well organized at the precinct level, and you've done a great job increasing your profile to voters in the state. Iowa is still super conservative, so it will be hard to unseat Triumph, but I think you've positioned yourself as one of the top two or three candidates."

"Time will soon tell," replied Silvia with a smile. "But I'm confident we gave this our best effort. I think it's time for me to go make another appearance downstairs, don't you agree?"

"I trust your instincts. But don't wear yourself out. The final tally probably won't be known for another four or five hours."

"Don't worry about that," said Silvia. "I will be totally exhausted by night's end, but I hope not to show it. All these trips between Iowa and New Hampshire in the last month can really drain a person. I'm looking forward to taking a couple days off in Phoenix."

"You definitely deserve it!"

At the hotel's campaign headquarters, Silvia's routine was to periodically go down to the ballroom, mingle with her supporters, and give interviews to the local and national media. She would change her attire every time, starting in blue jeans and different colors of the "Five-Ever" t-shirts, and then gradually increasing the professionalism of her attire until the final results of the caucus were tallied.

At 10 p.m., the results came in while Silvia and Professor were watching TV in Silvia's room:

1.	Triumph	33%
2.	DeRantis	18
3.	Silvia Rodriguez	17
4.	Hayley	8
5.	Scott	8
6.	Christee	8
7.	Spence	4
8.	Others	4

Before heading to the ballroom to address her supporters, Silvia hugged Professor, who whispered in her ear, "This is a great start, Silvia. I'm very proud of you."

Silvia exited the elevator and headed straight to the podium on stage. Her supporters in the ballroom immediately started clapping and cheering loudly once they saw Silvia. When the applause subsided, Silvia took the microphone with a big smile.

"Thanks to all of you in this room. Without your passionate support, we would not have been able to do what we did tonight. Third place is not our final goal, but it is a great start to a long election race. What we did… what you did for me… in Iowa is a total success. If you remember, a month ago the polls showed Triumph running away in Iowa with a commanding 48% of the vote, and only DeRantis within shouting distance at 28%. Two weeks ago, the numbers changed to Triumph at 40%, DeRantis at 22%, and an upstart called SlamRod entering the picture and quickly gaining ground at 11%. Today, the results in Iowa are nothing but positive.

"Though victory is not ours tonight, momentum is! I can guarantee you that when Triumph and DeRantis look in the mirror tonight, they will see us getting closer and closer. Let's all go home tonight and sleep well, knowing that we are committed to continue our momentum and our campaign of positive messages for our country, the greatest country in the world, the United States of America. Thank you again and God bless!"

As Silvia pulled away from the mic and waved to her crowd of supporters, the volume of their cheers almost shook the entire hotel.

101

GROSS OFFICE, JANUARY 28, 2024

The Washington weather was cold as Sam and Nick arrived at the same time at the GROSS office. Upon entering, they saw Straw with a worried look on his face. He motioned the two of them over to his desk.

"My daughter Stella had a friend over at our house last night," Straw said, his tone graver than normal. "This friend pulled me aside at the end of the night and said to me, 'My dad says that you work for a secret agency that spies on people.'"

As Straw paused with a look of concern on his face, Sam asked, "How did you respond?"

"I told her that he's not her dad."

Straw tried to keep a straight face, but broke up laughing at his own joke, his eyes welling up with tears.

"Good one, Straw. You deserve an Academy Award... you really had us going with that one!" said Nick.

"Better keep your day job, Straw. You'll never make it as a comedian," Sam retorted, as she and Nick returned to their desks shaking their heads.

102

CONCORD, NEW HAMPSHIRE, JANUARY 31, 2024

The time between the Iowa caucus and the New Hampshire primary flew by like the blink of an eye. Silvia was totally refreshed and recharged after taking one day off after the Iowa caucus, so she canceled the second day of her planned break and went straight to New Hampshire.

As usual, Silvia quickly acclimated herself to her new surroundings and endeared herself to everyone she met. She went snow skiing in the White Mountains at Bretton Woods. In an interview in the lodge at the top of the mountain, a crowd of skiers gathered around Silvia, who sported a coral pastel ski outfit.

"So, what do you think of New Hampshire, Ms. Rodriguez?" asked the local TV anchor.

"I love it! Look at this incredible view... I can see why New Hampshire is called the Switzerland of America. This landscape and scenery are simply breathtaking. And the powder here has been great. I should have expected that from the snowiest state in the U.S."

Each interview and public appearance by Silvia ended with cheers from the locals in attendance. Shouts of "SlamRod 5-Ever" and "Beat Triumph" spread like wildfire.

Silvia went from end to end of the state, finishing her campaigning at Minute Man Historical Park, the site of the opening battle of the revolution. She then went to meet Professor at the Hotel Concord to watch the results of the country's first primary. From their rooms in the hotel, Professor and Silvia had great views of the Merrimack River and the State House, a gold-domed building that dated back to the early 1800's.

Silvia went down to her campaign meeting rooms in the hotel shortly before the polls closed. An interviewer from Fox News asked her about her thoughts of the New Hampshire primary.

Silvia flashed her great smile and said, "I'll admit that I've never been to New Hampshire before this campaign. But after touring the state, this place and its people are incredible. I've always enjoyed the outdoors. Mountains, lakes, rivers, beautiful beaches, and the ocean… I love New England. Combine that with the great history of this place, and I really love New Hampshire! I hope the voters in New Hampshire like me half as much as I love them. If that happens, I'll be very happy with the outcome."

The night progressed and the final results were released late in the evening:

1.	Triumph	26%
2.	Rodriguez	22
3.	DeRantis	19
4.	Hayley	17
5.	Christee	10
6.	Scott	4
7.	Others	2

103

FEBRUARY 1, 2024

"Professor, what do you make of the results in New Hampshire?" asked Jefe over his burner phone.

"I think it shows that we are ending the first phase of the nomination process on a high note. I am somewhat concerned because historically, the Republican nominee wins either Iowa or New Hampshire. The Iowa winner has been the nominee in two of the last seven elections, and New Hampshire has been an even better outcome predictor, with the winner of its primary being the nominee in five of the last seven elections."

Professor continued, "Although Silvia did not win in either Iowa or New Hampshire, she has the next most valuable reward for her efforts... *momentum*. The absence of early success in primaries, especially for lesser-known candidates, usually results in an inability to raise funds, which is a fast-growing cancer leading to political demise. Based on this analysis, I could easily see Spence, Christee, and Scott wither away like weeds very quickly. This could also happen to Hayley, although she and Scott may stay in the race a bit longer just to increase the possibility that they could be considered for a VP role. Silvia is the only challenger who performed well in both Iowa and New Hampshire, which should give her real momentum and let her bloom like a flower."

"But Triumph still won the first two primaries," said Jefe. "Do you detect any flaws in his armor that will let us overtake him in the future?"

"Yes, I think some cracks are starting to show on the Triumph team. First, because of his legal troubles, Triumph has been laser-focused on keeping the loyalty of his base. This has been a winning strategy in the early primaries. But his failure to cultivate support beyond his base means he is headed for problems, clearly in the general election but possibly as well in future primaries.

"Second, Triumph's overall level of support and margin of victory have been steadily shrinking, in significant part due to Silvia's great efforts. I've looked closely at the Iowa voting data and the early exit polls from New Hampshire. It's clear that Triumph only maintains a big lead over other candidates when it comes to very conservative voters. Triumph's advantage starts to wither with moderate or somewhat conservative voters. His lead is even more scattered based on the income of the voters. Voters with incomes less than $100,000 still support Triumph by over twenty points, but those with higher incomes only support him by three points."

"So, what is next on the agenda for us?" asked Jefe.

"We are now into the second phase of the nomination process. With Iowa and New Hampshire done, there will be five primaries by March 3, the most important of which are South Carolina and Michigan. After that comes Super Tuesday on March 5, with fifteen primaries across the country that will select over a third of all delegates to the nominating convention. Basically, we are now in the phase of the election where we do a mad dash across the country making strategic in-person and media appearances as often as possible. Like the other remaining candidates, we'll also try to raise large sums of money from internet fundraising. We don't want anybody shining a spotlight on you as Silvia's real source of financial backing. Hopefully, we will build on our current momentum, because any candidate outside the top two or three after Super Tuesday probably needs to drop out of the race."

"Sounds like this will be an exhausting couple of months. Buena suerte!"

104

PENTAGON/WASHINGTON, D.C., FEBRUARY 2024

It took three weeks for decorated war veteran and SEAL combat trainer Lieutenant Commander Patrick Payne to get an appointment with Secretary of Defense Lloyd Boston, even though LCDR Payne had indicated that the meeting was "urgent." Payne arrived at the Pentagon early for the meeting. After fifteen minutes of waiting, he was given entry to the Secretary's office just as CIA Director Bill Burnside was leaving.

"Hey, Bill. You may want to sit in on this meeting unless you have another commitment. I think it's right up your alley," Secretary Boston said.

"I've got half an hour," said Director Burnside. "Happy to stick around."

"You don't mind do you, Lieutenant Commander Payne?"

"No sir."

After quick introductions, Secretary Boston asked, "So, what's on your mind Lieutenant Commander Payne?"

"Mr. Secretary, about fifteen years ago, one of our elite combat trainers attacked me for no apparent reason," lied Payne. "This guy had elite fighting and weapons skills, but he was emotionally unstable. He was like a time bomb waiting to explode. For the safety of our country, I thought he should be locked up for a long time. However, he was the son of Senator Class, so I was pressured not to press charges. I agreed, but on the condition that he go through the Clean Slate Protocol. I was promised that would 'fix' him forever and he would never be a danger again."

"What's the Clean Slate Protocol?" asked Burnside.

Secretary Boston responded, "It's a surgical procedure developed here at DOD. It effectively wipes certain periods from a person's memory. We haven't used it much, but it's been very successful in curbing the violent tendencies of certain people. This lets them live a normal life and not endanger others."

Boston turned to Payne and asked, "So, what's the issue, Lieutenant Commander Payne?"

"The issue is that I recently received evidence that Nick Class has broken the Clean Slate Protocol and has become a violent threat once again."

Opening a folder, Payne pulled out pictures of various crime scenes.

"Here are three citizens he killed about five years ago that I just learned about. Then here are some photos of two young men he shot in the knees a little bit later. And finally, I have it on good authority that he's one of the shooters who killed someone at the Knoxville synagogue a couple of years ago."

Boston and Burnside looked at the photos. "Do we know whether any of these killings or shootings were justified?" asked Boston.

"Permission to speak freely?" asked Payne.

"Granted."

"With all due respect, Mr. Secretary, I don't think that's relevant. The Clean Slate Protocol is only used on people who the country views as extremely dangerous and incapable of controlling their actions. Nick Class has broken the Clean Slate Protocol and, by definition, is a danger to our country. He needs to be eliminated for the protection of us all. With your authorization, I would be willing to carry out the mission."

"I think I'd like to get more information about these events," said Boston. "But I agree. The Clean Slate Protocol is applied to military assets we can't trust not to snap and go off on a violent rage."

"Lloyd, has that ever happened before?" Burnside asked.

"To my knowledge, no one has ever broken the Clean Slate Protocol before. This is a case of first impression. What do you think?" Boston asked the CIA Director.

"You are being asked to authorize Lieutenant Commander Payne to kill a U.S. citizen, and the son of a U.S. senator. I wouldn't do that without signoff from the president."

"Wow. When did the CIA develop a moral conscience?" joked Boston. "But I like your suggestion. Here's where we are, Lieutenant Commander Payne. You are going to provide me the full background on this matter, starting with what prompted Class to undergo the Clean Slate Protocol, plus all the details regarding the incidents of violence that you noted. You need to accompany that information with a written memo supporting your position that Class needs to be eliminated to protect our country. I will then submit the materials to the president. If he gives you the authorization to proceed, I will let you know. Until then, you are to stand down."

"Thank you, Mr. Secretary. You will have those files next week."

105

RICHMOND, VIRGINIA, MARCH 5, 2024

Silvia spent the weeks after the New Hampshire primary in a fast-paced blur of airplanes, public appearances, and hotels.

"I still love meeting the people, but everything is happening so fast that half of the time I don't even remember what city I'm in when I wake up," she confessed to Professor on one of their nightly Zoom calls. "Plus, I've gained at least five pounds eating at all these campaign events. If I never see another plate of rubber chicken, green beans, and stale dinner rolls, that would be fine with me!"

"You definitely deserve a few days off after we get the results tonight! You've done a great job working the campaign trail across the country. Let me say that I've really liked your recent statements that 'America needs a candidate who is positive and going somewhere. We want and need a candidate who has luggage, not baggage.' The crowd reaction when you said that made for a great soundbite for us. I'd also like to say that I'm impressed with your stamina on the campaign trail, and if you've gained five pounds, it sure doesn't show."

"Why Professor, I didn't think you focused on anything but polls and political strategy," replied Silvia playfully.

Professor's cheeks started to turn red. He finally composed himself and said, "Silvia, as attractive as you are on the outside, you are even more attractive on the inside. It has truly been a pleasure to work with you on this campaign.

"But let's get back to the business at hand. I think tonight's results will be a critical turning point for many candidates. Depending on the margins, I think a lot of candidates will drop out of the race if they don't finish in the top two or three."

"I agree with you, Professor. The fallout from tonight will be very interesting. No matter what happens, I can honestly say that I've given it my best effort."

106

RICHMOND, VIRGINIA, MARCH 5, 2024

Having traveled at a furious pace with campaign stops in California, Texas, and North Carolina, Silvia and Professor decided to finish the Super Tuesday stretch of the campaign in Richmond, the historic capitol of Virginia. The original plan, as in the past, was for their campaign headquarters on the night of the election to be in a ballroom of their hotel. Professor picked The Commonwealth, a historic hotel across from the Capitol in downtown Richmond as the preferred location. However, in mid-February, a large group of supportive students at the University of Richmond invited Silvia to spend the evening of Super Tuesday on campus, either outside in the large open space at Westhampton Green or, if unusually cold or wet weather occurred, indoors in the Robins basketball arena on campus.

Every other candidate spends election nights at fancy hotel ballrooms with their supporters. Professor thought the contrast of spending Super Tuesday with college students would add to Silvia's image as a fresh, new candidate on the presidential scene. Professor tried to convince Silvia only to commit two hours with the students, but Silvia disagreed.

"I want to stay up as long as my supporters," Silvia said.

"Let's see how the night goes," Professor suggested. "I've got a room in the nearby North Court student apartments dedicated to our use.

That's where I'm going to stay, and I hope you'll take a few breaks there during the night."

The Richmond weather was nice for early March, with clear skies and temperatures in the mid-40's. Though in the middle of the city, the beautiful University of Richmond campus was located at the bottom of a valley, surrounded by dense trees with a large lake in the center of campus. The secluded nature of the scenic campus created an 'island effect', and Professor never would have known that he was in the middle of an urban city if he hadn't witnessed it himself.

Despite its liberal reputation, Silvia was greeted with great warmth and excitement by a large crowd of students when she arrived at the Westhampton Green. The election party had clearly started a few hours in advance of her arrival. Large TV screens were set up in all corners of the open area so incoming election results across the country could be seen and heard. Portable bars were set up near the screens, and heat lamps were placed strategically in case the night became cooler than expected. Lots of "Silvia: Five-Ever" t-shirts were worn by students and supportive campaign signs were plentiful, with some Triumph and Burden signs sprinkled in between.

Silvia was greeted by the head of the Young Republicans chapter at the University of Richmond upon her arrival. Professor watched her work the crowd with ease. After quick introductions at a small podium stage, Silvia gave a very brief talk about her run for the presidency. She promised to give more talks as events unfolded during the night, but that her immediate desire was to mingle and get to know the students that had come out for the party. Professor saw the first of many solo cups of alcohol being raised to toast her magnetic presence.

Two hours later, Silvia took a break from engaging with the students and joined Professor in their room.

"I had forgotten how much college students can drink," exclaimed Silvia as she plopped down to rest on one of the beds. "But it sure is refreshing to talk with them. Their energy and enthusiasm are infectious! So, Professor, how are we doing?"

"Early results are filtering in from the eastern states. It looks like Triumph has the lead, but it's too close to call in Maine and Vermont... and it's you who is neck-to-neck with him. That's a great accomplishment! Though it's too early in lots of the other states, the results look very similar."

"That all sounds very positive," Silvia said.

"I agree," Professor said. "You have really resonated with the voters. It is clear that you are the preferred counterbalance to Triumph. No matter what the ultimate outcome tonight, I'm very proud of you!"

"Thanks, Professor! I'd be too nervous watching the TV in here, so I think I'll go out again and join the festivities."

"OK, but don't drink anything but bottled beer if you must drink alcohol... who knows what these college kids would put in their punch or in a Solo cup of tap beer? If any of the students have had too much to drink or act out of control, get away as fast as possible. Those optics don't help your image."

"Aye, aye, Professor. I will always follow your words of wisdom," Silvia said with a smile. She then went left to mingle with a young generation of supporters.

107

WASHINGTON, D.C., MARCH 5, 2024

Like most interested citizens in the capitol city, Straw and his wife Cherise spent much of Super Tuesday watching the election results pour in on TV.

"Silvia Rodriguez looks like she may give Triumph a real challenge in this race," said Cherise. "Her popularity has really skyrocketed these past few months."

Something Cherise said triggered neurons in Straw's brain. He stared at the TV, but his mind was clearly elsewhere.

Cherise looked at him and recognized the glazed look on his face. She let him ponder whatever thoughts were speeding through his brain, before gently snapping her fingers and saying, "Earth to Straw, Earth to Straw."

Straw snapped back to reality, with a gleam in his eyes. "Sorry Cherise, but I think I may be able to connect some missing dots to one of my puzzles. This might just be a simple twist of fate, but if this ain't the real thing, then it's close enough to pretend."

He stood up from the couch and said, "Give Stella a kiss for me in the morning and tell her I had to go to the office early. I'm going to head in now and see if those connections really exist. You're never going to learn what you don't want to know."

Despite the late hour of the night, Cherise didn't try to convince him otherwise. She knew Straw was like a wolf following the scent of his prey when he got that look in his eyes. She gave him a kiss on the cheek and said, "Fare you well, my honey. I love you more than words can tell."

Straw smiled and walked to his car in the garage.

108

RICHMOND, VIRGINIA, MARCH 6, 2024

Shortly after midnight, Silvia started the process of leaving the festivities on the University of Richmond campus. The coolness of the night temperatures, coupled with hours of drinking, had finally resulted in a stream of students leaving the outdoor party. As the party started to thin out, Silvia stepped up to the podium wearing a Richmond Spiders jacket a student had given her. She picked up the microphone and gave her final thoughts.

"Hi, it's time for me to go to my hotel. Before I leave, I want to thank everyone for coming. You are a fun and very interesting group, but I need my sleep! This evening inspired me about the intelligence and quality of this next generation of our leaders. I implore all these students and other young people to stay aware and to stay actively involved in politics. An informed and active electorate is the foundation of our democracy. I don't know the outcome yet of many of the Super Tuesday states. But whatever the outcome is, I feel like I came out a winner tonight for having the opportunity to spend this night with the bright and fun U of R students. The future of our country is in good hands. Go Spiders!"

The students gave their final roar of approval. Shouts of support for SlamRod continued well beyond Silvia's departure from the podium.

109

GROSS OFFICE, MARCH 6, 2024

Nick Class strolled into the GROSS office around 9:30 in the morning.

"Sorry I'm later than usual," Nick said to greet Samantha and Straw. "I stayed up much later than I expected last night watching the results from Super Tuesday."

Nick took a closer look at Straw, who appeared more disheveled than normal, with his five o'clock shadow showing up about eight hours early.

"Geez, Straw. You look terrible!" Nick twitched his nose and noted that the smell of coffee and pizza permeated the office as he walked in. "Have you been here all night?"

"Most of it. But I think it's been a productive use of time," Straw said, the expression on his face reflecting more energy than exhaustion.

"So, what's going on? What are you looking into?" Nick asked as he and Sam approached Straw's desk.

"Right now, the only thing clear about this case is how murky it is," Straw said. "But I'm starting to feel I know what is going on beneath the surface."

"Give us some details," urged Sam.

Straw stretched in his chair. "You know I've had a lingering view that one of Russia's nukes didn't get destroyed back in December by the Ukrainian missile attack. I'm convinced that this is true based on the lack of radar evidence showing incoming missiles from Ukraine, less radioactive discharge at the site than would be expected if two nukes had been destroyed, some of the guards dying of bullet wounds instead of a missile explosion, and Putrid's unusually quick condemnation of the attack. But I've struggled to figure out the location of the nuke and the plans for its use."

"It's scary to think a rogue nuke is floating out there that nobody knows about," said Sam. "I thought you were working on a connection with Salvador Santos, that cartel leader in Mexico. Is that still your focus?"

"Yes, I feel in my gut there's a connection to Santos. The first indication is the number of calls around the time of the supposed missile attack between Medvedev in Russia and a cell tower in Veracruz. While I could not trace the calls to a precise location, Santos lives in Veracruz. Second, I've always suspected Santos has something to hide, but he's very good at not letting things get traced back to him. So, last night I started looking deeply into some of the financial transactions engaged in by the banks and other companies he controls. I looked first at large transactions that were done by his affiliates, but all of those seemed above board. Then I started looking at what would be considered minor transactions for a multi-billionaire. And that's where I found something very interesting."

"What's that?" asked Nick, his interest growing with each word from Straw's mouth.

"In a few hours of digging last night, I found over 4,000 money transfers in the $9,000-$10,000 range from United States-based banks controlled by Santos. It is clear the parties to these transfers are trying hard to stay under the radar. So, I dug a little deeper and found that the recipient of the funds usually cuts a check in the exact same amount within a short period of time after receipt. Most of these checks are contributions to various Republican candidates, mostly for national offices. I then created an algorithm to ascertain the timing of these transactions. It showed that almost all of the money exchanges occurred in the six months before the Congressional elections that occur every two years."

"Where are you going with this, Straw?" asked Sam.

"Sometimes the obvious is hidden, but once in a while you get shown the light, in the strangest of places if you look at it right. I've been looking for connections for a long time. The money trail has finally opened my eyes," Straw said.

"What did you find?"

"I found that, by far, the largest amount of money went to the campaign coffers of Silvia Rodriguez. Some of these connected contributions go all the way back to her 2012 campaign to be governor of Arizona."

"But," interjected Sam, "could this just be a case of a super-rich guy who wants to help a fellow Hispanic woman in her career?"

"It could be as basic as that. But everyone has something to hide. So, I kept digging for a deeper connection. Sometimes, it's not the written word that provides clues, but pictures. A few hours ago, I found this photo of Ms. Rodriguez the night she was elected governor."

Straw handed a photo to Sam. Both she and Nick looked at it closely.

"I accessed some file video from a local TV station the night Rodriguez was elected governor. This is footage that never made the actual news, but shows her just before walking to the stage at the Arizona Biltmore to give her victory speech."

"Who's the guy she's hugging in the wings?" asked Nick.

"It's kind of a dark picture, but our facial recognition technology identified him as Professor Xavier Moody."

Nick held up his hands to indicate he didn't recognize the name, but Samantha said, "He's one of the advisors who led the Clanton and Olama campaigns."

"What's a Democrat strategist doing congratulating a Republican candidate?" Nick asked, still perplexed.

"That curious connection really spiked my interest," Straw said. "So, I kept digging and found these." He handed more pictures to Samantha. "These pics are from the 1985 'Ye Doomesday Booke', the Georgetown University yearbook. As you can see, the graduating class of 1985 had two persons of interest to me. Xavier Moody and Salvador Santos graduated that year. Here's something even more interesting… I found an interview of Moody, and he mentioned that having Santos as his roommate at Georgetown was one of his favorite college memories."

"OK, now the dots really are starting to connect! Did you find anything else?" Sam asked.

"Glad you asked!" Straw handed her two more pieces of paper. One was a photo of young girls at a recent birthday party, and the other was a printout of numbers. "This first one I just pulled from Instagram," Straw said.

"It looks just like a bunch of seven- or eight-year-old girls having fun at an amusement park?"

"Yes, but did you notice what one of the girls is wearing?"

Sam and Nick looked closer and then both exclaimed, "A SlamRod 5-Ever t-shirt! But, what's important about that?"

"Well, the girl wearing that shirt was tagged on the Instagram post as none other than Abriz Santos, Salvador's daughter."

"That could just be a simple coincidence," Nick said.

"I don't think so," said Straw. "Not when all of these 'coincidences' are put together. Plus, that last sheet is significant to me. I accessed Silvia's phone records. Over Thanksgiving in 2022, she made a phone call from none other than Veracruz, Mexico, where Santos lives."

"She might have just been vacationing there," Nick said.

"Yes, I don't want to be like Icarus and fly too close to the sun. But I looked closer and found that local news stations tracked her every move that holiday since she was a high-profile Congresswoman visiting Mexico. But, from every report that I found, Rodriguez arrived in Mexico City, went straight to her parents' house, and never left until returning to the airport. Therefore, it had to be a surreptitious trip for her cell phone to be in Veracruz."

"So, Straw. You've got a lot of dots of not-so-random connections. What do you think it all means?" asked Samantha.

"Well, I see with my heart, these things my eyes have seen, and I know that the truth must lie somewhere in between."

"English please, Straw!" Nick cried.

"My best guess is that Santos is bankrolling Rodriguez's campaign to be president, and that Santos' old roommate, Xavier Moody, is providing strategic assistance in the background. It's nothing I can prove in a court of law, but I feel confident in my conclusion. I think Santos wants Rodriguez as his puppet president!"

"Wow! That's quite an accusation, but I can see where you think that!" said Nick. "Just one question… where does your missing Russian nuke play into your analysis?"

The smile on Straw's face melted.

"That, I'm afraid, is something I don't have the vaguest idea about," he said dejectedly. "I don't know where it's going, and I don't know where it's been. But I'm going to keep looking!"

110

RICHMOND, VIRGINIA, MARCH 6, 2024

Silvia was exhausted and fell asleep in the car on the trip to The Commonwealth hotel. Upon arriving, Silvia entered through the front door of the hotel while Professor entered through an employee entrance. They soon met in their adjoining rooms.

"Great job tonight, Silvia. Get some sleep and we'll reconnect in the morning."

Silvia did not fight his suggestion and was fast asleep as soon as her head hit her pillow.

Six hours later, Silvia woke up from her deep slumber, splashed water on her face, and knocked on the door that connected her room to Professor's. She could hear the volume on his TV, so she knew that he was awake.

"Come in," chimed Professor in a muted voice, not wanting to awaken any other hotel guests.

Silvia walked in carrying a bottle of water, wearing sweatpants and a red, oversized University of Richmond Spiders t-shirt.

Wow, thought Professor. *A lot of women can look great when they get all dressed up and put on full make-up. But Silvia even looks great when exhausted and in sweatpants!*

"Mind if I make some coffee?" Silvia asked as she went to coffee maker in his room and inserted the strongest K-cup she could find.

When her coffee was made, she strode over to the couch and flopped down next to Professor in front of the TV.

"You didn't get any sleep last night, did you?" Silvia asked.

"No, I didn't. With that many primaries all at once, there are a lot of results that I need to digest and figure out our next steps. I can sleep all I want when I retire."

"So, what are the results? I'm anxious to know!"

"Not everything is final yet. Triumph appears to have a lead against you in both Maine and Vermont, but the margin is so slim in each state that a mandatory recount is required. In the other states, the common element is that you and Triumph have separated yourselves from the pack as the top two candidates. I think all the other candidates are just an afterthought at this point. So, the good news is that you are the only real challenger left to confront Triumph in the race. The bad news is that Triumph is still ahead of you in every one of these states."

"Hmmm, is this another one of those situations where close only counts in horseshoes and grenades?"

"I'm not ready to concede that yet," said Professor. "I want to dig deep into the exit polls when they are available. A lot of candidates are going to withdraw from the race in the near future. I want to see if we can capture the votes they are currently getting. There are still a lot of moving parts here."

"I get the sense that you are about to start your next sentence with a 'But.' Like, 'But, the results show we still have a big hill to climb' or 'But, the results are disappointing'… is that right?"

"Yes and no. There will never be anything disappointing about you or the campaign you have run, Silvia. The only disappointment to me right now is the frustration I get with that rabid, loyal block of voters in Triumph's base that support him like a cult leader."

Professor paused to take a sip of coffee. "The overall results of Super Tuesday show that you are within three points of Triumph, but that doesn't paint the whole picture. Here's the Super Tuesday tally as I see it:

Triumph	33%
Silvia	30
Hayley	13
DeRantis	12
Christee	9
Scott	2
Others	1

"So, we've got great momentum and we're getting closer. That's good, right?"

"Right, but the question we must face is whether it's good enough. I recently told Jefe about a saying in electoral politics… that if you are everyone's second choice you are no one's first choice. And sadly, not enough states award their nomination delegates proportionately to the results in that state. If that were the case, we'd be breathing down Triumph's neck right now and our momentum would give him lots of sleepless nights. But the fact remains that in a winner-take-all race for delegates, even though Triumph is only winning states by a small margin over you, he is way ahead of you in the current count for delegates. The reason is that some key states like Florida, New Jersey, Ohio, and Colorado award delegates strictly on a plurality-take-all basis. That will continue to kill us if we can't figure out a way to crack the rabid 'Always Triumphers.'"

"So, where does that leave us?" Silvia asked.

"Right now, it's to stay the course, keep our momentum, and look excited for the future and the upcoming primaries. The Georgia, Mississippi, and Washington primaries are in a week. If we want to have any chance of winning the presidency outright, we need to keep our supporters engaged and figure the best way to reach out to people who voted for candidates who are dropping out of the race. Our next step is to see if you can win Georgia. People there don't quite have the same love fest for Triumph since he was charged under the state racketeering statute with trying to overturn the 2020 election results in Georgia. That may give us an opening to win the state instead of finishing a close second."

Silvia stood up from the couch to stretch her tired body. "Guess it's time for me to get back on the campaign trail. Georgia, here I come."

"I'll update Jefe later today. Let me say it again, though. You have been incredible throughout this entire ordeal, Silvia. The country would be lucky to have you as its president. One way or another, we'll figure out how to get you past this immovable roadblock named Triumph and into the Oval Office."

"You've been great, too, Professor. Just let me know what I can do to help," Silvia said as she exited the room and closed the adjoining door.

111

MARCH 6, 2024

Professor answered his phone and was greeted by a bubbly Jefe.

"Congratulations, Professor. Silvia is making a remarkable climb in the race. If she keeps this momentum up, she'll soon be winning some state primaries and then, hopefully, the presidency."

"Thanks, but I don't want to burst your bubble, Jefe. Silvia has done an incredible job and voters really like her. But the system of primaries doesn't just declare the person who is doing best at the end the winner. It's more like a baseball game in which Triumph scored a lot of early runs. Just because Silvia starts scoring some runs in the last couple of innings, that doesn't mean she wins the game if she can't overtake Triumph's early lead."

"I'm surprised. I thought you would be a lot more optimistic after last night's results."

"The trouble is in the math. As I told Silvia last night, in electoral politics, first place is the only place that counts. So, despite her close second place finishes to Triumph yesterday, Triumph is in a commanding position in the all-important delegate count. I didn't tell Silvia this because I thought it would break her heart. I've been wracking my brain all day trying to get the math to work, but I just don't think we can capture enough delegates to overtake Triumph."

A deafening silence occurred as Jefe digested the news. He couldn't hide his disappointment when he finally spoke. "So, what is your proposal for the next steps going forward?"

"We have three more primaries coming up in six days. We need to let things play out for another week or two. At that time, we may need to pivot and change our strategy."

"What would our options be?" asked Jefe.

"If Silvia can't win the presidency outright, under any scenario we will need to 'eliminate' whoever is elected president. If Burden beats Triumph and Silvia was Triumph's VP, we would be in a bad predicament because we wouldn't have enough time to get Silvia back in Congress and then elected Speaker of the House."

"I don't like the risks of failure *or* delay under that scenario," Jefe said.

"I agree. The odds of getting our desired outcome during this election cycle, or shortly thereafter, increase significantly if we change our focus to getting Silvia elected as Speaker of the House in 2024. There's a much better chance that Republicans will maintain control of the House than there is of Triumph being the next president."

"Do you have a plan to get Silvia elected as Speaker of the House?"

"Yes. I need to discuss it with Silvia, but I'm confident we can get her elected as Speaker. That will give us an excellent chance of ascending to the presidency no matter who wins the upcoming election... at that point it simply becomes a matter of taking out the president and vice president and letting the succession rules of the Constitution put Silvia in place as president."

"I guess that makes Goliath key to obtaining our objective," Jefe said.

"Yes. Goliath is no longer just a contingency plan."

112

MARCH 14, 2024

"Silvia, thanks for making the time to talk with Jefe and me today," Professor said. "Let me get straight to the point. I know that you've given your heart and soul and lots of sweat in campaigning to be the president. But, in looking at all the factors involved, Jefe and I believe the best way to assure that happens is for you to drop out of the race and for us to use a different tactic."

"Are you sure, Professor?" asked Silvia. "I'm a competitor, and I think I can beat Triumph!"

"Nothing is ever for sure when it comes to elections. When the political landscape changes, we need to change with it. Otherwise, we will have a distorted view of reality. The reality, as I see it today, is that your best chance of becoming president is by having you serve as Speaker of the House."

"This decision pains me, Professor. Don't you agree that if Triumph is the Republican nominee, the general election will focus mainly on his legal problems and rehashing whether the 2020 election was stolen?"

"I agree with you, Silvia. In a perfect world, I would want the election to be focused on which candidate has a better plan for the future of our country. But the world is not perfect. Triumph has a commanding lead, and his trials and legal proceedings are dominating the news cycle. It's insane, but that's exactly what he wants, because it keeps solidifying his base. I know it's disappointing, but we need to change our strategy."

"This is very frustrating, Professor," Silvia said. "But you and Jefe have always taken great care of me. I trust you both and will do whatever you think is needed. What's the plan?"

For the next half-hour, Professor described in detail his plan to have Silvia withdraw from the presidential race, get re-elected to Congress, and eventually become the next Speaker of the House. After he was done presenting his proposed plan, Silvia reacted.

"That is quite some plan, Professor! But I do think it is viable. As I said before, I trust you one hundred percent. But, getting elected as Speaker only gets me closer to the presidency if the president and vice president can't perform their duties, right?"

"Correct, Silvia." Jefe said. "But you don't need to worry about those details. Professor and I will take care of that part of the equation. Sometimes the less you know, the better it is for you if you are ever asked."

Professor added, "Silvia, we have a lot of things to accomplish before the April filing deadline to get you on the Arizona primary ballot. The first thing we need to do is set up a quick, off-the-record meeting with Triumph. Let's go over the points you need to make to ensure the meeting goes as we desire."

113

MARCH 15, 2024

"Hi Silvia, how did your call with Triumph go?" asked Professor as he and Silvia talked on their designated burner phones.

"It went like clockwork. As you predicted, Triumph was ecstatic when I told him I wanted to meet in person to discuss my withdrawal from the race and my desire to unify the party. I also sense that he was very relieved. I think our gains in the primaries were really starting to worry him, although his ego's too big to admit it. He agreed to meet me at his Mar-a-Lago residence tomorrow night under cover of darkness to ensure secrecy from the media."

"Fantastic!" Professor said. "You know what to do when you get there, right?"

"Yes, Professor. I think I'm fully prepared. I'll let you know how it goes."

"Thank you, Silvia. I hate asking you to have this meeting with Triumph, but I think it's critical to the accomplishment of our end goal. Godspeed."

114

MAR-A-LAGO, MARCH 16, 2024

The next evening, Silvia arrived by private jet in Palm Beach where she was met by one of Triumph's staffers. He asked her to join him in an old Ford van that was nondescript except for the corporate logo "Larry's Laundromat… we wash all your dirty laundry" stenciled on each side door.

The staffer drove Silvia in silence to a side entrance for staff at Mar-a-Lago, the expansive resort used by Triumph as his "Winter White House." The driver took her into the resort and led her through a maze of hallways until they reached Triumph's private office.

Triumph quickly dismissed the driver and motioned for Silvia to take a seat on a long couch that ran along one side of the office. Silvia entered the office looking ravishing in a tight-fitting maroon dress with a plunging neckline. Her attire had been strategically selected to highlight her attractiveness, from the tips of her high heels to the top of her styled hair. Her designer accessories, including a color-coordinated Chanel purse and large, gold wristband, complemented her outfit perfectly.

"Thank you for meeting me on such short notice, Mr. Triumph," Silvia started with a feigned respect. "I really appreciate it."

"Call me 'Donald'," Triumph said with a twinkle in his eyes as he admired Silvia. "Unfortunately, my lawyers are requiring that you sign a Non-Disclosure Agreement before we continue any further with our discussions tonight," he said, pointing to a small pile of paper on the glass table in front of the couch. "Will that be a problem? I have been assured it's just a formality and full of boilerplate language."

"Normally, I would require my own attorney to review any legal documents. But I'm very familiar with NDAs, so give me a few minutes to review the document." Silvia put her Chanel purse on the glass table, picked up the stapled document, and started to study it, all while leaning slightly forward on the couch to tantalize Triumph.

After a few minutes of flipping pages, Silvia pronounced, "This document looks fine to me. Do you have a pen for me to sign? I would like to take a copy with me as well."

Triumph presented her with one of his White House pens and she signed two copies of the agreement. Silvia handed one copy to Triumph, then folded the other copy and put it in her Chanel purse. She sat back on the couch, crossing her legs in manner that caused her dress to ride up a few inches and provide an accentuated view of her legs. She shifted on the couch to address Triumph, who seated himself a short distance away.

"Let's discuss my proposal, Mr. Triumph… I mean 'Donald'," started Silvia.

"Not until I become a better host," said Triumph in a fake attempt at chivalry. "Can I offer you a drink?" he asked, walking over to the full bar in his office.

"No, thank you. I don't want to do anything that will take you away from Melancholia tonight."

"Don't worry about that," Triumph said quickly. "My wife is spending this week at Triumph Tower in New York."

"Still, no thank you. I don't want alcohol to affect our important business discussion tonight."

"Well, I hope you don't mind me having one," said Triumph as he poured himself a large glass of Augusta bourbon on the rocks. "Cheers," he said as he took a large drink from the glass. "What do you have on your mind?"

"As I said on the phone, despite being your only real challenger for the Republican nomination, I think it would be best for everyone, including for our country, if we unify. I propose to withdraw from the race so you can become the Republican nominee without any opposition, letting our party focus on beating Burden and the Democrats in the coming election."

"I'm not worried about winning the Republican nomination and don't really consider you a challenge," Triumph boasted. "But I agree it's best for everyone the less dissension we have in the GOP. I'm puzzled, however. What's in it for you to concede right now? You don't seem to be the type of person who does something for nothing in exchange."

"You are a good observer of people, Donald," lied Silvia, recrossing her legs. "I do want something in exchange for dropping out of the election, and that's your assurance that you will select me as your VP running mate."

Triumph bluffed, "It's too early for me to commit to that, Silvia. There are lots of considerations to take into account before I could do that."

"Well, I've looked very closely at this matter. Here's why I think any decision you make in selecting a VP points directly to me."

"OK, I'll hear you out," Triumph said, taking another drink of bourbon while letting his eyes roam.

"There are three basic decision trees in selecting a VP. One branch is to select a VP nominee who will follow the Hippocratic path and 'do no harm' to the slate. With a dominant presidential candidate, this is the safest approach. But I think we can both agree the upcoming election is likely to be very close. Let's face it. Burden has already beaten you once."

Before Triumph could respond, Silvia continued. "The second approach to selecting a VP is to pick someone you think will give you a big state or voting block that you might otherwise not win. While most VPs don't have the clout to affect an election outcome, it has happened. For instance, Landon Johnson helped JFK narrowly carry Johnson's home state of Texas in 1960 and win the White House.

"The third and final VP selection path is what I would call the 'Hail Mary.' This is a last-ditch attempt to save a campaign that is on the road to almost sure defeat. Picking a partner that breaks the political mold can bring huge media attention that can be very beneficial. However, there are also dangers… think about when John McClain chose little-known Alaska governor Sarah Painlin as his running mate. After a very brief honeymoon period, lots of questions were raised during the campaign about her preparedness for the White House, since a VP is always just a heartbeat away from being president."

"So, where do you come in?" asked Triumph, standing up to refill his bourbon.

"I'm the VP who can help you most in a tight race. With all humility, my success in the race shows I'm a rising star in the party. I've got great name recognition and, most importantly, I will draw a large portion of the Hispanic and female vote to our ticket. That's two voting blocs you desperately need."

Silvia paused to let her analysis sink in, but Triumph seemed distracted.

"Silvia, my concern is that you would clash with me too much. After what Spence failed to do for me on January 6, I need a VP who I can trust to do everything I ask. Do I have your pledge of loyalty and service?" Triumph rose from his seat and walked behind the end of the couch where Silvia was seated.

"Can I count on you to do that, Silvia?" he repeated from behind her. Before she could answer, Silvia felt Triumph's short, stubby hands grope clumsily at her breasts. Silvia instinctively yanked away and stood up to confront her aggressor.

"DONALD," she yelled with sarcasm in her voice. "Having sex with you would NEVER be part of our relationship."

Triumph seemed unfazed and uncaring about Silvia's reaction.

"You are a beautiful woman," he said, moving toward the front of the couch and reaching out to grab her. Triumph was a big, portly man and it was hard for Silvia to find space away from her attacker. When she got some separation by stepping to the side of the couch, Silvia kicked him as hard as she could in the groin. Triumph keeled over in pain, but managed to reach out and slap Silvia as she grabbed her purse and ran toward the door.

"You bitch!" he screamed. The long fingernails on his hand raked her cheek, drawing blood and leaving three scratch marks like she had been clawed by a bear. One of Triumph's security goons was there when she opened the door to flee. Not knowing what had happened inside, he didn't know whether to stop Silvia or not.

Silvia yelled at him, "You try to stop me from leaving and I'll sue you for assisting in a rape!"

That stopped the guard in his tracks. He stood motionless as Silvia ran to escape from the house. When she reached the front entry, she saw the driver who had picked her up at the airport standing next to the laundry van parked in the half-moon driveway. She jumped in the back seat and yelled, "Drive! I want out of here as fast as possible. Get me to the airport!"

Surprisingly, the driver didn't hesitate and immediately started to drive her back to the airport. Seeing in his rearview mirror that blood was dripping from Silvia's face, the driver pulled over to the side of the road and handed her his handkerchief. With a look of embarrassment and sorrow on his face, he sheepishly said, "Sorry for whatever happened in your meeting. Sometimes the boss can get a little out of control."

Silvia took the handkerchief and cried, "That's an understatement. He just tried to rape me! He'll be lucky if I don't add rape and assault to the ninety-one criminal charges he's already facing!" Trembling, Silvia pressed the handkerchief against her cheek to stop the bleeding.

115

WASHINGTON, D.C., MARCH 18, 2024

Silvia's campaign team alerted the news media to a press conference at her campaign headquarters that would involve an announcement of "critical significance" to the presidential race. Silvia carefully applied extra makeup and concealer to her face to hide almost all of Triumph's scratches as she got ready to face the horde of cameras and reporters that awaited her announcement.

Donald Triumph had not been in any communication with Silvia since their meeting had ended on a disastrous note two nights ago. He told his staff that he wanted to watch the announcement of Silvia alone in the solitude of his office, fearful that Silvia's message would soon derail all his political aspirations. He wasn't concerned about the legal implications of being accused of attempted rape or assault… he could always lie and assert that everything was a misunderstanding and fully consensual. He had been down that road before. It was embarrassing and costly, but nothing he and his squad of lawyers couldn't handle.

However, Silvia was a rising star in the party. She was liked and trusted by many. Accusations from her would carry a lot more weight and influence than the accusations of hookers and other women in his past. For the first time, Triumph felt vulnerable, and that his political career was about to end as he watched his TV screen.

The time came for the press conference to begin, and Silvia strode to a make-shift podium in her campaign quarters. Framed by numerous "Silvia 5-Ever", "SlamRod 5-Ever" and other campaign posters and placards in the background, Silvia started the press conference by flashing her magnetic smile.

"Ladies and gentlemen. Thank you very much for coming here today. I have a significant announcement to make. I hope it has been very clear to everyone during my career and this campaign that I love America very much. It is without a doubt the best and most important country in the world. Because of my love for America, and after much reflection and prayer, I have decided it is in the best interest of all that I withdraw immediately as a candidate for the presidency."

Silvia paused as there was a noticeable gasp in the audience. Many of her loyal staffers yelled "No!" and had tears form in their eyes. In Mar-a-Lago, Triumph dropped his drink in complete surprise at his great fortune, but didn't bother to clean up his spill. As usual, the mess Triumph made would soon be someone else's problem.

Silvia continued. "I want to, first, thank all my staffers and supporters here and throughout the country. I can never thank you enough for your loyalty and hard work. I will never forget you.

"Please do not feel abandoned by my decision today. I have always tried to act in the best interest of our country, and I think my withdrawal does exactly that. Our Republican party and our country need to be unified now more than ever. I hope that by withdrawing from the race, the Republican party can unify behind President Triumph, and that the general election can be a campaign where both sides focus on their plans to make our country even greater, even more prosperous, even more unified.

"Those are my goals, and I think I can best accomplish them by continuing to be a leader representing Arizona and the country in the House of Representatives. Therefore, in addition to announcing my withdrawal from the presidential race, I am also announcing my candidacy to be re-elected as an Arizona Congressman. That's all I have to say for now. God bless you and God bless the United States of America."

Before she could leave the podium, a reporter from FoxNews peppered her with a question. "Ms. Rodriguez, your announcement today must be welcome news to former President Triumph since you were his biggest challenger for the Republican nomination. I assume this also makes you the most likely person to be his vice president. Have you discussed this with Mr. Triumph?"

"No," Silvia lied. "I haven't. But I am not interested in the vice president post. I think my best opportunity for leadership that will have a positive impact on our country is just as I mentioned, as a member of Arizona's congressional delegation."

Silvia strode away from the podium, flashed her smile one last time to the reporters covering the presidential race, and began the next phase of Jefe's and Professor's plan to get her into the White House.

116

GROSS OFFICE, MARCH 19, 2024

Straw's face looked glum and dejected when Nick and Samantha arrived at the GROSS office. It was clear that he had heard the news about Silvia's withdrawal from the election.

"Straw, what do you think about Rodriguez's surprising withdrawal from the race to be president?" Nick asked.

"I'm tired and broken with words half-spoken, and lots of thoughts unclear. I need a box of rain to ease my pain. I can only conclude that her withdrawal means my theory of her being Santos' puppet president is wrong. If only I could be less blind, if only I knew what to find, it's bending my mind. Guess it really doesn't matter anyway. Sometimes false alarm is the only game in town."

Straw looked up and saw confusion on the faces of Nick and Sam. "For the life of me," Straw said, "I can't square her withdrawal from the race and her chance to be VP, with my theory that I was so confident was real." Straw rubbed his eyes and held his head in his hands like he was suffering a migraine headache.

117

WASHINGTON, D.C., JULY 4, 2024

After Silvia withdrew from the race, the other candidates followed suit in asserted efforts to unify the party. In reality, most of these candidates, with the exception of Christee, had only entered the race in the hope of being selected VP or being appointed by Triumph to a cabinet post. Without any competition, Triumph steamrolled through the remaining primaries and quickly gathered more than enough delegates to assure his nomination prior to the Republican National Committee convention in Milwaukee in mid-July.

Triumph took advantage of the patriotic July 4 holiday to host a news conference on the grounds of the Washington Monument to announce his selection of a VP running mate. With the Washington Monument behind him, Triumph stood before rows of reporters and cameras, his stringy strawberry hair blowing in the wind.

"In this historic setting I have a historic announcement to make. A lot of people, and a lot of really qualified people I might add, have expressed a desire to be my vice president. But one person stood out to me above all the rest. Today I am proud to announce that this person, and trust me, she's a really, really great woman, that will join me is someone all of you know very well from her service as governor of South Dakota.

She's a proven conservative who I expect will be loyal to me under all circumstances. I look forward to having her join our team to make America great again. So, I am pleased to announce that my running mate and the next vice president is Kristy Gnome."

118

JULY 4, 2024

"So, Professor, what do you think of Triumph's selection of Gnome as his VP?" asked Jefe to start their pre-arranged phone call.

"I think it was a logical choice. With what happened between Triumph and Silvia in their last meeting, and her public announcement that she had no interest in the VP position, Gnome can step in and try to be 'Silvia-lite'. She'll help attract some of the female vote, which is a polling area of weakness for Triumph, but unlike either Silvia or Hayley, Gnome won't help with the minority vote."

"Do you think it will be enough to overtake Burden and win in the general election?"

"I really don't think so. While Triumph has loyal supporters, I think lots of voters are going to think about whether they want to put a person in the highest office in the land who may very well become a convicted criminal. That's something that may happen in third world countries, but it would be immensely embarrassing for the United States of America."

"I guess we really don't care who wins," said Jefe. "Don't you think it's time you had your discussion with Triumph?"

"Yes, Jefe. I think it is time for me to connect with Triumph and make sure we are on the same wavelength. I'll line up a meeting when things have settled down after the holiday and he's done responding to questions about his VP selection. I'll let you know how it goes."

"Good. By the way, do you think Triumph has a clue that Silvia never wanted to be his VP when she met him and discussed it at Mar-a-Lago?"

"No. She played him perfectly, and he fell for it. Hook, line, and sinker."

"Great. Before we hang up, is Silvia still looking like a lock to be re-elected to Congress?"

"Yes, she seems to be a shoo-in. I expect her to win in a landslide."

"Excellent news. Thanks!"

119

MAR-A-LAGO, FLORIDA, JULY 10, 2024

Apart from his behind-the-scenes representation of Silvia on behalf of Jefe, Professor did not have any public role in connection with the 2024 election. Nevertheless, his reputation and clout as an elite electoral strategist meant that his phone calls would be answered by any candidate, even former President Donald Triumph. However, Professor did not want to have any conversation with Triumph until they actually met in person. So, Professor placed a call to Triumph's campaign coordinator and indicated that he had important information regarding the upcoming election that required an exclusive, in-person meeting with the former president. Triumph was going to take a break before the RNC convention in mid-July and play golf while staying at Mar-a-Lago. Triumph's campaign manager set up a private meeting for breakfast the morning of July 10.

Professor arrived at Triumph's beautiful Mar-a-Lago estate fifteen minutes before their meeting time. He was asked to wait in a room where fresh-brewed coffee and daily newspapers from Miami, Washington, and New York were available. Professor grabbed a cup of coffee and settled into a large, comfortable chair. About thirty minutes later, a Triumph employee entered the room, informed Professor that Triumph was ready for their meeting, and led Professor to Triumph's office.

Professor stood near the office door until the staffer left the room and shut the door behind him. The office appeared exactly as Silvia had described it to him. Triumph was sitting behind his desk in golf attire. He didn't apologize for the late start to the meeting, but instead motioned Professor to sit in a chair across from his desk.

As Professor walked toward the desk, Triumph eyed him over and said, "Xavier Moody, the renowned Democrat election strategist. You've piqued my curiosity. Why would you want to talk with a Republican? I admit, I've admired your work on past campaigns. Maybe you are coming here to work for me?"

Professor chuckled. "That will never happen. Let's focus on the business at hand."

Professor opened his cell phone. A video clip of Triumph's assault on Silvia played, showing him groping her before getting kicked in his groin, complete with expletives and other audio from the event.

"I knew I hadn't seen the last of that bitch," muttered Triumph under his breath as he got up from his chair and paced around the room anxiously. "What do you want? I don't react too kindly to blackmail."

"I have no desire to blackmail you, but you will sit down and listen to everything I tell you. If you don't agree to all of my requests, this video goes straight to the Washington Post, and your political and personal career is OVER!"

Triumph paused, contemplating whether he had any other options. He chose to sit down on the couch in the exact spot that Silvia had recorded her meeting with hidden mini cameras in her Chanel purse and bracelet.

Professor let a few seconds pass so the enormity of the situation would sink in with Triumph. He then said, "You are lucky, Mr. Triumph. If I had my way, this video would be released, and you'd spend the rest of your life behind bars for attempted rape. I personally think that is the best thing that could happen for our country as well. But Ms. Rodriguez has other thoughts, and I'm just serving as her messenger here. Here is what she requires and, I repeat, there are NO negotiations here. It is her way or the highway."

"So, what does the bitch want?" asked Triumph, unable to temper the rage he was feeling.

"First, if you call Silvia that again, I will personally beat the crap out of you to teach you a lesson you should have learned long ago about how to treat women."

Triumph started to rise from the couch as if ready to challenge Professor, but decided to back off.

When the testosterone in the room had settled down, Professor continued. "You're lucky. Silvia has only one request in exchange for never releasing this video. Whether you are elected or not, Silvia wants your assurance that you will use your influence to support her goal of becoming the next Speaker of the House."

Triumph started to protest, but Professor interjected, "You seem to have already forgotten… this is non-negotiable. I want you to look me in the eyes and tell me we have a deal. I also want you to see in my eyes how quickly I will make this recording public if you ever do anything but support her as the next Speaker."

Professor stared intently at Triumph, who looked at him and said, "I promise. But, how do you know that the Republicans will even control the House in 2024?"

"I'm more confident of that than your chances of beating Burden. But whether you win or lose, you will do whatever we ask to help Silvia get the votes to be Speaker. I'm now very confident that you will do that for her."

Professor started walking toward the office door. "And that concludes our meeting Mr. Triumph."

120

WASHINGTON, D.C., JULY 10, 2024

After arriving back home from his trip to Mar-a-Lago, Professor called Jefe on a burner phone.

"How did your meeting go with the former president?" asked Jefe.

"About as well as can be expected. It was priceless seeing the shocked look on his face when I played Silvia's video. I think Triumph appreciates how serious we are about releasing the recording if he doesn't cooperate with us. But, he's also a habitual liar. We may have to keep reminding him of the consequences of not complying with our wishes."

"Professor, you recently told me that you don't think Triumph will beat Burden. If that happens, will he really have any influence to help us get Silvia elected as Speaker?"

"Yes, I think so. His influence will be greater if he's the president. But even if he loses, there will be a strong base of people who still support him. So, his power within the party won't go away merely because he loses to Burden a second time. But heaven help us all if Triumph runs again in 2028!"

"I don't even want to think about that possibility," moaned Jefe.

121

AUGUST 20, 2024

Jefe watched with great interest as the campaign battle between Triumph and Burden unfolded. Despite their many attacks on the campaign trail, the Triumph/Gnome team had difficulty overcoming the slight lead Burden/Harris maintained in the polls. Jefe decided to call Professor for his updated assessment.

"Hi, Professor. Hope all is going well. I thought I'd ask for your quick analysis of how the election season is proceeding?"

"Sure thing, Jefe. All is good here and I hope it's the same for you and your family. On the election front, Silvia continues to enrapture Arizona voters and will have no difficulty getting elected to Congress. But, that's when our real challenge starts to get her elected as Speaker.

"On the presidential side, in addition to the economy getting stronger, the Democrats are counting their blessings every night that Triumph is the Republican nominee. Nightly media coverage of his legal trouble continues to display Triumph in a negative light, drain his finances, and weaken his attacks on Burden. Gnome is doing a great job and dominated in the recent VP debate with Harris, but no one pays as much attention to a VP. Bottom line: Triumph's transgressions and self-created problems are finally starting to haunt him, making him a nightmare for the Republican party and a dream come true for the Democrats. I don't see anything that will change this before the actual election in November."

122

DETROIT, MICHIGAN, AUGUST 23, 2024

Professor would quickly come to regret his last words to Jefe.

The Democratic National Convention in Chicago was anti-climactic since it was a foregone conclusion that Burden and Harris would lead the Democrat ticket. When the convention ended, the Democratic National Committee committed President Burden to attend campaign rallies in the neighboring states of Wisconsin and Michigan, two key swing states in which his margin of victory over Triumph was less than three percent in 2020.

An oppressive heat wave throughout the upper-Midwest caused reduced attendance at the first rally, despite the best efforts of Burden's campaign staff to utilize ice fans and other cooling devices. After the rally in Wisconsin, Burden mentioned to his aides that "anyone who doesn't believe in global warming or climate change hasn't been living in the Midwest."

Burden changed out of his sweat-soaked clothes on Air Force One as they headed to Detroit for the final campaign event of the day. Temperatures topped triple digits when they arrived in Detroit, and it felt even hotter due to the humidity. Not a cloud dotted the sky when Burden exited the plane. Unfortunately, the event was outdoors at a park near the GM plant to celebrate incentives in Burden's economic plan to support electronic vehicles like the Chevy Volt.

Despite the heat, the rally was well-attended. The audience reacted energetically to Burden's comments about how important the car industry and Motor City are to the economic success of the country. The people laughed at his jokes about the weather and how he felt tempted to jump in nearby Cass Lake or Lake Huron. Despite it being his second rally of the day, Burden felt energized by the enthusiasm of the supportive crowd and spoke longer than at the prior rally. When he finally walked off the podium to heartfelt cheers and clapping, Burden plopped down in the Town Car with a smile on his face.

"That was a good day's work," he said to his aides in the car, "but I'm glad for this air conditioning!"

On the way to the airport, Burden called his wife Jill, who had been at an educational fund raiser in Washington that prevented her from joining Burden on the campaign trail that day.

"Hello, FLOTUS," he said when she answered.

"Hello, POTUS," she chuckled in reply.

They proceeded to give each other updates of the day's events. After telling his wife the estimated time of his arrival back at the White House and saying he loved her, Burden hung up and rested his eyes for the remainder of the trip to the airport.

Burden's rest was short in duration as it seemed like just minutes before the Town Car was on the tarmac next to Air Force One. Burden grabbed a plastic bottle of water from the car, thanked the driver, and walked up the flight of steps to the door of the huge plane. At the top of the steps, he turned to wave and say something to the small crowd of his aides and reporters who were at the foot of the plane, but no words came from his mouth.

A look of confusion came over Burden's face and he blinked his eyes to clear up blurring in his vision. He suddenly felt numbness in his left arm, making him drop his water bottle. Burden instinctively reached to grab it, but lost his balance and tumbled head-first down the stairs in a manner that no stunt man would ever attempt. He landed at the bottom of the stairs in a thud, blood gushing from wounds to his head and mouth. Two teeth lay next to his body, which started to spasm upon hitting the ground. Aides rushed to his side as his body convulsed uncontrollably.

Burden's traveling doctor arrived at the scene as Burden's convulsions stopped. He quickly checked the president's vital signs and ordered some of the aides to stabilize Burden's head while treating his bloody head wound.

An ambulance pulled up to Air Force One. Burden's doctor helped load the president on a stretcher while stabilizing his head. The medics placed him carefully in the ambulance for transport to the nearest hospital. The ambulance departed the airport with the police escort that always accompanied the president leading the way, sirens blaring and lights flashing.

123

DETROIT, MICHIGAN, AUGUST 24, 2024

All of America, and most of the world, were glued to their TV sets awaiting word on the status of President Burden. Video of his horrific tumble down the stairs of Air Force One had permeated all TV stations and social media platforms. Vigils on his behalf quickly formed outside the White House and at churches and other locations across the country. Well-wishes poured in from Triumph, public officials, and world leaders. The nation waited… and waited… and waited.

The first official news from the hospital came approximately twelve hours after Burden's fall. The hospital's board room had been converted into a press room where the major national and local news stations were allowed to report. Hospital administrators had given minor updates through the night, but promised a more formal and complete announcement at the first opportunity.

At 10:05 a.m., the president of Hendry Ford Hospital, Rich DeNero, and Dr. Will Cutter, the head of its neurosurgery department, walked to the makeshift podium. The hospital president was the first to speak.

"Thank you all for being here under these unfortunate circumstances. Our report this morning will be brief and to the point based on the facts we know now. As the situation progresses, we will bring you updates."

He paused for a second as if to let the severity of the situation sink in, and then continued.

"Last night, President Burden arrived at Hendry Ford Hospital at 10:14 p.m. after suffering a fall. After his arrival, our medical staff, with the assistance of the president's physician who was at the scene of his fall, quickly diagnosed the president with three broken ribs, a punctured lung, a broken collarbone, and a traumatic brain injury from his fall. Our top-notch medical team, including one of the best neurosurgeons in the country, Dr. Will Cutter, who will speak next, immediately started treatment. I'll let Dr. Cutter describe in more detail the treatment that was provided, but I will say that the president arrived here in a coma and remains in one. At no time did the president's heart ever stop beating. He is now in the ICU, resting as comfortably as possible considering the nature of his injuries. Dr. Cutter, will you now please provide a description of the medical care that was provided to President Burden?"

Dr. Will Cutter, an attractive, tall, fit, forty-something doctor with a slightly receding hairline, stepped to the podium in his white coat with the confident swagger possessed by most surgeons.

"Thank you, President DeNero. You gave a very accurate description of the injuries suffered by President Burden. With respect to the treatment that was provided to President Burden, let me start with the easiest one first. One of President Burden's injuries from the fall was a pneumothorax… a punctured lung. Our trauma surgeon in the ER, Dr. Richard Rasch, successfully did a needle aspiration to remove excess air that had leaked between his lung and chest wall. We don't view this as providing any significant issues or concerns going forward."

Dr. Cutter paused and then continued. "As I said, that was the easy one. Much more serious and concerning was the traumatic brain injury suffered by the president. We did a number of scans and other tests and determined that the president had a complex brain bleed with lots of internal swelling. There was significant tearing of the brain's long connecting nerve fibers when the president's brain was injured as it shifted and rotated inside the hard skull because of his fall down the stairs. This is the cause of his coma, and it also means that the injury to the brain was not just localized, but was in multiple parts of the brain."

"As a result of this diagnosis, we readied the president as quickly as possible for surgery. Along with my team, I performed a complex surgery called a craniectomy to relieve the hemorrhaging that was occurring inside his brain. As I said, this is one of the more complicated forms of brain surgery and the procedure lasted approximately four hours. I am confident that we were able to relieve the internal bleeding and swelling. However, the next couple of days will be critical. As President DeNero stated, the president remains in a coma in ICU. That will help his brain and body to heal. However, I won't venture any prediction regarding how long the coma will last at this time."

Dr. Cutter moved back from the podium to let President DeNero give the final remarks.

"Thank you, Dr. Cutter. On behalf of Hendry Ford Hospital, I'm sure that the country feels fortunate that President Burden had one of the nation's best neurosurgeons in the world attending to him."

Before DeNero could continue, a question was shouted from the audience. "Dr. Cutter, can you tell us what the prognosis is for President Burden to make a full recovery?"

Cutter stepped back to the podium, but with less swagger to his step. His voice was somber as he said, "President Burden has suffered a severe brain injury. It's too early to tell, but if he recovers fully, it will only be after an extensive rehabilitation program, including with respect to his cognitive skills. I say this recognizing that each brain injury and rate of recovery is unique. The president's age does not help in this regard, but we also know that he is a determined fighter and should never be underestimated. Right now, let's all just give him our thoughts and prayers."

124

DETROIT, MICHIGAN, SEPTEMBER 6, 2024

President Joe Burden was one tough hombre. Two weeks after his fall down the stairs of Air Force One, Burden awoke from his coma at Hendry Ford Hospital. The coma had allowed his brain swelling to subside, but a lengthy recovery still awaited him.

In light of Burden's incapacity, Camelot Harris had been sworn in as acting president pursuant to the Constitution, becoming the first woman president in the history of the United States. Out of deference and respect to Burden during his coma, she had refrained from making any comment regarding her desire to serve as the Democrat's nominee for president in the upcoming general election should Burden not be able. However, top officials in the DNC, the strategic and coordinating arm of the Democrat party, had discussed alternatives immediately after Burden's admission to the hospital.

With Burden's acknowledgment that he was no longer physically able to serve, the DNC scrambled to adjust their ticket to compete with Triumph and Gnome on the Republican side. It was uniformly agreed that Harris would lead the ticket, but some dissension arose regarding her VP running mate. Some in the DNC wanted rising star Hakeem Jefreeze, the first African American party leader in the House in history. However, party leaders overall felt that the country was not ready for two people of color to be in the White House. Accordingly, the Democratic National Committee selected Chuck Scheemer, the Senate majority leader, to be a New York counterbalance to Triumph on the ticket.

125

WASHINGTON, D.C., SEPTEMBER 7, 2024

Defense Secretary Lloyd Boston placed a secure phone call to Lieutenant Commander Patrick Payne that was answered immediately.

"Lieutenant Commander Payne, I previously passed on your request regarding the Clean Slate Protocol matter to President Burden for his consideration. I have not received any response from him. In light of his current medical condition, there will obviously be some delay in getting an answer from President Harris. I will let you know when I get any updates."

"Thank you, Mr. Secretary."

126

WASHINGTON, D.C., NOVEMBER 4, 2024

It was the day before election day across the country. Jefe called Professor to get his insights on the presidential election, notwithstanding Silvia's withdrawal from the race.

"Professor, with election day being tomorrow, I'd like to get your predictions of the outcome. Do you anticipate any surprises?"

"As you know, when Burden fell out of the race, the entire dynamics of the election did a complete reversal. Triumph became the immediate front-runner by a healthy margin in the polls. Despite all his legal problems and divisive personality, he still has a comfortable lead in the polls."

"So, you are predicting a Triumph victory?"

"Yes, but I think it will be a tighter race than the polls currently show. But ultimately, I don't think America is ready for an inexperienced Black woman president, notwithstanding the energetic campaigning that former President Olama has done on her behalf."

"Even when the alternative is Triumph?"

"Yes, especially because he has the experience of previously serving as president. I know I'm preaching to the choir, but the parties in this country really need to do a better job of giving us higher quality candidates. Otherwise, there might be a real avenue for No Label or some other independent third party to step in and really shake things up."

"Are you going to be glad when the election is over, Professor?"

"I'm ready for it to be over, and I'm tired of seeing the same negative advertising every time I turn on the TV or listen to the radio. But I am a lot less stressed now that Silvia is out of the race! Silvia, by the way, will have no trouble regaining her House seat tomorrow. But overall, the political scientist side of me has enjoyed watching the race unfold."

"Do you fear for the future of America if Triumph wins again?"

"Of course. We know from experience that if you elect a clown, you are going to get a circus. Heaven help us all!"

"That is scary. I think you need to get Silvia elected as Speaker."

"That's next on my agenda, Jefe! Thankfully, it looks like the House will remain controlled by the Republicans, notwithstanding the view of many that it was going to flip to the Democrats."

127

NOVEMBER 21, 2024

In the aftermath of his election victory, Triumph was busy re-establishing his connections in the Capitol City, rewarding significant loyal donors with personal calls and appearances, filling his cabinet posts, and planning for his inauguration ceremony. Like his prior cabinet, Triumph's selections to fill the posts was based more on loyalty than talent, creating a large echo chamber. With his history of firing or chastising all who disagree with him, Triumph was circling himself with robotic supporters who blindly amplified and reinforced his positions inside a vacuum insulated from rebuttal.

With Triumph's cabinet largely finalized, it was time to think about governing the country and getting momentum on his legislative agenda once the transition of power formally occurred in January. However, nothing could happen legislatively in Congress after an election until the Speaker of the House was selected. Getting Silvia selected as Speaker was critical to the plans of Jefe, so he called Professor for a progress report.

"Professor, please remind me of the considerations that apply when the House elects its Speaker."

"Sure thing, Jefe," Professor said. "In general, the majority party needs to decide whether it wants someone in the Speaker role who will build bridges with the other party to try to accomplish things on a bi-partisan basis or, like so many times in the past, limit the Speaker role to just making sure the majority party position is advanced.

"In addition, the role of the Speaker will vary based on whether the Speaker and the president belong to the same party. If they do, like currently, then the primary role of the Speaker is usually to advance the president's platform. But if the Speaker and the president are from different parties, then the Speaker is normally the chief public opponent of the president's agenda. Think of how crazy Speaker Nancy Pelosee used to drive President Triumph during his first term in office.

"Finally, if the same party stays in the majority in the House, then frequently the incumbent Speaker continues."

Jefe interjected, "So, we now have Republicans who have stayed in control of the House along with Triumph as a president who is also a Republican. Doesn't that mean that current Speaker Mike Johnsen feels he's a shoo-in to continue as the next Speaker?"

"I'm sure he feels that way, but he's got a big surprise coming! I acknowledge that we may initially face some headwinds in trying to get Silvia selected as Speaker. Historically, this position is filled by the majority party from among its senior leaders. Although we have been at this for over a decade, Silvia has not been in Congress long enough to be considered a 'senior' leader."

"So, what's our best approach to get Silvia in?" Jefe asked.

"Normally, the only bargaining chip that the leading candidate can use to turn votes is either the threat or promise of committee posts. To my knowledge, no one has ever used money, in addition to presidential pressure, as the lever in this process… until now. With your funding support, Jefe, Silvia has helped a lot of the current members in the House get elected. I expect they will be loyal to her when she makes her wishes to become Speaker known. Let's be very honest here. Since House elections occur every two years, there's a saying that House members start campaigning for the next election the day after the current election. Though crazy, this means that anyone who can generate significant campaign contributions has an opportunity for influence."

"So, we bought some influence. But will this be enough to get Silvia selected Speaker?"

"Yes, because I think we have three key factors working in our favor. First, as we just discussed, House members engage in continuous campaigning, and we won't be subtle in reminding members of Silvia's funding assistance. Second, I will soon be calling President Triumph and calling in the chip we have with him to support Silvia as Speaker, or release the video of his physical assault on Silvia. Triumph obviously is riding high on his election victory, and he'll carry great clout when he informs Republican House members that he fully supports Silvia as the next Speaker. I can't wait to see the surprise on the face of Mike Johnsen when that happens!

"Third, despite her lack of seniority, Silvia has established herself as a known, loyal, and trustworthy rising star in the party. Her campaign for the presidency was inspiring to most everyone, including her willingness to challenge Triumph on various issues. And then, her selfless withdrawal from the race to help unify the party gained her even more admiration.

"Silvia has, I think, proven that she would be great under our system of checks and balances. They may not admit it in public, but I think most Republicans recognize that some checks are needed against Triumph due to his volatility. Triumph may surround himself with a rubber stamp cabinet. But in Congress, it won't be in the best interests of the country to have a rubber stamp Speaker like McCarthage or Johnsen. Republicans will get this with Silvia, and it will even come with Triumph's blessing thanks to the blackmail we have against him!"

"You sound very persuasive, Professor. Now, go make it happen!"

128

BLAIR HOUSE, WASHINGTON, D.C., NOVEMBER 22, 2024

Consistent with the grace of their administration, President Harris offered to meet with Triumph at the White House prior to Thanksgiving to engage in preliminary discussions of national security issues and other matters important to a seamless transition of power to a newly elected president. Former President Burden was also scheduled to make one of his first public appearances at the event since his fall, providing a great photo opportunity to help unify the country.

Professor took advantage of Triumph's meeting at the White House to schedule, with President Harris's consent, a meeting with Triumph immediately afterwards at the nearby Blair House. Located just across Pennsylvania Avenue from the White House, the Blair House is government-owned property for the exclusive use by the president and vice president. Foreign dignitaries stay there when visiting the U.S., and newly elected presidents often stay there in the days preceding their inauguration and the transfer of White House living premises.

Professor scheduled the meeting to occur in the Dillon Drawing Room, a room known for its unique Chinese print wallpaper and its vases from the Ming dynasty. Often used as a room to formally receive important foreign visitors, Professor thought this would be the perfect place to have an under-the-radar meeting with the new president. As a surprise to Triumph, Professor also arranged for Silvia to attend.

Professor didn't want to arrive at the same time as Silvia, so he showed up early and waited patiently for the others. Silvia arrived next, intentionally wearing the same tight-fitting maroon dress and carrying the same Chanel purse that comprised her outfit that tempted Triumph when they last met at Mar-a-Lago.

Professor and Silvia shared a hug and then sat next to the fireplace in the room, leaving Triumph with the chair directly opposite them. Triumph entered the room twenty minutes later, motioning to his Secret Service detail to stay outside the room.

"Good afternoon, Xavier," started Triumph. He gulped when he noticed Silvia. "Good afternoon, Silvia. I didn't know you would be here as well," Triumph stuttered, with a bead of sweat appearing on his forehead. He walked toward them, extending his hand.

Neither Professor nor Silvia accepted the offer of a handshake.

"Silvia," Triumph said in a condescending tone, "congratulations on your election victory. I would have thought things would be friendlier between us since we'll be working together."

"Let me make this perfectly clear, *Donald*," Silvia said sternly. "The only thing that exceeds my disgust for you is the love that I have for this country. I think I more than proved that when I never released the recording when you tried to rape me, then withdrew from the race to unify the party."

"I don't think 'rape' is the right word. It was more of a stumble," Triumph said.

"Stop the bullshit, *Donald*," Silvia said, quickly interrupting him. "Here's the reality of our situation. I find you disgusting and hope that we will never again be alone together. However, in public, I will do nothing but act supportive as we try to accomplish positive things for our country."

"I suppose you are recording me again today?"

"Absolutely. If for some reason Xavier couldn't attend today, my best defense against you is documenting your real behavior."

"You bitch!" shouted Triumph. "I don't take very well to blackmail."

"This is not blackmail," Professor said. "It's just a business negotiation. For the good of our country, we think Silvia could best serve as Speaker of the House. We also think it is in your best interest to help her get elected to that position."

"And if I don't agree to help?"

"If you break your prior promise to me," snarled Professor, "I think you know how I will respond. You can risk career-ending legal trouble based on the evidence we have against you. Or, you can help the country move forward. As Speaker, Silvia would be your ally in coordinating with the House on critical legislation. Seems like an easy choice to me, but you do have a history of doing idiotic things."

Triumph paused, infuriated.

"Don't be stupid, Mr. President," said Professor.

"OK, what exactly do you want from me?" asked Triumph, with the same glare as his infamous mug shot.

"Quite simple. First, we want you to sign this short letter proclaiming your support of Silvia for Speaker. Second, if you have any meetings with key House Republicans, we expect you to convince them to support Silvia for Speaker. Third, we want you to never mention this meeting or ever say anything contrary to your support of Silvia as Speaker."

"This will really piss off current Speaker Mike Johnsen."

"I'm confident you can deal with that situation," Professor said.

"What assurances do I have that there will never be a leak of that video?" Triumph asked.

"You have our words, which in our case is actually worth something."

Triumph scowled before he reluctantly signed the letter of support for Silvia. He then stormed out of the Dillon Drawing Room without saying another word.

129

WASHINGTON, D.C., NOVEMBER 25, 2024

The election over, lame duck President Harris was going over a long list of items to consider before her limited time in office ended. Among the requests were various pardons and a unique request regarding a Clean Slate Protocol matter.

I wonder what that is? thought President Harris.

She opened the file and was fascinated with the contents. Upon getting to the end of the file, President Harris called Secretary of Defense Lloyd Boston.

"Hi Lloyd," said President Harris. "I just reviewed the Nick Class Clean Slate Protocol file. I haven't been president long, but the one legacy I don't want is allowing a violent threat to endanger our country on my watch. You have my authorization for Lieutenant Commander Patrick Payne to eliminate Nick Class. I'll send you a signed authorization tomorrow."

The stunned silence on the other end of the phone was obvious. Finally, Secretary Boston said, "Thank you, Madame President," and hung up.

130

WASHINGTON, D.C., DECEMBER 16, 2024

After Thanksgiving, Silvia met with dozens of Republican House members behind the scenes to discuss her interest in becoming the next Speaker. She received positive feedback from the meetings. The vast majority of the members were persuaded to support Silvia as Speaker after seeing the letter from Triumph and being reminded of Silvia's fundraising impact on their election campaigns. Professor and Silvia decided the next step was for Silvia to meet with current Speaker Mike Johnsen in person.

Silvia arranged to meet Speaker Johnsen first thing on Monday morning. During her first stint in Congress, Silvia had always worked well with Johnsen, though she was much more moderate in her political beliefs. She arrived at his office in the Rayburn House Office Building carrying a box of a dozen fresh donuts from a local bakery. She flashed Johnsen her infectious smile, shook his hand, and offered him the box of donuts.

"Thanks for agreeing to meet with me early in the morning, Mike. I know you Louisiana congressmen don't often indulge in fresh donuts outside of Mardi Gras, but I was hoping you would make an exception today."

"Of course, Silvia," said Johnsen, opening the box and selecting a chocolate-covered donut. "Would you like some coffee? I've always got a fresh pot brewing."

"Thank you, that would be great."

Johnsen poured her a cup of hazelnut coffee and handed it to her with a smile. "So, what's on your mind today, Congresswoman Rodriguez?"

"Mike, I've always liked and respected you, so I'll be very direct. I didn't want this to catch you by surprise later, so I wanted to tell you in person that I am hoping to be the next Speaker."

Johnsen's eyes widened, but he kept his composure and smile.

"Silvia, you are clearly entitled to throw your name in the hat. But, I would counsel you against it. As you know, it took numerous ballots two years ago to get Kevin McCarthage re-elected as Speaker. Then later, our party took a lot of heat when he was removed and eventually replaced by me. I don't think Republicans want another inter-party battle for the Speaker position, and I think it's clear that I've consolidated support among the Republicans in Congress since then. Most importantly, I also have the support of President Triumph."

"I'm sorry to say, Mike, but the situation has changed. I've already had preliminary discussions with a number of our party members, and most have indicated support for me. And, I will say, it has helped to have a letter from President Triumph indicating his support for me as Speaker." Silvia pulled the letter from her purse to show him.

Surprise, fury, and outrage covered Johnsen's face. He swiped the letter from Silvia's hand and quickly read it.

"I don't believe this!" Johnsen cried in exasperation. "This has got to be a fake."

"I have Triumph on speed-dial if you want to call him for confirmation."

"I think you're bluffing. Call him up!"

Silvia pulled out her cell phone and, with the push of a button, called President-elect Triumph. She put it on speaker phone as it rang.

Triumph answered grumpily. "Hello, Silvia. Your timing is not great. What do you need?"

"Mr. President," Silvia said sweetly. "Sorry to bother you, but I have you on speaker phone, pardon the pun, with Mike Johnsen. I've just informed Mike that I intend to challenge him for the Speaker position, and I told him that I had your full support. He wanted to hear confirmation of that from you."

"Uh, Mike. Silvia's right. I think it's best that my new administration starts fresh with Congress, and having her as Speaker will help."

"Mr. President, you've got to be kidding me," said Johnsen, his irritation obvious. "I have championed your agenda ever since becoming Speaker, even when you weren't the president. How can you really believe that she'll be a better representative for you?"

"Sorry I didn't tell you earlier, Mike, but that's my decision. Gotta go now. They are waiting for me to tee off." The president then hung up.

Johnsen looked at Silvia. "Now I know why you surprised everyone and withdrew from the race."

Silvia didn't react to his statement. "Mike, I meant it when I said that I like you. I know this is shocking, but I'd like to give you some time to think about the current situation. Then, I'd ask for your support in my quest to be the next Speaker. In the meantime, I'm going to continue talking with House members to get their support. If you decide to cooperate with me instead of challenging me, I'll let you announce your change of heart any way that you would like. If you make this an easy transition, I promise you'll be happy with the committee assignments I give you."

Johnsen looked defeated when he said, "Let me digest things. I'll let you know in a few days." He then grabbed another donut and showed her to the door.

131

BALTIMORE, MARYLAND CITY JAIL, JANUARY 2, 2025

Luis Rojas and six other members of the Los Leones gang spent New Year's Eve in jail. New Baltimore Police Chief Richard Lorwey wanted to send a message that the city would start the year being "tough on crime/tough on drugs." Busted by police in the Baltimore harbor unloading a significant shipment of drugs from an unknown source, each of the gang members had been booked, read their Miranda rights, and then separately interrogated by Baltimore detectives trying to get to the source of the drugs. The gang members had all been taught to never talk to the police without the presence of counsel. The attorney would be readily provided and paid for by laundered money of the drug kingpin, which unbeknownst to the gang members, was Salvador Santos.

All the gang complied, except Luis Rojas. With one young child and another on the way, Rojas was looking to make a nest egg and then get out of the gang life. However, as a two-time offender, the current arrest almost assuredly meant that Rojas was going to serve significant time in prison... unless he cut a deal.

In his quest to avoid prison time, Rojas squealed to the authorities, giving details that he knew about the Los Leones connection to the drug pipeline from Mexico. He also mentioned that he was required to make multiple contributions to political candidates of drug money that had been deposited in his account. He named Silvia Rodriguez and other Republican members of the House of Representatives as recipients of his pass-through donations. He concluded the interrogation by stating that "Goliath will soon demolish David."

132

GROSS OFFICE, JANUARY 2, 2025

Details of the confession of Luis Rojas, and his accusations of drug money being used to influence Congressional candidates, quickly circulated among multiple intelligence agencies. Straw's computer notified him of this new information when he arrived at the GROSS office.

Straw read the intelligence reports twice, then sat back in his chair. A smile crossed his face. *"I knew there was a connection between Santos and Silvia Rodriguez. And this confirms my suspicions. Time to start digging some more."*

133

WASHINGTON, D.C., JANUARY 4, 2025

The morning the House of Representatives was scheduled to vote on the Speaker for the upcoming term, current Speaker Mike Johnsen held an impromptu press conference.

"Ladies and gentlemen, as you know, the House is scheduled to meet in a short time to vote on the next Speaker. I wanted to inform you that, for various reasons, I have decided to withdraw my name from consideration for this important position." Audible mumbles and gasps emanated from the press corps, who rarely showed surprise at announcements from the podium.

Johnsen continued, "I have discussed giving up my role as Speaker with the president and many current members of the House, and they fully support my decision. Serving as Speaker can, quite frankly, be very exhausting. I hope to spend the next term representing my constituents from Louisiana on important committee posts and having more time to spend with my family. I don't have time to address any questions since deliberations for my successor will begin shortly. I am confident that we will elect new, vibrant leadership to this position who will help advance the interests of both our party and the country during these challenging times. Thank you for your understanding and support."

134

U.S. CAPITOL BUILDING, HOUSE CHAMBER, JANUARY 4, 2025

Trial lawyers have a saying that you should never ask a question for which you do not already know the answer. Silvia had taken that wisdom and applied it to her quest to be the next Speaker.

Working countless hours in the background in the weeks before the House convened, Silvia was confident that she had the votes and that her selection as Speaker was a foregone conclusion. Some Democrats on the House floor were surprised how quickly the discussions favored Silvia as Johnsen's replacement, but they could do nothing to stop the groundswell of support that Silvia received. With endorsements from both Triumph and Johnsen, coupled with the swaying influence of her fundraising skills, the vote for Speaker became a mere formality. Silvia was elected on the first ballot.

135

JANUARY 4, 2025

"Congratulations on getting Silvia selected as Speaker, Professor. That's a fantastic accomplishment." Jefe said on a burner phone.

"Thank you, Jefe. I am very happy that everything fell into place as we had planned and hoped."

"Yes, and now it is time to focus on the next step on our agenda."

"I understand. How is construction going on Goliath?"

"Everything is on or ahead of schedule, which is great. Today, I would like to get your insights on Camp David. I remember you saying that President Clanton took you and other leaders of his campaign team there to celebrate his election victory."

"Yes! Anything in particular that you would like to know?"

"Not really. Just your observations about Camp David in general, its layout, and any security insights you can provide."

"OK, let me start with the basics," said Professor. "As you know, Camp David is the country retreat for POTUS. It is in the wooded hills of Catoctin Mountain Park in Maryland, near the towns of Thurmont and Emmitsburg, about sixty miles north-northwest of Washington, D.C.

"The president and his guests stay in plush, individual cabins. All events or activities occur nearby. The cabins are rustic, but very nice and would probably be rated five-stars. Though Camp David itself covers an expansive one hundred twenty-five acres of forested property, the area where the individual cabins are confined is relatively small. That way, no one has a long distance to go for meetings or to socialize with each other. All cabins are connected by curved, well-maintained, paved walking trails. Each cabin has access to an electric golf cart, and that is the usual means of transportation. Although events are within walkable distance, Camp David is hilly in places, so the carts help.

"From a security perspective, since living accommodations and events are limited to just a few acres of the camp, the vast remainder of the area is a buffer from outsiders. Though everyone understands Camp David is well-guarded, the wooded surroundings allow security personnel to remain unobtrusive. Camp David is located at the top of the Catoctin Mountain range, meaning that no one can look into the camp from a higher elevation. Its dense trees and forested vegetation are deep enough that no one on the outside can see what is happening inside the camp. Although the nearest town is only a few miles away, the topography of the camp on the mountaintop makes it very isolated.

"Ground ingress to the camp is limited to one road, with the gated and guarded entrance surrounded by formidable electric fencing that extends across the vast exterior of the camp. Helicopter traffic over Camp David is frequent, both for transportation to Camp David as well as security. Overall security for the Camp is provided by the Navy and Marine Corps.

"There are a lot of entertainment options at Camp David, but entertainment only comes after getting the work done. The president and whatever staff he brings to Camp David control the work agenda. Some work gets done in the guest cabins where one or more Cabinet officers or their top staff may gather to focus on a specific issue. When something is ready for presentation to the president, a meeting will most often be scheduled in the president's cabin, which is two or three times larger than the other cabins and is complete with its own outdoor pool and putting green. The largest of meetings are held in the Laurel Lodge conference room.

"Does that help you, Jefe?"

"I think so. Thank you! From what you've told me, it sounds like our plan will accomplish our goals if we can drop our 'gift' anywhere around the cabins, but especially near the president's cabin with the swimming pool."

136

GROSS OFFICE, JANUARY 4, 2025

"Isn't that an interesting coincidence?" said Straw to nobody in particular as the GROSS team debated what to do for lunch.

"What are you talking about, Straw?" asked Nick. "I thought you didn't believe in coincidences."

"I'll admit that sometimes random things occur, but most often I think there's a reason behind most actions and events… just like now."

"What are you talking about?" asked Sam.

"The quick election of Silvia Rodriguez as the next Speaker of the House."

"Why is that surprising? She looked like a rising star in the party, and lots of Republicans appreciated that she withdrew from the race so that a fight between her and Triumph didn't split the party."

"You are right, but I remain surprised by her decision to leave the race when she did. I also remain skeptical as to her real motives for leaving the race. Today, it's just surprising how quickly the House unified around her. It's even more surprising to hear that both Triumph and Johnsen formally pushed for her selection. Usually, the Speaker role goes to a member of the House with lots of seniority, and usually things are debated for longer than one morning. Heck, it took Kevin McCarthage four days and fifteen votes to get selected Speaker two years ago."

137

WASHINGTON, D.C., JANUARY 20, 2025

A gloomy and rainy day could do nothing to dampen the spirits of Triumph and his enthusiastic supporters during his inauguration as the 47th President of the United States. Triumph ordered his staff in advance of the event to ensure that the inauguration ceremony was filled with more pomp and circumstance than ever before. "Make it the biggest and best ever" were his exact words.

Consistent with history, the day started with the swearing-in ceremony on the west lawn of the Capitol. President Triumph and Vice President Gnome were given the oaths of office by the Chief Justice of the Supreme Court. After being sworn in, Triumph made one of the best speeches of his life when he gave his inaugural address. The speech was void of references to conspiracy theories, personal legal problems, or divisive comments about Democrats or other past targets. Instead, the speech was focused on a positive future for America and, somewhat surprisingly, mentioned his desire to work cooperatively with Democrats to move our country forward. Whether real or not, Triumph's focus on unifying the country for the good of all was welcomed by the crowd and received thunderous applause.

Following his inaugural address, President Triumph and VP Gnome lead the inaugural parade the approximate mile and a half from the Capitol to the White House. After watching the parade continue from his new and former residence, President Triumph had a brief break in the schedule to rest before attending the Presidential Inaugural Committee Ball and other black-tie events across town. The president seemed to relish every moment, including his performance in leading his lovely wife Meloncholia in the first dance at the Presidential Inaugural Committee Ball in front of a multitude of supporters. His dancing performance was greeted with more cheers, to which the president responded that "he wasn't quite ready to compete on Dancing With The Stars." Positivity, smiles, and laughter continued throughout the night.

138

WASHINGTON, D.C., JANUARY 23, 2025

Nick Class awoke before sunrise for his normal run through the neighborhood. While doing some pre-run stretches, Nick noticed, but paid little attention to, a plain black van parked two houses down from his brownstone.

Inside the van, Lieutenant Commander Patrick Payne marveled at the modifications he had made to the interior of the vehicle to turn it into his mobile sniper's nest. He had bolted a captain's chair two and a half feet from the rear window of the van. Connected to the chair at shoulder level was a sturdy eighteen-inch-wide oak slab that was anchored to the van's back door at the base of the window. All windows in the van had been darkened with tinted privacy glass. The back window of the van had undergone one other special modification — the cutting of a two-inch diameter circle in the window. The two-inch circle was covered with small flaps like a doggie door, through which the end of a sniper barrel could be placed while still giving the shooter the ability to make shooting adjustments.

Payne was sitting in his captain's chair at the back of the van. His sniper rifle of choice, an M110A1 CSASS made by Heckler & Koch, rested on the oak panel with the rifle's bipod providing critical stability. Payne had modified his weapon to include a detachable suppressor to reduce muzzle flash, and his folding front sight gave him perfect vision of his target through the back window of the van. Though not as accurate as bolt-action longer-range rifles, Payne didn't think his shot at Nick would ever come close to the eight-hundred-meter range of the weapon.

Payne had been tracking Nick for a week. Payne learned of Nick's routines… his early morning runs, drives to and from work at a real estate consulting firm, and the routes he took with both. Every time he saw Nick, Payne's blood boiled as his mind flashed back to their fateful encounter years ago when Nick beat him up in front of his SEAL trainees.

Revenge will soon be mine, thought Payne. He had determined that the best opportunity to terminate Nick would be outside of his brownstone at the start of his morning run, before the rest of the neighborhood was awake. *I can't believe I even have President Harris's authorization to do this,* smiled Payne.

Consistent with his traditional workout, Nick stood outside his house doing leg and windmill stretches before starting his morning run. Payne had parked the van in a perfect spot, giving him a clear shot at Nick. Payne looked through his scope, the end of his sniper rifle barely peeking out of the circular hole in the back window.

No problems with accuracy at this range, thought Payne as he focused his sighting for a straight shot at Nick's heart.

"Goodbye Nick Class," muttered Payne as his finger gently touched the trigger… and then stopped.

The only thing more satisfying that killing you here and now, thought Payne as he put the safety back on the rifle, *would be killing you when you watch me do it. Until we meet again, Nick Class… soon!*

139

GROSS OFFICE, JANUARY 23, 2025

"Well, our country has survived three days under the second-coming of the Triumph administration without any unusual drama or divisiveness," Nick said as he walked into the GROSS office. "Hope it all continues!"

"Well," Samantha chimed in, "the start of the new administration really hasn't happened yet. Everyone pretty much takes the whole week of inauguration off. In fact, we won't really know what the Triumph administration is going to try to accomplish until next week, after the president, vice president and all his cabinet meet in Camp David to define their specific objectives for the upcoming session of Congress."

"I guess time will tell. We can only cross our fingers and hope our government officials leave their egos and politics at the door, and instead try to govern for the good of our country."

"Well said, Nick. I couldn't agree with you more," said Straw. Then he suddenly swerved his head toward Samantha. "Wait a second. Did you say that the president's entire team is going to Camp David in a few days?"

"Yes, on Saturday," Sam said. "That's common for presidents to do at the start of their terms. Why? Is that important?"

"I don't know…" Straw turned to his screens, a far-away glazed look in his eyes as he pecked away furiously on his keyboard.

140

GOLIATH CAMPUS, JANUARY 24, 2025

Dmitri Federov woke up early and walked around the Goliath campus for the hundredth time, ensuring everything was in order.

"Is the 'package' ready to be delivered to Camp David?" Dmitri asked Jose Hernandez, the most trusted member of Los Leones who Dmitri had placed in charge to oversee security of the baby nuke in their possession.

"Yes, sir," replied Jose. "The carrier drone is ready to lift off with the 'package' whenever you give the green light."

"Gracias. The time is almost upon us. I expect to give you those orders tonight after everyone in Camp David is sound asleep."

141

CAMP DAVID, JANUARY 24, 2025

President Triumph and all his cabinet members arrived at Camp David as planned around sundown and checked into their respective cabins. After a late dinner together, they called it an early night in anticipation of a full day of meetings the next day.

The only person missing from the event was Vice President Gnome, who stayed back in Washington. Her eldest daughter had gone into labor much earlier than expected while visiting D.C. to attend the swearing-in ceremonies, and Gnome wanted to be present for the birth of her granddaughter. After a lengthy labor, the baby was born shortly before midnight. After posing for pictures holding the new infant alongside the healthy mother, Vice President Gnome went home around 1 a.m. In her Town Car on the way to her house, Gnome called the pilot of the executive branch's helicopter who was waiting to fly her to Camp David, to alert him to a change in plans.

"Ma'am," said the helicopter pilot, "there's a big weather system coming in. If you want to get to Camp David, we need to either leave now before it arrives, or wait until fourteen hundred hours when it should be safe to leave. That should get you there about an hour later."

"I'm totally beat and too old to pull an all-nighter," replied the vice president. "They don't really need me for the morning meetings, so I'll see you at fourteen hundred sharp, unless you let me know that a different time is needed because of the storm."

142

GOLIATH CAMPUS, SATURDAY MORNING, JANUARY 25, 2025

At 3 a.m. the local news broadcast an alert about an impending storm in the area. The alert flashed on the big screen TV monitor hanging on a side wall of the adult lounge that was presumably to be used by parents of Goliath campers, but nobody in the room paid any attention to it. Dmitri Federov and his core team of assistants had gathered there for a celebratory drink in advance of their historic mission.

Champagne glasses had been passed to all present when Dmitri raised his hand for silence as he wanted to speak with full attention.

"Gentleman, we are about to make history tonight. History that will change the world for the better. Before we initiate the launch, let us toast to our part of a great event!"

Before they could clink glasses and say "cheers," breaking news came on the TV screen showing Vice President Gnome along with the first public pictures of her holding her granddaughter. A quick interview followed of Gnome stating what a blessing it was to be with her daughter and granddaughter before going to Camp David.

No one was paying attention to the TV except for Jefe in Vera Cruz and Professor in Washington. They both immediately dialed Dmitri on his secure phone. Jefe's call went through first.

"Jefe, we are just about to put the plan in action. Vamos con Dios!" Dmitri exclaimed with great fervor.

"Dmitri," interrupted Jefe, "we must postpone. I repeat… we must postpone! The vice president is NOT in Camp David. We must wait until after she arrives. Hopefully that will be in a few hours. We may lose the surprise of an attack at night while they sleep, but the outcome should be the same. I will call you when the Goliath plan is ready to go. Wait until then."

"Yes, Jefe. Per your orders."

143

SATURDAY MORNING, JANUARY 25, 2025

At 5 a.m. two weather fronts collided in the Washington and neighboring Maryland area, creating a storm of staggering proportions that centered in the Catoctin mountains near Camp David. Howling winds caused the torrential rain to pour sideways across the black horizon. The darkness of the clouds racing across the sky was offset by blazing lightning strikes that zig-zagged like a strobe light with great frequency, and the ear-shattering blasts of the accompanying thunder awakened many people from their slumbers. Electricity in the area popped on and off like popcorn as old trees snapped and fell on power lines and blocked roads. Backup power generators kept the lights on at both Camp David and Goliath.

144

SATURDAY MORNING, JANUARY 25, 2025

Nick planned to sleep late on Saturday morning, but the peaceful silence of his home was shattered by the ring of his cell phone.

"We need you at the office immediately," Samantha said in a tone that indicated there was no alternative. "We'll fill you in when you get here."

Nick hopped out of bed, noticing that his clock radio was blinking. The clock on the oven in his kitchen was doing the same. It was clear the storm had caused a power outage in the area during the night, but Nick was thankful he currently had working electricity.

Concerned about the tone in Samantha's voice and the urgency of her request, Nick grabbed a Glock .45 from his dresser drawer. Just in case, he took an extra magazine from the drawer in the bottom of his desk.

Nick hopped in Sadie and headed to the GROSS office. He was slowed by some collapsed tree limbs in his neighborhood and water flooding some of the streets, but otherwise made good time thanks to very little traffic.

"What's up?" asked Nick as he hustled into the office, where he was greeted by a welcoming "woof" from Straw's dog, Cassidy.

The dog's energetic tailwagging was in stark contrast to the obvious tension in the office. Straw, in particular, looked very frazzled.

"I…I…I don't really know for sure," stuttered Straw. "But I think that something really bad is about to go down. I just can't prove any of it!"

"What are you thinking?" asked Nick while he patted Cassidy's head.

"Let me try to summarize so Straw can keep digging for more clues," Samantha said. "As you know, for a long time Straw has believed there might be a rogue nuclear device in existence and that it was somehow tied to Mexico… more specifically, to Salvador Santos. In addition, Straw thought Santos was funneling cash to try to influence elections in the U.S. That's why he was suspicious when Silvia Rodriguez quickly climbed the political ladder.

"The trouble with these theories is there's no real hard proof… just circumstantial evidence that Straw is using to connect the dots. Plus, Straw couldn't ever come up with a reason why people in Mexico needed a nuclear bomb. When Rodriguez withdrew from the presidential race, that also kind of derailed Straw's theory that Santos was pushing for her to be the next president."

"So, what has changed?" asked Nick.

Straw looked up from his monitors. "Two new items have really piqued my curiosity. What truth is proof against all lies?"

"Straw, please! Straight talk only," Samantha urged.

"Sorry," Straw said, trying to refocus. "The first thing raising my eyebrows was Rodriguez getting elected as Speaker on the first ballot, with the support of both Triumph and incumbent Speaker Johnsen. I'm not a political historian, but that seems odd for someone with such little tenure in Washington. I wonder if that's the quid pro quo for her surprising exit from the campaign. I was shocked when she got out of the race, and then surprised even more when she said she wasn't interested in being vice president. But maybe it was Triumph's promise of support for her being Speaker that enticed her to leave the race."

"With all due respect, Straw, that seems to be based on a lot of speculation, not facts," said Nick.

"You are right, Nick, but I think I'm really close to tying all the loose ends together… at least in my mind. I've thought for a while that Santos is the center of all my concerns."

"Do you think Santos has something that lets him control Triumph?" Nick asked.

"No, I don't believe there's any direct connection between Santos and Triumph. I'm really just focused on Santos. I've been intrigued whether someone like Santos could use his money and resources to infiltrate America's democracy. If I look at things through his lens, then I can see lots of favorable opportunities Santos could create by interjecting himself in our political system."

Straw paused for a second and then continued. "I've spent a lot of time digging into Santos's background… trying to think like him and understand him. The more I know about him, the more I conclude he is like the iceberg in Titanic. The part that you can see above water is beautiful and harmless. But the ninety percent that is beneath the surface is dangerous and can do treacherous things that are rarely seen. To the public he's a generous, smart, entrepreneurial businessman who became incredibly wealthy through hard work and diverse investments. But if you dig beneath the surface of his skin, you find that he's involved in lots of cartel activities and criminal enterprises that make money off people's weaknesses."

"I'm still confused," Samantha said. "If Santos is really trying to control the presidency, why wouldn't have Rodriguez just stayed in the race or at least positioned herself to be Triumph's vice president?"

"That question is a good one, Sam, and it baffled me for quite some time. When Rodriguez dropped out of the race, I thought she was gone and nothing was gonna bring her back to the presidency. But I think I've finally figured it out.

"Santos is a smart businessman who knows how to play the odds. Though Rodriguez was doing well in the primaries, she was still far from overtaking Triumph and his hardcore base of loyal supporters. So, I agreed with you and couldn't figure out why she wouldn't posture to become his VP. As vice president she would be positioned to be the leading Republican candidate in 2028 when Triumph would be term-limited from running again. Or, if something happened to Triumph before then, she would succeed to the presidency, just like Harris did after Burden's fall. That all made sense until I looked at it from Santos's perspective. If Santos's ultimate goal is to have her be his puppet president, then having Rodriguez as Triumph's VP puts all of his eggs in one basket.

"Let's remember that when Rodriguez withdrew from the race and announced that she wasn't interested in the VP post, Triumph was still behind Burden in the polls. Also remember that Burden had already beaten Triumph once before. So, making Silvia Triumph's VP was risky to Santos since a Burden victory in the general election would result in Rodriguez being without any role or position of influence in Washington. Plus, Burden hadn't fallen down the Air Force One stairs at the time, and no one could have predicted that he would have to exit the race.

"So, looking at things from Santos's perspective, the safest move at the time was for Rodriguez to be re-elected to the House. She was beloved in Arizona and would almost automatically be elected. Plus, the odds were good that the House would continue to be controlled by Republicans. This would give her a chance to then become Speaker of the House if she had some leverage over Triumph or Johnsen to have them support her in that position."

"I don't understand," Nick said. "Why is it important for her to be Speaker?"

Samantha answered his question. "Because under the succession rules of the Constitution, if both the president and vice president are unable to perform their roles, the next person up to serve as president is the Speaker of the House."

"WHOA," exclaimed Nick. "So, you think someone... Santos... is going to try to kill the president *and* vice president?" Nick shuddered at the thought.

"Yes," Straw said. "And I think that may even happen today."

"WHAT?" Nick said excitedly.

"What makes you think that?" Sam asked.

"I said earlier that two recent events raised my suspicion. The first was Rodriguez becoming Speaker under unusual circumstances. The second was the confession of Luis Rojas after the New Year's Day drug bust in Baltimore. I've watched his confession countless times. My focus was always on his statements that connected donations of drug money to Rodriguez and other political candidates."

"Can you really trust whatever a gang member says to try to keep from going to prison?" asked Nick.

"I always take the information I get with a grain of salt. I think I've become adept at being able to parse the chaff from the seed. Smart lies always contain an element of truth to be believable and two telltale signs of a liar are when the speaker blinks or his eyes cut away while talking.

"I've watched the video of Luis Rojas' confession multiple times. He never blinked unnaturally or cut his eyes away. I am convinced he was telling the truth. I also think I was wrong to focus on the drug money donations to the candidates. Now, I think the most important part of his confession was his final statement: 'Goliath will soon demolish David.'"

"What does that even mean?" Nick asked. "Sounds like hallucinogenic drug talk to me."

"I also didn't know what to think of that statement," admitted Straw. "Rojas is out of jail on bail, but I haven't been able to contact him for a more complete explanation. But here's my concern. The president, the vice president, and all their key advisors are at Camp David this weekend. What if that is the 'David' that Rojas said was going to be demolished by Goliath?

"So, I've been digging to find what 'Goliath' could be? For the last couple of years, there has been construction going on in Woodsboro, Maryland for a facility to provide underprivileged children the opportunity to go camping in the mountains."

"What's the significance of that?" asked Sam. "That all seems pretty harmless."

"The facility goes by the name Goliath, and Woodsboro is just about twelve miles from Camp David. I've also been unable to determine who own Goliath. That is suspicious to me in and of itself," said Straw as he kept pecking at his keyboard looking for additional information.

"So, you think Santos will try to kill the president and VP?" asked Nick. "But how?"

"I'm not positive, but this is where I think the stolen nuke may come into play. I had previously been trying to come up with a reason or plan why Santos or anyone else in Mexico might want to use a weapon of mass destruction against the United States. This led me down a bit of a rabbit hole. My best guess now is that the stolen nuke isn't intended to be used as a weapon of mass destruction, but rather as a weapon of assured destruction at Camp David. To kill all people on site."

"Have you alerted the White House and the military about this attack?"

"I've informed some of my contacts about my concerns, but it's a little difficult since GROSS does not officially exist. Plus, lots of cell towers have been knocked out by the storm, so it's really been hard getting in contact with people, including your dad, Nick.

"My contacts in the Pentagon and Langley all want more proof beyond my assassination conspiracy theory. I can appreciate their concern, but when it comes to the safety of the president, I really wish these people weren't as concerned about covering their own asses! It's not often terrorists give us a roadmap to their plans!"

"Straw, we all trust you and your ability to see things that others don't. I think that's why you're the best," said Sam.

"I agree one hundred percent!" Nick said. "So, what do we do next?"

"I think all we can do is drive to Goliath and knock on their door," Straw said. "Hopefully they will prove me wrong, but let's prepare for the opposite."

"Let's roll!"

145

SATURDAY MORNING, JANUARY 25, 2025

Straw, Sam, and Nick were walking to leave GROSS when the office door slammed open. Lieutenant Commander Patrick Payne rushed into the office, brandishing a SIG Sauer MCX assault rifle that he pointed directly at Nick.

"Stop where you are and put your hands above your heads," commanded Payne. "And shut up the dog before I do it," he threatened as Cassidy growled furiously.

The GROSS trio stopped in their tracks.

"Heel, Cassidy!" Straw ordered.

"Payne!" Nick uttered, their past flashing back in his mind. "What are you doing here?"

"Finally getting my revenge against you," Payne said. "I've waited a long time to get the pleasure of you watching me end your life."

"Payne, I've always known you were an asshole, but I never thought you were a murderer."

"Murderer? Not at all. I've got authorization from the president to kill you!"

Nick was shocked. "But… but Triumph hasn't even been in office a week."

"Not Triumph. Harris. She was convinced you were dangerous to our country since you broke the Clean Slate Protocol."

"Did Harris authorize you to kill my partners?" Nick asked, pointing to Sam and Straw.

"No, but I'm sure they'll just be viewed as 'collateral damage.'"

"Did Harris authorize you to kill President Triumph?" Sam asked.

"No, but what does that have to do with anything?" Payne asked, shaking his head quizzically.

"It has EVERYTHING to do with this," Straw yelled. "Do you know what we do here? We're not a real estate firm. That's just a façade. Our real work is preventing terrorism. And right now, we really need to go because we think the president is in imminent danger."

"You're bluffing," Payne said.

"Not at all," said Sam. "You shoot Nick, you might as well be shooting President Triumph."

"Look, we don't have much time to waste," Straw said. "If I show you some classified intelligence documents, will you believe us?"

Straw didn't wait for an answer, bravely turning around and walking back to his screens. He typed a few strokes on his keyboard and opened documents on his screens. "Take a quick look at these, but you gotta hurry."

Payne paused, not sure what to do.

"Payne, I've never liked you," Nick said, "but I always that you were first and foremost a patriot. If you kill us, then whatever happens today to Triumph is going to be on your shoulders. And I don't think you could live with that."

Payne walked over to Straw's monitors, keeping his assault rifle leveled at Nick. After glancing at some of the information, his brows slowly unfurrowed.

"I guess I kinda expected something like this after seeing the report about the guy you killed in Knoxville. Was that part of what you do here?"

The GROSS trio all nodded.

"Shit. Nick, you may be the luckiest man alive. But if I find out that you've been bluffing me, trust me. I will kill you, and I'll make it painful."

"Well, we're not bluffing and we really need to go," Nick replied. "We could also use some help if you want to join us."

"I wouldn't miss it," said Payne.

"Get in our car. We'll explain everything on our way to Camp David," Straw said, hurrying toward the door.

146

JANUARY 25, 2025

Nick, Sam, Straw, Payne, and Cassidy jumped into Sadie for the trip to Goliath. Though driving conditions were horrendous because of the storm, there were few cars on the road and Nick made good time once he reached the beltway.

As they drove, Sam briefed Payne while Straw continued his search for additional information to support his theory about an impending nuclear strike on Camp David. About thirty minutes from their destination, Straw suddenly said, "Bingo!"

"What did you find, Straw?" asked Sam from the back seat of Sadie, with Cassidy curled up between her and Payne.

Straw showed a photo on his laptop to Samantha. "It's a picture from eighteen months ago from the weekly newspaper in Thurmond, a city close to Camp David. It shows the beginning of construction of a new facility called *Goliath*."

"It looks just like a normal construction site photo to me," Samantha said after looking at Straw's screen. "What's important about this?"

"It's not the construction that's important. It's the person standing at the side of the construction site at the left edge of the photo. It's a little blurry, but my facial recognition tools say that is Dmitri Federov, the top assistant to Aleksandr Medvedev. Remember that Medvedev was the key contact person with Putrid regarding the Ukraine attack that supposedly destroyed the two Russian nukes?"

"Damn," whispered Samantha solemnly. "What would Federov be doing at the Goliath campus?"

"I'm afraid he'll be doing exactly as I feared," Straw replied.

"Straw, if Federov is on-site at Goliath, I'm sure he'll have others there as well to provide protection. If that's the case, we're going to need a lot more firepower than just the four of us in Sadie," commented Sam.

"Working on it," Straw said. "In about five minutes I'm going to need you to pull off the road to the right when you see a place called the Hideaway Bar."

"Do you really think we have time to pull over for a drink?" asked Nick curiously.

"I think that might be exactly what we need."

147

HIDEAWAY BAR, JANUARY 25, 2025

Nick pulled into the parking lot of the local bar as instructed by Straw. It was a typical dive bar, appropriately named the Hideaway Bar, with neon signs of beer companies showing through steel-barred windows to travelers on the highway. Notwithstanding the treacherous weather, the gravel parking lot was surprisingly full of large trucks and numerous motorcycles. The musty smell of cigarettes, marijuana, and mold and loud sounds of "Truckin" by the Grateful Dead greeted the group as they entered the dingy bar.

Despite being early in the afternoon, the rectangular bar against the side wall was filled with patrons sitting on worn wooden bar stools. The rest of the bar was comprised of rickety wood tables and chairs, two pool tables with faded felt, and a juke box that was kicking out the tunes. Upon closer inspection, cheaply framed photos of Grateful Dead concerts were hung haphazardly on available wall space. At least a dozen people in the bar wore tie-dyed shirts similar to what Straw had on.

The floor had a sticky, gummy feel to it as Nick strode to the middle of the bar. Nick could feel the stares of the bar clientele watch him as he walked, but the noise level did not subside. With a sense of urgency, Nick clapped his hands and said in a loud voice, "Ladies and gentlemen, ladies and gentlemen."

When no one paid him any attention, he repeated his words, only louder. Again, no response. Frustrated, Nick pulled out his Glock .45 and shot two shots into the ceiling. As some plaster from the ceiling fell near his feet, all the people in the bar turned their attention to Nick, at least half of them pulling out their own guns and aiming them at him.

"Maybe you'd better let me handle if from here, Nick," said Straw. "These are my people. Put your gun away."

Straw put his arm around Nick's shoulder as Nick put his gun away.

"Thanks for giving me your attention, and sorry to interrupt the party," Straw said to the crowd. "My friends and I are facing an emergency. Like Althea, our backs could really use some protection. We work for an anti-terrorist organization and our mission is to protect the United States of America. But there is now danger at our door. We think some foreign terrorists are in a facility a few miles from here. Some folks trust in reason, but terrorists trust in might, and I think they are getting ready to nuke Camp David, which is where the president and vice president are currently located. There's no time to convince the military to help us, so we could really use some additional manpower to help stop this plot."

A large, bearded man, at least 6'4" in height and weighing at least three hundred pounds, stepped forward with guns in both of his hands. Both forearms were heavily tattooed with Harley Davidson ink, skulls, and red roses. Wearing faded blue jeans, a Terrapin Station t-shirt, and a bandana holding back his long, straggly hair, it was clear that he was the leader of many of the patrons in the bar.

"It sounds like glorified insanity, and, like a song of Gomorrah, they are trying to blow the city off the map and leave nothing there but fire," he said. Straw nodded in agreement as if they were bonded like twins.

The leader of the bikers walked over to Straw and extended his hand.

"My name is Samson. What's your plan, brother?" he asked Straw, holding up his hands so others in the bar would remain silent.

"Love your t-shirt, Samson. Terrapin Station is a place of imagination and full potential, and we're gonna need some of both. My only plan is to drive up to this facility that they call Goliath and knock on the door. If I'm wrong, then hopefully false alarm is the only game in town, and they'll let us look over the place and make sure it isn't a terrorist hub. If I'm right, I think we'll be greeted with bullets instead of friendly smiles. It will be like a dark star about to crash with trouble ahead and trouble behind."

Samson looked at Straw quizzically and said, "That's one of the worst plans ever in the history of plans. It feels like we are rushing in like a bull without a clue. Hopefully, they won't be much of a matador when we get there. But we all know that there's a price for being free, and freedom don't come easy."

Straw looked at the biker leader. "I know that we are asking you to shadow box the apocalypse and fight a war you can't understand. I'm afraid there's going to be some fire on the mountain, and it may cost a lot to win, but even more to lose. Can we count on you to help us?"

A silence fell across the bar for seconds that seemed like an eternity. Nick couldn't tell whether it was due to apprehension, fear, confusion, or something else. Nick soon understood that the silence was due to the bikers, despite their carefree, beer-guzzling exterior, being first and foremost patriots who would risk death by going into battle whenever called. And, like all loyal Americans, the bikers fiercely hated terrorists.

"We can't let their deal go down. Let's go kick some ass!" yelled Samson, raising his gun to the sky. A chorus of "Hell ya!" and "Fuck the commies!" erupted from the others as they dashed to the front door.

"May the four winds blow you safely home!" yelled Straw as they departed the Hideaway.

"We will get by. We will survive!" replied Samson as he was pelted with a gust of wind and the sting of the rain. Even though rain was cascading down, the bikers did not hesitate as they sped out of the bar and jumped on their motorcycles.

"Let's ride. All gas, no brakes!" yelled the leader as they rode without fear toward Goliath.

148

GOLIATH CAMPUS, JANUARY 25, 2025

"Buckle up. It's going to be a wild ride!" yelled Straw as the GROSS team and Payne jumped into Sadie to continue their journey. "We are about to enter the eye of the hurricane."

It's easier to hide in plain sight in big cities than it is in rural areas, so Goliath was not difficult to find. With their newfound biker friends riding ahead of them like the first wave of Marines, Straw activated Sadie's turbo-drone and sped it ahead of everyone, giving them a visual of the Goliath campus in the distance.

The first sign of civilization the drone camera revealed consisted of farm machinery and construction equipment that were parked neatly on the perimeter of Goliath. Nick could see that significant landscaping remained to be done, and a large mound of freshly removed dirt sat next to a Caterpillar bulldozer at the edge of the campus.

Straw's drone quickly reached the main facility as Sadie's digital clock displayed the time as 2:50 p.m. Goliath looked more like a chic country club than a nonprofit facility for children. Nick looked in his rearview mirror and saw Samantha sizing up the expansive building, looking for access points, angles of advantage, and the location of security cameras. A state of the industry, high-tech polished steel elevator at the rear corner of the building caught Samantha's eye.

Massive boulders were placed in artistic positions throughout the front entry, providing both aesthetics and protection against vehicular attack. Nick noticed a fifty-caliber machine gun perched in a loft window to further protect the front of the Goliath campus. Nick's fingers started to clench and unclench instinctively.

"The drone's heat imager shows a lot of people inside the building," said Straw. "I'd guess there's probably thirty or forty people in there and they have started to scramble around."

From a military strategy perspective, it's generally preferable to assault a target from the rear, where there is often less protective security. However, in certain circumstances, there is no choice but to make a direct frontal confrontation. This was one of those times.

With no opportunity to plan in advance, the bikers arrived before Sadie and approached Goliath on the expansive half-moon driveway that provided access from the road to the front entry. The bikers must have looked threatening to those inside Goliath, because they did not wait for introductions before opening fire. Getting shot at from strategic and protected positions inside the house, the bikers were brave but unprotected from the onslaught of bullets. Machine gun fire dropped a number of the initial wave of bikers in their tracks, their dead or wounded bodies skidding across the driveway while the pelting rain quickly washed away the stains of their blood.

Seeing that the bikers needed protection, Straw made the drone fire both of its missiles at the Goliath entry, creating a loud explosion and fireball when the missiles hit with the front doors. As Sadie entered the front of the Goliath campus, Straw launched smoke camouflage cannisters to provide additional coverage to the remaining bikers. They were either scattering around to the back of Goliath or turning around for a return approach from the other direction, guns pulled.

"Stop here and let me out!" ordered Sam before Nick could drive closer to the main entry of Goliath. "I want to try to outflank them."

Nick slammed on the brakes and Sam exited the car before it came to a complete stop, doing a gymnastics tumble as she hit the ground. Sam quickly jumped to her feet and ran to the side of the building, carrying a Colt M-16 assault rifle and two .40 caliber universal machine pistols. Gunfire from the house greeted Sam, and she was forced to retreat to the side of the campus, running in a zig-zag pattern to avoid bullets until finding protective coverage next to the Caterpillar bulldozer.

Nick could see Sam returning fire with her assault rifle as he gunned Sadie forward to join the action in the center part of the Goliath campus. Coverage from Sadie's smoke grenades provided greater opportunity for the bikers to speed around the near perimeter of the Goliath facility, but their guns were useless against foes shooting from secure positions inside the mansion. Straw quickly tried to improve the odds, shooting fifty-caliber rounds out of Sadie's adjustable front grill gun port and opening Sadie's moon roof to simultaneously assault the mansion from the three Heckler & Koch submachine guns mounted at the top of Sadie. Though Sadie's weaponry caused significant damage to the front structure of Goliath, the number of enemy shooters inside the mansion still greatly outnumbered the GROSS team and the surviving bikers.

As Straw was adjusting Sadie's guns to optimize their effectiveness, Nick saw four bikers expertly maneuver their motorcycles up the front steps of Goliath and literally fly through the charred entry doors the drone had blasted. Nick couldn't see what happened, but heard numerous gun shots from inside the mansion. The battle inside continued for another ten seconds until Nick could no longer hear the roar of the Harleys inside the house.

149

GOLIATH CAMPUS, JANUARY 25, 2025

"Jefe," Dmitri said frantically the second that Jefe answered his burner phone. "We are under attack at Goliath!"

"Attack?!" asked a shocked Jefe. "Who's there?"

"I have no idea. Some of them just have street guns on motorcycles, but others are well-armed in a vehicle with high-tech weapons. I need to know NOW… should I commence the attack on Camp David?"

"Not yet!" yelled Jefe. "The VP is on a helicopter but won't arrive at Camp David for another five minutes. You need to hold off the attack for five more minutes. Then, but only then, you can start the attack. Call me immediately when the launch has been made."

"Yes, Jefe," said Dmitri and hung up the phone.

150

GOLIATH CAMPUS, JANUARY 25, 2025

Things were already chaotic at the front of Goliath… and then they got worse. A new fusillade of bullets pinged off Sadie. Nick was looking to find where the new attack was coming from when Straw yelled, "Sadie is armored, but she can't withstand an anti-tank guided missile. That's what they're aiming at us! Shiiiiiit!"

Nick looked out his window and saw the missile just before it hit his driver-side door. The sound of the impact and explosion was deafening. Sadie did a full flip in the air before landing upright, tossing Nick, Straw, and Payne around like bean bags. The explosion ripped the driver's door of Sadie apart, with pieces of flaming metal flying through the car. Smoke filled the car and Nick's door swung wobbly back and forth, connected to the chassis only by a thread.

As Sadie's sprinkler and ventilation systems kicked in to douse the fires and eliminate the smoke, Nick quickly checked on Straw. He looked dazed and bewildered, grasping his stomach area where a pattern of blood was starting to grow on his shirt.

"Are you OK?" asked Nick while choking on the swirling smoke and his ears ringing loudly. Straw looked at Nick and nodded affirmatively, though Nick could tell he was in pain.

Feeling powerless inside the car and not thinking clearly, Nick crept out of Sadie, landing hands first on the ground and pulling his body behind him as he heard bullets continue to ping off the car's exterior. Payne jumped out right behind Nick, his assault rifle blazing as he yelled and sprinted toward the front door.

The smoke outside of Sadie was starting to dissipate, which was bad since it no longer provided any cover to Nick as he sat outside the car, feeling concussed. Nick felt his body shudder back to life and the haze in his brain started to lift like the smoke around him. Feeling paralyzed and vulnerable outside the car, Nick reached for his universal machine pistols, but the UMPs were nowhere to be found. He looked up as the smoke cleared and saw a Hispanic-looking man pointing a laser-guided pistol at him, the red dot located on Nick's shirt near his heart. Defenseless, Nick waited for the sound of the bullet to end his life. Instead, a loud, vicious growl erupted from Cassidy as the dog jumped to Nick's side, causing the shooter to hesitate. A mini-second before the man could pull the trigger, a shot rang out and the man's head exploded from a bullet coming from the rear of Sadie.

The bikers were at the far end of the house, Payne was at the front of the house, and Sam was in a battle at the rear edge of the house, so Nick's mind couldn't compute what had happened. He glanced to his left to find the answer to the mystery shooter.

Nick's jaw dropped when he saw Blondie, gun still drawn and pointed at Nick's assailant. She looked him in the eyes, smiled, and gave him a thumbs up sign. She then ran to a nearby downed motorcycle, hopped on, and raced toward the far end of the house where a new round of gunfire had just started.

Too confused for words, Nick took his second chance at life to quickly recompose and assess the situation. Looking to his left, Nick saw Samantha engaged in a fierce gun battle as she knelt by a large tree near the bulldozer for cover. Nick could see that Sam was bleeding from a wound to her leg as she peeked around the tree to trigger off a round of shots at her assailants.

Suddenly, the gun in Sam's hand stopped making noise as she squeezed the trigger. Sam was out of bullets! Nick saw Sam reach for another thirty-round magazine as she slid behind the tree for cover, but she came up empty. Her eyes were wide as she looked around for any options to survive. Her eyes made contact with Nick's, and he gave her a palm's down "stay put" signal with his hands. Nick instinctively started running along the front of the house toward Sam. Weaponless himself, Nick didn't have a plan in mind of what to do when he got close to Sam, but he knew he had to try something.

Shots from the side of the house continued to spray bark off the mature tree that was shielding Sam. Recognizing the futility of continued shooting from their location, five gunmen ran from the house toward the tree to flush Sam out or get better angles to execute her. Nick could see that the men were heavily armed, with semi-automatics, handguns, and ammo belts visible to the naked eye. Nick was too far away to intercept the men, but he kept running. The five men raced in a line toward the side of Sam's protective tree until two of them had an angle to fire at her. As the two men pointed their weapons at a defenseless Sam, the whir of Straw's drone could be heard as Straw guided it at full speed into the shooters. Though the drone was not large, its turbo speed at impact immediately decapitated the first shooter and sent him and the kamikaze drone ricocheting into the other shooter, knocking him forcefully to the ground. The third gunman paused at the chaos created by the drone, but then continued to move into position to fire at Sam.

Nick felt a sense of desperation since he was still too far away to help when suddenly Cassidy sped past him and leaped full-speed at the gunman, sinking his teeth into the back of his neck. He stumbled to the ground as Cassidy's momentum caused the heroic dog to bounce off the man and tumble to a stop about ten yards away. This gave Nick, still sprinting at full speed, enough time to throw his body at the back of the other two gunmen. One of the gunmen dropped his weapon upon contact, so Nick turned his attention to the other shooter as they both scrambled to their feet.

The gunman fired an errant shot as he stood up, then raised his gun toward Nick a count too late. Nick karate chopped the man's arm, jarring his radial nerve and disarming him. Nick elbowed his torso and then jammed a thumb in the man's eye. Screaming in pain, Nick wrapped his right arm around his head and clasped his fingers with those in his left hand. A powerful sweep of his arms broke the man's neck with a loud crack.

By this time, the other gunman that Nick had tackled from behind was up and rushing toward the gun he had dropped. Nick beat him to the location and, using his Muay Thai training, punched him forcefully in the kidneys. As the man bent over in pain, Nick grabbed the back of his head and pulled it down to slam against Nick's raised knee, knocking him out cold.

Nick immediately picked up the gun from the ground. Cassidy was continuing his attack, fully occupying the attention of the bleeding gunman as he was scrambling on the ground to get away from the small dog's vicious growls and bites. The remaining gunman who had been knocked down by Straw's drone was still on the ground trying to recover from the surprise collision. He had a dazed look on his face as he raised his weapon in the direction of Nick. He was too slow, and Nick shot him between his eyes. Nick turned to the man being attacked by Cassidy and put two lethal bullets in his chest, taking special care to make sure his shots did not hit Cassidy.

151

GOLIATH CAMPUS, JANUARY 25, 2025

Nick and Cassidy raced to Sam, who was seated next to the tree, blood gushing from her leg. As Nick took off his belt to make a tourniquet, he heard an unusual sound in his ears that were still ringing… the distinctive whirring of a large drone engine. He looked up from Sam to see the doors of an underground shelter in the back yard of the Goliath compound opening and a large drone carrying what appeared to be a missile hovering a small distance above the ground. The drone elevated and flew away from Sam and Nick, providing Nick no opportunity to shoot it down.

Seeing the drone lift off from Goliath carrying a suspicious payload, Nick knew the top priority was intersecting the drone before it reached Camp David. With Cassidy by his side, Nick sprinted back to Sadie. They jumped into the car and found Straw holding his stomach to compress the blood flowing from a wound. It didn't look fatal, so Nick pressed on, hitting the button to open Sadie's trunk and activate its SAMs. The trunk door flipped open. Nick tried to adjust the elevation of the heat-seeking surface-to-air missiles, but the system jammed with a defective whirring sound.

"The anti-tank missile that hit Sadie must have messed up the aiming mechanism for the SAMs," Straw yelled. "If you shoot them now, they will go straight into the hillside and blow up before any heat seeking tracking can guide their path. You need to get them shot in the air headed that way." Straw pointed with a blood-soaked hand toward the departing path of the drone. "And you'd better do it fast before the drone gets out of range."

"Got it!" said Nick. He then shocked Straw by opening the passenger door and shoving Straw outside of the car. "Cassidy, stay with Straw!" Nick ordered and the dog immediately obeyed, jumping out of the car and taking a protective position on the ground next to his owner.

Nick turned the key and, thankfully, Sadie started. Looking in the rear-view mirror, Nick saw a mound of dirt that remained from the unfinished construction of the Goliath compound. Nick gunned Sadie in reverse and headed at top speed toward the hill of dirt, making sure not to hit Samantha as he sped past her. Upon hitting the dirt mound, Sadie went airborne with the back-end highest in the air as the weight of the engine dropped the front-end down. Nick hit the button to release the SAMs and saw them streak out of the trunk into the sky, speeding after the first heat-generating flying object in their path.

Nick didn't get the opportunity to hear if the SAMs would intercept the nuke-carrying drone. Instead, Sadie crashed into the hillside outside of Goliath. Nick was sent flying headfirst into Sadie's windshield, cracking it like a spiderweb. Nick was fading off into unconsciousness as Sadie flipped for what seemed to be an eternity before finally coming to rest upside down in the river flowing at the base of the hillside. Water rushed into Sadie through the driver's side door that had been blown up during the battle. As Sadie started to sink to the bottom of the river, Nick uttered in his last breaths, "Holy Mary, Mother of God, pray for us sinners now and at the moment of our death. Hail Mary, full of grace..." and then lost all consciousness.

152

JANUARY 25, 2025

Professor was watching a news channel on television, expecting to see a breaking story about a bombing at Camp David. Instead, his burner phone rang.

"Goliath failed!" Jefe cried. "You and Silvia need to lay very low. Destroy anything connecting you to me."

153

BETHESDA, MARYLAND, JANUARY 26, 2025

Nick awoke in a hospital room and looked to his side to see that he shared the room with Straw, who had Cherise sitting by his bedside holding his hand. Some of the equipment in the room was stamped "Property of Walter Reed National Military Medical Center," which Nick remembered was in nearby Bethesda, Maryland.

The bullet that hit Straw's stomach had also perforated his bowel, but luckily had missed his major arteries by mere centimeters. When Straw saw that Nick was awake, he proudly showed Nick his colostomy bag.

"Hey, they promise me the bag is temporary," said Straw smiling. "I don't want to be known as 'Bag Man Berry!'"

Nick's conversation with Straw was quickly interrupted when a doctor entered the room to check on Straw's condition. "You ought to go check on Sam. She's next door to us as you exit to the right," Straw advised.

Nick approached Sam's room just as a nurse was walking out the door.

"How is she?" Nick asked.

"She's recovering nicely," the nurse replied. "She had significant blood loss when the bullet pierced her femoral artery, but she's out of danger now."

"Great. Thank you," said Nick as he opened Sam's door.

Nick entered Sam's room and was surprised to see her talking quietly with Blondie.

"Sorry to interrupt," said Nick, "but I wanted to see how you are feeling, Sam."

"I'm doing fine, Nick, thanks mainly to you. Your tourniquet actually saved my life. It kept me from bleeding out before getting medical treatment."

"Glad I could help," Nick said.

"I also need to introduce you to my new friend… our new friend… Valerie Schomer, or as Straw calls her, 'Blondie.' She saved you not just once, but twice at Goliath."

Nick was stupefied and didn't know what to say as Valerie Schomer walked gracefully toward him to extend a welcoming handshake. It was the first time that Nick had ever seen her up close and Valerie did not disappoint. Unlike some women who look hot from far away, Valerie looked prettier the closer she got to Nick. Her attire and accessories clearly revealed that purple was her favorite color, and she wore it well. Her tanned skin gave off a healthy glow and she had sparkling, deep brown eyes and an easy smile. Surprisingly, her real hair color was brown instead of blond.

Nick tried to compose himself as he extended his arm and received Valerie's firm handshake. "I remember one time that you saved me when you shot that guy who had me in his gun sight. But what was the other time?"

"Valerie is the one who saved you from drowning in Sadie," Sam explained. "She saw what happened and rode a motorcycle down the hill to the river faster than I ever thought was possible. She then dove into the river and pulled you out of Sadie just before the entire car plunged to the bottom. You're lucky she's a great swimmer because she pulled you to the riverbank. She got you, me, and Straw all to this hospital."

"Wow! I guess I really do owe my life to you multiple times. Thanks! But who are you, Valerie? And, what were you doing at Goliath?"

"That's easy to answer, Nick," said Carson Class as he entered the hospital room and gave Nick a big, fatherly hug. "Valerie is part of Saving Our Country through Surveillance, or 'SOCS,' a second agency like

GROSS that kind of spies on our spy agencies. When I worked with President Plante to create GROSS, he was emphatic about the need for redundancies, So, SOCS was formed to be a counterpart to GROSS to increase our chances of stopping terrorist activity when the alphabet agencies fall short in their duties."

"Wow," said Nick again. "And we initially thought that 'Blondie' might be part of a terrorist organization!"

"Straw was off there," Sam chuckled.

Nick continued, "So, please tell me what happened after I plunged into the river. Did our SAMs work in time?"

"Yes," Carson said. "They took out the drone that was carrying the baby nuke a few miles from Camp David and the nuke never ignited. Our entire country owes all of you a huge debt of gratitude. But in light of the secrecy of our organizations, there will never be any public record of you foiling the attack. Still, you should sleep proudly tonight knowing that because of you, the presidency still belongs to the American people instead of a foreign terrorist."

"How did things end up at Goliath?" Nick asked. "We were vastly outnumbered. How did we ever get out alive?"

"Valerie is to thank for that as well. Like you at GROSS, her team at SOCS also put the pieces of the intelligence puzzle together to conclude that something fishy was happening at the Goliath campus. When she went to explore and saw the war going on at Goliath, she called her contacts at SOCS, and they sent in three helicopter gunships from the nearby military facility in Baltimore. For the record, the military documents will reflect their usage as a 'training exercise.'

"Well, these helicopters arrived shortly after you shot off the SAMs and a few shots from the big guns on the choppers made the folks inside Goliath surrender very quickly. Two of the helicopters were then used to transport you, Sam, Straw, and some wounded bikers to the military hospital here for the quickest care without attracting any public attention. The other helicopter stayed to ensure that none of the folks inside Goliath wanted to rethink their decision to surrender until we got a bus to take them all into federal custody."

"What about Payne?" Nick asked.

"He made it inside the facility before he was gunned down," Carson responded. "Sam told me what happened at GROSS. Since Payne was the only person officially affiliated with our military, he will go on record as a hero who led the stopping of the attempted attack on the president. He'll get a Medal of Honor and a hero's funeral at Arlington National Cemetery."

Straw entered Sam's hospital room during Carson's explanation. When Carson had concluded, Straw spoke up, "Thanks, Carson. What about our biker friends?"

"Unfortunately, only ten of the bikers survived. It's clear they gave their lives at a moment's notice when their country called, and their role in the attack was critical to the ultimate success of you thwarting the attempted assassination of the president and his cabinet. I promise you that all the bikers, survivors and casualties alike, will be rewarded for their valor with medals of honor, and that GROSS will take care of all of their families for life."

"Do you know if a biker named Samson survived?"

"I'm sorry, Straw. His body was found inside the entry of the Goliath mansion, along with a number of terrorists. He clearly put up quite a fight before he was killed."

Straw wiped a tear from his eyes. "Carson, we really appreciate you taking care of the bikers and their families. They are truly heroes."

154

POTOMAC, MARYLAND, JANUARY 27, 2025

The next afternoon, Samantha was released from the hospital. Carson arranged for a driver to chauffeur her. Instead of going home, Samantha instructed the driver to take her to the GROSS office and to wait for her while she finished a task. At the office, Samantha quickly typed a document on her computer and printed it.

Before leaving the office, Sam decided that it might be beneficial to make a quick change to her appearance. While in espionage training in the military, a make-up artist had shown Sam how to easily change her appearance to foil facial detection software. It took her almost an hour, but after lightening the color of her dark hair, giving herself a shorter haircut, placing a plastic insert into her mouth that caused her lips and mouth to appear enlarged, inserting blue-tinted contact lenses over her brown eyes, and finally applying makeup on her face to create highlights and shadows that previously did not exist, Sam almost did not recognize herself when she looked in the mirror. She then changed clothes to a stylish black jogging outfit with an oversized top under which she added a 'fat pouch' to complete the makeover process, making her look twenty pounds heavier.

Samantha took her document and disguise back to the driver. She directed him to take her to an upscale, wooded neighborhood in Potomac, Maryland. It was dusk when they arrived, so Sam had the driver cruise slowly around the neighborhood until she asked him to park outside of a house that looked like the residents were out of town based on the two days of newspapers that were still lying on the driveway.

"I have a very unique request," said Sam to the driver. "Would you please give me the keys to this car and call an Uber to take you wherever you need to go? I will get the car back to Carson tomorrow. I don't know how long my meeting tonight will take."

The driver looked perplexed, but handed Sam the keys. She gave him five one-hundred-dollar bills.

"Of course," Sam said, "you never took me here, correct?"

The driver, who was trusted by Carson, nodded in agreement.

As darkness fell, Sam walked with just a slight limp from her wound around the ritzy neighborhood as if she were just taking an evening stroll to stretch her legs. Wearing a low baseball cap that shielded her face from security or doorbell cameras, Sam made a couple of loops around the block, observing the layout of the houses and scoping areas of unlit access. When no car lights or other walkers were in the vicinity, Sam stealthily left the roadway and moved to the back of one of the large houses. She blended into the house's landscaping and continued to look closely at the backyard of the house that backed into her current location. She cased the other backyard for about fifteen minutes in silence, noting that two security guards roamed around the house in approximately five-minute intervals.

Staying in the shadows, Sam approached the back door of the house as the security guards finished their rounds at the rear of the house. Working quickly, Sam disabled the house's alarm system and then picked the backdoor lock to gain entry inside the residence. Once inside, Sam surveilled each floor of the large residence until she was comfortable that no one was inside the home. Sam then made herself comfortable in a chair in the family room off the front entry.

Interesting, Sam thought to herself. *All the Constitutional purists would be so outraged by my invasion of the Speaker's privacy tonight without any formal determination of "probable cause." But under the circumstances, I don't have any regrets over my actions tonight.*

While waiting, Sam placed a call.

"Carson," she said. "I'm in place and waiting for the Speaker. I'm sure things will go well."

"Great," replied Carson. "Keep me updated. After I hear back from you, I'll coordinate with my contacts at the CIA and Department of Defense. I'm sure once I give them Straw's final report, there will be very little chance that Salvador Santos will celebrate another birthday. I'll also make sure that President Triumph rescinds any termination order against Nick. I want to cool off a little before I give Camelot Harris a piece of my mind."

"Roger that."

After about an hour of sitting in relative darkness in Silvia's family room, Sam heard a car door open when Silvia was dropped off at her entry. Sam could hear some faint conversation between Silvia and the security guards and then the sounds of a key opening the front door. Out of habit, Silvia turned on the entry lights and reached to turn off the house alarm that did not go off.

Silvia looked quizzically at the alarm pad when Sam spoke up.

"Don't worry, Madame Speaker. And don't scream. The house alarm has been disabled."

Silvia jumped in surprise, but did not scream. She looked at Sam and then saw the gun with a silencer attached aimed directly at her.

"Don't even think about trying to run or yell," Sam said. "If you do, you're dead."

"OK, what do you want?" asked Silvia as she tried to compose herself. "I don't have much cash on hand, but you can take all that I have as well as my jewelry." She started taking off her watch and bracelets.

"This is not a robbery, Madame Speaker. This is about justice. Let me get to the point. I absolutely know that you were part of a conspiracy to kill the president and the vice president."

Silvia tried to assert her innocence, but Sam quickly cut her off. "Save it Madame Speaker. I'm not buying what you're selling. I also know that Salvador Santos has been financing this scheme that, fortunately for us, was foiled a few days ago."

Sam looked into Silvia's eyes for a reaction. Though she tried to hide it, Sam could see both fear and surprise in her eyes. Sam continued, controlling the narrative like an expert interrogator.

"My only problem, Madame Speaker, is that I don't have enough proof that would be admissible in a court of law to convict you, and maybe not enough to even arrest you. But you and I both know for certain that you are guilty! And, as a good friend of mine would say, what truth is proof against all lies?"

Sam pulled out her cell phone and turned the screen to Silvia. She played a live video stream from outside her parents' house in Mexico. The sight made Silvia's face turn pale.

"I have a confession for you to sign that details your role in this assassination conspiracy," Sam said. "I know it's not admissible, but if I ever go public with it, you will have a hard time proving that it is not accurate. I'm not looking to turn this into a legal battle.

"As I said before, this is all about justice. You will sign this confession letter tonight and leave the U.S. tomorrow for good, never to return. You can spin your departure any way you like. But if you ever set foot on U.S. soil again, I can guarantee that you and your parents will all pay the price. That's a promise."

Silvia thought it over, took a deep breath, then signed the confession without reading it. Before handing it to Sam, Silvia asked, "Don't you think the U.S. and the world would be better off with me as president instead of toxic Triumph?"

"My thoughts on that question are irrelevant," Sam said. "My guess is that you would just be a puppet president for your backer in Mexico. What I do know is that our democracy only works if our leaders attain their positions by valid votes of the people, not by subversive means like you tried." The irony of saving Donald Triumph, who himself had tried to subvert the electoral system in the previous election, was not lost on Samantha, but she did not waver in front of the Speaker.

"I will be gone by the end of the day tomorrow," Silvia said softly. "You won't have to worry about me returning."

Sam took the confession and confirmed Silvia had signed it. “Good. Xavier Moody will be the next person I visit. If I find out there’s been any contact between the two of you, need I remind you what happens to you and your family?”

Silvia nodded and Sam walked out the back door without Silvia making another sound.

THE END/EL FIN/WALSTIB

Special Thanks

This book is the culmination of the efforts of lots of people. In addition to the inspiration and critical comments from my nuclear family, special thanks go out to Ronnie Haggart, Chuck Work, Jody Beck, David Roll, Brian Walker, Tracy Dixon, Rene Larson, and Archway Publishing for their insights and assistance.